BROKEN
WING

Also by Thomas Lakeman

Chillwater Cove

The Shadow Catchers

BROKEN
WING

Thomas Lakeman

MINOTAUR BOOKS   NEW YORK

Lak

This is a work of fiction. All of the characters, organizations, and events portrayed in this novel are either products of the author's imagination or are used fictitiously.

BROKEN WING. Copyright © 2009 by Thomas Lakeman. All rights reserved. Printed in the United States of America. For information, address St. Martin's Press, 175 Fifth Avenue, New York, N.Y. 10010.

www.minotaurbooks.com

Library of Congress Cataloging-in-Publication Data

Lakeman, Thomas.
    Broken Wing / Thomas Lakeman.—1st ed.
        p. cm.
    ISBN-13: 978-0-312-38022-9
    ISBN-10: 0-312-38022-4
    1. Yeager, Mike (Fictitious character)—Fiction.   2. United States. Federal Bureau of Investigation—Officials and employees—Fiction.   3. Undercover operations—Fiction. 4. New Orleans (La.)—Fiction.   I. Title.
    PS3612.A53B76 2009
    813'.6—dc22

                                                                                    2008034141

First Edition: March 2009

10 9 8 7 6 5 4 3 2 1

For My Father

Acknowledgments

Like many Gulf Coast natives, I grew up with a crush on New Orleans—the kind of attraction you might feel toward a beautiful but indecent neighbor. I want to thank two dear friends, Bess and Steverson Moffat, for showing me that this amazing city is so much more than the sum of its scandals and tragedies; for taking me into their home and leading me through every wayward street; and for introducing me to Angelo Brocato's world-famous gelato.

As always, I am indebted to retired Special Agent Volney Hayes, formerly of the New Orleans field office of the FBI, for his professional and personal recollections. The first time he spoke to me of broken wings, I knew I had a title.

A childhood friend and sometime fellow thespian, Claudia Baylor, instructed me in the language of Italian hand gestures. Johnny Smiley, the St. Jude of ailing computers, once more gave me top-level access to Yoshi's brain.

Their wisdom was a gift to me; my mistakes are my own.

My gratitude to those who read and helped improve the manuscript: Bill Clarkson, Randy Davis, Victoria Forester, Scott Jolly, Mark Tapio Kines, Mary Leah Lowe and most especially my mother, Dr. Patricia Burchfield.

My beloved friend Keira Mallinger was brave enough to tell me when I almost let the story get away from me, and generous with the time and insight I needed to get the damn thing back on track. We shared the road to New Orleans and explored the ruins in silence.

My grandmother, Vieva Chason Crosby, died two weeks after I finished this book. To the very last, she continued to support my writing. She made me love reading. I am less without her.

Until I met Marian Young, I thought agents were people who shopped books around. Thanks to her, I now know they're really patron saints. I am equally blessed with an extraordinary editor, Kelley Ragland, and a first-rate team at Minotaur Books.

The city of New Orleans is battered but alive. The FBI is, at its best, a vital force for justice in our world. Everything else between these covers is fiction.

The Council of State will permit me to represent that it is exceedingly painful for an officer, who is intrusted with the destinies of a colony, to have nothing better to defend her than a band of deserters, of smugglers, and of rogues, who are ever ready, not only to abandon their flag, but to turn their arms against their country.

—Jean-Baptiste Le Moyne, Sieur de Bienville,
founder of New Orleans

Back in the French Quarter
A liquor store creole king
Was romancing a gypsy
With a Mardi Gras angel's broken wing.

—David J, "Hoagy Carmichael Never
Went to New Orleans"

I didn't shoot anybody, no sir.

—Alek Hidell

BROKEN
WING

ONE

There was dirt on the FBI director's hands: the dark soil of Arlington National Cemetery, worked deep into the pores and creases of the old man's skin. He got a little of it on me when we shook hands, and as he turned away I had to fight the urge to wipe my palm. The director kept a stoic face, but I could tell he was hurting. It wasn't just the traces of grave dirt that gave him away, or even the black band on his right sleeve. It was the way he avoided sitting in the mahogany armchair behind him, even though that chair was now—pending Senate confirmation—his. Instead, the acting director took his place beside me, in front of his predecessor's massive desk, as if both of us were awaiting orders from the Great Beyond.

"Less than an hour ago," the old man said, "I buried our late director. More than that . . ." He paused, steadying his voice. "I buried my friend."

The new director was lean and cautious, a lost greyhound in a city of junkyard dogs. Five foot four, shoe lifts included. If he did sit in the chair, his feet would dangle. His predecessor had been a very large man. I remembered how painfully that chair had creaked when he rose to say goodbye at our final meeting: a powerful grip, club-fingered with peripheral edema. A big-hearted, weak-hearted man.

"A great man," the acting director said, as if correcting me, "for whom justice was not merely a principle but a passion. And yet death was no respecter of his wisdom. The disease did not know the man it killed. Nature, my young friend, has no morality."

Silence. A rapid glance at the empty chair. Behind me, the door opened.

"While you were eating breakfast this morning—" He waited until the door had closed again. "I made a promise over his open grave. That his passion for justice will endure. That our fallen leader's unfinished work shall not be abandoned."

The new arrivals took their seats behind me. Two of them from the sound, men about my age. I knew who they were. One of them wasn't worth a backward glance. The other one I was simply afraid to look at.

"I'm told you are someone who can help me." The director folded his arms. "I wonder, Agent Yeager. I wonder if you can possibly know what it means to carry the burden of a dead man's dreams."

It took me a few seconds to realize that it was my turn to say something.

"He was a great man." I cleared my throat. "They were great dreams."

The director raised his eyebrows—as unimpressed as I was by my lame reply—then nodded to one of the men behind me.

"Special Agent Michael Francis Yeager." The voice was clean, correct: Uri Vitale, from the Office of Professional Responsibility. Among street agents, he was known simply as the Bastard. "Currently assigned to the Philadelphia Field Office, Crimes Against Children Unit. Twenty-year veteran. Thirty-six successful recoveries of abused and endangered children, ninety-two percent of arrests resulting in conviction . . . various awards and commendations . . ."

There was a silence as he turned the page.

"Current status—probationary." I could hear him smiling. "Did I leave anything out?"

"I made Eagle Scout when I was sixteen."

The director frowned and looked away.

"Last year," Vitale said, "you were placed on administrative leave after my office discovered that you had willfully mishandled subject interrogation in the matter of an abducted boy named Tonio Madrigal."

The director weighed my discomfort. "Do you deny this, Agent Yeager?"

"Yes," I said. "Vitale's office didn't 'discover' a damn thing. I came forward on my own. I'm not proud of myself, but those are the facts."

"The *facts* are that you pegged the boy's father without sufficient proof," Vitale answered. "When he wouldn't confess, you cooked evidence to frame him. After nearly a week of your infamous badgering, your suspect hanged himself in his cell."

"The father was an admitted child abuser," I said.

"He wasn't guilty of the crime you charged him with. And because you put the hat on the wrong man, the real kidnapper had sufficient time to torture little Tonio Madrigal to death." Vitale paused to let the venom settle in.

"How you managed to avoid misprision of a felony is beyond me. You ought to be behind bars."

I looked back at him: a round-faced squealer in shit-brown Armani, sneering like Torquemada's file clerk.

"No argument," I said. "That would have been the right thing to do."

Vitale shrank a little into the leather sofa.

"All right." The director raised his hand. "Uri, in all fairness, I didn't bring you here to resurrect the past. I'm mainly interested in the workup you did last April. Now what do you have for us?"

Vitale recovered himself. "Yeager's been clean since his reinstatement in January—six months of good behavior, for what it's worth. However, one or two interesting facts did come to light during our investigations."

Interesting facts scraped the back of my neck like razor burn. I braced myself for what was coming.

"Yeager's mother committed suicide when he was nine years old," Vitale said. "Bipolar disorder. Yeager apparently blamed himself. A fact he was reluctant to disclose during his recruitment interviews. Possibly because he feared that he'd inherited the condition from her. And, if so, that it might disqualify him." He drew himself in for the kill. "That was the reason, wasn't it?"

"Yes," I said.

"At least he's honest about it." Vitale rolled his eyes. "Personnel advises that Yeager's long overdue for rotation out of Crimes Against Children. Probably balancing right on the edge of total burnout."

"Possibly." The director narrowed his eyes. "What else?"

"He's not much of a family man," Vitale said. "Father died in eighty-five. One brother, three sisters. Hasn't seen any of them in the past two years."

"Four," I said.

"Beg pardon?"

"Four sisters," I said. "My mother was pregnant at the time of her death."

Vitale made a note in his file.

The director regarded me thoughtfully. "No family of your own, then?"

"Unmarried," Vitale said. "However, according to—"

"I can speak for myself," I said. "The answer's no. No wife, no family. I had a dog once, but it ran away."

"Well, it seems you've had your fair share of sorrow," the director said. "And yet, despite it all . . . here you are today. Can you explain why?"

"I promised a friend," I said. "She's getting an apartment in George-town. I said I'd help her move."

The ghost of a smile crossed the old man's lips. "Never mind the rest of the report, Uri. What's the final judgment on Yeager?"

"He's a true believer . . . a loner . . . and just dirty enough. We've got other names for you—but in my opinion, you won't find a better washout this side of Butte, Montana. He's perfect."

"As it happens, I agree." The director nodded to him. "Well done, Uri. Please leave the file with me when you go."

Vitale hesitated a moment before putting it on the desk.

"Yeager." Uri forced a smile down at me.

"Bastard." I didn't smile back.

The director waited until the door closed again before standing up to pour a glass of water.

"Not that I don't appreciate the free proctology exam," I said. "But when I heard I'd be meeting the director, I kind of expected something more like a commemorative photo."

"You have every right to be upset." He handed me the glass, not letting it touch the desk. "However, your anger at Agent Vitale is misplaced. I already had your file before you arrived. I could have spared you the ordeal."

"But you didn't."

"I wanted to see if you could face up to yourself," he said. "For the record, I believe that your handling of the Madrigal case was beneath contempt. Even if you did implicate yourself—even if you have reformed as well as you seem to have—I still consider your reinstatement to have been a gross error."

"So now I get to ask," I said. "Why *am* I still here?"

"Same old story." He nodded to the empty chair. "My boss overruled me."

I smiled in spite of myself. "The old man just won't let me go, will he?"

"Apparently not." He placed my file in his desk drawer, then locked it. "And Agent Vitale is right about something else. For what I need, you are the best I'm likely to find."

"Of course," I said. "The best for what?"

He looked down on me—a moment of decision.

"A walk in darkness." He sat down. "When a man enters pure darkness, either he lights his way through . . . or he falls. Agent Vitale believes you will fall."

"What do you believe?"

"I have my doubts." He gestured over my shoulder. "For what it's worth, the other man in this room thinks you'll do just fine."

"All respect, sir. He's been wrong before." I straightened my shoulders. "I wasn't lying about helping my friend move. If all this is just a test of my honesty—"

"It's not a question of how honest you can be." The voice behind me was familiar, easy, only slightly slurred. "What we're questioning, Mike, is how much you can take."

I turned in my chair to face him.

Art Kiplinger and I graduated Academy together and were both first office agents in New Orleans. Everybody thought we made quite a team: tall, steady Art, the born politico; and hard-charging Mike, a blue-eyed martyr on the cross of justice. For a while, it worked. The bad guys were scared of us.

Too scared. On the night before we were due to testify in a major organized crime trial, Art Kiplinger opened a box of Chinese takeout. The resulting explosion left me with ringing ears and singed eyebrows. What it did to Art required six units of blood and twelve hours in surgery. That was just to keep him alive.

"Good to see you, Mike." The left sleeve of Art's black suit was pinned to his shoulder. The eye above it was glass, a decent match for the right one looking at me. Plastic surgeons had almost completely restored the shape of his jaw: almost. The imperturbable smile was still entirely his own.

"You, too, Art." I was surprised by the catch in my voice. It had been years since I'd seen him last. "How's New Orleans?"

"Same as ever, only worse." He shrugged. "You've seen the news."

"Not so much since the storm." I gave an apologetic smile. "I keep worrying I'll see something familiar."

"It's all too damn familiar." Art took a sip of coffee. "A whole year since Katrina, and we're still fighting over who broke the damn levees. Someone needs to tell our elected officials that mea culpas don't turn the lights back on."

"Anything I can do to help?" The words were past my lips before I could stop them. The director seemed to take that as his cue.

"As a matter of fact . . ." He reached for a sealed file on his desk. "You could take a look at this for me, if you like."

I started to demur. Then I saw the names on the cover. "It's those two tourists, isn't it? The Brits?"

"Yes and no," the director replied. "Simon Burke and Amrita Narayan had tourist visas, but they weren't in New Orleans on vacation. Officially, they were volunteers for a nonprofit agency called Reconstruction International—home rebuilders, relief for displaced families. From all reports, they made friends very quickly."

"As well as a few enemies, I'm guessing."

"Apparently so."

My chest tightened as I took the folder from him.

"You're aware that our late director grew up in New Orleans," the director said. "And Hurricane Katrina . . . well, there's no doubt in my mind. The storm broke his heart." He refilled my glass. "As I said, nature has no morality. You can't arrest wind and water for killing people. But the things that men do . . ."

"Sweet Jesus." I stared at the first page.

Simon and Amrita had been missing for nearly three days before the NOPD finally got around to acting on a missing persons report. Then, on the morning of June twenty-third, a group of Katrina tourists pointed their video cameras into an abandoned home in the Lower Ninth Ward. And found Simon Burke.

He was nude, slumped against a brick fireplace, as if waiting for Santa. His abductors had shot him once in the head, but that was probably a mercy. There were traces of battery acid in his open cuts, and swelling in the groin from electrical burns. Also water in the lungs, probably inhaled after a few dunkings in the large plastic trough beside him. His face was a mass of bruises. A rubber ball gag had been stuffed into Burke's mouth. Not that he would have made much sense if he'd felt like talking: The killers had pulled out most of his teeth.

"They kept the teeth?" I asked through clenched jaws.

"That's only one of a hundred minor mysteries," Art said. "As you know, killers sometimes yank teeth to prevent dental identification. But then you have to wonder why they also left his wallet behind."

I examined a photo of the wallet. The cash and credit cards were still there, ditto the obligatory picture of his wife. There was, however, a wafer-thin indentation in one of the hidden compartments, roughly the size of a Scrabble tile.

From the pictures, Simon and Amrita looked like nice young people. Burke was a cheerful badass, a former Royal Marine who'd served in Kosovo and Iraq. Between tours of duty, his volunteer work had taken him to Malaysia, Rwanda, Afghanistan, and the Sudan. His wife, Dr. Amrita Narayan, was a refined beauty. Chestnut skin, rich dark hair, a licensed psychotherapist. Most passport photos have a way of making their subjects look punchy and exhausted. Burke and Narayan practically radiated optimism and adventure.

"Even before this happened," Art was saying, "the foreign press were already calling New Orleans a third world country—and a war zone to boot. Couldn't have happened at a worse time for the reconstruction effort."

"Can't imagine Simon and Amrita's families are too happy about it, either."

"Most definitely not," the director said. "Very few people know what I'm about to tell you, Mike. This man, Simon Burke—"

"He's a spook." I looked up. "Secret Intelligence Service, right? MI6?"

That got the director looking at me a little more closely. Art just smiled.

The director nodded. "How did you work that out?"

"The ball gag was removable, in case Simon wanted to talk. From the looks of things, it seems he managed to hold out longer than most people could tolerate. So I guess they weren't asking him about England's chances at the World Cup. Also, don't you think it's a little strange that his NGO kept sending him to build affordable housing in terrorist strongholds?"

"And the molars?" Art added.

"There's only one reason why anyone would want to hang on to an Englishman's teeth," I said, "and that's in case one of them happened to contain some kind of device—for instance, a GPS tracker. Since the bad guys didn't pull them all out, I'm guessing they stopped after they found one."

"You got this from looking at the crime scene photos," the director said with a measured look.

"Actually, sir, I got it from looking at you." I handed the file back. "No disrespect, but FBI directors don't often concern themselves much over the fate of charity volunteers."

"Possibly not," he said. "What concerns you, Mike?"

I took a careful breath before answering him. "What happened to Amrita?"

The director touched a button and the lights dimmed. A moment later, Dr. Narayan's face appeared on the video monitor. Her hair was pulled back, her hands pressed to her neck. She looked tired but otherwise betrayed little emotion. Razor lines of light fell on her between the boards of an old wooden shack.

"This will be the only communication." Amrita's accent was unpreten-tious middle-class London. "I am alive and unharmed. As you can see, I am not drugged or otherwise impaired . . ."

She's reading off a cue card, I noted. *They took her contact lenses away. Her eyes look a little swollen.*

Then there was a sudden jump cut: a two-hour shift in the direction of the sunlight. Now Amrita was crying hysterically.

"Why are you doing this?" Her breath raced, voice shaking. "Please, I can't—I don't know what it is you want. I don't know anything . . ." She gasped. "When I met you before, you seemed so . . . so . . . and now poor Sammy, I begged you to leave him alone . . . why did you . . ."

She shut her eyes tightly.

"We were trying to have a baby—"

The screen abruptly went dark. Both men were studying me as the lights came back on.

"Could I have some more water, please?"

The director swiftly complied.

"The second part of the statement . . ." I took a moment to collect myself. "It's an appeal to empathy. Amrita knew her abductor. She refers to her husband as Sammy, which I'm guessing is a nickname that the unsub would be expected to know. And she keeps asking *why*. It's like she still can't make herself believe that the person who killed her husband isn't a friend."

"We're pretty sure she was in the room when they tortured Burke," Art said. "You can see it better on digital enhancement. There's flecks of blood on her face."

"I saw them," I said. "Why are they keeping her alive?"

"We're not sure," Art said. "It's not likely her husband told her any-thing. They'd only met a few months ago. It was a whirlwind courtship—they left the altar and hopped straight on a plane. Apparently she didn't even know he was a spy."

"Hell of a honeymoon," I said. "Who was he spying on?"

"Take a look." Art handed me another file. "You'll recognize his smiling face on the very first page."

Did I ever.

"Emelio St. Clair Barca," the director said. "Last of the old-line Cosa Nostra kingpins in Orleans Parish . . . until you and Agent Kiplinger broke him, of course."

"Just his organization," I said. "Nobody's ever broken Emelio Barca."

Seeing him again gave me an involuntary chill. The photo was long-range surveillance of some lakeshore marina: a stout man in garish summer clothes, pacing the deck of a Bayliner with a beer in his hand. Noonday sun reflected off the deck and cabin windows, framing him in hard light. His salt-and-pepper hair was swept back, a wiseguy mane that had been unfashionable even in his glory days. But—I had to confess—there was something oddly assured about him. He strode that deck like Lord Nelson. *Christ, he's gotten old*, I thought. But not dead yet. Even from a mile away, you could still see the coyote gleam in his eyes: the last cruel survivor of a deadly pack.

There was something else in the picture: a pale shadow in the boat's aft porthole. Either light reflecting off the water, or something else.

"You've got that look in your eye," Art said. "You seeing something?"

"Nothing." I shook my head. "Good pictures, though. Looks like a . . . Moretti beer. Cold, too." I put the photo down. "So what's the son of a bitch doing, showing his face after twenty years on the lam?"

"We think Barca's trying to reactivate his organization," Art said. "Most of the local gang leaders got domed to Houston and other cities, so we figure he's taking advantage of the power vacuum. The working theory is that he's bribing half the gangs to make war on the other half."

"You've got an informant." I nodded. "How close?"

Art held his thumb and forefinger about an inch apart. "The informant gave us the proof-of-life video. And here's the point of it all: Barca's not ransoming Narayan. He's selling her. To whom, and for how much, we don't know. But it's all coming down in less than a month."

"So you want me to go back to New Orleans," I said. "Stop the sale."

The right side of Art's face tensed. "No, Mike. We want you to make sure it happens."

The director stared at the floor.

"Go to hell," I said.

"Already been there." Art gave me a pained look. "God knows we've assured the British government that Amrita's safety will be given the highest priority. But if we pull her out now—if that's even possible—we'll never find Barca's connection. And you know I want this bastard. I've been chasing his tail ever since he . . . well, did this to me." He gestured to his empty sleeve. "The informant can only do so much. We've got to put one of our own guys inside."

"So call in a specialist," I said. "Somebody who knows how to infiltrate an organization like this, without blowing his cover."

"I did," Art said. "That's him lying dead in the Lower Ninth Ward."

I laughed. "And you think I'm gonna succeed where James Bond Jr. failed?"

"You're the man for the job. This guy can smell undercover a mile away. What we need is somebody who's—"

"Expendable?" I asked.

"Credible," he said. "If Barca thinks you've gone dirty, you won't have to infiltrate. He'll take you in."

I looked to the director. "Sir, are you buying this bullshit?"

"Mike, please." The director lifted his chin. "You investigated Barca for two years. Perhaps he believes you developed some sort of . . . connection."

"There's no connection, sir. The only thing Emelio Barca wants from me is my head on the prow of his boat." I turned to Art. "And he's not going to believe I've 'gone dirty,' six months after getting a second chance."

"Well, then, I guess you're going to have to blow that second chance," Art said. "Take a bribe, score some coke—"

"Drown a few puppies?"

"Just make it look real, Mike. I'm sure you can figure out a way to do that."

I took a long drink of water.

"So I become a broken wing," I said. "And after it's all over? Do I get a third chance?"

Neither one of them answered.

"Guess it was a pretty dumb question," I said finally.

"Please understand," the director said. "You can stop this man Barca. You can bring this woman home again. Once it's clear that justice can prevail in New Orleans . . . hope will be reborn." He cleared his throat. "You're very brave to agree to this."

"I haven't agreed to anything yet—sir." I set the file on his desk. "I'm not entirely sure I will."

"Ah." The director gave me a gray-eyed stare. "If this is about your career . . . I can personally assure you that your record will be wiped clean after this is over."

"All respect, screw my career. I don't take assignments based on how shiny they make me look."

He smiled thinly. "Would it be so terrible if you did?"

I opened my mouth to answer—then took a breath. "How long do I have to think it over?"

The two men exchanged glances. The old man was clearly peeved. Art squinted like I'd made a bad chess move.

"I could give you till Doomsday," Art said. "It's Amrita Narayan who's a little short on time."

"Understood." I was halfway out of my chair.

"You may not credit this." The director's eyes followed me to the door. "My predecessor always believed the day would come when his confidence in you would finally be rewarded. Agent Yeager, I believe that day has arrived."

I looked back at him: a little man, terrified and alone.

"Too bad he's not here to tell me that himself," I said.

TWO

Art accompanied me out of the secure area. I steadied the guard's clipboard while Art meticulously signed us out.

"People are always telling me it could have been worse. I could have lost my right arm." He set down the pen, flexing his wrist. "Too bad I'm actually left-handed."

"No damn justice." I walked slowly enough to let him keep pace, hopefully without seeming too obvious about it. "How'd I make out in there?"

"You were almost polite," he said. "Particularly when you asked the director if he was buying my bullshit."

"I respect you too much to lie, Artie. Your informant stinks, whoever he is. Even if I do pretend to be a broken wing, no way is Barca clasping me to his bosom."

"The informant's high-value. Carefully vetted. And that is the second thing you've been wrong about today."

"Only two? I'm on fire." I dropped my voice. "There's something you're not telling me about this case."

"There's a lot I'm not telling you—at least not until after you say yes." He walked ahead of me to the elevators. "The case is a heartbreaker, Mike. You'll be standing there with your hand on your nine-millimeter while Emelio Barca negotiates for the life of an innocent woman. Helping him past every obstacle you've been trained to set in his way. Not to mention that you'll be surrounded by guys who will be watching you sneeze."

"And if I sneeze the wrong way?"

"If you die, you disappear. No one can ever know what happened to you. That's the deal with suicide jobs. On the small chance that it works . . ." He shrugged. "Life goes on. A little better, maybe. You've heard about this bill working its way through the Senate? Levin-Marcato?"

I nodded. "Six billion dollars for rebuilding New Orleans. Think it's got a snowball's chance of passing?"

"Not with things as they are," he said. "Not until the city's been declared safe for a hundred thousand construction workers and a half million new families. Short of that, New Orleans is America's Baghdad. Congress won't touch us. Neither will the corporations."

"So, in a way, this is really about money."

"For me, it's about the place where I raised my children," he said. "You tell me what it's about for you."

"I can tell you it's not about clearing my record. I don't know what gave the director the balls to think that."

"The director thinks it because it's true." Art pressed the DOWN button. "You stepped on your dick with the Madrigal case, right? And you've done some good things since then. The trouble is, it doesn't equal out. Some things the Bureau doesn't forgive. Not unless you're willing to donate a pint of blood for the cause." He paused. "You wouldn't be pretending to be a broken wing. You are a broken wing. Get past it."

He looked away. The glass eye continued to stare.

"Then I guess this is my chance to get right with the angels," I said. "Maybe I don't want it, all the same."

"You do want it," he said flatly. "You just don't want to have to face the people who can give it to you."

I nodded. "You're asking me because I've got nobody to shed tears when I turn up dead on Florida Avenue?"

"No," he said. "I'm asking you because you were the one who was smart enough not to open that Chinese takeout."

The elevator doors opened. He didn't follow me in.

"Art," I said. "You told me I was wrong about two things. What was the first thing?"

"Not here." He considered a moment. "I'll send you the case file. If you're as half as good as you used to be . . . you'll work it out."

Then the door closed between us.

If you die, you disappear. *Artie always did have a gift for the brass tacks,* I thought as I sweated my way up Pennsylvania Avenue. It was just before noon, a real scorcher in our nation's capital. Somewhere in Arlington, military backhoes were pouring dirt on the late director's coffin. Somewhere in Louisiana, Amrita Narayan was getting an education in hell. You die, you disappear. That's the deal.

He'd called it a heartbreaker, a suicide job. Still, there had to be a reason why Art thought the whole crazy gambit would work—and a damned good reason for thinking I'd say yes. Not just because of Madrigal, or the director's ham-handed amnesty deal, or even Amrita's cries for the baby she and Simon would never have. Art knew those things would gnaw at me, and they did, but he also knew they might not be enough to convince me to approach Emelio Barca with an offer to betray myself. Kiplinger had to be keeping something else in his hip pocket. He never bet on anything less than a sure thing.

Except that Art hadn't said anything about approaching Barca. *He'll take you in*; as if I were some kind of charity case. Which meant the informant had to be someone Barca trusted, somebody in a position to confirm my disciplinary status . . . or, at the very least, plead for my life. The trouble was, Barca never trusted anyone. So maybe Art was bluffing, and there was no high-value informant. Or maybe it was simply that Barca didn't need that much persuading: because I was a broken wing, a burnout, available at fire-sale prices.

"Barca," I muttered. "Why the Christ did he have to show up now?" I got so lost in self-revelation that I narrowly avoided getting clipped by a number 35 bus on Wisconsin Avenue. I was in Georgetown.

Peggy had picked a pretty nice place to live, I thought as I approached the brick red town house on Congress Court. A step up from the slum she'd rented back in Philly. Between her latest promotion and the settlement she'd made after her last case, it seemed like she could afford it now. I heard a blow-dryer in the bathroom as I let myself in. My black weekend bag sat alone on the floor, untouched. The place still had that yuppie-bait smell: Murphy's Oil Soap, fresh Colonial White paint. A nice place for Supervising Special Agent Peggy Jean Weaver to begin her new life on the chief inspector's staff.

No one can ever know.

The hair dryer shut off.

"Hey, is that you?" Peggy asked from the bathroom.

"It's J. Edgar Hoover," I said. "I've come to borrow some of your filmy lingerie."

"Sorry, but I've got plans for it," she said. "Turn around, Yeager. I'm not ready for you yet."

I obeyed, thinking how nothing seemed to make Peggy quite so happy as the chance to boss me around, and nothing ever seemed to make me quite so happy as the chance to be bossed by her. Probably that's why we always made such a good team. I hated to think what it might imply about our love life.

"I thought you'd get back before me," she said. "Did you catch up with your friend at headquarters?"

"We caught up," I said. "Do you mind if I don't have this conversation staring at a blank wall?"

"Two seconds. We're only getting one chance at this. I want it to be perfect." She laughed. "Okay, hotshot. See what you've gotten yourself into."

I turned. Then I whistled.

In my seven years working with Peggy Weaver, I'd seen her in body armor, in hiking shorts, in various skillful variations on FBI office-drab. Once in a glorious while, I'd seen her naked. But nothing could have prepared me for what she'd put on that morning.

The dress was white: just enough below the knee to work for daytime, just enough off the shoulders to advertise that killer body. Her full auburn hair was still curled from the dryer, falling around her heart-shaped face like shade on a warm day. She had on makeup, but not much. She didn't need much. For a bare second, I caught just a glance of the small-town Tennessee girl Peggy had been before the FBI took her.

"Well?" She raised an eyebrow.

"Oh, you look good." I barely breathed.

"Don't I just." She fixed an earring. "Look, we're not due at the chapel until one o'clock, but I honestly think we should leave now. Before one of us loses his nerve."

I took her by the hand.

"Let's get some lunch first," I said. "Big decisions make me hungry."

THREE

All the TVs in the hotel bar carried footage of the late director's funeral—endless loops of a massive flag-draped coffin and three former U.S. presidents bowed in prayer. Meanwhile, people kept stopping to congratulate me and Peggy for a wedding that hadn't happened yet. One of them even sent champagne. Peggy drank it by herself while I ordered root beers. We mostly talked about work, the details of a job she was leaving to me until her replacement came along. Somehow, the subject of our future—even for the next thirty minutes—kept avoiding us.

"The Cherry Hill porn." Peggy stopped her champagne flute an inch from her lips. "The more I think about it, there's no way that evidence could have been misfiled. Those Cherry Hill guys will pay anything to avoid an indictment. I think we've got ourselves a mole."

"I think we've got incompetent evidence clerks," I said. "So what have they got you working on while I'm tracking down kiddie porn back in Helladelphia?"

She made an indifferent gesture. "Still getting my sea legs, I guess. Internal Affairs, congressional liaison . . ."

"Sounds kind of sexy when you say it like that." I rattled my glass. Seconds later, the barmaid returned with another five-dollar Hires. "How was the funeral, by the way?"

"Sad." Peggy eyed the waitress. "Humid."

"I should have been there," I said. "The old man was my first supervisor. Hell, we even had lunch together once."

"You'd have been like a bored kid at church," she said. "And I remember you telling me about that lunch. You said the way he ate, you were afraid to get your hands close to his mouth."

"I said that? God, I'm cruel."

"Not to interrupt the guilt break." She cast a look around. "But should we maybe find a restaurant that doesn't have a forty-minute wait? I'm getting a little antsy here."

"I'm sorry. You're hungry, aren't you?"

"Sure, Yeager. That's it. Hungry." She gave me a dull stare. "And, of course, every girl dreams of celebrating her wedding day in a Foggy Bottom bar."

"Hey, check it out. You're on TV." I pointed. "Funeral at ten, wedding at one. How'd you get changed out of that black dress so fast?"

"Seven years of undercover experience." Peggy kept her eyes fixed on me.

"Okay, now I know why the camera's staying on you. Is that the senator by your side?"

Then she looked up.

Even in a crowd of Washington power players, there was something about Senator James Seaweather of Pennsylvania that never failed to catch the eye. Maybe it was his voting record on the environment, but more likely he was just plain handsome. Smooth ebony skin, nice suits, an easy way with reporters. Oval Office written all over his chiseled features.

"I heard a rumor he was gay," I said.

Peggy laughed. "The senator? Who started that one?"

"Me. Just now." I pointed. "Seriously, check out the way he's smiling at the president. That's passion."

"That's politics," she said, "and if he is gay, it's his own business." Then she looked back at me. "But he's not."

"And you know this because . . . ?" I raised an eyebrow.

"He has five children. For the record, it was his youngest daughter who wanted me at the funeral." Peggy pointed to the child, a solemn six-year-old in black organdy. "It was her first time back in public. The family thought it might calm her if I was there."

"Did it?"

"A little. She was scared of the rifles."

On-screen, the child held Peggy's hand tightly in her own. I remembered how she'd looked the last time I saw her: terrified, covered only by an FBI Windbreaker, moments after Peggy had rescued her from a North Philly basement cage.

"He's single again, right? Incriminating testimony from an intern? Nasty divorce?"

"He's a widower," Peggy said. "We're invited to his town house this weekend. If you can make it back here."

"Did you tell him we were getting married?"

"No." Finally she took a drink. "Are we?"

The news went to commercial. A moment later, the TVs switched over to coverage of the Tour de France.

"Why wouldn't we be?" I felt a sudden ache in my jaw.

"Well." She set her glass down. "Ever since we got here, you've been doing color commentary on that funeral like Dan Marino. You're also chewing your ice—which you only do when you're nervous. And you won't meet my eyes."

"I have not been chewing my ice," I said.

She pointed. "Check your glass."

I looked. "Jesus, no wonder my gums hurt."

"Don't make them any worse." She took my hand, cool from the glass. "You were almost fine this morning. So I'm guessing something happened during your meeting at headquarters."

I didn't answer. Peggy reached over and brushed a lock of hair from my face.

"Want to tell your friend and partner what's going on?" she asked softly. "Or is this one of those things I have to figure out, so you don't have to break a confidence?"

"Are those my only choices?" It was no good; she wasn't laughing. "It's like this, Peg. I get a call from an old friend who finds out I'm coming to the District—"

"By some strange coincidence," she said.

"Or not. And hey, the new director heard I was coming around, and he wants to say hi . . . and damned if OPR doesn't have a copy of my personnel file on hand . . ."

"You got hot-boxed." She sighed. "Oh boy. Where are they sending you?"

I stopped myself from reaching for my glass. "I haven't said yes to anything, Peg."

"Something tells me you haven't said no, either." She waited. "Seriously, Mike. How far away?"

"Why does that matter?"

"It matters a lot if I'm about to be your wife," she said. "Two hours away means a daily commute. Six hours is a weekend relationship. Farther than that . . ." Then the wheels started turning. "Jesus. It's New Orleans, isn't it? There's nowhere else it could be."

"Damn," I said. "How . . . ?"

"You know the territory. They're hungry for warm bodies. Tell me I'm wrong and I'll drop the subject."

I looked at my watch. "We should probably drop it anyway. We're going to be late to the chapel."

"We are late," she said. "Tell me I'm wrong, Mike."

I sighed. "You're not."

"Okay." She thought a moment. "This old friend who approached you. This wouldn't by some chance be the guy who . . . ?"

"Exploding dim sum." I nodded. "Art Kiplinger."

Then she let go of my hand.

"Say no," she told me.

"Because you don't want me more than six hours away."

She laughed. "I'd like my husband to live in the same time zone as me, sure. And if he's getting TDY'd, I'd like to believe it's a step up, instead of the ninth circle of Hell. Either way, it's a bad move for you. Trust me."

"Hold on. Did you just say 'step up'?" My voice tightened. "What's that? I'm on the bricks? I'm supposed to follow your lead like a faithful hound?"

"That's not what I—"

"Oh, I think you nailed it." I breathed out. "We don't all get promoted every eighteen months on the button, Peg. We don't all have U.S. senators for angels. And God knows we don't all win our fortunes in a lawsuit. So if you don't mind—"

"The Avalon College money is going into a scholarship fund," she said, "and you know damn well I've worked my ass off for everything else. Stop trying to piss me off, okay? I'm not impressed."

"Don't turn this around. You just called me a loser."

"I'm not apologizing for something I didn't say." She shook her head. "You're too smart and capable for me to pity. So don't pity yourself. This albatross you keep carrying around . . . all this guilt from the Madrigal case?"

"Some things the Bureau doesn't forgive," I said. "So I've heard."

"Try forgiving yourself," she replied. "Guilt is a dangerous vice in our line of work. You turn every case into the Passion of the Mike, and it's going to blindside you one day—and most likely get somebody killed to boot. At the very least, it lets guys like Kiplinger push your buttons. Maybe because you feel bad about surviving the explosion—which you shouldn't. Possibly because you think he's a better man than you are. Which he's not."

"You've never even met him."

"I've met you," she said. "Tell him no, Mike."

"Right," I said. "So is this advice from my former supervisor? Or instructions from my future wife?"

I hated the words as soon as I'd said them. Her lip was set, her hazel eyes smoking. And that was not good. Nothing made Peggy Jean angrier than losing control. I waited for her to explode. Instead she simply took out her cell phone and dialed.

"Peg—"

"Hold that thought." Her voice brightened. "Hi, it's Peggy Weaver . . . yes, ma'am, the couple from Philadelphia. Well—" She threw me a look. "Actually, it seems like today isn't the day. No, no, don't worry. Frankly, I'm not really sure myself. I'll let you know."

She closed the phone.

"I'm sorry." I stopped, not knowing what to say. "I'm an idiot, okay? I shouldn't have brought this up in a bar."

"Oh, you thought we'd have a table by now?" Her voice coiled. "You didn't bring this up, Mike. I had to worm it out of you. And you didn't bring me to a bar. You brought me to the hotel where you knew you'd be sleeping after I kicked you out. Very convenient."

"I didn't plan this."

"You improvise well," she said. "Do you want to marry me, or not?"

"Am I nuts? You just canceled the wedding."

"I canceled the chapel. You get to decide about the wedding."

I rolled my eyes. "If I didn't want to be married . . ."

"Maybe you do," she said. "To somebody, anyhow. But I'm not entirely sure that person is me."

Finally I realized just how many people in the bar were trying not to look our way.

"New Orleans is the one place you've never talked about," she said when I didn't reply. "Secrets mean unfinished business. I'm not blaming you for it, God knows, but this isn't the first time we've tried to get to the altar. And we keep not getting there. If Kiplinger isn't the reason you're going back—then maybe it's someone else. Somebody I don't know about."

You do want it, Art said. *You just don't want to face the people who can give it to you.* Then I thought: *Jesus, she's right.*

"Mike?" She shook her head, her voice aching. "Mike, you need to tell me if you still want us to be together."

It would have been enough to say yes. Or to say anything, as long as I didn't hesitate. But that last revelation was still hitting me hard, and the words came too late.

"I do love you," I said. "But if you're right about me . . . if guilt is all that motivates me . . ."

"Don't," she said. "Please."

"I think you need somebody else," I said.

Her breath seized, as if she'd been punched.

"That was stupid," I said. "Peggy, there's something I have to tell you."

"Omigod! We *found* you!"

We both turned in the direction of the young people coming our way: Special Agent Yoshiro Hiraka—"Yoshi" on everything but his Bureau creds—and his wife, Shoreh. Yoshi was twenty-six but looked seventeen, which probably had something to do with his permanently tousled hair. Shoreh was, by her own description, a PAP—Persian American Princess. They wore T-shirts from the Smithsonian Air and Space Museum. Their newborn daughter, Rina, hung from Yoshi's stomach in a puppy pack.

"I am *so* sorry about this." Shoreh swept down into a leather armchair. "I was totally panicked when I lost the directions to the chapel—and Yoshi was all 'Don't worry, I can GPS it' or whatever . . ."

"It's okay," Peggy said. "You haven't missed anything."

"Oh, *look* at you. You are so *beautiful*." Shoreh gasped. "Mike is so much more romantic than Yoshi. *We* had to get married at a *Star Wars* convention, if you can believe that."

"Don't be fooled. She wanted a Klingon ceremony." He looked down at Peggy. "Boss, you okay?"

"I'm fine." She got up. "I'm going home to change my clothes. Mike will explain. If you can pry it out of him."

"Peg . . ."

She was already gone.

"Honey." Shoreh was stroking her daughter's arm. "Are you sure Rina's okay? She looks like she might have heat stroke."

"She's asleep. What else do babies do after two hours in an IMAX theater?" He sat down, wiping perspiration away. "Okay. Explain as in 'This is all good, and we're both just pretending to be miserable'? Or the scary kind of explaining?"

"That one," I said.

He winced. "Want me to track her down? I can probably ping her from her cell phone."

I tossed down a twenty, then threw another on top of it.

"Let her go," I said. "Peggy's had enough pinging for one day."

FOUR

I was pacing my hotel room for a cell phone signal when I heard the knock at the door. I nearly tripped over myself trying to answer it—then realized that Peggy probably wouldn't be tapping with her fingernails in her current frame of mind.

"Special delivery." A hotel employee, an ash blond woman of thirty, stood before me—pouting, as if I'd kept her waiting. Her brass name-plate read LILI. She held up my weekend bag; a padded mailer envelope was tucked against her left breast. "Where do you want this, hon? The bed?"

"The desk." I held out a ten from my wallet. "Here. Smallest I've got."

"Keep it. I see what I want right here." She set the bag on the bed. As she passed, I caught a familiar mingled scent: honey roasted peanuts and expensive cigars, masked by perfume.

"You're not from the bell staff," I said.

"It's a free country. I can be from anywhere I want." As she knelt at the minibar, I was suddenly aware that she had a shape—the kind that Iowa corn lobbyists pay money to watch.

"I recognize the fragrance," I said. "Either you've got a jones for Monte-cristos, or you work in the bar downstairs."

She laughed. "Well, now, give the man a teddy bear. I was only serving you root beer for half an hour."

"I had other things on my mind."

"Don't we all." She rummaged through liquor bottles. "Jack Daniel's, Jim Beam . . . nah. Sick of those boys. You feel like cracking open the Mumm's? Guess not. You didn't touch your lady friend's champagne."

I closed the refrigerator. "That's enough."

She pouted. "You mean the FBI won't let you expense one little bottle of booze?"

"What makes you think I'm . . . ?"

The barmaid smiled frankly. She'd caught me noticing her cleavage.

"I see enough of you people to know. Even when they're wearin' white. Plus we could all hear every blessed word you two were saying. Why do you think I switched over to ESPN?"

"Thank you for that. I'm calling security."

"Don't sulk, now. It's not attractive in a man." She opened a Sam Adams. "You may not have noticed me—but she sure did. Like she knows your type . . . and it ain't her."

I took my hand from the phone. "On second thought, screw it. I'm throwing you out myself."

"One little beer." She'd thrust it into my hand before I could stop her. "Take the edge off."

I put it on the desk, feeling its cool echo on my palm. "I left forty dollars in the ashtray downstairs. If it's money you want, go collect it. If it's something else . . ."

"You mean you can't figure me out?" She smiled. "Go on, baby. Profile me. I need it bad."

Get her out of here. Now. The warning voice in my head sounded just a little too much like Peggy to suit me.

"You asked for it." I pointed to her nameplate. "How do you pronounce that? Like the flower they give out at funerals?"

"Uh-uh. Lee-lee. Like two Confederate generals."

"Something tells me two wouldn't be enough to satisfy you." I stared into her eyes, coal-mine black. "Well, Lili-not-like-the-flower, how's your favorite baby sister in West Virginia?"

"Married and pregnant," she said. "How'd you get me?"

"Your nickname's the kind that toddlers give to their big sisters. I figure you must like her, or it wouldn't have stuck all those years. Only you changed the spelling when you came to D.C., so it wouldn't sound too much like somebody's bichon frise. Gives it a little sophistication."

"West Virginia, huh?"

"Somewhere between Parkersburg and Wheeling," I said. "You didn't pay for that perfume. More likely a gift from a recent K Street conquest. You wear it in case he can steal an hour for a matinee. It's the same brand his wife likes—he's just that careful. Only she got the good stuff. You had to settle for the eau de toilette."

She widened her eyes the way somebody might watch a knife juggler at work, more fascinated than afraid.

"Not bad," she said. "Except his wife had to switch to my brand. It makes her sneeze, but I wasn't gonna change. And I did get the good stuff. Believe it." She sniffed her wrist. "Or can't you tell the difference?"

"It's all feline anal secretions and distilled whale vomit to me," I said. "Had enough?"

"Got more?" Her eyes danced over me.

"The boyfriend doesn't know you're playing him. He wants to leave his wife for you. When you say no, he gets angry."

"They all get angry when you say no. Come on, tiger, you can do better. Tear me wide open." She laughed easily. "Tell me what's gonna happen in the next fifteen minutes."

At some point in the last few seconds, Lili had gotten way too close. She wasn't moving, so I stepped back.

"I'm not a tarot card reader," I said. "I don't predict the future."

"I bet I can." She advanced, countering me. "Even if you had followed that pretty lady to the altar today? It wasn't gonna last. Two months . . . six months, tops. You just can't help yourself when it comes to women."

Suddenly my throat was dry. "Then why are you here?"

"Because I'm what you really want," she said. "And I'm here to give you exactly what you're looking for."

As she said it, she brushed her thigh against me—a quick and sinuous move, practiced and yet absolutely effective. It drew the heat straight through me.

"Get out," I said. "This isn't funny. Go."

She didn't back away—just put her hand on her hip, like I was the most pathetic virgin ever to blow his shot at a pretty girl. Then she stroked the hair from my eyes . . . just as Peggy had done an hour before.

"Don't worry about the beer," she said. "I won't tell if you don't."

I kept my back to the desk until the door closed, my heart running a solid hundred-forty. Then my eyes found my cell phone, resting on the edge of the desk.

1 MISSED CALL, it read. Peggy's number.

"Oh, Christ." Tears on my face. My back arched and knotted like a snake impaled on a cast-iron fence.

Peggy Jean.

I took a few breaths to calm myself. Opened the phone, closed it again. One fucking bar: Never have an argument when your signal is weak. Too much chance that she'll think you hung up on her. *Why didn't I hear it ring?* I finally got smart enough to call from the hotel phone.

"Mike?" It was Yoshi, answering Peggy's cell. His voice had the flat echo of her empty apartment. "Jesus, you're bold."

"Sorry. I thought she called."

"She did. Be extremely glad you didn't answer." He dropped to a whisper. "Did they bring your stuff? Boss-lady was very insistent that nothing got left behind."

I looked at the bag, the envelope beside it. "Yeah. How'd this Bureau file wind up at the town house? Did Peggy see it?"

"The messenger came just as she and Shoreh started making voodoo dolls. So, no."

"Any chance of getting her on the phone?"

"Hang on." A door closed, muffling him. "Not unless you want to leave my baby without a father. It's never a good sign when my wife starts cursing in Farsi."

I sighed. "I guess Peg's got a right to be mad."

"Would I be hiding in a closet if she were just mad? Seriously, Mike. There's fifty states in the Union. See if you can find one that's outside her jurisdiction."

I started to speak, then found I couldn't.

"You guys have been going around and around on this marriage deal ever since I've known you," he said, relenting. "But you've never once turned your backs on each other. Think about that that, and . . . I dunno, go visit the Lincoln Memorial. He knew all about civil wars."

"He also died five days after that war ended," I said. "Please thank her for not tossing my bag into the Potomac."

"She knows the EPA rules too well for that," he said. "Courage, chief."

I hung up. Then I noticed the open bottle, sweating beads of cool water. Samuel Adams, Brewer and Patriot. *Wonder which of those two careers gave him more trouble?* I carried the beer into the bathroom, emptied it slowly until the foam disappeared. After that, all I could smell was Lili's perfume.

Inside the envelope was the Narayan file.

I skimmed through Burke's CV, then dove straight to the data on Amrita. North London girl, child of wealthy immigrants; a first at the University of Leicester, Ph.D. in experimental and clinical psychology from Oxford. By all accounts, an outgoing and very popular young woman. Twenty-six years old. Christ, I thought: When did that start to sound so young?

Young . . . and idealistic. She'd given up a lot when she ran away to build Katrina cottages with her new husband. Amrita's therapeutic practice was just starting to take off, and her previous fiancé—an arranged match through her family—was a well-heeled tax solicitor in London. Then along came charming Sammy Burke, and she threw it all right out the window.

I'd worked with guys like Burke. They were always fun to be around, good to have at your back in a fight, and they never got close to anyone unless it was somehow useful to their cover. Without knowing the details, I could guess how the romance had developed. He'd zeroed right in on whatever she had that made her special. Maybe it was her psychology training, or her family's money, or maybe it simply that she was pretty and sincere and put people at ease. He'd caught her in a weak moment—a fight with her dull-witted fiancé, a pregnancy scare after a one-night stand—and snapped her up before she could get her head back on straight. He'd never stopped to consider that his work might be dangerous for her; they never do. I never did, when I was young and foolhardy like Simon Burke.

So, midway through a steamy summer night, they tortured him to death and made her watch. Not to make him talk, because he never would, but to get something out of her. She was the valuable one. It was very possible that whatever Simon needed from her was something that Emelio Barca needed, too.

I had to admit, it sounded like Barca. He loved to find dramatic ways of hurting people. He didn't whack his enemies in alleyways; he hung them up on lampposts like Mardi Gras beads. He was cruel and unpredictable, at times even inspired. Witness the attempted murder of two federal agents, something that had seemed impossible until Barca came within an inch of pulling it off. It was his swan song, but he didn't give a shit: He'd shown us that we weren't bulletproof.

So maybe the FBI hadn't really caught him on camera after all. Maybe he'd allowed himself to be seen. Which was why his hair was so neat and his clothes were so loud. Barca was showing us all that New Orleans was still his town, screw the indictments.

Or maybe, I thought, he was only showing me.

Peggy guessed that there was someone for me back in New Orleans, and she was right. She also liked to say that everyone has to eat—and she was right about that, too. Barca didn't look like he'd missed any meals. Somebody had to be taking care of him, and it wasn't some goombah with a .38 stuffed into his sagging jeans. For that he needed someone he trusted—which, in Barca's equation, meant someone he could bully around. And it seemed he'd found a way to bring her home to him.

Barca, you shit.

I examined the surveillance photo again. There was no way I could be right about this. Sofia couldn't be in the picture. She was legally dead, living under a new name in Niknak, Alaska, or West Dogpatch, Wyoming. Three kids by a guy who sold John Deeres and called her Honey Bunny. After everything I'd done to get her free, she couldn't have come back to him of her own accord. It couldn't be her.

But it was her. And she was in the picture. One of the first things they taught me in photo analysis was not to see human faces everywhere you look. That head of Jesus on the potato chip is usually just a grease stain. So when I'd first seen light reflecting off that porthole in the surveillance photo, I'd allowed myself to believe it was just that: dark reflections off the water, a sinuous curve of light from the sun. When really it was her dark hair, her pale neck, the roundness of her cheek. Hidden in shadow, avoiding the cameras.

Sofia.

I grabbed the hotel phone.

"Kiplinger," he answered.

"You've got me," I said. "I want in."

"Hang on," he said. "Call me from your cell."

"I don't think I've got a signal—"

"Yes, you do," he said. "Five bars."

Damned if he wasn't right about that.

"I see you got the file," he said when I called back.

"Oh, I got it, all right. Why the hell did you send it to that particular address?"

"Your romance with Agent Weaver is quite possibly the Bureau's worst-kept secret," he said. "Why didn't you tell the director you had a personal conflict?"

"I had to find out if it really was a conflict," I said.

"And?"

"I don't want to talk about it." I exhaled. "So I was wrong about my connection to Barca. I'm surprised you and Vitale didn't fling it out with the rest of my dirty laundry."

"Vitale doesn't know. I figured I owed you the chance to bring it up yourself." He paused. "Which you now have."

"Does the director know?"

"He'll have to, once you've signed on. Have you?"

"I just said so. Why do you have to tell him anything?"

He gave a short laugh. "You don't think it's any of his business that you once hooked up with the daughter of Emelio Barca?"

I sat on the edge of the bed, feeling the weight of the bag beside me. "That's not how it happened."

"Well, at least now I know why you didn't go through with that wedding today." Art sounded almost pleased. "I did say you were smart enough to figure it out."

"We have to change the ops plan. If Sofia's your informant—"

"The informant's identity is not up for discussion." His voice was clean and firm. "Keep in mind that I have a very good team working this investigation, whose toes I do not want stepped on Yeager-style. Especially since you don't have any official connection to this case."

"I've got a bit too close a connection for safety," I said. "If Sofia's with her father, then infiltrating me is the absolute worst thing we can do."

"All respect, Mike, this is not your operation. You get on board, you're doing it on my terms. Understood?"

"Yes," I said. "Why do you even need to ask?"

"Because you keep acting like a man who's hedging his bets," he replied. "Once you agree to this—and you just did—there's parts of the deal you cannot control. No matter how wild your paranoia gets, you have to trust your old partner to know what he's doing and watch your back."

"I trust you, Art. You know that."

"Good. You ought to. Remember that and we'll be fine."

"I still think we should give ourselves time to cover our bases. I'll need a couple of days to clean up my mess here."

A careful silence. "You didn't tell Weaver, did you?"

"No." I decided not to mention how much she'd guessed on her own. "But Peggy's liable to get suspicious unless I can give her a better good-bye than the lame-ass one I left her with. Also, I'm supposed to serve as interim supervisor for the Crimes Against Children squad in Philly."

"Forget about that. It's dead."

"I'm not gonna do it, don't worry. It's just a few loose ends—some missing kiddie porn from our evidence locker."

"Uh-huh."

"Could be something for Vitale's crew." I lowered my voice. "I think we may have a mole in our field office."

"Mike, listen to me. Stay calm."

"I'm calm," I said. "I can handle this."

"I know." He sighed. "That's not what I'm talking about."

There was a sharp rap on the door.

"Swell," I said. "Lili's returned to raid the minibar."

"Mike—"

"Call you back." As I closed the phone, the rapping became a knock, harsh and insistent. Then a pounding.

"Michael Francis Yeager." A man's voice. Cop voice. "Open the door slowly. Then put your hands in the air."

"Oh, you rotten bastards," I whispered.

A key rattled in the lock. A moment later, the door flung wide. Three D.C. police entered, watching me with cautious fury, hunters on wild prey.

"Michael Yeager," the lead officer intoned, "you have the right to remain silent. Anything you say during questioning can and will be used against you in a court of law."

The other two cops tried to take my upper arms. I jerked them away as a fourth man came through the door.

"You have the right to an attorney—"

"Vitale," I said to his smug face, "what the hell is this?"

"Illegal transportation of criminal evidence across state lines," he said. "Among other things. Don't worry, the warrants are proper. The hotel manager signed everything."

"Oh, Christ," I said. "Not this. Please, not like this."

"You're a grown man, Yeager. Suck it up."

"Agent Vitale, we got it." One of the cops was poking at my weekend bag. "Should we take it in, or—"

Vitale shook his head. "Open it. Here. I'd like the news crew to capture his face at the exact moment he sees . . ."

The cop unzipped the bag, upended it. Out with my underwear fell the CD-ROMs. And flash drives. And printed photographs. Child pornography: sheet after tape after megabyte, still bagged for evidence. It spilled over the bedsheets, onto the rug. The Cherry Hill porn. All of it.

"Nicely handled," I said to Vitale.

"Thank you," he answered. "The girl had a gram of coke ready for you. It probably would have been easier just to fuck her and get high. But you had to go and be pure about it." He shrugged. "Like the lady said. She was here to give you what you really wanted."

Then the fearless white light of the local TV news crew was in my eyes. I could hear the dull click of handcuffs, ready to bind me.

Just make it look good, Art said. Aye, aye, Captain.

"Vitale," I said. "Here's something for the cameras."

He saw me swing, but he just couldn't duck in time.

At least I got to watch the Bastard's nose bleed before the cops landed on my ass.

FIVE

Two weeks later, I was working lunchtime security at Della's Original Oyster House on the corner of Bourbon and Iberville. There weren't too many people in New Orleans I could call out of the blue and say, *Hi, I'm under federal indictment, I need a job.* Thank God for Al and Della Crawford.

I'd known Al since the old days, when I was a rookie agent and he was working homicide in the Eighth District. He said they were lucky to have me: He was busy rebuilding their home in the Lower Ninth and didn't like to leave his wife alone, even in the daytime. I was pretty sure that Al only said that so I wouldn't feel like I was receiving charity. Which I definitely was. The indictment might have been phony, but the bail money I had to cough up was absolutely real.

The oyster house hadn't changed much in the past twenty years. Brass-rail bar, tall secluded booths, a friendly smell of Tabasco and beer. NEVER CLOSED read the illuminated sign over the door—though usually at least one of the neon letters was broken, so that it often read EVER CLOSED or NEVER CLOSE (or my personal favorite, EVE LOSED). The fact was, it never *had* closed, not for Katrina or Camille or even Betsy in 1965. Vendella Crawford—Della to friends and customers—was a true survivor.

"Excuse me." A tiny white-haired woman with an enormous blue cocktail was trying to get my attention. "Sir?"

I briefly took my attention from the TV over the bar. Three mildly inebriated middle-aged ladies smiled at me.

"I don't mean to bother you." She blushed a little. "But are you . . . I mean, are you . . . ?"

Here we go again, I thought. Vitale's office had done a swell job of putting my face all over the tabloids. I'd received plenty of hate mail over the past couple of weeks, as well as a fairly serious marriage proposal from a woman in prison. Even disgraced former FBI agents had groupies, it seemed.

"Yes?" I asked, a grumpy celebrity facing autograph hounds.

"I just wanted to know . . ." The tourist pinched her eyebrows together, embarrassed. "Do you really have to watch the TV? Because my friends and I would like to hear some Louis Armstrong music on the jukebox."

"Satchmo's not recording anymore," I said. "Died in '71. Sorry to break it to you." I turned away.

"Oh." She wasn't ready for that one. "Well, it's just that the television . . . you've got it turned up a little loud, and . . ."

I shook my head, deeply affronted. "Ma'am, that is a United States senator on C-SPAN. Please show some respect."

The tourist shrank behind her Sani-Flush margarita.

Senator James Seaweather was, in fact, chairing a special hearing on the Levin-Marcato bill. He had some serious political muscle with him on the rostrum, and for good reason: It was crunch time for a committee vote, and the battle wasn't going his way. New Orleans's future hung in the balance.

"If this bill becomes law, as some of my colleagues seem to think inevitable"—the senator punched each phrase home with his thumb—"then we must not only consider the potential benefits, but also the risks to human liberties, and the human costs. Which are almost certainly going to be heavy. And my question to you, sir, is this. Do you truly believe that our most cherished freedoms can be bought for a little money?"

The witness smiled, a balding little man in a pale gray suit. "Well, Senator," he said, "we are talking about an awful lot of money."

Laughter erupted through the Russell Caucus Room, silenced by the chair's gavel. I hadn't caught the witness's name. Somebody from one of the big corporations that were loading in on the reconstruction deal. He didn't seem too concerned about the future of his investment.

"You are offering an awful lot of money to rebuild New Orleans." The senator smiled back. "And you are also asking for an awful lot in return. The whole thing's awful, if you ask me."

"Oh, snap. Good one, Jimmy." Then I felt the blood rise to my neck. Seaweather was leaning away from the microphone to whisper to someone behind him. The person answering his call was none other than Special Agent Peggy Jean Weaver of the FBI. She bent close to his ear and said something that made him nod and smile.

"Now if we could take a look at the reorganization pl—"

Then the screen went dark. Della Crawford—a steel-haired Creole woman, fine-looking at sixty—was standing behind me, holding the remote.

"He was just getting to the reorganization plan," I said.

"I don't pay you room and board to watch TV." She snapped her fingers at me. "Come on, G-man. We got trouble over on the other side."

Tell me that woman needs a bodyguard, I thought as I followed her into the next room.

There were two halves to the restaurant, with separate entrances on Iberville and Bourbon. By some sacred and unspoken commandment, the large dining room was reserved for tourists, the small one for locals. At that moment, a crazed-looking homeless guy with saucer eyes was crashing the party. He was leather-skinned, wearing a faded Spider-Man T-shirt and a pair of moldy shorts. He also was chattering like automatic gunfire over the heads of two finely dressed people in the corner.

"Ain't a fit place for these children. And I wanna know how you can live with yaself"—he swallowed a huge gulp of air—"knowin' what you done. Wife took my kids and you people took my VA money, and the Coast Guard made me leave my dog to drown in the flood. Now you got me back on the street and back on the pipe, and I been waitin' *ten months* for you to—"

"Buddy." I got between him and the two diners. "Come on."

"Rebuild this damn city and I *ain't* your buddy, sir, this man is a criminal. He belongs in jail. You understand?"

"I understand. Relax." I looked down at the person he was spitting at. A prosperous white guy with Just-for-Men hair and fleshy lips, dressed in a sky blue summer suit. "Sir, do you know this person?"

"Obviously not." The man threw me a sullen glance. His date, a pretty dark-haired girl in a thin white dress, kept her back to me. Her right hand clung to a cosmopolitan. "I don't even know what he's talking about."

"He says you belong in jail." I put my hand on the homeless guy's shoulder. "You know something, Spider-Man, or are you just spinning a web?"

He recoiled. "Get your hands off me, y'damn lunatic! I do not give you permission to touch me, understand? I'm a war veteran, and I—"

Now I was part of the act. Della was frowning at me, clearly displeased. A dapper young man in a black shirt and sunglasses watched me from the bar, enjoying the show.

"Want you to *arrest that man*." Sweat rose from the homeless guy like a cloud of steam.

"Look, will you just *get rid* of him?" The man in the baby blue suit was turning pink. "Do your damn job, all right?"

Then I saw why his date was holding on to her glass so tightly. Nervous perspiration on her shoulders: She was shaking from shoulder to fingertip.

"It's okay," I whispered close to Spider-Man's ear. "Leave him to me. I'll take him down for you."

The homeless guy stared at me for a second, as if uncertain whether I was pulling his leg.

"You'll do it proper?"

"Swear on my mother's grave." I nodded. "The guy's dead meat, okay? You don't have to worry anymore."

After a moment's rapt consideration, Spider-Man wandered out through the open door.

"What did you just say to him?" the white man asked.

"He's gone, isn't he? Why do you care?"

"I care because I think I know what you said."

"Well, then, why'd you ask?" I circled around for a look at the girl. "All I did was promise I'd beat the shit out of you."

"What?"

I knelt down to look at her. She was painted up pretty, a real doll. Her eyes were two black mirrors, staring at nothing.

"You want to let me have that glass?" I smiled at her. "It's okay, sweetheart. Nobody's gonna hurt you."

"Do—you—mind?" But the man had lost some of his blooded indignation. He'd figured out where I was going. "I come here for good food and privacy. Not to—"

"Stick a pipe in it, sir."

"Mike," Della said.

I pried the drink out of the girl's hand. She drew her arms close to her body, shielding herself.

I sniffed the glass. "Better fire your bartender."

Della set a hand on her hip. "What's wrong with the drink?"

"I'm sure it's delicious," I said. "The kid's underage."

That got the girl's attention. "I am not."

"Look." The gentleman seemed to have rediscovered his manners.

"There's no need to raise our voices. This young lady is a family friend in trouble, and I—"

"What's her name?"

He hesitated.

"Outside." I pointed to the door. "Or you'll be getting some broken teeth on your shrimp étouffée."

The girl tried to bolt. I put a hand on her thin shoulder. She was terrified. Now I could see where she'd tried to hide her tracks with makeup.

"Easy. Easy." I nodded Della over to her.

"Check, please?" The man pushed his chair back.

"No, no, it's on me. In fact—" I took out my wallet. "How much do you want for the kid? Fifty bucks? A hundred? No, wait. Seventy-five?"

He feigned indignation. "Now, really."

"My money's as good as yours." I checked my funds. "What there is of it, anyway. Come on, I'll take her off your hands. What's the going rate for a drug-addicted child prostitute these days?"

"Please don't say that." The girl stared up at me, desperate. "I'm not a whore."

Della took hold of her. The man anxiously looked to the exits. Most of the diners had stopped eating a long time ago.

"Suit yourself," he said. "We'll take it outside."

"*Mike.*" Della's voice was filled with warning.

I didn't answer as he walked ahead of me to the exit. I met him on Iberville, away from the crowds.

"I know who you are." He was calm, almost cordial. "Do you know who I am?"

"Yeah. You're my first child molester of the day."

He smiled. "Actually, I'm in the district attorney's office."

"I should resist pounding you because you're a lawyer?"

"I have friends in Washington." He squinted in the noonday sun. "Including the prosecutors in your upcoming trial. So don't lecture me about child endangerment, Mr. Yeager. I know how you got that money you were waving at me."

"Agent Yeager," I answered.

"Not anymore, you're not," he said. "And you only had forty dollars in your wallet. You sure you want to take this all the way?"

I thought about it. "What about the girl?"

"She decided to sit down at my table. No idea why. Never saw her before in my life." He shrugged. "If you're ready to be reasonable, I might be willing to pass the good word along to my contacts at federal district court."

"You're offering to intervene on my behalf in an evidence-tampering trial if I let you walk on solicitation of a minor."

"What choice do you have? Right now you can't even give me a ticket for loitering." He buttoned his jacket. "I wouldn't risk my neck over the kid. Two hours from now, she'll be back on the street, peddling her cute little—"

I drove my fist straight into those fat lips. The attorney's eyes rolled back, startled. I caught him in the gut with my left. Then I took his head in both hands and threw it against the old brick wall. His skull made a dull sound, like a bag of sand. He went down faster than a Mardi Gras drunk, spitting his lunch onto the sidewalk. I knelt down and grabbed him by the collar, aiming his mouth away from me.

"Here's a good word," I said. "Stay away from children."

"Mike!" Della stared cold fury at me. "For God's sake, release that man this instant! Are you insane?"

Now my hands were starting to throb. People stood in the doorway. From the corner of my eye, I thought I could see the girl beginning to smile.

"Everybody, let's get back to eatin'." Della turned back to her clientele. "Come on, it ain't like you never saw a fight in the Quarter before."

I watched the attorney pull himself to his feet. That nice blue suit, covered in his own barf. I considered following him. Then I felt fingers tapping me on the shoulder.

"You left your wallet inside the restaurant." It was the man in the dark shades.

I took it from him. "Thanks."

"My pleasure." He offered me a saturnine grin. "You might want to be gone when the police arrive. No rush, of course. It usually takes them a few hours to find their asses and elbows." He peered over his sunglasses, showing pale green eyes. "Well done, by the way. Nice to find a man of conviction."

Then he was gone. The lawyer had meanwhile skulked into the shadows. Probably dove into a titty bar to see if he could still score. I dreaded going back into the restaurant, knowing that Della was waiting for me. She'd make me clean up that vomit. As I slipped the wallet into my back pocket, I noticed that it felt uncomfortably bulky.

It was stuffed with cash. Ten crisp new portraits of Ulysses S. Grant stared gravely at me. A vintage calling card was enclosed with the money, printed in elegant script:

MLLE. JOSEPHINE DE BONANGE
BASIN AND ST. LOUIS STREETS
WILL RECEIVE DISCREET CALLERS AT ANY TIME

Aujourd'hui, someone had written on the back, a man's handwriting; *a l'heure verte*. Today at the green hour. Whatever the hell that meant.

"Mike." Della, standing in the doorway. "You done stuck me with this child. Come in and help me deal with her."

I pocketed my wallet and went inside to face the consequences.

SIX

Between the girl, Child Protective Services, and a restaurant full of nervous customers, the whole mess took nearly an hour to sort out. By then, it was just me and Della in the Iberville room.

"Well, you sure earned your money today." She stood behind the bar, shucking oysters for the dinner crowd. "How'd you know she was fifteen? She looked old enough to fool everybody else."

"It's something in their eyes," I said. "Even the ones who've been in the life for a while. It's like they know how they're supposed to behave, but they don't know why."

"Sure you ain't talkin' about yourself?" She put the shucking knife down. "You know you didn't make one bit of difference. That child will be back on the street again by end of day."

It sounded cynical when the lawyer said it. Della just looked tired.

"It made a difference," I said.

"Yeah. To my bottom line." She took off her gloves and wordlessly refilled my bowl of pork rinds. "In case you didn't notice, I ain't been so prosperous since the storm. Today was the first decent lunch shift I've had since I don't know when. Word gets around when there's trouble, Mike. It does."

"Let the word go forth." I took a mouthful of pork rinds. They were locally made, pepper-spiced, and you couldn't get them anywhere but Della's. I washed them down with a Big Shot root beer. "Tell me something. Do you enjoy watching human slime prey on innocent children? Thinking they can get away with it because they've got money and the system is corrupt?"

She bit her lip before answering. "I cook for people. If I wanted to make my living judging people, I woulda become a judge." She turned away to wash her hands. "How'd you like it if I started in on you?"

I stopped eating. "What's the verdict?"

"You didn't come down here to clean up New Orleans." She shut the water off. "Who were you really hoping to find in my restaurant?"

Something in her voice froze me to the bar stool. A moment later, the door crashed open behind me. I turned, ready for the NOPD goon squad. Instead, the doorway was filled by a broad-chested black man in a yellow golf shirt. His face was hot with distress, halfway to rage, and for a second I was convinced I was about to die. Then his eyes settled on me, and his grin broke wide—a smile so wholehearted, so completely generous, that you would never know it belonged to a homicide cop. Detective Sergeant A. E. Crawford, retired.

Big Al.

"Mike, thank God!" He laughed deep from the soles of his size fourteen shoes. "Shit, woman, you about gave me a stroke! From the way you were hollerin' on the phone, I thought I was gonna have to knock somebody's jaw in for him."

I smiled back as Al set a two-foot section of lead pipe on the bar.

"But damn, Yeager." He pulled me into a bear hug. "It is good to know you're here protectin' my beautiful wife! Feels just like old times, don't it?"

"Yup." I coughed, trying to refill my lungs. "Feels like you just separated a rib, too."

"If you boys are done huggin' on each other . . ." Della stared coldly. "Mike wasn't protectin' me from nobody, Al. Fact is, Mike is the trouble I'm in."

"What happened?" Al's hand rested on my neck.

"That ol' fishlips-lookin' lawyer had a new girl in here. Your buddy Mike made him puke on the sidewalk."

"Damn." Al couldn't suppress a grin. "I always said that guy was a merlin. Only wish I'd been here to see it."

"That 'merlin' has friends in the health department. *And* the liquor board. What do you think's gonna happen to us if they shut me down?"

"Bring 'em on, baby. You're married to a detective in the mighty Eighth District."

"Not since you retired, I ain't." She sighed. "You take Mike with you to the house so I can get some work done. Least he can't do any damage to the Lower Nine that ain't been done already."

Al looked worried. "What are you gonna do here alone?"

"Shuck oysters and curse the day we met." She threw me a sour look. "You really wanna know what my verdict is on you, Mike Yeager? You won't like it."

I nodded timidly.

"Guilty of havin' a guilty conscience," she said. "I saw that hoodlum stick a bunch of money in your wallet. You do know who he is, right?"

"No idea."

"You best make it your business to find out. When you take money from a man—"

"Nobody paid me a dime to beat up Fishlips."

"I ain't talkin' about him. Or the girl. You know damn well who I mean. Been a long time since she tended bar up in here."

"Sofia." I waited. "Della, she's dead."

She eyed me coolly. Al looked away.

"That's right. Dead." She picked up the knife. "And then, lo she rose from the grave, like Jesus and New Orleans. And here you up and come, callin' out for her like John the Baptist."

"I think you're getting your Bible mixed up." I tried to wink and it came out a nervous twitch. Della let me get to the door before speaking.

"You think maybe I should have said Judas?"

I turned. She wasn't smiling.

"Don't you try and start it up with that woman again. You heard she was dead, leave her be dead. She ain't your sweet young thing to play with, like in the old days."

"You've seen her?"

"I don't see what don't concern me." She gave a warning nod to her husband. "Talk some sense into him, Al. Tell him how John the Baptist wound up."

"Come on, Yeager." Al shepherded me out the door. "Let's go set the universe to rights."

Driving across the St. Claude Avenue drawbridge was always an exercise in mild terror. Its metal grating dug into the tire treads of Al's green minivan, making it buck and swerve like the bridge was trying to dump us both into the Industrial Canal. It aggravated the sick feeling in my stomach, which I had been trying to blame on Vendella's pork rinds.

"I thought I was doing the right thing," I said. "Della hates me now, doesn't she?"

Al laughed. "She loves you, Mike. She's only just tryin' to save you from yourself."

"Good luck with that."

Finally we were on the other side. As we turned onto Deslonde, Al waved cheerfully to a couple of uniformed guards protecting an abandoned gas station. They didn't wave back. Their armored transport vehicle was gunmetal gray. A strange logo was decaled on where you'd normally expect to see an American flag: three red triangles on a black semicircle.

"Not the National Guard?" I asked.

"Private security. Those boys act like they run the show, nowadays." He shook his head. "Okay, home again."

We drove the streets in silence. I'd seen the destruction on TV—but it was nothing like being there, even a year later. Some of the homes in the Lower Ninth Ward were at least partly on their foundations, their rusted cars parked in gutted-out garages. Spray-painted *X*'s marked the ones that had been checked for bodies. Other buildings had collapsed, or floated partway into adjoining lots. Most of them were just plain gone.

"It's the quiet that gets to me." Al lowered his voice. "You remember how it was before Katrina—and her hellcat baby sister, Rita. Bad roads, sure. Drugs and gangs, you bet. But these were my friends here, they were homeowners. We had pride in this neck of the woods. You could get a nice meal on every block, you could hear music at night . . . it was a lively place."

Now it was like a trailer park on the surface of the moon, I thought as we bounced along that mass of potholes called Jourdan Avenue. "This is about where that kidnapping was, isn't it? Those two charity volunteers?"

"Near about. We can take a look if you're interested."

"If we've got time, sure."

"Time is just about all we have left." He pointed to the concrete flood wall along the levee. "Those dark sections are where they repaired the breaches. I was in the CBD when the trouble came, near to the Dome. And wasn't *that* a pig's eye. Della was here with her niece. It came up around her ankles, and she said right away—'We need to get out of here. Now.' By the time she finished that sentence, it was up to her hips."

"How long did it take for you to find each other?"

"Too long." He filled his chest, as if bracing himself against some heavy memory. Then he pulled the minivan over. We were at the Florida Avenue rail bridge, halfway between the river and the lake. "Okay. That's the house where I found that poor English fella."

I raised my eyebrow. "You were on the scene?"

"I was first cop on the scene. Retired cop, anyhow. These tourists come runnin' into my yard yellin', 'We found somebody who got killed in the hurricane.' Like anything stays fresh around here for two days, let alone nine months." He shook his head in disbelief. "I guess some people think that's how we handle our dead in New Orleans. Leave 'em to rot."

We both fell silent as he tore away the crime scene tape.

There were still a few yellowing letters in the rusting mailbox, addressed to Kendrick and Rosemary Duplessis. Just walking in the front door was enough to make me feel like a grave robber. Even a year later, the stink of mold was everywhere. Plaster had fallen from the walls, revealing the wooden lathing underneath. Children's crayon drawings were trampled in long-dried mud. The furnishings were gone—except for a family portrait, propped against the far wall. Right next to it was a smoked glass tube: crack pipe.

The floorboards were stained black where Simon Burke had died.

"Who lived here?" My voice sounded dry and stale in the dusty air.

"Nice people," Al said. "Kenny worked for an auto body shop in Bywater. Rosey cut ladies' hair in her dining room."

"Kids?"

"One son. That's their grandkids' crayon pictures on the ground. Nobody's seen hide nor hair of 'em since the storm. Somebody told me they made it to Houston, but you never can tell. So many people just up and disappeared."

I studied the family picture against the wall: Kenny and Rosey, two boys, and a young woman who was evidently their mother. The children's father was not in the picture.

"The evidence teams didn't want any help from me," Al was saying. "They picked this place over pretty good, I guess. Although how they managed to miss that rifle shell casing . . ."

"Rifle?"

He nodded. "Five-point-five-six caliber. Military weapon, if I'm not mistaken. The casing had some kind of plastic jacket on it. Bright red, like a lady's lipstick. That's how sloppy these Fifth District boys are. Can't see for shit."

I paused to consider that. The crime scene report Art gave me didn't mention rifle casings, 5.56 or otherwise—and I was pretty sure that the kill shot to Burke's head was from a 9 mm.

"Where'd you find the casing?" I asked.

"Out back." Al raised his eyebrow. "Michael F. Yeager, please tell me you're not tryin' to work this case."

"Just morbid curiosity." I sniffed the air. "Jesus, what is that smell?"

"Refrigerator." He cocked a thumb into the kitchen. "Most people had theirs hauled away long ago. Ken and Rosey just never came back for it. Probably full of rotten pork. Kenny did love his ham and biscuits."

I knew that smell from a hundred murder scenes. As I approached the old refrigerator, the cold dread that had been rising through me suddenly swelled.

"Mike, don't—"

"Cover your nose." Before I could stop myself, I gripped the handle and pulled hard. The door came open with a sticky sound. A noxious stink of ancient meat filled the air. No dead bodies in there: just rows of plastic containers, blackened and grotesquely swollen with rot. Shoals of maggots spilled to the ground and immediately began crawling for darkness. The smell practically knocked me to the ground.

"Jesus, let's get the hell out of here." Al pressed his hat to his face. I followed him at a trot.

Al and Della Crawford lived at the ironically named intersection of Flood Street and Law. For the next couple of hours, I helped him with the stud framing of his new home—a smaller version of the one that had vanished in the deluge. Afterward, we drank sweet tea in the shade of his trailer, an oasis of suburbia in the midst of a dead land.

"Were you lying to Della before?" The lawn chair creaked a little as Big Al settled into it. "Or do you really not know who that green-eyed fellow was who gave you the money?"

"I wouldn't be too good at my job if I didn't," I said. "Graziano Amadeo Barca—Grady to friends and associates. Don Emelio's beloved third son by his second wife."

"Also Sofia Barca's not-so-beloved half brother," he said. "Those Sicilians are gettin' pretty bold lately, aren't they? Thought you FBI boys dealt 'em out a long time ago."

"So did I." I handed the calling card to him. "This came with the cash."

He studied it closely. "Looks like a Storyville card."

"Yeah? How's that?"

"Well, you recall that Storyville was the old-time red-light district, right where the Iberville projects are today. Back then, even hookers had calling cards. You could probably get some money for it on eBay."

"I seriously doubt the card's authentic, Al. Take a closer look at the address. Basin and St. Louis?"

"St. Louis Cemetery Number One." He chuckled. "I guess Miss Bonange really *is* receiving discreet callers anytime."

"Bonange was the maiden name of Sofia Barca's mother," I said. "Also the name of her father's marina on the north shore. It seems they want to meet me at the 'green hour.' Maybe Barca's turned environmentalist?"

"Probably just has a taste for strange liquor." Al handed the card back. "The 'green hour' is when people used to drink absinthe. Green booze, green hour. Fancy way of saying five o'clock. You sure you want to keep that appointment? You never know who might decide to show up."

"I'm not in business with Emelio Barca," I said.

"I believe you. And I don't blame you for keepin' the money, times bein' what they are." He leaned in to catch my eye. "But you kind of dodged my question. Is Della right about you trying to get back with Sofia?"

"She's in the past," I said.

"Your past has a hard time staying that way," he said. "I know how stuck you were on that girl. Can't blame you too much. She was a heartbreaker."

"Yeah." I nodded. "Broke a few plates and glasses, too. Everybody always wondered why Della kept her behind the bar, with those butterfingers of hers."

"That's easy. She was kind to people. Folks can get drunk anyplace. But Sofia? No matter how busy she got, she always—"

"Listened," I said.

"You should know." He smiled. "Tiny little dancer, we called her. Black hair, black eyes . . . always wore black, too. Remember how we used to joke around that her other job was as a professional mourner?"

"God knows the irony of that has stayed with me through the years." I shook my head. "I really screwed her over, didn't I?"

"You did what you had to." He looked at me soberly. "When you reported on the death of that uncle of hers . . . you did what nobody else could. You broke the mob in New Orleans."

"For all the good it did." I sighed. "Yeah, I guess I owe my FBI career to old Uncle Paulie, rest in peace. And I'd do anything to undo the harm that report of mine caused."

"Anything?"

I didn't answer. Al just shook his head.

"Damn it, Della was right. You did come down for Sofia."

"I swear to God—"

"Forget it. It's too late. I've seen it in your face." He leaned in. "Take this from your old friend, Big Al. Go easy down here. No 'undoing' anything in my hometown, okay? We've had Betsy and Katrina and Rita. We do not need Hurricane Mike."

I smiled. "What's Al short for, anyway? Alibi?"

He put his head back and laughed. No one had ever correctly guessed Al's full given name, and he always gave a different answer each time you asked. Aloysius, Al Jazeera, Allakazam—the answers got more creative with the years.

"Alzheimer's," he said. "Or is it? I can never remember anymore." His smile let me know that he wasn't going to probe if I didn't feel like talking. Then again, that was usually how he got people to talk.

"I don't need to make trouble, Al. I've got plenty enough of my own."

"So I heard." He nodded gravely. "People say . . . terrible things about you now. That you've gone dishonest. That you took money from child abusers to steal evidence. It doesn't make you look too good."

"Nope." I swatted a mosquito. "Does it change the way you feel about me?"

"We'll always be friends," he answered simply. "I guess I wouldn't be much of a friend if I didn't give you a chance to say it ain't so."

I fumbled in silence for a few agonizing seconds. Then finally he let me off the hook, and we went to talking about other things. I had no choice but to maintain my cover. But it hurt like hell to let Al Crawford think I was crooked.

SEVEN

At a quarter to five I stood at the crossroads of Basin and St. Louis, watching tourists and mourners wander in and out of the cemetery. The text message I'd sent to Art was still on my screen:

> Contact made
> 5pm today
> How do I do this?

I told myself that I was only waiting for Kiplinger's reply—although I knew full well what his answer would be, even before it finally arrived.

> Any way you can
> G-d be with you

I made sure to delete both messages before walking through the cemetery gates.

You did what you had to, Al said. *Any way you can,* Art wrote. And what had Lili-the-barmaid told me in that Washington hotel room? *You just can't help yourself when it comes to women.* It would have been nice to believe them all, especially where Sofia was concerned. It would also have been a complete lie. At the end of the day, I did what I thought was the least of all possible evils. Not the same thing as doing right. And I chose my method as carefully as any surgeon chooses a scalpel.

When I first met her, I thought my intelligence had to be wrong. No way could she be Barca's daughter. Sofia vaguely resembled our only photo of her—taken when she was ten—and she'd kept the name her late mother gave her, although the surname was different for obvious reasons. But she was nothing at all like her father. Right from the start, she trusted me as easily as if we'd shared a cradle. We cruised the Quarter like school run-aways, partners in crime, and each night I'd go home and file my daily report on her.

As far as she knew, I was in charge of security for a local bank. It was an easy cover, and it explained why I kept a .38 under my jacket. I tried to give the impression that my job didn't make me happy, that I was open to temptation. There were times when I wasn't entirely sure I was pretend-ing. On paper, my assignment was to keep tabs on Sofia in case her father tried to get in touch. In reality, I knew my job was to find out her secrets. My supervisor dropped hints that he didn't much care how I got the goods, as long as they came gift-wrapped. I told myself it was all right to be her friend, because she wasn't a focus of the investigation, and because we weren't sleeping together. Both of which were true enough, for a while.

In those days, she lived at Algiers Point and took the ferry to work. Some nights I'd ride back with her, just to make sure she got home safe. Even then, I couldn't help noticing how cautious she was in public. She said that her dad owned a marina on the north shore of Lake Pontchartrain. I knew she didn't like him, even though everyone else seemed to. She even told me that I'd like him, if we ever met. He was a naturally charismatic person. All of that went into my 302s.

Still, there were a few other things about Sofia that I didn't put into my daily reports.

To begin with, there was no denying that Sofia was a mediocre bar-tender. She mixed the drinks according to whim, and her hurricanes tasted like rancid Kool-Aid. And she had a tendency to drop things, spilling beer and crawfish all over her customers' laps. They laughed and forgave her because she listened, as Al said, because she was friendly and kind, but also because she always seemed just a little bit lost.

She was also, let's face it, an incredibly bad singer. Sofia had gotten one chance from Della on open-mike night—two off-key verses of "God Bless the Child" was as much as anyone could take—and that was it for her per-forming career. She loved music, though, and she knew good from bad. She'd picked Harry Connick Jr. for a rising star, when I thought he was only our district attorney's pampered son. Sofia also had a head for money, which was another reason Della kept her close to the till. In a couple of years she probably would have started her own club, maybe even managed a few bands. Sofia sometimes said that music had nearly destroyed her on her sixteenth birthday, but it had also saved her life. She was vague on the details. I did notice the scar on the inside of her right wrist.

There was so much more that my supervisor didn't know, that I didn't want him to know. Like the echoes of sadness that sometimes fell between Sofia's words, even when she was happy, like rain on a clear day. That wild-rose scent about her. The violin curve of her back. Those unbelievable Italian hand gestures that seemed to follow her conversation like subtitles. The way she laughed in her sleep, and cried after making love. How could I put those things into a report?

I convinced myself that it was an accident, that it wouldn't have happened if it hadn't rained that December night. But it did rain, heavy and unmerciful. Nobody was coming into the restaurant, and she was alone, listening to Nanci Griffith on the jukebox. Some country-folk song about finding love once in a very blue moon. I thought it was sad and sweet right up to the fifteenth time she played it, and then it started to make me insane. She forced me to pay for every song. I protested that I needed my quarters for the laundry, but she just kept making me hand them over. My laundry, she said, would only get dirty again. The song would be guaranteed to stay in my head forever. She was right about that, too.

Sofia was going through hard times. She told me that her Uncle Paulie wasn't doing well, some financial troubles with the family. I let her carry on talking as if it were just a squabble over Grandma's crystal. Sofia said that Uncle Paulie was the only person who ever stood up for her. Inside, my heart was beating a Gene Krupa solo. I was getting close.

Just before dawn, I told her that I would stand up for her, if she ever needed me to. Stupid and young as I was, I actually meant it. Stupid and young as she was, she believed me absolutely. Then she kissed me, hard and needing. Seconds later, Della came roaring in through the back door. Della didn't seem to care that she'd caught me and Sofia with our hands up each other's shirts. All she wanted was some help carrying in the live oysters. Finally, she took pity and sent us both away. Sofia and I spent most of the next forty-eight hours on her futon in Algiers Point, wrapped around each other like saltwater taffy. That was how it began.

That was how it went on. After that her secrets flowed like water. Mine held like a concrete dam. One day over breakfast, Sofia finally told me who her father really was. I said that I didn't judge her for it. The look of gratitude she gave me caught in my throat like a shard of glass.

It all started to break right around Mardi Gras. I asked her if she liked the parades and she said yes, but I couldn't help noticing how she always seemed to keep one eye on the floats and another on the crowd. We were lined up for Orpheus when a female cousin of hers approached us, chastising Sofia for being out of touch for so long. The cousin went on to say how much better Sofia's arm was looking, how sorry her father was that it had to happen like that, in front of everyone. Sofia barely masked her hostility. Later, when we were under the covers, she told me how she had gotten the scar on her wrist.

Parties at the marina were always a big deal, she said, and her father liked to spend money where people could see it. He'd paid a fortune for her Sweet Sixteen, even though she had asked him not to. He'd hired two different bands—a jazz combo and a Jimmy Buffett tribute group—because he knew music was important to her. He had tried, unsuccessfully, to hire Jimmy Buffett. Then, at the height of the celebration, her dad presented her with an original 1956 Gibson Les Paul Custom electric guitar: the Black Beauty.

By then he had a belly full of liquor. There was homemade wine at every table, very strong, and glasses were never empty. She'd never seen him so happy. Finally—around one o'clock in the morning—the wine began to run low, the musicians ended their final set, and the guests showed signs of wanting to leave. Her father hated it when parties ended too soon. He said that, in his youth, his friends had no money but they never stopped celebrating. He decided that there should be more wine and more music. He sent two of Sofia's male friends out on a booze run, even though it was early Sunday and there were blue laws. Then he asked Sofia to play a song on the expensive guitar he'd bought for her.

There was just one problem: Sofia played guitar about as well as she could sing; which is to say, not at all. She told her father so. She told him a few more times, in as many ways as she could think of. Then she finally gave up, laughing from exhaustion and giddy terror.

No one was really sure when it stopped being a game. Her father went quiet, always a terrible sign. He began to wonder aloud if perhaps he had made a poor choice. Maybe the guitar wasn't suited to his daughter's fine tastes. Maybe she just didn't like the color. Sofia explained that it was a classic instrument, it was gorgeous, but she couldn't play well enough to deserve such a gift. Her father accused her of trying to refuse his love for her. He demanded a song as proof that he was mistaken. Someday, when he was old and deaf, he would need the memory of her playing guitar for him on her sixteenth birthday, to comfort him in his final days. He had to know that he was truly loved.

Sofia finally picked up the guitar and strummed a few sappy chords about the cat in the cradle and the silver spoon. Some of her friends laughed and applauded nervously. Her father's smile died a slow death. Then she put the Gibson into her father's lap and said if that wasn't enough to comfort him in his old age, perhaps he should hire a more expensive daughter. He blankly accepted a kiss on the cheek. Then he told her to pour him another glass of wine.

As she told me the story, Sofia took my finger and ran it very softly along the ridge of the scar.

The boys hadn't returned with the beer—maybe they'd been arrested; they were underage, after all—and there was only enough wine left for one full glass. Her father would have it. Sofia obediently reached across the glass patio table for the pitcher—and, as she did, he brought the guitar swiftly and smoothly down on her arm. Twice. He wasn't angry when he did it, she told me, not even on the second stroke. Anger meant weakness, and her father was very strong. Which explained the scar. And why she always dropped the platters at work. And why she never saw much of her friends and relatives after that—at least, not the ones who stood by and watched it happen.

Uncle Paulie had not watched it happen. When he finally came back from paying the musicians, Paulie went so pale that his face looked blue. Without raising his voice, he said something in Italian that instantly stayed her father's hand. Then he drove Sofia to North Shore Hospital, where their family doctor was given a great deal of cash to set the arm she had broken while diving in the lake.

Sofia said that she would always remember what Paulie told her that night. Live through this, he said, any way you can. That's how you show your father who's stronger: Live through it. She knew that Paulie did not dare say more. Her father had friends at the hospital who would tell him everything.

Before he left her, Uncle Paulie asked Sofia if she needed anything. She suggested that her father's heart and lungs might be nice, but she'd settle for her Sony Walkman. He brought it to her along with the tapes she liked best, and she listened to Nanci Griffith singing "Once in a Very Blue Moon" in a morphine haze. That was how she lived through it.

I asked her if she was playing the song for her Uncle Paulie on that night in the bar. No, she said. Just for you.

That spring turned out to be a hot one, and the FBI brass was sending down most of the heat. Time for some serious indictments in the Barca investigation, fuck or walk. Time for Agent Yeager to be a hero. By slow and easy steps, I convinced Sofia that she needed to reconcile with her family. If there was trouble, I promised her, I'd be at her side. I'd catch her if she fell. So, in perfect trust, she finally took me to the marina. Just as she predicted, I hit it off with her dad right away. Most of the others were blandly indifferent to me: I wasn't Italian, and apparently her boyfriends never lasted very long. Only Uncle Paulie seemed to perceive the threat this German boy represented, as though I were the first Visigoth to come riding over the Palatine Hill. I don't know if he ever expressed his doubts about me to the don. All I know is that Paulie Barca was dead less than a week after Sofia introduced us.

After that, Barca took me under his wing with perverse gusto. At first I worried that I was being coddled while his henchmen dug my grave. However, it soon became clear that Paulie's death had created a void—one that I, against all logic, was beginning to fill. Night after night, the two of us shot the breeze in his cramped study, drinking stolen whiskey while he talked through a haze of unfiltered Camels. The don told me a lot about his childhood and a little about his business practices. I laughed at his punch lines, feverishly waiting for the ice pick in the back of my neck.

By the end of April, Sofia was talking fairly seriously about getting us both out of New Orleans. I didn't sense jealousy or resentment in her: I sensed fear. Something bad was coming down the wind that she could sense, even if I couldn't. It was our last chance to break free, start over, live the way we chose, instead of the way our parents chose for us. Or just live, period.

It bothered me that Sofia still thought I was a bank detective. It bothered me more that she believed I was capable of doing better. I finally admitted that I wanted to go to graduate school—which I did—and study outdoor photography like Ansel Adams. After that, she wouldn't leave me alone until I got the applications and put a portfolio together. We were supposed to look through that portfolio on the night I finally told her who I really was.

I think I may have tried to convince her that my report to the FBI would help Sofia get revenge for Uncle Paulie. I hope and pray that's not what I said. She let me get through the whole speech, and then she said one word: okay. It wasn't: *okay, I forgive you*. Or even: *okay, go to hell*. It was much more practical than that: *okay, we have to leave now*. She got all the cash she'd saved—like I said, she was good with money—and then I drove her to the bus station. By then she'd figured out that I wasn't coming with her.

I didn't know where her bus was going. We agreed it was better that way. She wouldn't let me carry her bag. Instead she took it under her weak right arm, fractured and healed in two places, and said that I didn't need to care about her anymore. I told her that I would always care about her, that her safety was everything to me. Then Sofia Barca looked at me with her dark, lonely eyes and spoke the only harsh words I'd ever heard her say to me. She said that maybe she'd have been safer if I'd cared a little less, and listened a little more.

The next morning, I told my supervisor what I'd done.

I expected to be fired, even prosecuted. Instead, my boss took me to lunch. The service at Galatoire's was impeccable, the food outstanding. I couldn't swallow a bite. The old man ate like a starved Viking. Over prime rib and béarnaise sauce, he told me that my liaison with the Barca girl was a youthful indiscretion. What mattered was that I'd gotten her father cold. I shouldn't trouble my conscience over how the information came to me.

I guess I did all right for the team. In the end, we netted forty-two of Barca's soldiers and lieutenants, the best month's work I ever did. We got just about everybody who mattered, except for Emelio Barca himself. Ten years later, my supervisor became the director of the FBI. Ten years after that, he dropped dead of a heart attack. Ungrateful child that I was, I didn't even go to his funeral.

I came back tipsy from Galatoire's that afternoon, and made an excuse to leave early so I could stay that way. That night I got stinking drunk. I took my photography portfolio to a Dumpster. Then I stayed up till dawn in a booth at Della's, refusing all company, throwing back Jim Beam and listening to Nanci Griffith. Somewhere around the third time through, I finally realized that the song wasn't about falling in love. It was about someone who's trying to offer kindness to a brokenhearted woman, even though he was the one who broke it. How there are times when a broken heart is all that ex-lovers have left to share. She had been playing it for me.

Care a little less. Listen a little more. Name two things that Michael F. Yeager cannot do to save a life.

That was my last bottle of whiskey, and the last coin I ever put into a jukebox. After that, if anyone ever offered me a drink, I'd say no. If that song ever happened to play within earshot, I'd either turn if off or get up and leave. And I would be damned if anybody ever got me on the ferry to Algiers. Those were things I knew about Sofia that had never gone into my daily reports to the FBI, that I would try my best to carry with me to the grave.

EIGHT

"This place is so *cool*," a ten-year-old girl was saying as she and her sister raced among the tombs. "It's like you're at the Haunted Mansion in Disney World. But it's *real*."

"There's nowhere to pee," her younger sister said anxiously. "Where's Mommy?"

St. Louis Cemetery No. 1 is a pocket-sized necropolis on the northern edge of the Vieux Carré. The twin-chambered tombs are packed together like slum tenements, protected by angry-looking iron fences with arrow-pointed spikes. The crypts are reusable: Heat and humidity rapidly cook the coffins to ash, making room for new bodies in the upper deck. The caretakers refer to these vaults as "ovens" with no discernible sense of irony. Death has always been a routine business in New Orleans.

Mademoiselle de Bonange was waiting for me in a crypt along the cemetery wall, surrounded by the men of her family. Some dirt-daubers had built a nest in the shade of her memorial stone; a few wasps crawled lazily around it. Josephine's elaborately carved epitaph was juicy enough for the jacket blurb of a gothic romance novel:

Here lies the mortal dust of our dear fallen
JOSEPHINE LUCIE DE BONANGE
April 1, 1886–December 6, 1904
Taken in the blossom of youth from a family who truly loved her
and reduced to her degraded avocation by a base rascal
whose name is unfit to be recorded here.
"I kissed thee ere I killed thee."—Wm. Shakespeare

For a loving family, they sure laid it on pretty thick. I had just barely read to the bottom when I heard a muffled ringtone. It took me a few seconds to realize that the music was coming from inside the crypt.

I checked my watch: five o'clock on the button. I shot a quick glance around me to make sure no tourists or nuns were watching, then pushed aside a loose brick and reached in. I wasn't sure if I was more afraid of getting stung by a wasp or making contact with Mademoiselle Josephine's mortal dust.

My hand touched plastic. I pulled out the disposable phone and answered it on the fourth ring.

"You recognize my voice?" came the answer.

"How's your father?" I responded.

"He sends his regards," Grady replied. "Take a moment to appreciate the headstone. It's a masterpiece of its kind. The decorative flowers carved into the border. Medlar fruits—symbols of prostitution—entwined with lilies, symbols of virginity. The pure and the profane, united in death. Remarkable, isn't it?"

"Are we doing business, or is this a floral arrangement class?"

"It's a stickup," he said. "Turn around."

I could smell cordite even before I saw him. A remorseless-looking Hispanic man in a sleeveless T-shirt calmly aimed his 9 mm at me.

"Guess I don't get to keep the five hundred, huh?"

"Just cooperate," Grady said. "If you're playing square with us, you'll get it all back with interest."

The gunman didn't get his scars in prison. They were puckered circles, bullet wounds. A small blue skull was tattooed on his chest, with the number 316 in the center. I recognized it instantly: Battalion 316. Honduran death squad.

I tossed my wallet onto the pavement, then my keys, hearing the laughter of tourists from a short distance off. I silently wished them away as I threw down my own cell phone, keeping the disposable phone at my ear.

"*Los zapatos,*" the gunman said. "*Y la correa.*"

"He says he wants my shoes and belt."

"Better listen to him. The guy's CIA-trained to kill assholes like you." Grady sounded amused. "Oh, and by the way? If you're wearing a fucking wire, Mikey, you're going to wish you'd been the one to open up that box of Chinese."

The line went dead. I threw down the second phone, then removed my belt and shoes. The gunman silently watched me with all the emotion of an alligator gar.

"That's as far as I go without a brass pole," I said.

Then the shooter's eyes darted to the side. The two young girls stood screaming at us.

"Kids, get back!" I yelled.

"Mommy that guy's got a g—"

The last thing I felt was a wasp on my neck.

I came to in darkness, awakened by the noise of an outboard engine pounding against water. From the pitch-and-yaw motion, I guessed I was in a speedboat making crazy Ivans around Lake Pontchartrain. Felt like I might be in the forward compartment. The wasp sting—or whatever it was that knocked me out—itched like crazy, but I couldn't reach it. My hands were cuffed behind me. At least I still had all my teeth.

Finally the boat cruised to a stop. Then the hatch opened, and the smell of gasoline gave way to the stink of low tide. I was lifted to the deck of a darkened boathouse.

"Wakey wakey." A match flared in the shadows. "You're a lucky fellow, Mr. Yeager. My father gave strict orders not to lay a finger on you. Otherwise I could have saved myself a dart."

"What happened to . . ." My voice slurred. "The girls?"

"The girls. The girls." The red coal of a cigarette illuminated Grady Barca's poisonous green eyes. "I forget, Ciro. Did we finally decide to shoot them . . . or what?"

Ciro, the Honduran gunsel, merely shrugged and pushed me out into a gray twilight. BONANGELA MARINA read the flaking sign over the board-walk. A few pleasure boats still hung in their slips, strewn with debris. Many more were half-buried along the shore, canvas sails covering them like body bags. I remembered the place very well. Somewhere beyond the line of magnolias and live oaks was the clubhouse, with its various changing rooms and laundries that Barca had once used for warehousing drugs. Beyond that was the old colonial residence: the famous Bonange mansion on the north shore of Lake Pontchartrain.

"Cheer up." Grady tossed his cigarette down. "Those girls at the cemetery wet their pants and ran home to Mummy. They'll have nightmares about scary brown men with big fat guns for a few weeks, but they'll be fine. As will you too, my friend. *La vie vaut la peine,* eh? Life is worth all the sorrow."

We passed a checkpoint of armed guards—Hondurans like Ciro, hard-muscled guys who didn't fuck around. My cuffs were removed and I got a final, very thorough body search. Then my belongings were handed back to me. The money was there, but my cell phone looked like someone had taken a claw hammer to it. Finally I was left alone in the great drawing room. No lights. All the curtains were drawn. The air smelled musty, not the toxic mold of Katrina. Something far older, like grave rot.

According to legend, Sieur de Bonange had built his remote sugar plantation in 1752 as a hedge against his principal business, which was slave auctioning. The house had a stone basement, a very rare thing in colonial Louisiana, where he could hide his human merchandise from the English invaders. The foundations had subsided long ago, creating a pronounced sag in the hardwood floors. The parlor was cluttered to the ceiling with enough bad Victorian art for a really sad episode of *Antiques Roadshow*.

As I stood in the dark, one of the white marble statues started to move toward me. I was still freaking out on that when it flattened me with a left hook to my gut.

Sweet Jesus. The air screamed out of me. I reeled away, watching red flowers dance across my field of vision. Then a second slablike blow knocked me straight to the floor. A sharp kick to my ribs.

The statue was laughing.

"Been waiting twenty years for that," he said in his deep, rasping voice. "Always worried I might be a little disappointed when the day finally came."

I sucked air into my lungs. "So . . . how do you feel?"

"Fantastic." He rubbed his fists. "Thanks for asking."

As I ached to my feet, I got a better look at the massive figure standing over me. The years had worked hard on him, but he'd held on like Primo Carnera in the eleventh round. The conqueror's gleam in his eye. The wolfish curl of his mouth. That thick sweep of white hair, not a strand of it lost to age. Emelio St. Clair Barca, last great crime boss of Orleans Parish. Standing ready to kick the everlasting shit out of me.

"Now I know why you ordered Grady . . . not to hurt me." I fell backward into a chair. "I'd have ducked if I'd known it was you. I thought you were just a crummy statue."

Barca's laugh was heavy with acid. "You mean, like that commendatore in *Don Giovanni*? You didn't invite me to dinner, I invited you." He whistled a tune from Mozart's opera as he turned on a Coleman lamp. It hissed like an opossum guarding its nest, throwing cadaverous light over the room.

"So what happens now? You kill me?"

"I wasn't going to. I probably will, though, now that you're bein' such a pussy about it." He frowned. "That was a kindness, Mike. A kiss on the forehead compared to what you deserve. But it just so happens that I need to borrow that brain of yours for a while. You all right? You gonna puke?"

"I wouldn't want to mess the place up," I said. "Everything's so lovely."

"It's a fuckin' mess. No women in the place. We just moved back in a few days ago." Barca settled into a plastic-sheeted sofa. "We're puttin' generators in. You ready for that absinthe now? I guess to God you are."

"I'll pass."

"Somebody told me you quit drinkin'. What happened, the FBI turn you into some kind of *fanook*? Jesus, I thought you'd at least hit back a little. There's nothing but shame for a man who won't defend himself." He waved with two fingers as the two men entered the room. "You remember my youngest boy, right?"

"I remember he smeared jelly toast in my hair the day we met." I nodded to Grady. "Of course, he did make his bones at the age of thirteen. So I guess I got off lucky."

"Twelve, actually." Grady smiled. "Pop said my first hit didn't count, since I hadn't taken First Communion yet."

"Respect for religion is important." Barca snapped his fingers. "*Assenzio due*, Grady. Do that thing with the liquor."

Green-eyed Grady set to an elaborate ritual. From the side table he took a tall bottle of absinthe—the real thing, an ancient Pernod Fils—and poured out two glasses. He placed a slotted spoon on each one, weighted with a sugar cube. Then, using a small pitcher, he dribbled water over the spoons, dissolving the sugar grain by grain. He did it with such slow and intense concentration that I thought he might have fallen asleep. Then another drop of water went in—plop.

"Like Chinese fuckin' water torture," Barca observed. "The Grand Canyon eroded faster than my son pours. Tastes unbelievable when it's done right, though. Releases the, I dunno, the—"

"Essential oils," Grady answered.

Barca rolled his eyes: whatever. "So what the fuck, Mikey. Are you really crooked now, like I keep hearin'? Or am I gonna have to feed you to the gators down in Bayou Sauvage?"

Ciro cracked his knuckles, one by one. Another drop of water. Barca waited for my answer.

"What do you keep hearing?" I asked finally.

"Oh, the TV news people all say you took a bribe. But then I got friends who are friends with the Cherry Hill crew out of Philadelphia. They claim they never paid you one red cent for that kiddie porn."

"See, that's what I could never get right. First you get the money, then you hand over the porn." I shrugged. "What else would you expect them to say? They're under indictment, same as me."

"How about you answer the question."

"It's true," I said. "I took a bribe."

He stared at me for several seconds before waving it off.

"Eh, you're all *oobatz* up north." He turned to Grady. "Hurry up with that, okay? I'm thirsty."

"You can't rush perfection." Grady looked up. "Ask him about the assistant district attorney, Papa."

Barca laughed. "Oh, that was beautiful. I been waitin' years to pay off that chicken-plucker. Then Mikey—bam! Coldcocks him in broad daylight. How'd it feel when you finally got to deck a child molester, instead of just reading him his Mirandas?"

"Fantastic," I said with complete sincerity.

"Imagine feeling that way all the time." A chill light kindled in his eyes. "I always knew you were a vigilante, even in the old days. You remember . . . ? Back when you thought you could get away with fucking me in the ass?" His smile drew tight, like a cobra's. "That shame you put on my baby girl, Sofia? I can't imagine what gave you the figs to come back to my town, after the way you treated me and mine."

Another drop of water. Two. Ciro checked the slide lock on his 9 mm.

"I didn't know it was your town anymore," I said. "I just thought . . ."

Drip. Drip.

"You thought what?" Barca asked. "Who asks you to think?"

"I just . . ." I rubbed the sore place on my neck. "I need money, Barca."

"I should say the hell you do." He nodded slowly. "How much?"

"A lot. I've got legal troubles."

Grady looked up. "He's not lying, Pop. Yeager had to cash in his retirement, just to make bail." He returned to his preparations. "You should see where he lives now. Sleeps between cases of vodka in the storeroom of the oyster house."

"And then he goes and punches out an assistant fucking DA," Barca said. "I'm gonna sell peanuts at your trial, Mikey. It's gonna be one hell of a show. Whattya think, Ciro? Think we oughta sell peanuts?"

Ciro didn't seem to think anything. He simply watched me, a patient snake on an exhausted mouse.

Barca stretched. "Face up, Michael. Your, pardon the expression, life is a joke. You're lookin' at twenty years in a federal pen . . . right next to every hardcase you ever sent up. And you got nobody. Even that female agent you traveled with in Philly—word is, she's gettin' her ass slapped by a moolie politician. How's it feel to know you're wearing a pair of fuckin' horns?"

"Like crap," I said.

"It should," he replied. "You dishonored yourself for nothing. And I'm perfectly within my rights to kill you now. Say it."

"You're within your rights to kill me."

He burned red. "Say it like you mean it, or I will."

Something in the way Grady and Ciro edged away convinced me that the old man wasn't joking.

"I deserve to die for what I did to you and Sofia." I looked straight at him. "So why not just get it over with? You'd be doing me a favor."

He seemed genuinely touched by the question. "Because you're *valuable*, Mikey. Don't you think you have value to me? I know you swore an oath to destroy me and all my kind. And I wouldn't have much respect for a man who could throw his oath out the window—like that." He flung an invisible object into the air. "But I can see you're in trouble. It's disgraceful, the way the FBI tossed you out, like a used rubber. So I say to myself, 'Emelio, forgive. This man was once a friend of yours. He might have been family. Raise him up.' "

I smiled. "How are you planning to 'raise me up'?"

"Our family has lawyers on the payroll." It was Grady who answered. "Not your typical shysters. These are high-powered defense attorneys who will work on contingency. The Justice Department will cower before them like women. By the time we're done with your civil suit for wrongful prosecution, you'll own the damned Robert F. Kennedy Building."

"And that's just to get you on your feet," Barca said. "I aim to take this city back. Half the gangs in New Orleans are working for me now. The other half will either fall in line, or—" He snapped his fingers, aiming his index finger like a pistol. "There's a lot of takings, with this federal money coming down the pike. A lot of construction, a lot of garbage to collect. A whole fat lot of new government bureaucrats to bag. I don't speak their language, Mikey. You do. You could carve out a nice earning for yourself, working for me."

"What would you want from me?"

He stared at me for a long time, an old fighter who knew his enemies well.

"Go bring my daughter home," he said.

For several seconds there was only the hiss of the Coleman lantern and the sound of dripping water. Barca reddened, as if struggling to master himself. When he spoke again, his voice was choked with sorrow.

"During the bad years, when I was forced to run and hide for my life . . . my Sofia, she didn't do so well on her own. Her mother, rest in peace, suffered from dark moods. Runs on that side of the family. And now she . . ." He gestured to Grady, unable to continue.

"Thanks to the continuing FBI surveillance," Grady said, "we've had to rely on middlemen to represent our interests in Orleans Parish. One of these individuals—a colorful gent named Damien 'Magpie' Corveau—enjoyed a particularly close relationship with our family. The arrangement has been . . . mostly satisfactory up to this point."

"Fuckin' son of a French halfbreed." Barca could hardly contain himself. "My daughter took up with that quadroon, can you believe it? Probably got enough drugs in his bloodstream to open up a Walgreens pharmacy. I thought it was bad enough when she spread her legs for a kraut like you, Mike. No disrespect."

"None taken."

"The worst part is, I *trusted* the two of them together. This is the failing of my old age. Trusting too much." He threw me a close look, keen as razors. "I just want to hear from her own lips if this is what she wants. To be with that useless *bookyak*. I have to know he's not forcing her. I think he knocks her around."

"I'm not a button man, Barca. If this is a hit—"

"No, no. Please. It's what you do best. A recovery. Thing is, we can't get to her. We're not even sure where she is. I got a call through a few days ago, she sounded scared. Tell the truth, she sounded *fuori di testa*, drunk out of her mind. Then her boyfriend made her hang up the phone." He placed a hand on his heart. "I'm worried, Mike. I want Sofia here, back at the marina, where maybe a doctor can look at her."

My breath came a little tight. "What happened to her?"

"You tell me, Mike. You're the one who ran out on my little girl when she needed you, twenty years back." He said it out straight as an iron poker. "We finally ready here, genius?"

"Oh, yes." Grady smiled. The green liquid had turned semiopaque. He passed it to his father with a flourish. "Last chance, Yeager. You're missing a real New Orleans treat."

I shook my head. Grady sipped his absinthe with religious reverence. Barca knocked his back like a shot of bourbon.

"Christ Almighty, that is beautiful." Barca wiped his lips. "So you gonna do me this favor? Go out and bring my baby Sofia back to me? Maybe look after her a little?"

"When do you need me to go?"

"Right now." He shifted his bulk, a bull elephant preparing a charge. "Grady and Ciro will come along in case there's trouble. I am not telling you how to handle this. However, if you can do to Corveau what you did to that pedophile lawyer, I'll gladly change those ten Grants in your wallet to Ben Franklins."

I stood up. "Just so we understand, I have limits. I'll bring Sofia home, but that's as far as it goes."

Barca smiled patiently, as if I'd just said something incredibly naive.

"Mike has limits. Such a talker he is. Just so *you* understand . . ." He calmly cracked his knuckles. "I know who you are this time, down to the last hair on your Hitler-loving ass. And you owe me. If you think, then I own your thoughts. If you take a piss, then you owe me for the piss. If this idea somehow displeases you . . ."

He held out his hand, and Ciro stepped forward to hand something to his boss. In the dim light, it looked like a strand of pearls.

"This is what I took from the last guy who thought he could talk his way out of trouble with me."

He threw it at me like Mardi Gras beads. They rattled in my hands, smooth and shiny. Then I realized what it was I was holding, and it was all I could do to keep my mouth shut.

Human teeth, strung on a wire. A mouthful of them.

"Now get your ass on the highway," he said.

NINE

We took the Causeway back to the city. I insisted on driving: It was the best way to make sure I wouldn't get popped, at least while the vehicle was still in motion. Grady rode shotgun. Ciro sat directly behind me, staring intently at the back of my head.

"So why am I the one who gets to pick your sister up from her boyfriend's? Isn't that a brother's duty?"

"Half brother." Grady shuffled a new deck of cards. "God knows I've pulled that thankless job often enough in the past. You get that girl out of trouble, she dives right back in. Her and Magpie . . . both of them headed straight for the morgue."

I had to fight the urge to ask how the years had treated Sofia. Instead I shook my head, as if she barely mattered.

"Why do they call him Magpie?" I asked. "He likes to line his nest with tinfoil?"

"He steals," Grady said. "Money, drugs—anything you've got. Lives on the misery of others like a scavenger bird. Wouldn't take him lightly, though. He has protection."

"What kind of protection?"

"A gang called Rize. A small but very efficient crew in the Black Pearl. Magpie used our money to buy his people one of those big houses on St. Charles. Parties with them almost every night. Disgusting."

"You don't like parties?"

"I don't like people." He fanned out the cards. "Here, pick one."

"We're doing a magic trick?"

"Take the fucking card," he said.

I tapped one in the middle. He grinned, as if I'd just given myself away.

Then he held it out for me: a tarot card. It showed a man lying facedown, his back pierced with daggers.

"Ten of Swords," he said. "Someone near and dear has recently betrayed you. You don't even have a clue who the traitor is. And just when you start to believe things can't possibly get any worse—"

He turned the card around—and when he flipped it again, it had changed. Now it showed a horned devil, holding a naked man and woman in chains. *Il Diavolo*, it read.

"Look who turns up."

"That's great," I said. "Now make Ciro disappear and I'll get you booked at my niece's birthday party."

Ciro glanced up at the mention of his name. *"Donde estamos que van?"*

"We're going to the Black Pearl neighborhood," I said. *"La Perla Negra,* Ciro. Sound good?"

"Magpie isn't stupid enough to hide there," Grady said. "He knows he isn't safe from us in his own neighborhood."

"Maybe hiding's not his style," I answered. "When people are in danger, they don't necessarily want to *be* safe. They want to *feel* safe. Why do you think New Orleans keeps on building levees?"

"Well said." He tossed the Devil card away and it vanished. A moment later, he plucked another one out of thin air. "I've often wondered why you have such little regard for your own safety, Yeager. Can't imagine it's going to end well for you. Of course . . ."

He turned the card. Now the two young people were cowering before a skeleton holding a scythe: *La Morte.*

"Since when has it ever ended well for anyone?" he asked.

Black Pearl had been a relatively genteel area before the storm. According to some, it was once the home of the fabled House of the Rising Sun; hence the name of its local gang, Rize. The area hadn't exactly fallen on hard times—not like the Lower Ninth, anyway—but the poststorm chaos had brought in a new wave of drug money, and with it all the terrors of gangland capitalism.

You could hear the noise from several blocks away: jaw-rattling house music, a lot of threats mixed in with the cheers. Not a typical New Orleans revel, but a hard-core monster's ball. Either the cops had been paid to leave it alone, or they had the good sense to keep the hell away.

The street in front of the Victorian mansion was completely packed with human traffic. I parked in a side alley, out of sight.

"Does Corveau know about me?" I asked.

"Not that I'm aware," Grady answered. "He certainly doesn't know about your connection to us."

"Good enough." I got out from behind the wheel. "I'm going in alone."

"My father's instructions—"

"Were to me, not to you. I'm sure you're handy enough with blow darts, or whatever you jabbed into my neck. And Ciro looks pretty scary, as long he's got his opponent handcuffed naked to a chair. But we're easily out-numbered twenty to one. We just don't have the firepower to fight our way in."

Grady seemed amused. "And you think you'll just blend in with the crowd?"

"Like Pat Boone opening for R. Kelly, I'm sure. Still they won't see me as a threat if I'm alone."

Grady seemed to appreciate the logic: Better you than me. "I warn you, my father doesn't like surprises. If you can't handle this quietly—"

"I don't like surprises, either. Be here when I get back."

I left them waiting in the car. Then I turned the corner and waded straight into the mob on the front lawn.

If the New Orleans gangs were anything like the ones I'd dealt with in Philly, then the house party was mainly camouflage. The noise would drown out any surveillance, and the crowd provided plenty of cover in case the shit went down. You could spot the real gangbangers straight away: They were the ones who kept looking around as if they might die any second. It took me less than a minute to draw the kind of attention that a wounded bird gets from an army of cats.

"Who let the fuckin' narc . . ."

"Cracker alert."

"Somebody get Deadman."

By the time I got to the porch, it was already too late to back out. The crowd simply closed in around me. Somebody bumped my elbow, then another guy took me by the shoulder. Next thing I knew, I was cheek to chest with a human mountain in a Hornets jersey. The search I'd gotten from Barca's men seemed positively demure compared to the wall of flesh now prodding me from every side. Then an iron grip on my throat cut off my air. Someone was laughing insanely.

"Fucking cop," the big guy said. "Been waiting for this."

"Leave him be." A cool voice, cutting through the din. "Back off, K-Man. Put him down."

I found myself looking into the graveyard eyes of a young black man. He was about my height, all muscle and bone. Despite the press and swirl of bodies all around us—and the steam of an August night—there was not a bead of perspiration on his face. He might have been a bronze sculpture. People seemed to know that it was best to make room for him.

"Long way from home, ain'tcha?" His eyes flew over me, scanning for signs of danger. "You're a little lost, daddy. Best take it on down St. Charles. Streetcar don't come this way no more."

"He's *cop,* Deadman!" K-Man the giant held me by my windpipe, ready to shake me like a bobblehead doll. "Same cocksuckers that wasted my man Cleanhead. We got to make an example."

"We ain't *got* to do shit. Cappin' this man ain't gonna bring Cleanhead's junkie ass back to life." Deadman shook his head at me, disgusted. "If you're cop, then I guess we can't touch you. Are you cop?"

I shook my head.

"An honest white man," he said. "Leave him go."

A chorus of disapproval from the men holding me.

"Aw, fuck that noise, Deadman."

"You arguin' with me, baby doll?" Deadman turned to face his comrade. "Come on, snowflake. You want to party?"

"Shit." K-Man's grip loosened. I fell to the front steps, gasping.

"That's better." Deadman spat on the ground, an inch from my face. "Now get this crazy fucker off the property. If he is a narc, he's the dumbest one yet."

"Came . . . to see Corveau." I had to clear my throat to breathe properly. "Your boss. Magpie."

At the sound of the name, several of the partygoers shifted a little anxiously.

"Magpie." Deadman's face was expressionless. "What's that? Some damn thing from a bakery?"

"I'm here on business from . . . his boss." I pulled myself carefully to my feet. "Our friend on the north shore. I came to negotiate. For his daughter."

That seemed to strike K-Man as funny. Deadman wasn't amused. "What's your name, asshole?"

"Yeager," I said.

Deadman hesitated for a moment, as if wondering whether it might not be better to kill me and be done with it. Then he simply turned his back and walked up the front steps.

"It's your funeral," he said to me. "Come on up."

The party only went up to the second floor. The mansion's third floor was all business. We passed a room where two armed men in latex gloves and respirator masks carefully weighed out rocks of cocaine like so many lemon drops. I kept my eyes forward like I hadn't seen a thing.

Deadman knocked on a door at the far end of the hall. A moment later, it was answered by a beefy guy in a wheelchair. His legs were missing from the knees down, but he had plenty to compensate him. An AR-15 5.56 lay across his lap. Deadman seemed to regard him with special deference.

"So this is the clown you were telling me about." As the bodyguard cast a cold eye on me, I noticed the tattoo on his arm: the winged fleur-de-lis insignia of the Army 82nd Airborne. "Is he carrying?"

Deadman shook his head. "Says he's from the north shore, Sarge. I thought the boss should decide whether we ice him or not."

"He's expected." Sarge opened the door. "In you go, cornbread."

Grady told me that Magpie stole things. Judging from my first view of the inner sanctum, that was like saying Rodin sculpted things, or that Miles Davis played things on the trumpet. I felt like I'd walked into Tupac Shakur's estate sale. There was Cristal in the Sub-Zero wine case and powdered cocaine in a gigantic brandy snifter. A Martin acoustic gathered dust in the arms of an immense teddy bear, HAPPY VALENTINE'S DAY tied in a bow around its furry neck. Big-screen projection TVs were lined up against the wall. Also a dozen DVD players in their boxes. Cash was stuffed into black gym bags—two million, maybe three—as were piles of designer clothing, still on their wooden hangers. There was polished gold on the mirrors, and gold leaf on the bedroom door, and gold pretty much everywhere you could cram it in. A pair of intricately carved elephant tusks flanked the doorway, ten feet high. Never mind where he found them, I mused: How the hell did he get them into the house?

"They're from Ghana. Nineteenth century, if I'm not mistaken." The voice behind me was rich espresso. "I see you have a taste for fine art."

"Not exactly." I turned to face him. "I just keep thinking about poor Dumbo having to wear dentures."

He laughed broadly. Damien "Magpie" Corveau was taller than me, coffee-skinned, with only a few silver hairs in his dark beard. His black silk shirt and gold earring gave him the raffish air of a freebooter; it wouldn't have surprised me to see a cutlass in his hand. He crossed the room with a panther's deliberate pace—so deliberate, in fact, that I barely noticed how carefully he'd shut the bedroom door behind him. He studied me briefly, then threw a dagger glance at his bodyguard.

"Deadman says he's clean," the guard said. "I haven't searched him yet."

"No need. I'm sure Deadman knows his business."

That didn't sit too well with the sergeant—but finally he nodded and wheeled himself from the room.

"You seem like a better class of thug than Barca's usual." Magpie poured out two glasses of Rémy-Martin, then set one down before me. "Where'd they dig you up, friend?"

"In a graveyard." I didn't touch the glass. "Sorry to bother you this late. I didn't realize you were packing to leave."

He raised an eyebrow. "Who's leaving?"

"Any guy who keeps his cash in his luggage probably isn't running for chair of the local neighborhood association. I just figured you might be in some kind of trouble."

"We're all in some kind of trouble," he said. "Exactly what kind were you thinking of?"

"Could be anything in your case. Cops. Rival gangs. Loss of manhood. Maybe you heard I was coming and got scared."

We both had a laugh at that. Magpie laughed just a fraction of a second longer. Then he drank.

"Not me, brother. I'm steady here. Thanks all the same."

"You sure? Seems like you're gonna have a bitch of a time getting all this swag through airport security. Maybe I could lighten the load."

"Ah." He smiled. "By the weight of one woman, perhaps?"

"Not a bad suggestion," I said. "If that's your offer, I'm sure my employer will be pleased."

"No doubt." He finished his glass. "Let me see if I have this right. Your boss habitually crushes his daughter for his amusement—throws her out with the morning trash—and now he's suddenly overwhelmed with fatherly concern? No disrespect to my old business partner, but dogs take better care of their bones than Emelio Barca cares for his children."

"That's probably a generous assessment," I said. "All the same, my instructions are that she's coming with me. With your blessing, of course."

"Of course. And if I decide to shoot you instead?"

"Then I'll be dead," I said. "I won't insult you by pretending I've got an army hidden in the bushes. Or that I'm prepared to offer you a dump truck full of money as compensation. It's going to happen, that's all. And if the man I represent isn't enough to command your respect—"

"Hold." Magpie smiled indulgently, as if I were a toddler charging at him with my tiny fists. "My friend, I have shown your employer more respect over the years than he has ever earned from me. Back when the Barcas were living in the bayous—feeding on whatever crawled out of the mud—who do you think kept on doing business with him? And did that job for him in the Nine a few weeks back? And helped him get on top again, when nobody else in six parishes knew his name?" He held out his hands. "Personally, I should think he'd be grateful to me."

"Probably he should. Maybe you should call him and remind him of that."

"You're no gangster." He eyed me curiously. "Too much life in the eyes. Even if you are in the game, you haven't been there long. Not a portrait painter, are you? I can always stand to have my portrait done."

"Some people used to think I was a bank detective," I said. "Why does it matter to you?"

"We all have to live with the destiny we choose. You build a city below sea level, and someday people are going to drown. And you . . ." He tilted his head at me. "You say you want to take this girl back to the father who mistreated her. Why? What sort of man does that?"

"We do what we do."

"No we don't, friend. We do what we give ourselves permission to do." He looked at me sadly. "I suspect that you are a basically decent person who's thrown in his lot with the devil. Perhaps you think Barca has some kind of hold on you. He doesn't, you know. You could accept my friendship in place of his. Turn right around and walk out that door, clean in the sight of God. And do some kindness to a woman who's seen far too little of it in her lifetime."

"Mr. Corveau, I walk out that door and I'm dead. You must think I got my brains knocked loose in that scuffle with your bodyguards."

"That isn't really the point I was making," he said. "You strike me as someone who cares a little more than he thinks. And a lot more than he listens."

Now I understood why they called him Magpie. I'd expected him to pick my pocket. I hadn't expected him to steal my thoughts.

"I'm just trying to work off a debt." I stretched. "Now if you don't mind, I'd like to inspect the merchandise."

"Not going to happen, friend."

"Why? You stole her fair and square, and now she's your bottom bitch?"

He could break me in half, or impale me on his elephant tusks, but at least I'd thrown him off his head game—and made him cast a sudden look at the closed door behind him.

"You keep a civil tongue." His voice was cold steel, carefully tempered. "Wasn't anybody stolen. She came to me here, and I keep her safe here, and she's free to come and go as she pleases. I treat her with all the love and respect she deserves. That is the life I've given her."

"She must be constantly thanking you for that," I said. "Oh, and I'm sure you love her, too."

"More than some men who've crossed her path." His tone grew brooding. "Yes, I love her. Not that it's any business of yours."

"Why?"

He stared darkly at me. "What do you mean, why?"

"What do you love about her?" I scratched an imaginary itch on my temple. "I mean, I'm sure she's a nice part of your collection—but come on, you're a guy with his own elephant parts. You don't need her . . . unless it's just as a bargaining chip with her dad. Guess that's reason enough to love anybody."

"I don't have to dignify that question," he said. "She's my light and my love and my lady, that's all. Don't presume to speak of her so airily. Or I might have to force you to apologize."

"I'll go you one better," I said. "Bring her out here and I'll apologize to her in person."

"Now you're being a comedian."

"Serious as a heart attack." I pointed to the bedroom. "You said she's free to come and go. All right, Magpie. Open the door and let's see if she flies away."

He seemed to consider it. "What if she tells you that she's happy where she is?"

"Then you'll never see me again," I said. "And I hope to God you're right. Sounds like this girl could use a break."

He briefly studied me, as if trying to peer through dense fog. Then a shadow passed over his face.

"Honey?" He called back over his shoulder, not taking his eyes off me. "Honey lamb, you awake?"

No answer. Something slid and fell on the other side of the door. Now he was looking worried.

"Give me a second." He started to rise.

I pushed past him to the door. The knob didn't turn.

"Open it," I said.

"It's not locked on my side," Magpie said. "When there's strangers around, she shuts herself away—"

Before he could stop me, I reared back and hurled myself at the latch. The lock was new, but thank God the door was old. It splintered at the rail and flew open.

"Sofia?" Then I saw her.

She was nearly lost within the enormous bed. Nude except for a red thong, which fit her loosely and somehow made her seem even more vulnerable. I could see her ribs and backbone pull against her skin. The scar on her right wrist that had never faded. And the red mark left by a tourniquet on her right arm, the vein freshly bruised from the needle. Her eyes were half open, dark and sightless. Her breasts scarcely rose with each narcotic breath.

A cell phone lay open on the carpet. I picked it up. No signal.

"Call nine-one-one," I told him. "Now."

"Calm, now." His brow furrowed, astonished. "This isn't an emergency. She's resting, that's all. So just you back away from her. I don't care who you claim to work for."

He started to reach for me—then he must have seen something in my eyes that made him stop.

"We're getting her to a hospital." I knelt down, took her wrist. It was cool, her pulse barely a whisper. Sofia's head lolled into my chest. "Come on, sweetie. Wake up, all right? We have to go now."

"God damn you." Cheated rage burned in Corveau's eyes. "I know who you are. The man from the FBI. Sofia told me all about you. That bastard who—"

"Yes!" I said. "Now will you please help me get her out of here?"

"No." He shook his head gravely. "I'm not putting her in some Katrina hospital with crack addicts and lowlife scum. This is where she belongs now. I'm the only one who can keep her safe. And I'll kill you before I let you take her from me, Mr. Yeager. Don't you think your boss knew that when he sent you here?"

"Somebody's sure going to a hospital tonight. And if you don't—" Then

I stopped myself. Something had changed in the party down below. The cheering had turned to yells.

As I looked at Sofia, her eyes opened wide.

"*Boss!*" The bodyguard's voice. "We've got trouble downstairs!"

I reached to pick Sofia up—then turned to see a .357 Magnum in Magpie's hands.

"Leave her be," he said. "She's not for you."

I got to Corveau's arm before he could squeeze the trigger, cracking it against the doorjamb. His bones made a satisfying sound. *Tough muscle,* I thought. Grabbing hold of him was like trying to ride a hammerhead. He slammed me against a mirror, shattering it into my back. A piece of glass fell into my hand and I thrust it into his side. He didn't yell—but he instantly let me fall. Then, while he was still off balance, I threw him down over my leg. His head struck the tile floor good and hard. I grabbed the gun and struck him with the butt twice across the temple. He was dazed now, but he'd be up again in a second. Then I would die. Or I could end it with the gun. I wondered how I'd feel after killing him. It chilled me a little to realize that it probably wouldn't bother me at all.

"*Boss.*"

The Magnum would be enough to stop the guy in the wheelchair, and maybe Deadman if I was lucky and quick—but I'd have to kill them, too. Six rounds just weren't enough to get through that crowd.

I took off my jacket and put it around her.

"Sofia." I leaned in close to her. "Sofia, it's Mike."

"Mike . . . ?" Her voice was as pale as twilight.

"There's no time to explain. People are coming with guns. Tell me how to get us out of here."

"The . . . landing." She gestured aimlessly to the window.

The door was rattling. Magpie rolled on the floor, trying to raise himself. I picked Sofia up, light as a sleeping child.

"*Open the fuck up.*" The outer door shook on its frame, spilling shadows from the hallway. "Open or I will fire!"

"Mike." Sofia began to slide through my arms, a broken toy. "Don't . . ."

"What's that, Sofia?" I tried to keep the Magnum aimed as I fumbled with the window latch. "Don't what?"

"Please don't take me back to my father," she said.

Then the door crashed wide open.

TEN

The trouble that Magpie's guard mentioned was turning out to be mine as much as theirs. A riot squad from the NOPD—twenty-five or more—had surrounded the house. Nobody was being arrested: The cops were firing rubber bullets and busting heads. The gangbangers were firing back with real live ammo. Sofia and I were exposed on the third-floor balcony, a shot that any clown could make with his eyes shut.

"Sofia." I half-carried, half-pulled her along the narrow railing. "I need you to wake up, okay? We've got maybe fifteen seconds before Magpie's guys figure out we're h—"

A blast of gunfire exploded glass from the window, less than two feet from my head.

"So I was wrong about that," I said.

"*Sophie*?" Corveau screamed like Jacques Brel playing Stanley Kowalski. "*Sophie ma vie, pour l'amour de Dieu, ne me quitte pas!*"

"What's he saying? He's got heartburn?"

"He's begging me not to leave him," she said.

Magpie had followed us onto the balcony, cradling an automatic rifle in his good arm. Even so, he hadn't seen us yet. I aimed the Magnum. Sofia pushed my hand aside.

"Don't," she said.

Then he turned and smiled.

"There you are, you damned slut!"

I pulled her down just in time to keep us both from getting sprayed with bullets.

I raised the gun again.

"Mike!" Sofia cried.

I shot the bulb out over his head. Sparks and shards of glass rained down on Magpie. As he shielded himself, I hustled Sofia to the far end of the balcony. We looked fifty feet down at a frantic mob, surrounded by a phalanx of plastic shields.

"How the hell do we get down from here?"

"The other way," Sofia said. "Should have gone the other way—"

"*Up there!*" A dark-uniformed cop aimed a riot gun at us. "*Drop your weapon or you will be fired on!*"

"Top of the world, Ma." I hurled the Magnum at him. The policeman instinctively ducked. One of the kids in the crowd grabbed the gun, and that started a scuffle. "Sofia, can you stand up?"

"If I hold on to something." She swayed against the balcony, looking very green.

I pointed to a side roof, seven feet down. "We leap down to the roof, another jump to the ground, with any luck we can escape through the bushes. Think you can make it?"

She nodded.

"*Sophie ma belle?*" Corveau again.

"Good Christ, he's in love." I hauled her over the balcony. Then I leapt down after her.

I landed badly on my ankle. Sofia wasn't with me. I spotted her on the ground, stumbling headlong for a dark space between the hedges and the pool house. What she didn't see was that one of the riot cops had already tagged her.

God help me. I jumped down just in time to see him strike her sideways with his rifle stock.

"I told you to get down, bitch! Lie flat on the ground."

"Officer?" I walked up, a smiling citizen.

"Sir, back off."

He raised his gun, too late to keep me from dragging it out of his hands. I slammed the butt into his rib cage, then knocked his visor off on the upswing.

Sofia was bent double on the ground.

"Guess those drugs wear off pretty fast when the adrenaline kicks in." I knelt down to help her up.

"Go to hell." She took my hand. "Thanks for not letting him shoot me, I guess."

"Relax. It's just a marker gun. Doesn't fire bullets." I examined the rifle. "The ammunition is nice, friendly—"

Then we both turned to the same noise: a popping sound. A milky fog swirled in the yellow street lamps.

"CS gas," I said. "Cover your eyes."

We were running before I finished the sentence, but it was already too late. A crowd of people had broken through the fence into the backyard. They swept over us, dragging us apart. Some of the men and women were already gagging from the tear gas. Others flung themselves into the swimming pool.

"Sofia!" I knew I had maybe five seconds before the gas hit my eyes. "Sofia!"

Then I saw her. The running crowd had crushed her against the garden wall. I tried to push my way to her—then a clawlike hand swung me around.

"I'll kill before I let you take her from me." It was Corveau, glass and blood streaming down his face. "Kill you."

He had his hands on my throat. I squeezed the trigger of the rifle I was holding. Bright red liquid flew upward across Corveau's face. At first I thought I'd shot him—but when he started screaming, I knew it was only pepper spray, marked with dye. Unfortunately, I'd caught a dose of it in my own eyes.

Crap. A needle of agony. My left eye swelled shut almost instantly. The right one was a tear-streaked haze. I let Corveau fall, then ran to Sofia. She lay fetal, vainly shielding herself with my brown leather jacket.

"Stop." A gun at my back. "Put both hands—"

I turned just in time to see his pale blue eyes. Then the policeman jerked backward as blood and bone painted the inside of his cracked visor. Two more shots killed him before he hit the ground.

"Come on." It was Ciro, gripping his 9 mm two-handed. "Through the bushes. The car's in the alley."

"Thought you couldn't speak English."

"Chingate." Ciro moved to cover us both. "That Spanish enough for you, asshole?"

The car was already moving as I pushed Sofia into the backseat. I could barely see Grady behind the wheel. Mucus ran freely from my nostrils; my lungs felt like I'd inhaled fire ants. Ripping both eyes out suddenly seemed like a great idea.

"Sofia?" It was all I had breath enough to say.

"She's here." Ciro jumped into the front passenger seat. "They got a roadblock at the end of this alley. We can try and crash it, or we can ditch the car and shoot our way out."

"This piece of shit couldn't break through a line of trash cans." Grady spoke as idly as if he were playing a video game. "Yeager, can you see well enough to aim?"

"He's blind," Ciro said. "Give him the shotgun. Even he can't miss with that."

"Purple house." It was Sofia speaking, an agonized whisper.

Grady laughed. "What the fuck? Purple haze? What are you on this time, Sofia?"

"Purple . . . house." She took me by the collar. "Magpie keeps it for us. Safe house. Car in the driveway . . ." She gasped.

"It's okay." I turned to Grady. "She says—"

"I heard her." Grady slammed on the brakes. "All right, we'll take my junkie sister's word for it. But the keys had better be in the fucking ignition. I'm not hiding out while these assholes go door-to-door."

Ciro and Grady hustled the two of us into the backyard of a house adjoining the alley. I heard breaking glass. Then we were pushed inside. A dog instantly started barking at us.

"*No mames!* God, I hate fucking dogs." I heard the safety of Ciro's weapon slide off.

"Don't shoot her!" Sofia struggled for breath. "I know where the car keys are—and you don't. Leave my dog alone."

Silence. "Shit, they're all over the neighborhood. We got to move."

"They won't come into the house," I said. "They're not equipped for search and seizure. They probably have authorization to disperse the mob, but that's all."

"I don't care to find out what they're authorized to do," Grady said. "Where are the keys, Sofia?"

No answer.

"Grady," I said. "Is there any milk or beer in the fridge?"

He laughed. "Yeah. Are you thirsty?"

"Just give it to me."

A moment later the carton was in my hand. I poured milk over my eyes, then rubbed it into my face and hands. After a few seconds, I could just barely see again.

"What the fuck was that all about?"

"Pepper spray isn't water soluble. Milk dissolves the . . . Sofia?"

She'd fallen to the ground. The dog—a beagle—was nosing her cheeks. Grady was staring through the kitchen window.

"Christ, she's gone into toxic shock. How long were you just going to stand there?"

I heard a car engine roar into life.

"Sounds like Ciro got the engine running." Grady lifted Sofia like a rolled-up carpet. "Come on, we're in business. You can bring the dog, if you like."

Ciro drove slow and casual until we were well away from the police cordon. A lot more backup had arrived on the scene. I also noticed EMT wagons and a camera van for WWL-TV.

"Anybody want to lay bets on what's going to be leading tomorrow's news?" Grady asked as blue lights retreated in our rearview mirror.

"We have to get her to an emergency room," I said. "She's losing consciousness again."

"Half the junk in her system is counteracting the other half," Grady observed. "We're not going to a hospital. Last thing we need is some pimple-faced intern asking questions."

"I really don't give a rat's ass what questions get asked. She's taken a lungful of CS gas. There could be pulmonary damage. And that's on top of whatever shit Corveau's been feeding her. Frankly, I'd rather take my chances with the EMTs back there."

"Who do you think called the cops?"

"What do you mean?"

"Just what I said." Grady lit a cigarette. "It all happened while you were inside. You didn't happen to push a panic button, did you . . . FBI man?"

"Go to hell."

Sofia awoke with a sudden jerk. Then a spray of thin liquid burst from her mouth and nose.

Ciro grimaced. "Hey, if she's gonna *cutear* all over the place, I say fuck her."

"Grady," I said. "If she dies while we're fighting traffic on the Causeway, it's not going to look good for any of us."

Sofia began to cough, convulsing. I put a hand on her back to steady her.

"Is she dying?" Grady glanced into the rearview mirror. "If she's going to die, it's probably better we get rid of her now. I'm not getting pulled over in a hot car with a dead junkie in the backseat."

"The smoke isn't helping," I said. "Ditch the cigarette."

Grady laughed. "Or what?"

"How about I put it straight into your eye," I said coolly.

Daggers of smoke shot from his nostrils—then he lowered the window and tossed the cigarette.

"We've got a boat waiting for us at the West End yacht harbor," Grady said as he rolled the window back up, "and our own doctor. If she can make it that far, she'll be fine."

Sofia was shivering. She didn't resist as I drew her close to me.

"Where are we going?" she whispered, softly as a child.

"I'm so sorry," I said. "We're taking you home."

ELEVEN

The doctor—Anthony R. Petrie, M.D.—was waiting at the yacht club as promised, on the deck of a pleasure craft. He and a male nurse took Sofia into the cabin for treatment. I wasn't allowed to follow her. For a moment, I wasn't altogether certain that I'd even be making the trip back. Not alive, anyway. As the boat left harbor, Grady was looking at me with a new and fascinated suspicion.

"How was Magpie when you left him?" Grady walked a coin across his knuckles, then back again.

"Let's see." I wiped my face with an alcohol-soaked cloth. It stung my eyes, but not nearly as badly as the pepper spray had. "Broken forearm—at least the ulna, although I'm pretty sure I got the radius, too—as well as a face full of glass from a lightbulb and a good healthy shot of riot gas. Think that's enough to earn the grand your old man promised me?"

"I already told you, he doesn't like surprises." Grady glanced sideways at me. "What do you think happened tonight? Why did that riot crew suddenly decide to show up?"

"Beats the hell out of me," I said. "Look, I can see we're never going to be braiding each other's hair. But you have to admit that if I was going to flip on you, I probably would have chosen a method that was less likely to get me killed in the process."

He considered it.

"I'd love to," he said finally.

"Love to what?"

"Beat the hell out of you." He threw the coin at me. "Penny for your thoughts, G-man."

But the coin never touched me. He'd made it disappear.

"We're clear," Ciro said from the boat deck. "No pursuit."

The generators appeared to be in good working order as our boat docked at the marina. Every damn light was visible from a mile away. Which I would have normally called an insane risk, except that it didn't begin to compare to the insanity I'd already experienced that night. I was fairly sure it was Barca's silhouette in the second-story window. I could practically feel him grinning down on us, ear to ear.

There were a lot of new faces on the property, loading pallets of food and ten-gallon cans of gasoline into the house. *Barca's laying in for a siege,* I thought. *Or an invasion.* Sofia was carried into the kitchen on a stretcher. When I tried to follow, the door slammed shut in my face.

"Yeager." Grady motioned me into the parlor. "Wait here."

"For what?"

"Your reward." He winked. "What else?"

Then he left me alone. For fifteen minutes I listened to creaking boards and stomping feet on the second story—then decided, *Screw this; if I'm going to get shot, I might as well take it in the face like a man.* I went up the back stairs, stalking the lion in his den. The stairwell was pitch-black, forcing me to negotiate my way by touch. As I approached the second floor, I heard men whispering. All I could see of them was shadows.

"I ask you a simple fuckin' question." Barca's voice, his anger bridled. "One request, and you turn your back? Jesus, Mary, and Joseph, whatever happened to loyalty?"

"Look, even I get followed sometimes." The second voice was a young man's, cautiously respectful, masking a low note of arrogance. "The call to the police definitely came from inside the house. That's all I can tell you without putting my assets at risk."

"Oh. That's all you can tell me. Thank you very much, you little turd. You think your ass is covered here? If the police get to our friend Magpie—"

"The cops are nowhere on that whole business. Neither is the FBI. If you want to know which way the wind is blowing . . ." Then his voice dropped. The only phrase I could remotely understand sounded like "canned mouse." "If you've got any sources inside Pandora, now's the time to use them."

"Yeah. I got a source. You."

"Uh-uh. I open those files, they're gonna know it was me. You've gotta do this some other way."

"Right. You see the boat come in tonight?"

The second man hesitated. "Yes."

"You know who was on that boat, right? In this very house, as we fuckin' speak?" Long silence. "You are gonna help me on this thing. You think you have a choice in the matter, but you don't. It got made for you a long time ago."

Another silence. "Are you really going to move ahead on the exchange? Because I promise you, these people will eat you for dinner."

"Yeah? Well, it so happens I got a pretty goddamn big appetite of my own. Now get the fuck out of here. Go learn some respect."

Then a door opened. As it did, a thin edge of light swept along the floor, briefly lighting a pair of men's black dress shoes. Bostonians, from the look of them. Then darkness again. Footsteps coming my way.

"What the fuck are you doing up here?"

I nearly jumped a foot out of my skin. Grady was at my heels.

"Thought I told you to wait in the parlor." He passed me on his way up the stairs. "If I were you, Mike, I wouldn't be in such a hurry to do this meeting."

I followed him down the darkened hall. Nobody else was there. Grady knocked on the study door.

"Yeah." Barca's voice on the other side.

"I brought Mike." Grady's eyes telegraphed the unspoken ending to that sentence: *and he's a fucking rat.*

"Send him in."

Grady seemed oddly pleased with himself, as if I were about to get a spanking in the principal's office.

I had to squint as I went in. My eyes, still adjusted for darkness, were stung by the glare of a naked hundred-watt bulb. Barca's office seemed prosaic after my visit to Corveau's gilded mansion: battered furniture and acrylic paintings of pelicans and a Catalina calendar from 1986. I wasn't fooled. More blood and treasure had been stolen in that dusty room than Magpie could fit into a thousand St. Charles mansions. As the door closed behind me, I felt—I can't deny it—a deep surge of nostalgia. I could still smell the Camels of twenty years past.

The man himself was enthroned in an oxblood armchair, brooding under a private thundercloud. It took me a moment to realize who was sitting next to him: Constantino Barca, the don's uncle. Long ago, he'd been Carlos Marcello's most feared enforcer, a soldier of unimpeachable loyalty.

They called him "the Mute" because he famously refused to utter a single word during his testimony before Robert Kennedy's Senate investigation. He was rumored to have played more than a minor part in the death of Bobby's elder brother. Now Uncle Connie and his nephew sat over glasses of pinkish water and what appeared to be a game of checkers in progress.

"You look like you're still gettin' used to the light again, Mikey. Where you been hiding out?" Barca pointed to a chair. "You get the thing done like I told you? My son says you fucked it up."

"Your daughter's downstairs." I sat down, trying to angle myself so that I wasn't staring straight into the lamplight. It forced me to keep my back to the open doorway. "Corveau's not enjoying life very much right now. If Grady wants to call that fucking up . . . well, he wanted to leave her behind to die."

Barca stared at me keenly.

"You have a Peychaud's with us." Reaching to the table beside him, he shook a few shots of purple liquid into a glass from an ornate bottle, then poured seltzer water over it. "Good for a sour stomach. It's got a little kick to it, but not much. You won't be breaking your temperance pledge too bad."

"Thanks." I took one god-awful whiff and set the glass down. Barca noticed but didn't comment.

"So these cops who crashed the party tonight." Barca pushed a black checker—then thought better and took the move back. "Any idea what was behind it?"

"Some politician screwed the pooch," I said. "If it was up to the cops, they wouldn't have relied on riot control gear in a high-risk felony bust. They'd have sent in a SWAT team with MP4 assault rifles and flashbangs. My guess is that the mayor's people are desperate to show that they're still in control of the city."

"Yeah, they showed everybody, all right." The answer seemed only to partly satisfy him. "Guess you did okay, Mikey."

"You think?"

"Coulda gone worse. Tonight I'm gonna sleep better, knowin' my girl's finally safe from that nutcase." He made his move, decisively this time. "Too bad I still got to deal with the nutcase. Maybe it's time to end our business arrangement with Magpie. È vero, Connie?"

Constantino Barca raised his hawklike head. "Che?"

"Relax, zio. Consider your next move. I'm about to double-jump you."

He shook his head sadly. "Shame. You remember what a cowboy my Uncle Connie used to be. One by one, we're all fading away. Anyhow, Mike, there's a G in that envelope on my desk. Take it with my blessing. Ciro or somebody will drive you back over the lake."

"Is that all?"

"It's a thousand bucks more than you woke up with this morning." He sneered at my complete lack of gratitude. "I'll also keep my promise about the lawyer, of course. Don't you worry."

Then he went back to his game. For a moment I wasn't sure whether to leave. It seemed like a dangerous moment to end the conversation.

"You still here?" He didn't look up.

"What I meant to say was . . . is that really all you wanted?"

"What else would there be?"

"Well . . ." I took a breath. "Earlier today, you said there was room for me in your organization."

"Earlier today, you said you had limits." He held up his finger like a Roman statue. "If a man is loyal, then he has no limits. You want to know how you fucked up tonight?"

"Sure."

"Corveau is still alive," he said.

"You didn't tell me otherwise."

"Exactly. You stayed inside your limits. Therefore, you are not loyal. Got it?" He seemed to think I didn't. "Magpie now thinks I'm the one who tipped off those pigs. So who knows what the maniac's gonna try and do to me now."

"I don't think—"

"No, you *do* think. The trouble is, you still think too much like FBI. In my profession, we don't wait for arrest warrants and jury verdicts. We plan, we assess, we improvise, and we do what's necessary. *Capisce?*"

"Isn't my FBI training what you wanted me for?"

"I *wanted* you because I thought you might like a chance to set things straight with me and my daughter." A knife's edge tore through his voice. "Jesus, will you try and see things from my perspective? Twenty years ago, you stabbed me in the fuckin' back. Through my baby girl, no less. I don't like thinking that you might be able to do that again. So tell me. What's it gonna take to convince me of your loyalty?"

"I brought your daughter to you. And you're home free. Isn't that enough?"

"What's free? Free lunch, free beer? I don't know free. I know safe. Right now that ain't me."

"You're free to kill Magpie," I said. "That's the real reason you wanted Sofia back, right? Now he doesn't have a hostage anymore. You can take him down any time you like."

He laughed, a throttled noise like a rope tightening.

"You're a cold bastard," he said. "Take him down, Santa Maria. All I said is, maybe we should end our business affairs. Now you want to ice him?" He shook his head, deeply affronted. "Get the fuck out of here, Mike. You're not amusing me anymore."

The light made it hard to read their faces. But I'd caught the rapid glance that passed between him and his uncle. The Mute did a pretty convincing imitation of Alzheimer's, but I could feel his radar on me. Something was on the boil, and like as not I was about to get tossed into the pot. I decided to go on the assault.

"How close were you to Corveau?" I asked.

"Close. Loved him like a son. So fuckin' what?"

"Seems like you're careless with your friends," I said. "Maybe that's why you have so few of them left. Why you had to rely on guys like Magpie in the first place. And I'm pretty sure it's why your daughter—"

"That's far enough." Barca sliced the air. "You made your point, okay? Back off."

"My point is that you demand loyalty, but you're not very good at inspiring it." I braced myself: Suddenly I badly wanted that shot of Peychaud's. "I've seen what twenty years of living under your 'protection' has done to your daughter. She was naked, Barca. Covered with bruises. She'd fixed maybe fifteen minutes before I got there—"

"You're the one who fixed her," he said. "Took her innocence away. Fucked her so that no decent man would ever take her off my hands."

"Respectfully—"

"This for your respect." Barca obscenely forked his nose with two fingers. "She is mine, all right? *Mine*, you . . . *pompinaio tedesco*. Do you understand that, you German prick? You took my dearest, most cherished joy and . . . made her a whore, a stinking *puta*, I should *crush* your nuts for that. If you don't like breathing, just you speak of my daughter again with such . . . *lust* . . . and I'll squeeze you out like a cockroach. I'll . . ."

There it was, the famous Barca temper, scalding hot. I shrank into my chair.

"... eat you for dinner, do you understand, I can ..."

"Emelio." Constantino looked up, worried. *"Che cazzo stai dicendo?"*

"Niente." Barca stepped on his rage. I seized the opportunity to catch my breath.

"Sometimes ... I say things that I shouldn't." I managed to keep my voice steady. "Forgive me, Don Emelio."

Barca looked up, sniffing for hidden traps.

"You know what really pisses me off about you?" His voice was still smoking. "Even when you were doing a job on my daughter, I always liked you. I *liked* you. So why'd you have to go be a rat, huh? I had the whole city right there in my hands. Another year or two, and I'd have had the whole territory, Houston to Miami. I was gonna do important things. Then you come along, and tear it all away, like a child from its mother's tit. So what the fuck, Mikey? What the fuck?"

"I thought I was doing my duty," I said. "For what it's worth ... I've always liked you, too." I nodded to him. *"Padrino."*

The use of Barca's honorific seemed to soothe him. He stared at me a moment, the wheels turning swiftly.

"You knew I'd kill you if you came back. Yet still you came." Barca drummed his fingers, brooding. "Perhaps there is a way I can assure myself of your loyalty, after all."

"I thought I did that already."

"Bringing Sofia home was just for the money. My forgiveness costs a little more." He smiled. "You still care for my daughter, don't you?"

"She's all right."

"Oh, I think she's more than that to you. Much more. What if I could return her to you? Make her yours again?"

An odd light danced in his eyes. He seemed happy in a way that made me extremely uncomfortable.

"What if you could?" I asked.

"You must have a few contacts left in the FBI," he said. "This business with Corveau makes me think ... no, it's stupid. I'm asking too much of you. Still ..."

"What is it?"

"A small business affair I'm working on," he said. "Have you seen those new security guards running around town? The uniforms with the red circle, and the ..."

I nodded.

"What are they calling themselves? Such strange names these outfits have nowadays." Barca looked up. "Kadmos. That was it. Kadmos Security."

At least now I understood what the reference to "canned mouse" was all about.

"What do you want to know about them?"

"Nothing so much," he said. "Nothing that would force an honest man such as yourself to betray his limits. All I want to know is if these Kadmos people are trying to kill me."

I pondered it. "Why would they be trying to—"

"Maybe they're not. That would be fine news, eh? It's nothing serious. But if I'm gonna gamble on something, it's good to know what's in the other guy's hand." He snapped his fingers. "Oh, and if you run across anything called 'Pandora's Box' with my name on it . . . you be sure and tell me, okay?"

"If I do, I will. That's all you wanted?"

He laughed. "Well, I'd love it if you could find out what your old friends in the FBI are doing. There are times when I worry that partner of yours . . . you know, the old thorn in my side, the Christ-murderer . . ."

"Kiplinger." I felt a sick thud in my gut.

"Exactly. Kiplinger. I worry he might try to plant an informant inside my crew." Barca smiled and winked. "But we won't let that happen. Will we, Mikey?"

"No, sir." I stood up to go. "Excuse me."

"You forgot your money," he said.

Violet afterimages of the lamp were floating past me. As I reached for the envelope, Barca took me fiercely by the wrist.

"Do we have a deal?" He said it without flourish or ornament. "I need to know right now."

"I just want to check on Sofia," I said.

"Please do." He smiled. "She's all yours."

"All right," I answered. "Then I'm yours."

He released me, raising both hands in generosity.

"*Bene,*" he said. "Welcome home, Michael."

He stood up to face me. Somehow, I actually summoned up the balls to accept his embrace. Then I picked up my glass and knocked back the bitters in one straight shot. It tasted like a Chanel No. 5 and soda, but the acid feeling in my stomach instantly vanished.

"You a good boy." Uncle Connie grinned.

TWELVE

Sofia's doctor met me in the winter kitchen. His instruments were set up across the enormous butcher's block. As I watched him pack his things, I couldn't help wondering if he was the one who'd set Sofia's arm on her sixteenth birthday.

"Your girl's got a nasty little monkey on her back." Dr. Petrie was a spare-looking man with a morgue attendant's muscular hands and an air of cold disdain. "She'll be detoxing for the next few days. It won't be pretty. My advice is to buy plenty of diapers."

I winced. "Can't you do anything to make it easier?"

"I've got her on clonidine and baclofen," he said. "We could bring her through the worst of it with rapid detox, but that would require intubation under general anesthesia—and, of course, the old man is dead-set against hospital care. Never mind rehab. Are you by chance the husband?"

"No," I said. "I don't think there is a husband."

"She's going to need someone to keep her from hurting herself," he said. "Withdrawal can trigger psychotic depression, and she's had a hard ride. Unfortunately, my nurse and I have to return to the hospital tomorrow morning. Is there anyone you trust to look after her?"

"Not in this bunch," I said.

"Swear to God. No amount of money is worth this." He shook his head in disgust. "Go on. You can see her now."

Sofia's bed had been set up in a tiny room off the kitchen. It seemed to have served as a pantry but was most likely built as the cook's quarters. The men of her family had chosen it for security, not comfort: The only window was set high in the wall, too small for even a child to squeeze through. Sofia sat up in bed, awake and agitated. She didn't meet my eyes.

"Hello," I said.

"Hey." She held herself as if warding off the cold, although it was easily seventy-two degrees inside. "I wasn't sure if you were really there or if I only imagined you."

"I'm here," I said.

Then she looked at me.

Time hadn't changed her so much. She had a woman's body now, not a girl's, as if she had blossomed in sorrow. And though it was clear she hadn't been treated well for some time, there was a kind of fragile allure to her. A sense of immediacy in her dark eyes, no barriers between us. A few gray hairs, a few lines: The years were nothing. I had to remind myself why it was better to keep my distance.

"Yes, you are here, aren't you?" She took a careful breath. "And now you can go."

"Sofia—"

"I guess I didn't hallucinate you breaking Magpie's arm, either? Or smashing his face in with that gun? That was all real, too."

"Well, golly Moses. If only I'd known he was your boyfriend, I guess I would have let him kill us both."

"He's not my boyfriend."

"Do you have sex with him?"

"That's none of your damn business." She stared coldly at me. "You're going to kill him, aren't you? He's been expecting it for weeks."

I couldn't stop myself from laughing.

"Why is that funny to you?"

"Do you have any idea how much pain and misery I went through tonight, trying *not* to kill your precious Magpie?"

"Poor you." She looked down. "If you don't kill him, someone will. It's what happens to everyone who tries to come between me and my father."

"That's junkie paranoia talking," I said. "Just because Corveau was measuring out your fixes doesn't mean he was looking out for you."

"God, you're charming." She narrowed her eyes at me. "Now seriously, will you please fuck off?"

"In a minute, I will. Just tell me this. If you care so much about Magpie, why did you let me take you away from him?"

"He's losing control," she said. "He was . . . starting to frighten me. I guess I didn't think you'd actually bring me here."

"I didn't have a choice," I said.

"Strange. Isn't that what you told me the last time we said good-bye?"

For a moment, neither one of us spoke. I saw shadows pass beneath the door. I moved closer to her.

"How are you feeling?" I asked in a low whisper.

"Like I'm about two seconds away from crawling out of my skin," she said. "I'm scared."

"The next week's going to be hard for you," I said. "Believe me, I know how it feels to—"

"Oh. You know what heroin withdrawal feels like? Because that would be interesting." She waited. "Please don't act like you've been there if you haven't. It makes you sound like a Baptist missionary."

"Lutheran," I said. "I have been there. Just not on your end of the room, that's all. My mother . . ." I fell silent.

"I remember." Her voice softened a little. "I don't want to die, Mike."

"You're going to need help getting through this. I'd like to be the person helping you."

"If you want to help me, get me out of here." She half-smiled. "But you can't do that, can you? You came here to work for my father. Bought and paid for."

"I made a deal with your father," I said, "but I came here for you."

She stopped. "Why?"

"I just do. I . . ."

The feet were still behind the door. *To hell with it,* I thought.

"I came back to ask your forgiveness," I said finally. "I wanted to know if—"

"Mike." Sofia leaned in. "*Why?*"

"I still . . . care about you," I said. "I still love you."

She held her black eyes on me, trembling a little, as if she were afraid to believe me.

"Christ Almighty." She sighed. "I wish to God I was still the girl you put on that bus twenty years ago. I'd have forgiven you in a heartbeat. But I just don't have it in me anymore. Why aren't you telling me the truth?"

"That is the truth."

She shook her head in disbelief. "Here's the truth. My father gave me to Corveau. I was a *gift*. And as soon as they put me back together again, he'll give me to someone else. Probably you."

I looked away. "You're comparing me to Corveau?"

She drew a pained breath, released it. "You're not going to want to hear this, but they do come a lot worse than Magpie. He took care of me. Tried to, anyway. Maybe it was just to satisfy his ego . . . because I was part of his collection . . ." Her voice faltered a little. "You're a nice guy, Mike. But I tell you, I'd rather get hurt by Magpie . . . or my father . . . or my father's *button men* . . . than by a nice guy like you. You made me trust you. That's something even my father couldn't do to me."

I took a breath. "Maybe now isn't the right time to—"

Then the tears came. She abruptly shut her eyes, pressing her palms against her head.

"Sweetie." I reached out to take her arm. She knocked my hand back with surprising strength.

"Look, will you please *get the hell away*?"

I stood up. "I'm going to get the doctor."

She put her head down against the blanket, sobbing quietly.

"I know you mean well," she said. "I'm just . . . not up to being in the same room with you. I'm sorry."

"No," I said. "I'm the sorry one."

A moment later Grady came in, holding a cardboard box. "Time to go." He sneered at his sister. "Oh, dear. Little princess has the shakes. Sure you want to kick like this, Sofia? I could send Ciro out to fetch you a nickel's worth of black tar. Put you right back on that fast ride to the graveyard."

"You can't talk to me that way."

"I can talk to a whore any way I want to." Grady's tone was strangely matter-of-fact. "You don't respect yourself, how can you expect others to treat you any better? Do you know what you do to our father? You know how you make him suffer?"

"Not enough," she answered. "He hasn't suffered enough."

"Grady," I started to say.

"Stay out of this, Mike." He shoved the box into my arms. "Here's your shit from the boat. You're taking a car this time." He waited. "For Christ's sake, stop staring at my sister's tits and get the hell out."

Sofia looked terrified—for herself or for me, I couldn't tell.

"You get out," I said. "Or I'll leave you in a lot worse shape than Corveau."

Grady smiled, and I was instantly sorry he had. His smile was the one a baby porpoise sees right before the shark takes him. A Barca's smile. He gave it directly to his sister.

"Sounds like Mike needs to hear the whole truth," he said. "Think he'll still want you after he knows everything?"

She didn't answer. Finally he left.

"He used to be such a nice kid," I said.

"He's right about me," she said. "Mike—"

"You don't owe me any explanations. And he's dead wrong about you." I looked at her. "I'll leave you alone now."

"If you—" Sofia stopped. "Mike, the box is moving."

"Yeah. I didn't think you'd want to leave her behind." I set the box down on the bed, allowing it to fall open. "What's her name, anyway?"

The beagle instantly jumped up onto Sofia's lap, pestering her with kisses. When Sofia smiled, it was like the first light after a longer and terrible darkness.

"Josie," she said.

THIRTEEN

A green Eldorado was idling in the driveway, but no one was standing nearby. I was about to go back into the house when I realized I was being watched from the shadows.

"Hello?" My voice didn't carry far in the steamy night air, but I could hear a man's footsteps treading the gravel. Thin soles: dress shoes. "Heck of a night, huh?"

No answer. A moment later, Grady came down from the house.

"You preaching to the armadillos, St. Francis?" His eyes made a rapid check over my shoulder.

I turned back in the direction he was looking, saw nothing. "You're driving? I thought Ciro was my ride home."

"Count your blessings. If it was Ciro, you'd be dead by now." He got into the car.

As we drove away, I stole a glance into my sideview mirror. A silhouetted figure watched me from the mist, then vanished into dark night air.

We stopped at the gate, and two men climbed into the backseat. Not Ciro's Hondurans but old-school Sicilian toughs, wearing silk shirts and lightweight .22s in the summer heat.

"We're good?" Grady asked one of them. "Our prize package nicely bedded down for the night?"

"*Sì, signore. Come i morti.*" Yes, sir. Like the dead. The guard smiled at me with clean yellow teeth.

Nobody said a word after that until we were halfway over the Lake Pontchartrain Causeway.

"So why didn't my father kill you?" Grady asked idly. "He was dead set on it when you went up there."

"I made him lose his temper," I said. "Something I learned with my own dad. They can't hit you and yell at you at the same time. Makes them look weak."

"Don't get cocky." He lit a cigarette. "You dodged a bullet tonight. That doesn't make you bulletproof."

"Grady, you've had a lot of chances to kill me and I'm still here. Your father once tried to blow me up, and I'm still here. I figure I must be doing something right."

"You got it all wrong, Mike. My father *had* to set that bomb to save his life." He blew smoke. "You know how bad things got after you shafted us? The commission was this close to icing my father once they found out he let FBI get inside. My older brothers—dead. I myself had to grow up in a fucking swamp. So understand this, please. If we let you live, it's because we need you. The minute we stop needing you . . . *auf wiedersehen* to your kraut ass."

"So . . . what? You're mad at me because you didn't get to go to your high school prom?"

"You know, we really shouldn't fight." Grady smiled pleasantly. "I always looked up to you. Even when you were disrespecting me in front of my sister tonight."

"No disrespect intended. Leave her alone and we're fine."

He threw a glance my way. "Aren't you the least bit curious to know what she's been—?"

"No," I said.

"It's best you don't get too hot and bothered for Sofia. Don't misunderstand me, it's not fraternal jealousy. I just don't want to see you screw yourself up, when the future has so many other lovely things to offer."

"Such as?"

"My friendship," he said. "You know my father's going to retake New Orleans. It's his legacy. I've spent years preparing for the day I inherit that legacy—and with his blessing, I'm damned well going to do it. Consider that as you plan your next move."

"Which is what?"

"You're going back to the FBI." The way he said it, I wasn't sure if it was a question, a statement, or a command.

"Yeah? Even though I don't work there anymore?"

"Yes," he said. "You'll be asked to betray my father. You may even be tempted to drop a dime, for old time's sake. Of course, if you admit to knowing anything about us—if you admit to knowing the letters of the fucking *alphabet*, Mike—trust me on this, we'll know."

Grady pulled into a crossover between the bridge's two spans. The lights of Metairie glittered from a mile away.

"This is the last free ride you're getting," he said. "Report back when you have something to report. Change cell phones at least once a day. Don't bother calling us with the new number, we'll know it before you do. If anybody picks up your trail, we will sever our ties with you. The immediate result of which is that you will be dead."

"Understood," I said.

"One last thing." He took a drag on his cigarette. "You got a watch on?"

I held up my wrist. "What, your father never taught you how to tell t—"

A needle of pain shot through me as Grady deftly planted the end of his cigarette on the back of my hand.

"That hurt?" He smiled. "Good. Remember that the next time you feel like throwing down."

A smell of charred skin rose into the air. Grady's bodyguards seemed mildly disappointed when I didn't strike back.

"Now get out of my sight," he said.

"You're leaving me here?"

"You've got a thousand dollars in your pocket. Surely somebody can be persuaded to take you back to your lovely storage room." He smiled. "And Mike?"

"Yeah."

"Sofia will suffer for every mistake you make," he said. "My father has a sentimental attachment to my sister. I don't. If you turn out to be a screwup or a traitor, I will be required to cause her pain. It will be your fault. Don't make me prove to you just how helpless you really are."

I waited until Grady's taillights were well out of view before starting my long walk home.

FOURTEEN

Three days later, I stood in the lobby of the New Orleans field office of the FBI. Neither I nor the young uniformed guard was having much success with my attempts to unlock the electronic door to Investigations.

"Maybe if you kind of drag it through." He demonstrated with a flick of his wrist. "You want me to try?"

"I'm fine." I swiped the card, then punched in my four-digit PIN. A red light blinked three times. "My code number obviously isn't working anymore. Let's just sign me in, okay?"

"It's like I said, Age . . . um, Mr. Yeager. The new regs don't allow us to bypass the gate unless a supervisor walks you through." He gave me a worried look. "Don't try it too many times or it'll set off a security alert."

I looked around. I was starting to draw a crowd. "Let's call a supervisor."

"Okay. What's your squad assignment?"

"I already told you, I don't have one." I lowered my voice to a whisper. "Try Agent Kiplinger."

"Sorry?"

"Agent. Kiplinger."

It was my first visit to FBI New Orleans Division since the new building went up near Lakefront Airport. Just walking in the door had been an education. The exterior was faced with red granite and polarized glass, ready to withstand anything short of field artillery. The agents all looked like high school kids on their way to a Model United Nations assembly. Then there was the magical security door that wouldn't let me through.

"Yeager." Art leaned through the open door.

"Special Agent Kiplinger." The guard tried to offer him a clipboard. "We need you to sign for—"

Art didn't reply as he turned back to the secure area. I caught the door just as it was about to fall shut again.

"Sorry about the trouble," the guard called after us.

The presence of a broken wing in an FBI field office is often deeply unnerving to other agents, something on the order of seeing Martin Luther inside the Vatican. We used to get a lot of these burnouts, back when New Orleans was a disciplinary office. They were either hard-asses from the Hoover era or head-case narcs who'd maintained their covers just a little too well. We spoke of them as "on the bricks," as if someone had cleaned them off the sidewalk. No one ever had to point them out to us. There was just this clammy dead-man-walking air about them, a smell of too many cigarettes and beer before breakfast. Nobody ever accepted their invitations to lunch. Nobody ever met their eyes.

That's how everyone was looking at me as I followed Art back to his office: I was that guy on the bricks.

"So I scored us a couple of rocks in the Nine," I said cheerfully at the top of my voice. "Or are you still snorting that primo Colombian blue-flake you swiped last year?"

Agent Kiplinger merely frowned as he expertly tapped a ten-digit passcode into the keypad next to his office door.

"That's artistry." I walked in. "And to think I couldn't get through the door with four lousy num—"

He shut the door behind me. "Are you nuts? Where the hell have you been?"

"Nice view of the golf course," I said.

"We'll go hit nine holes after work," he said. "Seriously, Yeager. The last communication I had from you was a text message, three days ago. I thought you were going to turn up floating in the London Avenue Canal."

"Gee, Dad. Susie and I were having so much fun at the drive-in, we just lost track of the time." I sat down. "I'm fine, thanks. I've been doing what you and the director assigned me to do."

"You've been to Barca's place?"

"A couple of times in the past few days."

"And?"

"I think I'm in trouble," I said. "Why did you bring me here? It's not safe."

"There are things we have to talk about that can only be discussed inside this building." He suddenly noticed my bandaged wrist. "What happened to your hand?"

"Cigarette burn. What happened to yours?"

"Sorry I asked." He gave a tense frown. "Don't worry about coming here, okay? You're covered. They're kicking me up to ASAC so I can coordinate operations between squads. As far as anybody on the floor knows, this is a mandatory post-termination debrief. Look a little pissed off when you leave."

"Somehow I don't think that's going to be a problem," I said. "*Mazel tov* on the promotion, by the way."

"*Kine ahora.*" There was a knock at the door.

"Who's that?" I asked.

"Your handler." He moved past me to answer it. "God knows you can use one."

"My what?" I put my hand on the doorknob. "Hold on. I report to you, Art. We never talked about any babysitters."

"We're about to talk about it right now," he said. "You mind?"

I backed away and he opened the door. Somehow I managed to keep my face on straight when I saw who was standing on the other side.

"Mike," Art said. "Say hello to Special Agent Noah Delacroix."

At first glance, he seemed no different from any of the other Model UN kids. He was a little taller than me, dark-featured and well groomed, with a confident posture and intensely watchful eyes. The young man bore himself with straight-out-of-academy earnestness, the kind that usually comes with a trust fund attached. His shoes were cleaned and polished, no trace of sand or broken shell. Black Bostonians.

"A pleasure." Noah extended his hand. "I've heard a lot about you over the years. Nice to meet a legend in the flesh."

Even I get followed sometimes. It was the same voice I'd heard talking to Barca. Noah's grip was cold blue steel. I gripped back.

"I thought it was high time the two of you got acquainted." Art closed the door. "Noah's only been on my team for a month, but he's already burning up the place. We'll probably both be working for him someday."

"Gives me something to look forward to, I guess." I unobtrusively flexed my sore hand as I sat down. "This is why you called me in, Art? So I can meet the freshman class?"

"Not exactly." Art took a seat behind his desk. "I assume you've been following the news about the Black Pearl raid?"

"I have. 'Major Drug Bust in St. Charles Crackhouse,' was it? 'Heroic Burnout Cops Winning Hearts and Minds'?"

"Try 'Dead Cop in Post-Katrina Clusterfuck,' " Art said. "For the record, the murdered policeman's name was Ray Lenahan. He left a wife and two kids, if that means anything to you."

"It does," I said. "So what?"

"So this." Noah handed me a color surveillance photo from his file folder: It showed me and Sofia running away from the dead cop. Ciro was nowhere in sight. "Can you tell us who the shooter was?"

There was no sign of threat when he asked the question. But as he watched for my response, I could hear Grady's voice, sharp as ice, *Sofia will suffer for every mistake you make.*

"Mike?" Art waited. "Are you . . . ?"

"No idea." I shook my head. "Sorry."

Art pursed his lip and said nothing.

"Hang on." Noah gave a patronizing smile. "You fled the scene of a riot, hand in hand with a mobster's daughter, and you want us to believe you saw nothing?"

"Here." I took out my ballpoint pen and drew a circle around my eyes. "In the land of the blind, the one-eyed man is king. Both of my eyes were full of pepper spray. So tell me, genius. What was I seeing?"

He gave Art a flat look: *Can you talk sense to this guy?*

"The Black Pearl raid has put a big fat spotlight on the cracks in our law enforcement structure," Art said. "Two fatalities, three dozen serious injuries. Meanwhile, the NOPD are exhausted and demoralized. Working out of trailers and using porta-potties. Quitting in droves, like your friend Crawford. The casualties only confirm what everyone's been saying, Mike. We're losing this war."

"Big Al didn't quit, he retired. He's rebuilding his house."

"Remind me to send him a pot of jam."

"What I don't understand is what you were doing with Barca's daughter in the first place," Noah said, "when your assignment is supposed to be tracking down Amrita Narayan."

There was an odd tightness in Noah's voice as he fired the question. I knew it well: I often made the same sound when I was trying not to betray anger.

"Barca wanted me to bring his daughter home," I replied. "It was necessary to establish my cover."

"You're sure that's all it was?" He pulled himself up. "Seriously. What's your real interest in Sofia Barca?"

"Artie, am I crazy, or is this kid breaking my balls?"

"Probably a little of both," he said. "Agent Delacroix, would you mind getting the NOPD meeting started for me? Tell everyone I'll be along in a few minutes."

It took Noah less than a quarter second to regain his dutiful smile. "No problem." He said it like it was his favorite expression. "I'm really not trying to give you grief on this thing, Mike. We're all on the same team, right?"

"Apparently so." I didn't meet his eyes as he left.

Art closed the door. "What's your beef with Noah? I could have sworn you jumped a foot out of your skin when he walked in the door."

I was that close to ratting Noah out, so help me—but damned if Grady hadn't predicted I'd find myself in that exact situation. *Predicted, hell. He fucking well knew.* Something told me the kid knew it, too.

"I'm not thrilled about working for Boy Scouts," I said with what I hoped was a convincing degree of irritation.

"I seem to recall you recently bragging that you used to be a Boy Scout." He reached under his desk. "Want some water?"

"Only if it's cold."

"You think the taxpayers are gonna foot the bill for a refrigerator?" He picked up a bottled water, then expertly twisted the cap off with one hand.

"Show-off," I said.

Art smiled. "Noah's good. Young, but good. Twenty years ago, you'd have thought he was serious competition."

"Maybe I do now." Then I noticed what was on Art's credenza: a prosthetic arm. "That's an interesting trophy. They gave it to you for marksmanship?"

He exhaled a distracted laugh. "That's my excuse for staying in the field. It works fine, as long as I don't mind looking like the Abraham Lincoln robot at Disneyland."

I picked it up. An electronic fingerprint reader was next to the arm. The credenza's sliding door had a combination lock.

"How do you shoot nowadays?"

"Same way I do everything else." He held up his remaining hand. "Who killed Officer Lenahan, Mike?"

"It's like I told the kid. I couldn't see."

"Save it for somebody who doesn't know you." He took a long drink of water. "Pepper spray or not, I've seen you pick out a sniper's angle of fire before the body hit the ground. So don't bullshit me on this."

"Okay, but you do realize that narrows down my list of possible responses to zero."

He thought about it. "Do I at least get to know why you're stonewalling?"

"Do I get to know who called in the police raid?"

"Wish I could tell you, but it's strictly need to know."

"Fair enough," I said. "We done here?"

He took my measure. "There was an anonymous tip to the police, saying it looked like trouble between rival gangs. We vouched for the intelligence. That was the extent of the FBI's involvement." He waited. "Satisfied?"

"Did the tip come from the informant?"

"Jesus Christ, Mike. Why are you asking?"

"How else could you vouch for the information?" I put the fake arm down. "To your knowledge, is Magpie Corveau at any stage of contact with federal or local law enforcement?"

"No."

"You're saying no because you're not allowed to discuss it with me."

"I'm saying no because he's not in contact with anyone. Damien Corveau is dead."

I blinked. "How?"

"Somebody crushed his windpipe during the raid." Art gave an indifferent shrug. "He was the other fatality I referred to. His name hasn't been released to the media yet."

"Need to know?"

"Need to know," Art said.

"It might interest you to hear that Magpie was the one who kidnapped Narayan at Barca's request. At least, I'm pretty sure that's what happened."

"What gave you that idea?"

"Lucky guess. Or maybe because Magpie told me he'd recently done a job for Barca in the Lower Ninth Ward." I raised an eyebrow. "Have you turned up any other bodies besides Simon Burke's?"

He distractedly shook his head.

"You will," I said. "Start looking for the son of Kendrick and Rosemary Duplessis. They own the house where the kidnappers took Simon and Amrita. Their son—"

"Evander," he replied. "His gang name is Cleanhead. He's a founding member of Rize."

"Not anymore," I said. "His homedogs seem to think the cops killed

Cleanhead. I'm guessing he was murdered by his own team, to prevent us from questioning him. He's the only direct link between the crime scene and the kidnappers."

Art narrowed his eye. "How do you figure?"

"You don't pick a house for a job like that unless you know for a fact that the owners won't be coming home. Also, Cleanhead got sentimental. Smoked a crack pipe for auld lang syne, then propped his family's picture up against the wall."

"And you believe he's dead because . . ."

"A five-five-six shell casing was found at the scene," I said. "With a red polymer jacket to prevent overheating. I'm pretty sure it's the APLP. Stands for armor-piercing, limited-penetration—"

"I'm quite familiar with the APLP, thanks."

"Shreds human flesh like hamburger," I said. "Corveau's bodyguard was packing just such a weapon the other night—and he's former military. So here's my question, Art. Why isn't that shell casing in the crime scene report? Because it's looking to me like you might have buried some evidence."

"Christ." He gave me a weary look. "As you can see, the NOPD is in kind of a mess lately. I'm filtering the information in case the wrong people start looking at the case file. Otherwise I'd have read you in on it sooner."

I nodded. "Kind of like when you didn't 'read me in' on what Vitale and the Capitol Police were planning for me?"

"That was not my call," he said. "We had to make sure your cover was airtight. The director didn't think you'd be able to pull it off if you saw it coming. In any case, I'm sorry." He waited. "Do you accept my apology?"

"Like you said, it wasn't your call." I sat down. "If you don't trust me, I can't function. Simple as that."

"Do not make this personal," he said. "I'm getting killed over this dead cop thing. Your name hasn't been mentioned outside this room—yet. But if that surveillance photo gets into the wrong hands . . ."

"Is that a threat?"

"It's a risk," he said. "Don't make it any worse."

"You're saying you don't trust your own people."

He frowned. "If you mean Delacroix, he's been vetted."

"So were Robert Hanssen and Aldrich Ames."

"So were you," he said. "I know you're not crooked, Mike. Still, I do think you ought to tell me what Barca's got you working on. Besides bringing his daughter home, I mean. I think you owe your old partner that much."

I exhaled. "Kadmos."

"The security company?"

"Barca wants to know if they're trying to kill him. He also asked me to find out if his name shows up in connection to something called Pandora's Box."

Art thought a moment. "He's got to know he's on the list. He's probably just testing you."

"What list?"

He judged me for a second—then walked past me to the credenza. He pressed his index finger into the reader and opened the combination lock. Then he handed me a single page from a red file. Sure enough, Emelio Barca topped the list, followed by Damien "Magpie" Corveau. Many other names had been obliterated with a black marker.

"Pandora's Box is our hundred-most-wanted list," he said. "The worst of the worst, the real stone killers. Our organizational theory experts swear up and down that if we take these guys, the drug networks will collapse."

"Who's collapsing so far?"

"We are," Art said. "We take them in, sixty days later they're back on the street. Witnesses recant or mysteriously disappear. Still the murder rate keeps climbing. So what do we do?"

"Get a bigger box?"

"Get a better list," he answered. "For that we need information—and our informants are getting whacked as fast as we can develop them. Some people think this is random chaos. I don't. I see Emelio Barca's guiding hand. He can only flourish in a failed system, and right now we're on the verge of one. Which is probably why he's so worried about Pandora."

I handed the sheet back. "So where's the real list?"

"That is the—"

"Half the names on this memo are redacted, and most of the others are small-time crooks. Am I not getting the grown-up version because you think it would interfere with my cover? Or are you worried I might actually feed the information to Barca? Don't say 'need to know,' or so help me I'll smack you with your own fake arm."

He replaced the sheet and locked the credenza.

"There are questions you don't ask an agent working undercover," he said finally. "Because then you're responsible for knowing the answer. Like whether he only smoked the joint, or sold it to kids. Or if he only watched the shooting, or—"

"Ask the question, Artie."

"I think I just did."

"I didn't pull the trigger," I answered. "I saw Lenahan take the bullet. To be perfectly frank, I didn't stick around to cry over the body. At that moment, my only concern was getting Sofia the hell out. You knew I'd do anything to protect her when you handed me the assignment. In fact, something tells me you were counting on it."

He smiled thinly. "That's the price I pay for having Mike Yeager on the case?"

"It's the price I pay," I said. "For God's sake, please don't pull me out again unless it's critical. Next time, I might just show up in a pine box."

"Mike." Art watched me walk to the door. "What are you going to tell Barca about Kadmos?"

"What should I say? *Are* they trying to kill him?"

"You can't tell him what you don't know," he mused. "It's probably better you keep it that way."

I let that one work in my gut for a few seconds.

"You're the boss," I said with an indifferent nod.

"Thanks." He smiled, a little sadly. "Listen, if you're uncomfortable having Agent Delacroix on your detail—"

"He's all right."

"Really? Why the sudden change of heart?"

I opened the door.

"We can always use another pair of hands," I said. "Mind if I get one of those warm bottled waters for the road?"

He pitched it to me and I caught it by the cap. I nodded and saluted. Art didn't respond—but from the credenza, his prosthetic arm seemed to return the wave.

FIFTEEN

I caught up with Noah in the seminar room, which was packed to the walls with men and women in police uniforms. You could taste frustration in the air like aluminum foil on your teeth. Noah refereed from the podium.

". . . getting our asses kicked," a red-faced lieutenant was saying. "I pick up the newspaper and the mayor's people are calling us racist thugs—like *we're* the ones who started the shit? Like one of *our* guys didn't get shot? I'm not asking for any medals—but *come on*, guys. A little support here."

A chorus of anger. At least half the room was with him. Maybe more in a few seconds, depending on how Noah answered.

"Look, I'm as pissed off as you are about Lenahan," Noah said. "To me it proves two things. One, we have to start coordinating our efforts. Two, you guys deserve a lot better support than you've been getting under the current political administ—"

"You're saying the problem will get solved if the federal government is in charge?" The lieutenant shook his head, amazed. "After you guys did such an amazing job in Iraq."

"This is going to be a federal operation," Noah answered plainly. "Phase One of Levin-Marcato nationalizes all law enforcement activity in New Orleans. Phase Two is the money, and we don't get the money until we solve the gang problem. You're objecting to this?"

"I'm objecting to the fact that you're talking like this Levin-Marcato thing is already a law, and it's not." The lieutenant appealed to the room. "Am I the only person in this room who cares that we're letting these clowns take over our city?"

Evidently he wasn't. A grumbling wave rippled through the room; any second it could turn to shouting. Then I noticed the one person in the room who didn't seem the least upset by any of it. A young woman, standing against the far wall.

"Unless somebody in here has six billion dollars to spend on reconstruction, we'd better hope and pray that it does pass." Noah's voice cut through the noise. "God help us all if it doesn't, because then there won't be a city left to fight over."

The lieutenant wasn't satisfied. "What happened at Black Pearl—"

"Was everybody's mistake," Noah said. "We lost because we underestimated the enemy. We're at war, guys. If we want to win, then we have to abandon this image we have of mobsters as fat old men with thirty-eights stuck in their pants. Or even as strung-out teenagers with AK-47s. Today's gangster is better organized, better armed, and even better trained than anything our side can bring to bear. Believe it. If we're not prepared to match them—dollar for dollar, weapon for weapon, tactic for tactic—then we may as well admit we lost this war a long time ago." He paused for effect. "Or should we maybe all pull together and save our city?"

Noah said it with such boldness that I was almost tempted to believe that he meant every word. Maybe he did. Scattered applause broke through the room, led by the young woman. Pretty soon they were all clapping. Then she turned and saw me.

She was ice-blond confidence in a black suit. Her hair was lighter, her makeup less trashy, and the hillbilly attitude was gone—but it was her, all right: the barmaid from the Washington hotel.

"Now if we can get back to the business at hand," Noah said as the applause died down. "A few minutes ago I handed out some packets . . ."

Noah absently wiped his hands on his trousers before retrieving his file. There was a sound of pages turning; the room was back under control. Damned if the woman in black didn't smile at me.

I approached Noah as the room cleared after the meeting.

"Glad to know we're doing something about organized crime in New Orleans," I said. "We should talk."

"Not here." He didn't look at me. "The coffee shop near Lakefront Airport. I'll buy lunch."

"I'm supposed to eat with friends across the lake." I said it casually, like it wasn't a big deal. He nodded as if he couldn't care less either way.

"I'll see you in twenty minutes," he said. "Excuse me."

He strode away. Lili was waiting for me just outside the auditorium door.

"You get around," I said. "Nice look."

"Thanks." She was more formal than she'd been in Washington. The sultry, fuck-off look in her eyes hadn't gone away. "How do you think the discussion went?"

"I think the discussion's a long way from being over. The respect of these men doesn't come cheap."

"Don't worry," she said. "We can afford it."

The badge around her neck wasn't FBI. Beneath the visitor's pass, dangling between her breasts, was that same logo I'd seen on the security vehicle in the Lower Ninth: three red triangles, like teeth, descending into a black horizon.

"I knew Lili wasn't your real name," I said, "but . . . Kadmos? Your parents must have been reading a lot of Marvel Comics when you were born."

"Please tell me you're not using the old pretending-to-read-the-badge trick as an excuse to check out my rack." She gave me a weary look. "Kadmos is the company I work for. Kadmos Security Solutions. We handle consulting and outsourcing for most of the law enforcement agencies in New Orleans nowadays. Firearms training, medical services, facilities management—basically, we do the heavy lifting so your people can keep above the fray."

"So what you did in Washington . . ."

"A favor," she said. "To a friend."

"Must be quite a friendship," I said. "I suppose the gentlemanly thing would be to tell you that I don't hold a grudge. That you were simply—as you put it—doing the heavy lifting. Then again, my friends tell me I'm not a gentleman."

"Your friends underestimate you." She looked away. "For what it's worth, I tried to go easy on you. I could tell you were getting scared."

"Maybe I should have tipped more for bringing in my luggage," I said. "Seems like you're the kind of woman who gives good value for the money."

"I get paid by the same taxpayers as you, Mike. Just a little better, that's all." She scanned the space around me. "It wasn't your fault that you couldn't see through my cover. I had very good teachers."

"Exactly how wrong was I about you?"

"Well . . ." She pursed her lips. "I'm from southern Ohio, not West

Virginia, but that's close enough. And I wouldn't wear that perfume in a million years. As it happens, though, I do have a baby sister who used to call me Lili."

"How about the married boyfriend who makes occasional booty calls?"

She smiled without humor. "We've reached an understanding."

I stared her down. "Vitale told me you were ready to snort coke with me and do the nasty. Was that something else the taxpayers are footing the bill for?"

"You'll never know, will you?" She walked away. Then she stopped. "You want to know my real name?"

"I'd actually rather see you buried up to your neck in fire ants." I smiled politely. "Of course, since you're a subcontractor for the federal government, I suppose that would technically constitute an abuse of funds."

"I'm Leah Varnado," she said, "but you go on calling me Lili. You sound almost sweet when you say it."

As I turned to the men's room, Leah walked away down the hall. A moment later, Supervising Special Agent Art Kiplinger idly crossed her path, and they started talking. Their facial expressions suggested that it was all about work; their body language implied that it wasn't. He kept taking little steps forward and she kept touching her hair. Then they went their separate ways. The whole exchange had lasted less than a minute. If either one of them had seen me watching, they gave absolutely no sign of it.

SIXTEEN

I'd just barely gotten used to the Bureau's air-conditioning, and now that I was back on the pavement, the heat was dragging me down like an asphalt blanket. A jogger with maybe 1 percent body fat ran past me. *How the hell do they do it?* I asked myself, not for the first or the hundredth time. *How does anyone live here?* Then I remembered: They don't. Not so much anymore.

Agent Delacroix waited for me outside the airport's main hangar, next to the famous Fountain of the Winds. Like everything else in New Orleans, the fountain had taken a beating. Its four concrete statues seemed to be shielding themselves from the wind instead of causing it.

"I've got ten minutes." Noah peeled the lid from a foam cup. "What do you have for me?"

"Nothing. It seems like we should get to know each other."

"In ten minutes?"

"Bigger mistakes have been made in less time," I said. "For instance, I didn't give you up to Kiplinger."

He didn't meet my eyes. "You're smarter than you look."

"A smart man would have stayed in Philadelphia. I guess I can take it for granted that Barca knows the real reason I'm in New Orleans?"

Noah nodded. "He's known it since you got here—well, since I told him, anyway. He says it doesn't matter, as long as you remember he owns you now."

"You and me both," I said. "How many sides are you playing for, Noah? Are you a bad agent who sold out to the mob, or a bad mobster with a fake badge?"

"At least I've got the badge." He took a long pull off his coffee. Drank it black, I noticed. "There's never just two sides in any war, Mike. What's your point?"

"Let's just skip over any bullshit about your loyalty to the Bureau," I said. "I overheard you talking to Barca the other night about Pandora's Box. And Kadmos. So I guess I caught the job you were afraid to take. Is there any background you can give me, or am I flying blind here?"

"Like you said—you caught the job, not me. I'm sure you'll do fine. All those years of experience have to count for something. And if they don't—"

"Sofia will suffer," I said. "So what's Barca got on you? How's he ensuring your loyalty?"

Noah smiled.

"Let's take a walk," he said. "I'll spot you an extra five minutes."

We went up to the observation deck, where our view consisted of the empty runway and a corpse-white sky over Lake Pontchartrain.

"Doesn't sound like the New Orleans police are too crazy about placing themselves under federal command." I followed him up the concrete staircase. "Think they'll get in line with Levin-Marcato?"

Noah shrugged, as if it were small potatoes. "Do they have a choice?"

"Probably not. Anyway, you did all right in that meeting. If I didn't know better, I'd have said you were cool as a lemon sno-ball."

"How do you know I wasn't?"

"Your palms were sweating," I said. "Don't be hard on yourself. When I was your age, I couldn't get through a five-minute debrief without stammering. Never mind keeping a whole roomful of angry cops in line."

"Yeah? And how old were you when you were my age?"

"Young," I said. "Twenty-three, right?"

"That's what it says on my birth certificate."

"I figured you had to be shrink-wrap fresh from the Academy. I take it you had my old pal Bill Bly for firearms training?"

"Yeah, Bill's good. Still has that burn mark on his cheek from a shell fragment he took in ninety-one. Got no complaints about Captain Bly. The NATs say he's tough as gator shit, but he'll sure teach you how to drive a nail in with that MP5 submachine gun."

He said it without cracking a smile. I got the definite impression the kid was winding me up.

"Bill didn't qualify you on the five-five-six assault rifle?"

"FBI doesn't require proficiency on the five-five-six, Mike. But yeah, I can handle it well enough. Are you going to keep on asking these coy little questions to trip me up? Or do you want to take a shot at something that really matters?"

"Just trying to get a sense of my handler's résumé."

"My résumé." He took a breath. "I grew up in Colorado Springs. Valedictorian, St. Mary's High School, class of 2000. Go Pirates. Earned my B.A. from Colorado State, magna cum, double major in poli sci and criminal justice. Got an early academy slot and immediate transfer to my first office of preference."

"Family?"

"Two brothers, one sister. I'm the baby. Mom's a tax accountant, Dad teaches history at the Air Force Academy. Work doesn't give me much time to travel home."

"Not if you're gonna make Organized Crime squad at twenty-three." I nodded. "Which we can no doubt attribute solely to talent and hard work."

"That and my staggeringly good looks," he said. "You made OC during your rookie year, didn't you?"

I shrugged. "I wouldn't recommend my method."

"Which was what?"

I didn't answer right away. We had reached the top of the stairs, and I was trying not to seem winded. Noah looked ready to go six more flights.

"You've read the newspapers about me," I said finally, "and I'm sure you've seen my personnel file. What else can I tell you that you don't already know?"

"Oh, you have no idea what I know about you, Mike. Trust me, it'd make your eyes pop."

"Try me."

"Let's start with something simple," he said. "Root beer."

"God's gift to mortals," I said. "What about it?"

"You have this weird thing about always drinking the local root beer. Your friends think it's strange—but they figure it makes you happy, so knock yourself out." He shrugged: takes all kinds. "What they don't know is that you can barely stand the stuff. Your old man drank root beer when he was trying to kick the bottle, and now you drink it whenever you're tempted to order scotch. You keep that god-awful dark brown toothpaste flavor in your mouth just so you won't be tempted to ask for something you actually want. You're scared of what you want. For you, root beer's not a beverage. It's self-flagellation."

"The flavor's grown on me over the years."

"Whatever." He finished his coffee. "After the Madrigal case, you saved some kids in Nevada from a psychopath. That's in the official case report. It got you back on active duty and brought some nice publicity to the Bureau. What isn't in the report is that you also hooked up with the kids' schoolteacher—which very nearly got her killed. You have a bad habit of getting women killed. Maybe it has something to do with your mom, who knows. I'm no psychiatrist."

"So you think Mommy and Daddy is what makes me tick."

"I know what doesn't," he said. "Barca thinks you'll fall in line because you want his daughter. I don't. Whatever motivates you, it's not true love for the girl you left behind." As he said this, the wind caught his empty foam cup; he let it go. "You want some background on this Pandora's Box thing? Tell me what your real interest in Sofia Barca is, and I'll give you some shit worth knowing."

"You keep coming back to her." I grabbed the cup before it flew off the ledge. "Why are you so hot to talk about my connection to Sofia? Is it because she's your boss's daughter? Or is she—"

"It's nothing," he said. "She's nothing."

"Yet it really torks you off to think about her and me. Why?"

He shrugged it off. "I have to get back to work. Don't call me again unless you actually have something to say."

I let him get halfway down the stairs before speaking.

"I got Sofia into trouble," I said. "That's my interest in her."

He stopped at the first landing.

"It was partly because of me that her uncle got killed," I went on. "I thought I'd be a nice guy, give him a chance to testify against his *padrino*. Paulie knew he was a dead man either way, but he still refused. Old-school loyalty. I finally convinced him it was the only way to ensure that Sofia would ever be safe from her father's wrath. So we worked out a deal to get both of them into witness protection. What I didn't know at the time was that Barca put a tail on his brother. Two days later, Paolo Barca fell a hundred and fifty-three feet into the Mississippi River."

"That's how you got Sofia into trouble," Noah said.

"I got her into trouble by making her pregnant." I walked down the steps toward him. "That's why he decided to do the deal. He didn't want her raising her child inside the mob. And I—"

"Didn't want a child at all." Noah nodded. "What do you think happened to the kid?"

"She got an abortion. At least . . . that's what she said." I tossed Noah's coffee cup into the trash. "So what's some shit worth knowing?"

"You're going to meet somebody very important at lunch today," he said. "Don't look too surprised when you see who it is. And don't be surprised when your girlfriend's name comes up."

"My girlfriend?"

"Weaver," he said. "She's wired in on this Pandora's Box thing—and not in a way you're going to like."

He started to walk away. I put a hand on his shoulder.

"Noah—"

Half a second later, his fist connected with the right side of my jaw. *Left-handed*. I went tumbling down the stairs. I pulled myself up against the metal trash can—then picked it up and hurled it at him. He calmly ducked and waded back into me. For several seconds we grappled like two bears fighting over a potato chip bag. Then he got me one in the ribs and threw me down. *Kid's strong. Nice uppercut.* As I lay against the concrete stairwell, I realized that Noah hadn't so much as broken a sweat. Meanwhile, my own heart was going like a bad case of engine knock.

"You want to know what makes you tick?" Noah wrung his bruised fists. "I can sum it up in one word. Guilt. Probably the most useless emotion of all. That pain you're feeling right now? That's your own pain, fuckhead. Deal with it."

"Maybe guilt is all that keeps us from turning into complete assholes." I pulled myself up. "Hell, look at you."

"What about me?" He threw me his paper napkin. I used it to wipe the blood from my lip.

"You're so completely sure you've got everybody fooled," I said. "So arrogant, so good at the straight-arrow routine. Yet . . ."

"Yet what?"

"It's like you know how you're supposed to behave—but you don't know why." I nodded. "And I don't give a crap what your birth certificate says. No way in hell are you twenty-three years old. More like—"

He smiled.

"Nineteen." I exhaled. "Oh, Christ."

He smiled. "Like your worst nightmare come true, isn't it?"

"Close enough." I rubbed my jaw. "So what do I call you? Is Noah Delacroix your real name?"

"As far as the FBI's concerned." He walked away from me. "But I'll be damned if I'm going to call you Daddy."

I lay still as his footsteps disappeared down the stairwell, listening to those last words echoing away.

Hell and damnation.

We all do insane things in moments of insanity. The thing I wanted to do—in spite of the corkscrew fear twisting through my spine—was to call Noah back. Apologize. Start the conversation over, play the cable TV version: *I can't change the way things started for us, son . . . but there's still time to get the rest of our story right.* Then he smiles and puts one arm around me: *You got a deal, Pop.* Of course, that was always my first impulse after my own father and I got into a scrap. I didn't want to believe that we had such violence in us. I wanted so badly to apologize before the anger had a chance to settle into hate.

But he was gone. Noah couldn't get away from me fast enough. And no wonder: While we were busy trying to kill each other, he'd planted a listening device on me. A ballpoint pen that was only slightly heavier than the one I'd used in Art's office. It didn't bother me that he'd staged the fight, since it also gave me a chance to steal his wallet.

He wasn't lying. Noah Francis Delacroix was in fact the name on his driver's license. Guess I should have been flattered that she'd given him my middle name. Blood type, O negative: rare type, same as mine. He even kept a fifty-dollar bill tucked away for emergencies. Just like his old man. Just like his father.

"Sofia," I whispered. "God, baby, did I ever mess you up."

I took a breath: *Freak out later, Mikey. For God's sake, back to work.* I studied the contents of Noah's wallet and kept what I needed. Then I returned to the coffee shop and placed it next to the cash register, where it would almost certainly be found by some honest citizen. The pen would be fine once I removed the transmitter inside. No need to waste a good pen.

SEVENTEEN

The north shore of Lake Pontchartrain is a mere twenty-six miles from New Orleans. From a cultural standpoint, it might as well be five hundred. The people there are more typically southern than folks in the Big Easy: You're likelier to eat KFC for dinner than red beans and rice. There is also a quietness to the place, a deep green tranquility, that is utterly missing across the lake. Once, long ago, I had to make a grocery run in the middle of a surveillance job in Mandeville. I was in a hurry, so I slipped on the freshly waxed floor of the Pak-A-Sak and wound up ass over teakettle. As I lay on my back, beer bottles foaming and spinning around, the elderly proprietor smiled down on me. "Look like somebody took him a *tomble*," he said in his amused Florida Parishes accent. That is the north shore attitude in a nutshell: Bad things happen when you don't slow down.

I was surprised to find cars parked along the private road to the marina, among them a black stretch limo. Balloons bobbed around the iron gate—red, white, and green. Early Doobie Brothers floated from the house on a haze of barbecue smoke.

"Cheer up, Yeager. You're going to a party." Grady snapped his fingers in my ear. "What happened, you lose something?"

"More like something found me." I pointed to the balloons. "Who's the guest of honor?"

"You," Grady said. "King for a day, you are."

As I walked behind him, one of Grady's men approached us. They exchanged tense words in rapid-fire Italian. One word peppered the conversation: *medicina*. When Grady returned to me, he looked more than a little pissed off.

"Everything all right?" I noticed that the guard hadn't left the way he came. He was hauling ass down the path that led to the swamp, down to the old slave cabins.

"No worries." Grady lit a cigarette. "Eyes front, now. Curiosity killed the cat."

"Funny," I said. "I thought he died of lung cancer."

There was a lot of muscle at the barbecue. A few of them were goombahs of the old school—geriatrics like Uncle Connie or Marco "Red Eye" Ugolino, so called because he reportedly never slept while traveling to a hit. Now he dozed in the sun like an old hunting dog. Their younger counterparts strutted around the barbecue pit like hungry coyotes. The rest were civilians, members of Barca's extended family. All the older women had the names of saints or movie stars from the Cinecittà days. The younger girls were named Morgan or Heather or Zoë. The men of every age were called Tommy and Petey and Paulie and Tony and Joey and Sammy. Sofia was nowhere among them.

I finally caught up with her in the old Edwardian greenhouse. She was alone, pulling weeds from a terra-cotta planter, her skin glowing in filtered sunlight. Her dress had attracted some warmth from the humid air, forcing it to cling to her. Seeing her brought a painful reminder of her agony over the past three days. She was still very tired, very pale.

"Hey." She smiled timidly. "Here comes trouble."

"I brought you something from the barbecue." I held out a plate. "Sausage and crab meat. You hungry?"

"Nah," she said. "You should eat it while you can. My family's like piranhas when there's free food around."

She was looking a little better than when I'd left her the day before. The first twenty-four hours had been a pure nightmare. The second day, she was nearly comatose. Gradually, the poison released its clawlike grasp, and what little sleep she got was full and natural. Today, she seemed almost like her old self. Her hair, freshly washed, was tied back. Her dress was long-sleeved, covering her bruises.

"I'll eat when you do," I said. "What are you doing out here? Was it the noise at the party?"

"It's always loud around here," she said. "This used to be the only place I could hide from my father. The flowers, you know . . . bother his allergies. I was thinking I might do something out here, but then I got too tired. And it's nothing but weeds now."

"You should rest," I said.

"I'll rest when you do." She gave me a wan smile. "Why do you keep trying it on with me, Mike? You know I can't stand the sight of you. And after the way I yelled at you the other night, you've gotta be wishing you'd left me for the cops."

"I'm a glutton for punishment," I said. "Where's Josie? Somebody should be eating this food."

"You spoil that dog." She whistled. "Josie? Josephine?"

An anxious shadow passed across Sofia's face, vanishing as soon as the beagle trotted up.

"My father's been bragging on you all morning." Sofia tossed a piece of crab; Josie caught it in midair. "What did you do to make him like you again? Convert to Catholicism?"

"We settled it like men," I said. "Hot fudge sundaes at Angelo Brocato's. I got rainbow sprinkles. Your father seems to prefer decorating his gelato with human teeth."

She winced. "That's not funny, Mike."

"No argument there." I sat on the concrete bench. "Today we're gonna head down to the Quarter and get novelty T-shirts made. Got any ideas what mine should say?"

"How about 'Card-Carrying Moron'?"

"See now, I was thinking more along the lines of 'World's Greatest Absentee Dad.'"

Sofia's hand stopped in midthrow. The dog stole the meat right out of her fingers.

"Unless you think that's too much for a T-shirt," I said.

"Mike . . ." A terrified warning look in her eyes.

"Can we talk here?" I asked. "Are we safe?"

"Nobody's safe anywhere," she said.

"Just answer me this." I lowered my voice. "Is Noah . . . ?"

"Yes." She paled. "God, I'm sorry. I should have told you before. I was so scared."

"Guess that was the little secret Grady kept hinting about." I smiled weakly. "You Roman Catholics, swear to God."

"You've met him?"

"He's my FBI handler. For what it's worth, he makes a pretty convincing G-man. Any idea how he was able to fake his way in? Bureau security procedures are pretty damn tight."

She shook her head. "It's been a long time since my son told me any-thing about his business. Even my dad can't always control him the way he used to, and that's saying a lot."

"It is." I looked at her. "Don't you mean 'our son'?"

She raised an eyebrow. "Do you want him to be 'our son'?"

"I never wanted him in the first place," I said. "So I guess I really don't have any claim to him."

For a moment, we both concentrated our attention on Josie.

"I was so angry at you," she said, ending the silence. "I wanted to get rid of everything that connected me to you. But then I thought . . . that baby didn't do anything to me, you know? It wasn't his fault he had stupid par-ents. With Uncle Paulie dead, that little bump in my belly . . . he was all I had left." She shivered. "So I lied to you about the abortion. Flat-out lied. And then . . ."

"Then I shoved you on a bus and ran for cover."

"Yeah." She threw me a dark look. "Then you did that."

I avoided her eyes. "How did you wind up back here?"

"Oh—six months after I ran away, my brother finally caught up with me. In a New Mexico Dairy Queen, of all places." She shook her head. "Lit-tle Noah kind of paid me back for saving his life. Grady and my dad, they were gonna kill me. Then Papa found out I had a baby in me, and it was a boy, and . . . I guess he thought it was a mortal sin to murder his unborn grandchild. So I got a stay of execution. Then I had to live to nurse the baby, and then . . ." She scratched her dog behind the ears. "By then, my father had found other uses for me."

My first impulse was to put my arm around her. Though I knew that would be painful for someone in detox, and something told me I didn't have the right.

"At least you don't have to worry about that anymore," I said awk-wardly. "Magpie's dead."

"Yeah?" She seemed more relieved than I'd expected her to be.

"I don't know how long you were with him, or if he ever told you any-thing about his business . . ."

She glanced up. "Why?"

"No reason." I looked around. "Did you ever meet someone named Am-rita Narayan? Or maybe her husband, Simon Burke?"

She didn't answer.

"It's okay," I said. "Just making conversation."

"Uh-huh. Maybe we should stop having this conversation."

"You think someone's listening?"

"I'm listening," she said. "I don't like what I'm hearing. It sounds too much like the way you used to fish around for an invitation to meet my family."

"Sorry I asked." I stood up.

"You're leaving?" Her eyes followed me anxiously.

"Your father wants me to meet some people. I'll only be gone for a little while." Then I saw the desperation in her face. "Are you going to be all right?"

She nodded.

"I only spoke to Amrita one time," she said abruptly. "While Magpie was keeping her for my dad. I liked her right away. She was smart. She reminded me a little of myself at that age. Right down to her bad choices in men."

"Was she in good shape?"

"No. Very bad shape, in fact."

I sat down again. "The guards were talking to your brother about her when I arrived. She might be somewhere here on the property. The slave cabins, I'm thinking."

"What were they saying?"

"My Italian's not good. One of them seemed to be saying that Amrita's medicines were running out."

Sofia paled. "Anxiety medications. That's what they mean. If she doesn't get them, she has panic attacks."

"Did she tell you she was trying to have a child?"

She paused slightly. "Yes. It wasn't . . . going well."

"And was her neck swollen? A dry rash on her legs?"

"A little." She looked at me. "How—"

"All of those symptoms are consistent with Graves' disease. A thyroid condition. The treatment is radioactive iodine. In which case Amrita's white blood cell count is probably next to zero." I threw the paper plate into an empty planter. "Can you imagine what she's going through right now, locked up in one of those old cabins in the swamp?"

"Yes." She looked at me. "As a matter of fact, I can."

I nodded, understanding. "Do you want her suffering at your father's hands the same way you did?"

She pressed a hand to her forehead. "Mike, don't do this to me. I'm in enough trouble already."

"Don't worry about it. Seriously." I pointed to the blade-shaped leaves in the planter. "By the way, what do you call those weeds you've been pulling?"

"It's just gypsywort," she said. "I was—"

"*Lycopus americanus,*" I said. "Also known as bugleweed. Grows in wetlands like the ones around here. Kind of a strange thing to find in a greenhouse, though."

"My mother used them in her teas. They're for pain."

"If I'm not mistaken," I said, "they're also used as an herbal remedy for thyroid troubles."

"Smart-ass." Sofia's eyes flashed fire. "You do know it's really annoying when you do that, right? Ask questions when you already know the answer? What did you do with your childhood, memorize the encyclopedia?"

"Sofia, I'm just talking."

She flicked her fingers under her chin, a gesture of disbelief. "Right. And I'm just a bartender from Algiers. And you're a bank detective who wants to study photography."

"I guess I deserve that. But—"

"Don't start me thinking about what you deserve. I might get ideas." With an effort, she pulled herself to her feet.

"If I'm wrong about you, Sofia, then I'm about to give you the power to kill me. Maybe you'd like that." I stood close to her. "I don't think I am wrong. I think you are the same person I knew twenty years ago. As loving—and as decent—as you ever were. I don't think you want Amrita to die."

She trembled a little, not speaking.

"Tell me where she is," I said. "I can help you save her."

"Something tells me that's not your highest priority," she said.

"You're right, darling. You're my highest priority. Now maybe that's only out of guilt, and maybe guilt really is a useless emotion. On the other hand—maybe you and I have always seen things the same way. Neither one of us can stand to do nothing while an innocent person gets hurt."

"Yeah?" She backed away a little. "That's you and me?"

"Damn straight." I countered her. "The other night, someone told the police there was going to be trouble at Magpie's. An FBI informant. At first I couldn't figure out why an informant would risk his cover for something like that. Then I realized the informant was probably trying to protect me."

She almost laughed. "Not too self-centered, are you?"

"The raid distracted Magpie's men just long enough to help us both get away. Which is why I'm still alive to look after you—and why you're still here to look after Amrita." I showed her the phone in my shirt pocket. "Here's the cell phone you were holding when I found you. The last outgoing call is to a detective lieutenant at the NOPD. It's not a published number."

She paled. "What are you going to do with it?"

By way of answer, I took the cover off the back, then removed the SIM card and bent it until it broke in two. Then I dropped the phone into the stone fountain beside her.

"What am I going to do with what?" I asked quietly.

We were nearly touching, our skin damp from the heat. Close enough to feel her breath on me, close enough to catch just a little of her scent over the flowers surrounding us.

"Sofia," I whispered. "Why did you make that call?"

Her lips parted, moving toward my cheek.

"Mike—"

Then Josie started barking. We turned to see Ciro standing in the door-way, balancing a rifle on his hip.

"*Se la van a robar.*" He grinned. "She's so beautiful, somebody's gonna rob her away. Back to the party, *mamacita.* Show them your pretty face."

Sofia seemed terrified to get too close to Ciro. As she walked past him into the sunlight, she lost her balance and stumbled to the ground. I moved to help her, and Ciro's rifle fell between us.

"You want her?" He grinned. "You got the stones to reach for her? Go ahead and try."

I held up my hands and said nothing. He walked ahead of me, whistling.

"Didn't think so," he said. "It's a *pinche* miracle you had the spunk to knock her up, dude."

The whole time he was speaking to me, I kept my eyes on Sofia. She'd pulled herself painfully to her feet, retrieving the fallen gypsywort leaves. Then she continued on to the house, watching me desperately as the steel muzzle of Ciro's rifle drove us apart.

EIGHTEEN

A subtle change seemed to have taken place over the past few days: I was no longer being followed from room to room like an American tourist in Pyongyang. Barca's guards were still eyeballing me, but evidently they'd been given orders to quit slamming doors in my face. As I found my way to Barca's private study, I could hear the boss in heated conversation.

"You can't come barging down into my territory and not pay tribute," Barca was saying. "It's not polite. And it's sure as shit not how things get done in New Orleans."

"It's not going to be like in the old days, Emelio." The new guy's voice was vaguely familiar to me. He spoke in tones that were cultured and companionable yet also faintly condescending: somewhere between an NPR pundit and a Western civ professor who never gave A's. "We won't get anywhere with the reconstruction effort if fifty cents on every dollar has to go for bribes and kickbacks."

"Do I look like some city hall bagman to you? Did I say kickback? I'm talking about respect here. I'm doing you a favor, Marty. I didn't have to approach you with this deal. And yet you're still dicking me around on percentages. At this rate, we're never gonna— Hey, Mike. How's it hanging?"

He said those last few words as I rapped on the open door. It might have been my imagination, but he seemed almost happy to see me. Grady, playing bartender for the room, did not.

"You sent for me," I said. "Am I interrupting?"

Barca shook his head. "Grab a chair. We were just about to get around to you."

Noah was dead-on when he said I'd be meeting somebody important.

Two of them, in fact. The bald-headed fellow with the glasses was even smaller than he'd looked in Senator Seaweather's hearing. The woman beside him was sharp, hawk-featured. I recognized her as the lead defense attorney in a case where a once popular actor had been acquitted on a charge of murdering his once living wife. Between the two of them, their shoes probably cost more than I'd ever made working for the government.

"This is your man?" The gentleman said it to Barca, not me. His voice registered cold amusement.

"Yeah, Mikey's a friend of mine. Good guy." He pointed. "Mike, you know this rascal?"

I nodded, instantly aware of my place in the room. *Friend of mine* identified me as an associate of Barca's, not necessarily an important one. *Good guy* meant that I could be relied on to keep my goddamn mouth shut.

"I'm Martin Telford Campbell. Chairman and CEO of the Roanoke Group. President and founder of Kadmos Security Solutions." He didn't offer his hand. Campbell took a sip from a crystal glass, then looked up to Grady. "This is excellent scotch. I wonder if I could have just a touch less water?"

Grady instantly and politely complied with a fresh glass. Only a rapid flash of his green eyes indicated what he thought Campbell could do with his scotch and water.

"I'm assuming you already know me by reputation." Campbell sampled his whiskey again, evidently satisfied. "You won't drink with us, Mr. Yeager?"

I shook my head.

"You do know how to *talk*, don't you?"

I made sure to get a nod from Barca before answering.

"Yes, sir. My understanding is that your company's ponying up for the reconstruction on a dollar-for-dollar basis with the federal government. I take it your stockholders are happy about that?"

"I have no stockholders. They tend to interfere." He looked to Barca. "Are you certain you're comfortable having him in the room at this stage?"

"I've checked Mike out plenty." Barca seemed slightly affronted. "If I wasn't comfortable with him in the room, he'd be dead already."

"Excuse me," I said. "Since we're all talking about me, do you mind if I ask what the hell is going on?"

Campbell raised an eyebrow. The lawyer soured. Barca seemed to be trying very hard not to smile.

"By all means," Campbell said.

"Thank you," I said. "What the hell is going on?"

"We need you for a special job." Barca nodded to the window. "Grady, alla sudden I can hear a lot of squalling from the lake. You wanna go down the shore and make sure your nieces and nephews aren't drowning each other?"

Grady stopped, stunned, but he dutifully nodded. "At once, Papa." He threw me a parting look that could curl a tarantula's legs.

"My son and Mike don't get along," Barca explained once the door closed. "Grady thinks Mike's a *fugazy*. Only Mike knows what he thinks of Grady."

"I don't have a problem with him," I said.

"Good to know. Here's the point of it, Mike. Campbell's crew and mine are gonna be doin' some business. We've got something of his that he lost on the roadside, so to speak. Understand?"

"Do I need to?"

"Probably it's best you don't. Anyway, the pain-in-the-ass negotiations are almost done, although I can't say I'm too happy about where we ended up—this is what happens when you get lawyers involved—and now we're ready for execution. We need you to execute."

"Assuming our concerns about you can be answered," Martin Telford Campbell said. "It seems you've been hanging out with the wrong crowd, Mr. Yeager."

"That's just what my father always said."

Campbell smiled patiently. "Does your father also know you badged in at the FBI field office at eleven twenty-six this morning?"

I regarded him evenly. "One, my father's dead. Two, I couldn't have badged in because I no longer have a badge. Three, my boss ordered me to report to the FBI."

"Of course. That would be—" He glanced at a slip of paper in his hand. "Special Agent Arthur Kiplinger."

"Kiplinger's a former colleague. My boss is right here in this room." I nodded to Barca.

"He's not lying. I told him to go." Barca seemed pleased by my deference. "How's that business we talked about, anyway?"

I took a careful look at our two visitors. It wasn't Campbell who bothered me but the lawyer. I'd seen her gobble up district attorneys with anchovy sauce.

"It's under control," I said. "So what else can I tell you about myself, Mr. Campbell? I'd mention the state of my laundry, but I'm worried you'll show me pictures of my underwear."

"It's all necessary," he said. "Certain . . . collateral is about to change hands. Your job would be to ensure the safe transfer of that collateral. And while Emelio is confident in your abilities . . . you'll understand if my standards are a little more fastidious."

"I always wash my hands after I visit the restroom," I said. "Do I get to know what this 'certain collateral' is?"

"Not from me, you don't." Campbell stood up, nodding to the attorney. "He's all yours. Now if you don't mind . . ."

He left the room. Barca's eyes followed him suspiciously.

"What the fuck is 'fastidious'?"

"It means fussy, Mr. Barca." The lawyer's accent was Oxbridge English, edged like a sacrificial knife. "Mr. Yeager, I'm Dolores Lincoln."

"I know you, Ms. Lincoln."

"I think not," she said. "Let's not begin on the wrong foot. If you think to tell anyone that you saw me or Mr. Campbell in this room, life in prison will seem a mercy to you. So will death itself. Do we understand each other?"

"Yup."

"I've been reviewing the discovery materials for your upcoming trial," she said. "Would you mind if I offer my professional assessment?"

I shook my head, puzzled by Barca's lack of response. If he'd seen through my cover, then he had to know the government case against me was a load of crap.

"The government's case against you is rubbish," Lincoln said, echoing my unspoken thoughts. "They've got you stuffing child pornography into a suitcase and driving it from Philadelphia to Washington in the boot of your nineteen fifty-six Nash Rambler. They have also enlisted the cooperation of your alleged partner in this misadventure—an unsavory gentleman from Cherry Hill, Pennsylvania, who has agreed to testify in exchange for immunity."

"Casey Pappadoulas," Barca offered. "They call him 'Fat Poppa' in Philly."

"So it's a bad case," I said. "Good news for me, right?"

"Hardly," she answered. "Your prosecutors would sell their children to win a conviction. They're certainly not above bribing this Fat Poppa to testify against you. How much were you paid in exchange for the evidence in question?"

"Objection, your honor." I attempted a smile. "Prejudicial line of questioning."

"Withdrawn," she said without humor. "Did you and Mr. Pappadoulas ever have any conversations concerning money?"

"We had a conversation concerning fifty thousand dollars," I said.

"Fifty thousand is hardly worth sacrificing your integrity for, now is it?"

"I buy a lot of scratch cards."

"Where and when did this conversation take place?"

"Lee's Hoagie House on Bustleton Avenue," I said. "The evening of June twenty-ninth. If you're ever there, I highly recommend the cheese steak. Do not let anyone talk you into putting provolone on your sandwich. It's not authentic without Cheez Whiz."

"I'll keep that in mind," she said. "Mr. Yeager, are you prepared to spend the next twenty-five years to life in prison?"

"On a charge of mishandling evidence?"

"As my beloved grandfather used to say, you're being a bit of a mug. In spite of their shoddy little parade of evidence, the government expects to convict you. I believe they will."

"And if I can't see that coming with my own two eyes, then I'm a mug."

"You would likely say 'sap' or 'rube.' But yes, most definitely. The lead prosecutor has gone so far as to boast that you'll . . . what was the expression? 'Feel the love' at the Supermax penitentiary in Florence, Colorado."

Suddenly I was lost for a response. Art and I hadn't talked about that one during my prep work for the assignment.

"How are they—"

"Your recent decision to assault an assistant district attorney didn't help. He's been making calls. Officially, no judge has been assigned to your case. Off the record, I can assure you that the judge will likely be Harold D. Edgewater."

Hatchet Harry, I thought. *Oh, Jesus.*

"A man with a, shall we say, stringent reputation for applying harsh penalties to corrupt law enforcement officers such as yourself." She consulted her notes. "Prosecution is seeking additional indictments for criminal conspiracy under the RICO laws—"

"What?"

"Spare me your astonishment," she said. "There's something else.

Apparently the FBI has evidence you were involved in the recent murder of a New Orleans policeman. Something about surveillance photographs."

I did my best imitation of a man who's never heard the words "surveillance photographs" before in his life.

"If you insist on entering a plea of not guilty, the prosecution will seek to introduce the photograph as evidence of criminal conspiracy." She took a polite sip of her drink. "I'm afraid your friends in the FBI are only too happy to cooperate with the prosecution. They seem to consider you an embarrassment. In fact, only one agent has so far declined to testify against you. One . . . Margaret Weaver?"

Damned if Noah didn't call that one on the money.

"Peggy," I said. "Nobody calls her Margaret. She's taking up for me?"

"The FBI may not give her a choice. If she's issued a subpoena, what do you think she'll say about you?"

"The truth." I sighed. "Unfortunately."

"Yes, I'm aware there's a personal connection between you. Would you mind explaining—"

"No."

Campbell and Barca looked at me.

"I'm sorry. Do you mean to say . . . ?"

"I'm not explaining my 'personal connection' to Peggy Weaver. I don't care if you got Cain acquitted for murdering Abel. My private life—"

"Is a thing of the past," she said. "A woman scorned, Mr. Yeager. Agent Weaver was your supervisor—and a bride left standing at the altar. Her testimony could sink you. Are you seriously refusing to take steps to neutralize that threat?"

"I'd like to see anybody stop Peggy Weaver from telling the truth in a court of law," I said. "And you better watch your ass before you drop any more hints about 'neutralizing' her, lady. Better people than you have tried."

"Mike." Barca was getting his quiet voice, his deadly voice. Any second and he'd start looking around for blunt instruments. "If you know what's good for you, please . . . shut the fuck up."

"First the FBI kicks me out because I'm dirty, then you want to kick me out because I'm not dirty enough. Let me put it to you plainly. I make mistakes. I've gotten people killed. Sometimes my hunting instincts are a little fucked up, and other times I'm a little too efficient for my own damn good." I took a breath. "But when I give my loyalty to someone, I try to make it mean something. If that isn't good enough—as my beloved grandfather used to say, up yours. I'm through auditioning."

"Well." Ms. Lincoln drew herself upright. "I don't know whether to walk out or applaud. Do I stand a chance of making your list, Mr. Yeager?"

"Not bloody likely," I said. "So what's the verdict? Am I crooked enough for you and your boss, 'Specs' Campbell?"

She frowned, drily irritated.

"Right," she finally said with a precise nod. "Mr. Barca, has Mr. Yeager not been apprised of our arrangement?"

"He didn't give me a fucking chance," he said. "Mikey, you got it all wrong. She don't work for Campbell, she works for me. This lady here is your lawyer."

I looked back to her. Dolores Lincoln smiled with quiet pride.

"If you'll have me," she said. "For what it's worth, I believe that my firm is quite capable of incinerating the federal government's case against you. I daresay they'll be begging your forgiveness by the time I'm done." She arched an eyebrow. "Now don't you think we ought to begin talking about bringing the American criminal justice system to its knees?"

I took a hard breath, gave a punch-drunk laugh.

"Where do I sign?"

"About fucking time." Barca stood up. "All this talk about steak sandwiches is making me hungry."

NINETEEN

Most of the party guests left as soon as the food ran out. Finally it was just the members of Barca's inner circle sitting on the back porch, as the afternoon turned to sultry dusk: Grady, Ciro, Uncle Connie . . . and me. While everybody else was refilling their drinks, Barca pulled me aside to a glass patio table. It was covered with deep scratches. I realized with a dull shock that it was almost certainly the same one where he'd broken his daughter's arm on her sixteenth birthday.

"So I know about you," he said as he fiddled with the bug zapper. "I know you were sent down here to spy on me. And even now you're thinking, 'Is that old man bluffing?' I don't have to bluff, Mikey. I know they sent you to bust me on this kidnapping thing."

"That's what you know, huh?"

"Yeah. From Noah. He's a phony agent, and you're a phony hoodlum. Funny old world, eh?" Barca grinned widely. "You think this trial thing is bullshit. Let me relieve your remaining doubts. They're doing a job on you. The Feds, they're setting you up. I brought the lawyer down here so you could hear it from somebody who's got no motive to lie."

"Barca, I don't know what angle you're playing—"

"Kiplinger *told* you the case was gonna be rigged so you'd play along. Look at me." He waited for my full attention. "This is real. If you don't want to take the fall for something you didn't do . . . get back on the side of the angels, okay? I'll take care of you."

"Whose angels are we talking about?" I laughed sharply. "And why the hell do you want to take care of me? Maybe I could have helped you once, but not anymore. I'm damaged goods."

"You're family." He filled his glass with wine from a plastic pitcher. "As much anger as I got against you . . . I got twice that much cause for rage against my daughter. But she's forgiven now, and so are you." He drank deep. "When you get to be my age, you start thinking about what you're gonna leave behind. And who am I gonna leave it to? My oldest boy died in prison. Another got killed in a fight with those bughouse Irish from Boston. Grady does a fine job steering the ship, no complaints there. But that ain't enough. I wanna aim higher."

"What about Noah? Can't he help you aim higher?"

Barca's face darkened. "Someday, maybe. Right now he's still going through that whole teenage rebellion thing."

"How so?"

"Eh, it all started with this FBI scam. Thinks he's gotten too smart for his family. Noah's a good kid, though. He'll pull through." Barca laughed. "Aw, look at you, G-man. Completely poleaxed to find out you're a daddy after all these years. Like lookin' in the fucking mirror when you see your son become a man, huh? Bet you can't wait to get close to him."

"Dunno. I got close enough to his left hook earlier on."

"Huh?"

"Nothing." I pointed. "Let me have some of that wine."

"Sure you can handle it?"

"Better than root beer," I said. "My father gave me my first beer when I was five. I think the kraut boy can hold down a little Italian wine."

He cautiously filled my cup. I took it down in one long pull. It had been twenty years since my last real drink, and I'd always wondered if falling off the wagon would be as much like a descent into oblivion as I'd always feared. Or as much like heaven as I'd dreamed of. The truth was that I barely felt it. I was the same Mike Yeager as before. The only difference was that fruity taste in my mouth, sour and cheap.

"Let's try that again," I said.

Barca obliged. "You better stay sharp. Things are about to come down."

"Yes, Mother." I drank more slowly, feeling the wine warm my head. "You want me to guarantee the handover of Amrita Narayan. She's the collateral, right? What did Campbell do, hire you to kidnap her?"

"Actually, he hired us to take care of the husband. Which I was happy to do, 'cause I always thought he was a fuckin' rat. The wife was just lagniappe." He couldn't suppress a grin. "I had Magpie's crew do the heavy lifting. They were gonna pop her, too. Then Ciro roughs her up a little, she starts screaming that she can't die, she's too valuable. So I think, what the fuck, let's pass the word back to Campbell's crew, see what her market value is. Noah gives 'em a call—and what do you know? Turns out they do want her after all."

"Are you going to sell her to Campbell?"

"If you think it's a good deal, sure. If it's not, I gotta know. You were supposed to find some stuff out for me."

"I haven't forgotten." I put the cup down. "For what it's worth, I've tangled with Kadmos before. Really, it was my partner's case. Agent Weaver."

"The ex-girlfriend."

"That's right." I nodded cautiously, hearing the weight Barca put on that "ex." "We had some reason to think that Kadmos might have been involved in a criminal abduction case back in Tennessee, but we never could lay a glove on them. I'm not saying they're clean. I'm just saying they have good attorneys—and a lot of influence in Washington."

"Don't I know it. Fucking cheapskates." He pursed his lip, frustrated. "So am I crazy to walk into this deal? Noah thinks it's bad news."

You can't tell him what you don't know. Something about the flip way Art said that was still burning my ass.

"I still don't know enough to advise you," I said. "What do you think they want with Amrita?"

Barca made an indifferent gesture: who knows, who cares. "I never trusted that limey husband of hers—and with good reason, it turns out. Maybe he told her something so she'd give him a blow job. All I know is, they want the girl pretty bad. Got a lot of money on the table. But if I hand her over, maybe they gotta cover their tracks. Maybe I get popped."

As he spoke the words, a dragonfly electrocuted itself on the bug zapper, a brilliant blue flash in the fading light. Barca barely glanced at it.

"Noah can't do this for me, Mike. He's too young and excitable. You're old and crafty like me. You gotta tell me if I'm about to die."

"I already said I don't know." I swallowed the last of my wine. "But I do know how I'm going to find out."

"Yeah? How's that?"

"I know how I'm going to get to Kiplinger," I said.

Barca's gaze tightened, and for an instant I could tell precisely what he was thinking: *What was that you were saying before about loyalty?*

I cleared my throat. "I think we should consider—"

Then his face suddenly brightened.

"Noah! Get your fucking ass over here."

Now that he'd changed out of his dull Bureau suit into a black shirt and khakis, it was easier to see just how young Noah really was. He sullenly allowed his grandfather to kiss him on both cheeks.

"Sorry I couldn't be here for the barbecue, Grandpa. Had some things to take care of in the city."

"Eh, that's okay. You say hello to your father?"

Noah looked away. "Hey."

"Hello," I answered.

"Been waiting a long time to see you two together." Barca beamed. "A force to be reckoned with, this kid is, Mikey. He's got your brains and my balls. Gonna take over the world someday." He waved Noah to a chair. "Your dad was just telling us . . . what were you saying, Mike? What was it we should consider?"

Noah and I both looked up as Sofia approached, leading Uncle Connie to a chair. Barca barely noticed her.

"I was saying that we ought to consider finding out more about our hostage before we hand her over. Grady, when's the transaction supposed to take place?"

"Soon." As Grady joined us, his eyes passed over the empty cup in front of me.

I turned to Noah. "Do we have a victimology on Amrita?"

"Yes," Noah said. "But there's nothing—"

"What's alla sudden these words I don't know?" Barca furrowed his brow. "What's victimology, like fortune-telling? You kill a guy and read his entrails?"

"It's like a written study of the victim's history and behavior, Grandpa." Noah gave me a barbed look. "There's nothing in Narayan's history that indicates she knows anything important. Her husband was the former MI6 spook, not her—and I promise you—anything he had of value, we got out of him."

"How do you know?" I asked. "Were you there when they tortured him?"

Noah merely gave me a distant smile. Sofia, I could tell, was beginning to tense up.

"You called him 'former' MI6," I went on. "Who was he working for at the time of his death?"

"He was a special contractor from Kadmos," Grady answered. "One of Campbell's people, hired by the Feds, sent to spy on us. Damn government outsources everything nowadays."

"Amrita does not know a thing." Noah made a decisive slice of his hand. "Kadmos is just tying up its loose ends, that's all. Trying to avoid embarrassment over Burke."

"Mike's got a point." Grady sneered. "How do you know all this? You holding back on us, you little prick?"

Noah glowered at his uncle. "I just know."

"Have you talked to Amrita?" I looked to Barca. "I mean, you're giving her over anyway, it seems kind of stupid not to hear what the girl has to say."

Barca only seemed to be half-listening. "Sofia, come here into the light, where I can see you better. It's like you're a ghost or something."

"I'm all right, Papa." She shrank away.

"I'll decide what you are. Sit next to Mike, okay? Give him some more wine."

Noah looked up, smoldering. "Grandfather—"

"Shut up," Barca said distractedly. "Go on, baby. Be with Mike now. He has my blessing."

Avoiding my eyes, Sofia charted a fearful course to me between her brother and Noah.

"I'm not thirsty," I said in a low voice. Nevertheless she had already taken my cup from me. Sofia hesitated only slightly as she reached across the glass table for the pitcher. Then she dutifully poured the wine.

"That's a good girl." Barca nodded, very pleased. "Fill it up, now. We don't deny anything to family."

It's okay, I tried to say to Sofia with my eyes. She didn't look back, merely smoothed her dress and sat beside me. I didn't touch my cup.

"You really think there's some value in talking to the girl?" Barca seemed utterly unaware of the tension he'd caused. "I mean, I'm all for it, but my understanding is she don't have too much to say. Grady says she's crazy in the head."

"You're not going to get very far by mistreating her," I said. "She's only going to spill her secrets to somebody she trusts. It also sounds like you've blown your chance at that. Maybe if I sit down with her—"

"Don't do it." Noah had been on the boil ever since Sofia sat next to me, and now the steam was rising. "Don't let him near her, Grandpa. I promise you, it's nothing but an FBI trick."

Grady raised a watchful eyebrow. I smiled back like I'd just taken a gentle poke in the ribs.

"Guess you don't know too much about your father's legal situation," his grandfather said. "It's the FBI who's been playing tricks on Mike."

"Yeah, I remember. Let me see if I can remember something else." Noah stood up, a prosecutor before a hostile witness. " 'I, Michael Francis Yeager, do solemnly swear to support, uphold, and defend the Constitution of the United States of America against all enemies, foreign and domestic.' " He tilted his head at me. "You remember the next line?"

I nodded. " 'To obey the lawful orders and directives of those appointed before and above me—and that I enter into this office without any mental reservation whatsoever—' "

" 'So help me God.' " Noah smiled. "Your oath, old man. You still believe it?"

"When I said it, I meant it. What about you?"

"I had my fingers crossed." Noah seemed to take his point as proven. "You can think whatever you want, but I'm right about this. He might be lousy at keeping his promises, but he still wants to keep them. So bad, he can taste it."

"Noah," Sofia started to say, "please don't start—"

"Oh, now you're his character witness, because he brought you home from a crack house?" Noah gave a venomous laugh. "Look at you sitting there next to him, like his—"

"Easy," I said, feeling my own temperature rise.

"Like his whore." Noah said it plain as bricks. "Ever since I was a baby, I've had to hear all about the great Mike Yeager. My father, the hero FBI agent. And just look at him now. What gives him the right to come back here—"

"Noah." Barca spoke in a voice of cold command. "Sit."

With what must have been a supreme effort, Noah forced himself back into his wooden deck chair.

"He is your father," Barca said. "Whatever harm he may have done . . . whatever kind of man you think he is . . . you owe him that respect. You understand?"

"Yes, sir." Noah stared at the deck.

"Good. Now apologize to him."

"That isn't—" I held up my hand to protest.

"Apologize, Noah." Barca didn't raise his voice. *Chiedi scusa.*

Noah fumed, biting his lip. When he finally spoke, the words seemed to tear their way out of him.

"I'm sorry," Noah said in a choked voice. "I'm really sorry . . . but he's still a fucking traitor."

"For chrissakes, Noah." Grady leaned in.

"No. I know you all think you've got him in your pocket, but you're *wrong*. The bastard spent maybe half an hour behind closed doors with Kiplinger today, God only knows what they talked about." He pointed at me. "Added to which, he stole my wallet. He's got my goddamn Bureau ID. Make him empty his pockets, Grandpa. Make him show you."

I didn't blink. "Son, you need to calm down."

"Mike, do you have his wallet?" Grady asked wearily.

"Not really, no. I'd check around the airport observation deck. Probably fell out while he was planting a wire on me."

The words were out before I could be certain of their effect. All at once, the temperature seemed to drop thirty degrees. Sofia took a terrified breath.

"A wire?" Barca looked up with renewed interest. "You put a wire on your own father? Who told you to do this?"

"It was to protect us, Grandpa. The family. I had to know for sure if he was—"

Suddenly Sofia was standing up.

"—still working for the Feds—" Then Noah saw too late what was coming.

"Daddy, no!" Sofia screamed.

No matter how many times I'd heard about Barca's wrath, there was no comparing it to the actual thing. I only thought he was angry when he screamed at me in his study. I only thought he was angry when he planted that bomb for me and Art. One moment Barca was sitting in his chair, holding a cup of wine. A bare second later the cup flew away, spraying liquid against the bug zapper. Electricity turned the air blue. Now Emelio Barca was on his feet, and the cedar chair was in his hands. Then it shattered like firewood, frozen in staccato light as he broke it against his grandson's back.

After that, it was as if a grenade had exploded. Grady backed away. Uncle Connie stared vacantly, a spectator watching a fight on television. I'd half-expected Noah to fight back—he sure as hell had the reflexes—but he simply rolled on the wooden deck, unresisting, as Barca tore the arm from his chair and prepared to swing it down.

"Daddy, please." Sofia took his arm. "Daddy, please don't, please don't, please . . ."

He shook her off like a kitten from a branch. I caught her in my arms as she fell.

"Barca," I said. "Leave him alone."

For a second I thought he would turn on me. Yet the old man stayed his hand.

"He should apologize to you." Barca looked halfway at me over his shoulder, still wielding the chair arm. "You're his father."

"I'm his father," I said. "I'll decide his punishment."

I could hear in my own voice that I meant it. I also could see in Barca's eyes that he believed me. He dropped the chair arm and stumbled back into the house. After a moment's uncertainty, Grady followed, staring as if he'd just seen an alligator retreat from a rabbit.

"You okay?" I asked Noah. "Can you stand up?"

She went over to Noah, who lay curled on the wooden deck.

"Baby?" She reached over to him. "Noah, can you talk to me, sweetie? Are you all right?"

She put her arm over him. For a moment, he accepted her embrace, shaking from head to toe.

"Noah," she said, cooing. "Are you—"

"Fucking whore." He pushed her away, launching himself to his feet, and ran away into the twilight shadows.

Then there was only the noise of cicadas and Sofia's tears.

"Dear girl," Constantino Barca said in his soft, wandering voice. "When do we eat again?"

TWENTY

For long seconds Sofia and I crouched on the deck, surrounded by the chair's broken fragments. A riot of outraged feelings broke inside me: the rush of guilt that I had indirectly caused Noah's humiliation; the urge to chase him down and kick his ass for calling his mother a whore. Strongest of all was the desire to sweep Sofia into my arms and run like hell for that bus I'd missed twenty years ago, to still her sorrow as I held her by the shoulders.

"Sofia," I whispered. "Come on. Let's—"

"You go to hell," she said—and tore herself from me as she ran away after him.

I found her down by the shore, wandering along the concrete floodwall. A pair of lights, red and green, spun away into the mist.

"He's gone," she said. "Took one of the boats. He just—"

"Sofia, come inside. He'll be all right."

"He doesn't have a license, Mike. He doesn't even have a boating license."

I couldn't help myself. "Doesn't seem like he ever waits for permission to do anything, does he?"

Her eyes swung back at me.

"You should talk," she said in cold fury. "You did real well with that part about gaining Amrita's trust, Mike. Even my father was impressed."

"I meant what I said before. I want to help her—"

"Help her? You stood there and watched our son take a beating, Mike. *Our* son. How are you going to stick your neck out for anyone if you won't help your own child?"

"Sofia, when I woke up this morning, I didn't even know 'our son' existed. And what I've seen of him so far is not exactly awakening my parental instincts." I exhaled. "My *child*? Whatever Noah is, he's no child."

She paused for a moment, biting her lip. "Did you take his ID?" Sofia asked. "Did you?"

"Yes," I said. "I needed to know if the ID was a fake or the real thing. It's back in his wallet now, same as before. All he has to do is go find it."

"It's funny you didn't mention that sooner." She shook her head. "You were pretty quick to shoot back about him planting that wire, though. It reminds me of the way Grady and I used to run to my father, when we were kids. 'He hit me, Papa.' 'Yeah, Papa, but she took my comic books.' It always ended with somebody getting a beating."

"I had to change the subject fast. If your father had started to listen to Noah—"

"So you threw your son into the path of the oncoming train," she said. "Never mind what you thought you had to do. Or how you feel about him. Is that how a father ought to treat his son?"

"No." I took a breath. "I wish I hadn't done it."

She stared into my eyes for a moment before speaking. I could feel her breath, warm on my face.

"I knew it would hit you hard when you found out," she said. "He's had years to anticipate meeting you, and you've had one day. But think about this. The worst thing Noah said to you today—the absolute worst—was to accuse you of still believing in the oath you took to the FBI." She put her hands on her hips. "You're the only guy I've ever met who's actually afraid that his son might find out he's a decent man."

I laughed. "Who thinks I'm decent?"

"I do," she said. "For God's sake, start acting that way."

She stared at me for a moment. The rising moon shone on her face, wet with tears. A button had broken during the struggle with her father, leaving her throat bare. I pressed my hands against her face and kissed her.

The wine hadn't made me drunk. Staring Barca down hadn't made me angry. But the moment I felt Sofia's soft lips against mine, twenty years of lost time ripped through me like hot wire. For a moment, she looked back at me with stunned anger.

"I'm sorry," I said. "I shouldn't have done that. I—"

Then she took me by the back of my neck and drew me to her.

Her mouth parted sweetly, responding to me. We pressed together; her hands sought my back. Sofia and I probed each other, hungry as teenagers. Then she abruptly broke away.

"What is it?"

I looked back in the direction she was staring. The red coal of a cigarette glowed in the distance, then faded away.

"Grady." I waited. "Is he still there?"

For several seconds we only clung to each other.

"I don't know." She seemed to recover herself. "Are you . . . going away now?"

"I'll come back," I said. "Will you be all right till then?"

She nodded.

"Amrita." Her voice dropped low. "Tell me the truth, Mike. Are you going to save her? Will you promise to?"

"Yes," I said.

She leaned up to me, breathing into my ear.

"Talk to Deadman," she said. "Tell him I said it's all right. He—"

She never finished the sentence. The cigarette glowed in the breeze, closer now. Sofia released me and backed away into the shadows. As if the wind had suddenly taken her from me, she was gone.

TWENTY–ONE

I'd only told half the truth to Sofia—which, as my father never failed to remind me, was just as bad as a complete lie. The ID card was still in Noah's wallet, but not the card's microprocessor. Given that—and ten bucks for a prepaid cell phone—I was in business.

FBI security cards are designed with special countermeasures against fraud. Each one contains an imbedded silicon chip with volatile memory, a kind of mini computer with its own power source. Every time the card passes a security checkpoint, this microprocessor contacts the network, verifying the user's identity and resetting the codes. If the chip is tampered with in any way, the card will be invalid the next time someone tries to use it.

There are, however, ways of getting around this—and it seemed as if Noah had already done some of my work for me.

"It's not FBI issue," Special Agent Yoshi Hiraka was telling me on the phone as I sat in the mildewed basement of the UNO Computer Lab. "In fact, it's a generation ahead of anything we're even talking about developing in the next couple of years."

"So what exactly is it?" I asked, trying not to disturb the pale-faced student sleeping in the next cubicle.

"No idea, but it sure is cute." A few decisive keystrokes. "I'm losing a little integrity on the snooping circuit, Mike. Can you check contact number five on the I/O pins?"

Whatever those are, I thought as I attempted to comply. Under Yoshi's patient instruction, I'd installed the chip in my own expired FBI card, then plugged it into a reader/writer I'd lifted from the lab's Tech Support room. Now it was wired into a desktop computer, linked to Yoshi over a secure network connection. A whirl of numbers and symbols flashed over the screen, controlled by Agent Hiraka's unseen hand.

"Yoshi, what exactly are you doing to this card?"

"For some moments there are no words," he answered in a voice that sounded like true love. "How did you come by this magical thing, anyway? Somebody told me you were a bouncer at a New Orleans strip club or something."

"Oyster bar. We're upgrading our online gift shop." Suddenly an image flashed by on the screen. "Hang on. Whatever you're doing, stop. I'm seeing something."

The river of data froze over. The kid in the next cubicle grunted something about his underwear itching, turned over in his chair, and went back to sleep. Now there was something entirely new on my computer monitor.

```
MTC-11226300000313-X
KSS TECHNOLOGIES, LTD.
ENTER LOGIN:
```

The image beneath it was the Kadmos Security logo.

"What is this, Yosh?"

"Looks like a serial number and manufacturer's stamp," he said. "KSS Technologies apparently left themselves a back door, so they could play with their own toys without any pain-in-the-ass government interference."

"What's the login?"

"That would be the thing we need to know," Yoshi said. "If you gave me the chip and a couple of days, I could probably tease the information out. How soon does your New Orleans oyster bar need its advanced smart card technology?"

"Soon." I thought for a moment. MTC were the initials for Martin Telford Campbell, the big boss himself. The card had to pertain to something mission-critical. "How many letters in the login?"

"No more than thirteen, including punctuation marks and blank spaces."

"Try 'Pandora's Box,'" I said.

The letters typed themselves onto the screen.

"You better be sure about this," Yoshi said. "If we hit one stroke wrong . . ."

Then a word appeared on the screen: AUTHORIZED.

"Son of a bitch," Yoshi said.

The screen now showed Noah Delacroix's face and vital stats. *Handsome kid*, I thought absently. *Smiles at the camera like he means it*.

"Holy Mary, this is sweet. Mike, I don't know what this technology is—but if it were legal, I'd marry it."

"What are all those dates and times?" I asked.

"Those are the times this Noah guy badged in and out over the last thirty days," Yoshi said. "That's not the cool part. The cool part is that everything on the chip is user-editable."

"The chip is edible?"

"Editable. I can rewrite any of the personal data. Just a few keystrokes and I can give anybody—you, me, the Dalai Lama—immediate access to any FBI field office worldwide. If I'm right, it's what every hacker dreams about at night—a skeleton key to the entire federal intelligence infrastructure."

"How can it possibly do that?"

"Because it's freaking sweet, that's why. It doesn't just supply information to the network, it issues commands. I could probably make you FBI director right now if you wanted the job."

"I think I'd rather be a bouncer in a strip club." I thought a moment. "Yoshi, if an agent—or someone posing as an agent—has this card, what would be the risks of using it?"

"The golden rule of technology is that you never permit your own inventions to pass beyond your control," he said. "You can bet this KSS Technologies outfit is going to keep tabs on their little bundle of joy. It's easily worth killing for."

There's never just two sides in any war. "Does the card contain a record of other identities that might have been created along the way?"

"There's a BIN file here . . . looks like it might be . . . yeah. Here you go."

A new face and name suddenly appeared on the monitor.

"Friendly looking guy," he said. "Who is he?"

As I saw the face staring back at me, I dimly recalled the wafer-thin indentation in that wallet I'd inspected in the FBI director's office. Just about the same size as the computer chip.

"His name was Simon Burke," I said. "He's dead."

After I got off the phone with Yoshi, I went to the university library to check Noah's bona fides. There was, it seemed, a twenty-three-year-old

Noah Delacroix from Colorado Springs with a degree from CSU. The same one who'd somehow survived the grueling FBI application process— background interviews, polygraph test, psych eval—as well as the sixteen bone-breaking, soul-tormenting weeks of training that followed. Of course it was possible, though unlikely, that all the documents were faked, that Noah had never actually walked through the Academy door. If so, there was an easy way to find out.

On a pretext of assisting with reference checks, I managed to speak with the Academy's senior firearms instructor, my old friend and colleague Bill Bly. Agent Bly described SAT Delacroix to a *T*. Apparently they called Noah "the blue-eyed killer" because he tackled every obstacle like a Siberian wolf assaulting its prey. He was respected, not popular. Noah gave the impression of somebody who was there to do a job and nothing more. Before we got off the phone—Bill's grandkids were due for dinner that evening—he remarked, with no detectable irony, that Noah and I would get along like a house on fire if we ever met. We were forged in the same furnace.

So it seemed that Barca wasn't entirely right when he called Noah a phony agent. It wasn't just the card that got him into the FBI, either. Noah had graduated Academy in December, but he didn't take possession of the smart card until the following June. Even if it had helped him fake his way through Bureau security, it couldn't leapfrog him into a slot on the Organized Crime squad. There was just no way in hell a silicon chip was ever going to fool an old lion like Art Kiplinger.

Noah had to have someone scamming for him on the inside.

And this is my son. Jesus, Mary, and Joseph. Thoughts kept hitting me like they'd been shot in with a nail gun. When Noah took his first steps, I was coordinating drug raids with DEA in Kansas City, Missouri. By the time he was old enough to read, I'd moved up to Kidnapping in the Chicago field office. During his teenage years—those wrenching, thin-skinned years of desire and rejection—I was settled in Philadelphia, protecting the lives of children who were not my own. Peggy and I had never once talked about kids, even when we were seriously talking marriage. I'd convinced myself I was better off than my colleagues who had families. I didn't have to picture my own son or daughter when I looked at confiscated images or crime scene photos. I had no school conferences or skinned knees to distract me, no demands to read *Go Dog, Go* for the fiftieth time. I could stay up all night writing reports and prepping for court appearances. I was streamlined and focused, free to devote myself entirely to the cause of justice. All the while, Noah was out there, growing up without a father and preparing for the day when he'd finally confront me.

Like lookin' in the fucking mirror when you see your son become a man, huh? The trouble was, I knew only too well how manhood came to the Barcas. *Like your worst nightmare come true, isn't it?* No argument there. Dolores Lincoln was right about me: I was a goddamn mug.

It was a few minutes before nine o'clock when I got back to the Bureau. My own photograph was now imbedded in the chip, and a storm was coming south across the lake. I used the card at the field office parking lot and the gate swung right up. So far, so good. Then I straightened my tie and walked straight through the FBI's front door. Half a dozen cameras would see me come and go, but that was no matter. After what Yoshi told me, it wasn't Bureau security I was worried about. Kadmos would be watching, too.

Ten minutes later, I was staring at Art Kiplinger's office door.

I must have looked like an idiot standing there, but I couldn't make myself go in. As long as I didn't open that door, I was still an undercover agent doing his duty. Once I walked through . . . I didn't know what I would be.

"Can I help you?"

I turned to see a gnomelike woman staring at me, pushing a file cart down the hall. I felt a little like a coach passenger caught wandering around in first class.

"You looking for Kiplinger?" she asked.

"Just looking for caffeine." I casually went into the supervisors' break room and poured myself a cup of coffee. "Do you know where the creamer is?"

"In the cabinet. It's the fake powder." She watched me get it down from the shelf. "Kiplinger went home an hour ago. Religious observance with his family, he said."

"Shabbos on Wednesday." I stirred the creamer around. "That's what I call devout."

"Hah?"

"Just ask him if he's free for golf on Friday evening."

"Ask him yourself. I'm not an answering machine." She pushed her cart down the hall. "Shabbos, he says."

I held the cup to my lips, then pretended to be suddenly fascinated by a sign-up sheet for the annual interagency softball tournament. The clerk turned the corner; I counted three. Then I poured the coffee down the sink, breathed a silent prayer, walked straight up to the keypad outside of Art's office door, and tapped in the ten-digit code I'd seen him use a few hours before. Seconds later, I was in.

When Art tossed me the water bottle, I'd worried that he might have only given me a partial print. But God—or somebody—was with me, and I got a nice clean impression off his index finger. After that, the hardest part was getting the bottle out of the building without smudging it. I did the whole job at a Kinko's in Metairie: set the print with Super Glue, scanned it into a computer, printed it to a transparency slide, and built up the dummy with wood glue so that it had nice clean ridges. Now I had myself a counterfeit fingerprint. Now all the damned thing had to do was work.

I attached it to my finger with a drop of spirit glue, then pressed it into the fingerprint reader. There was a quiet click as I opened the combination lock. The drawer slid open. Two words stared at me from a red folder at the back of the drawer: PANDORA'S BOX. Inside was an inch-thick report, neatly bound.

Art was understating his troubles, I realized as I scanned the report. There were close to two hundred known gang leaders and drug traffickers on the roster. Collectively, they were responsible for hundreds of deaths each year, as well as tens of millions in drug revenue. It was a swell report, though. The supporting documentation included a wealth of biographical detail. Dates of birth, criminal records, known associates, even behavioral profiles. Kiplinger's people had done a pretty good job, I thought, except that they hadn't: Kadmos Security had compiled the whole shooting match.

And, not just for the love of country, it seemed. The report included an invoice; its bottom-line number nearly blew my retinas out. The cover memo was addressed to Supervising Special Agent Kiplinger, with three names copied: the FBI director, the special agent in charge of the New Orleans field office, and good old Martin Telford Campbell. The memo was signed by Kadmos's lead consultant in New Orleans, Leah Varnado. Her cell number was included in case SSA Kiplinger had any questions.

Talk to Deadman, Sofia told me—and there he was, about fifty names down from the top of the list. True name, Charles Wesley Carmichael, age twenty-six. New Orleans native, born and raised in St. Claude, attended McDonough 35 High School. His next entry was an eyebrow-raiser: PFC, 82nd Airborne Division, United States Army. Known associates included

Corveau's legless bodyguard—t/n Staff Sgt. Delaney F. Harper—and Evander "Cleanhead" Duplessis. All 82nd Airborne. Say what you wanted to about Magpie, he knew how to recruit high-grade muscle.

I was briefly tempted to stuff the entire report into my jacket and see if I could sneak it out of the building, but something told me that might be a bridge too far. I had to start thinking about how I was going to get my butt out of there. I was about to do just that when I saw a report with my name on it.

PSYCHOLOGICAL PROFILE, SA MICHAEL FRANCIS YEAGER. Boy, did those words jump right out at you.

> Yeager's primary affect stems from an obsessive identifica-
> tion with the victim. His behavioral history demonstrates
> that he will ignore all other considerations—mission in-
> tegrity, respect for authority and the law, even his own per-
> sonal safety—if he believes himself to be directly
> responsible for the victim's welfare. Obviously, this trait
> can be exploited. If the correct circumstances are forced
> upon him, Yeager has no choice: He *must* act to defend the
> subject in jeopardy.

The report was unsigned, addressed to no one. A series of numbers was penciled into the margin:

128.02

I knew the numbers very well. They were straight out of the FBI's Crime Classification Manual. All 100-level categories referred to various forms of homicide, from sadistic murder to killing for hire. The number 128.02 was the designation for hero homicide: the kind of unsub who commits a murder so he can be the guy to solve it . . . or intentionally puts a victim in danger, just so he can be the one to ride to the rescue. Likely suspects for hero homicide included firefighters, security guards, and former law enforcement. I had to admit, I did not like seeing that classification next to my name.

As I read on, a stray line jumped out at me:

> Yeager's supervisor confided that, at her urging, he began
> psychological counseling in the EAP program in the after-

math of the Madrigal case. The psychiatrist's records currently remain under seal of patient confidentiality . . .

The report didn't name its sources, but in this case it didn't need to. I'd had a few supervisors tell me it was time to see a shrink—but only one who answered to the feminine pronoun.

A moment later, Art's office phone rang, nearly jerking me out of my skin.

I approached the telephone with caution. The caller ID was the cell number for Rachel Kiplinger, Art's wife. The clerk also said he'd been gone for an hour. Wherever he was, it wasn't with his family at Touro Synagogue.

That was all the encouragement I needed to get out. I replaced the file, locked the drawer, then wiped everything down for safety. There was a low rumbling sound outside the office. When I finally got the courage to open the door, I saw it was just some guy pushing a carpet sweeper. He didn't seem to care that I'd just burst out of a supervisor's office with nervous sweat on my face and a piece of plastic stuck to my finger. I should have been relieved by that, but I wasn't. Part of me really wanted the armed guards to bring me down.

TWENTY-TWO

An hour later I was pacing along South Shore Harbor, a stone's throw from Lakeshore Airport, when my cell phone rang. I had to force myself to answer.

"Mike?" Peggy's voice, somewhere between frustration and relief. "I was surprised to see you'd called."

"I almost didn't." I breathed. "It's good to hear you."

"You too. I—where are you? You sound like you're in the middle of a war zone."

"This is the kind of rain we get down here," I said. "I could go somewhere and call you back—"

"No. I'm . . . still working." Pause. "It was dumb of me to call back when I don't have time to talk. I just thought . . ."

"You figured it might be easier if we didn't have to talk long." A crash of lightning. I ducked under a storm-damaged shelter. "How's the new life treating you?"

"I'm still dealing with bits and pieces of the old one, I guess. They gave Crimes Against Children to Doug Vennerbeck."

"I thought he was dead."

"No, just living in Delaware. It's not a good sign for the team. With me in Washington and you . . . where you are . . . it's just Yoshi and Tabitha left. Everybody else is getting thrown to the four winds."

"So I'm the guy who broke up the band, huh? Call me Yoko."

She was silent for several seconds.

"Peggy . . ."

"I'm here," she said. "I'm sorry. This is more difficult than I thought it would be. You . . . always turn smart-ass when it starts to hurt."

"I guess it hasn't been easy for me, either."

"Mike, *I'm* hurting. You hurt me." Her voice fell a little. "All these years together . . . I guess I didn't know you had it in you."

"I'm sorry," I said. "Believe me when I say I haven't felt very good about myself since then."

"You haven't felt good about yourself for a long time," she said, almost gently. "I think I must be part of the reason why you're so unhappy."

"Since when do I need reasons to be unhappy?"

"I'm serious, Mike. We haven't wanted to face this. Even so, it's pretty obvious you've been sticking it out for my sake these past few years. Because you knew how much I needed you. Now I can see how badly you wanted to get out."

"That's no excuse for treating you like shit."

"No, it's not." She took a long breath. "I should go."

"I can call you back," I said. "Unless you've got plans for tonight . . ."

"Um." She seemed to be fighting for control. "I don't think that's a very good idea."

Now the rain was really coming down hot and heavy. I pressed the phone to my ear, straining to listen.

"So you're telling me it's over," I said.

"It's too soon," she answered. "I don't want to hurt your feelings . . . but my mind's been on other things lately. These hearings have started to move into uncharted waters."

"I saw you on TV," I said. "You looked good. I can see a series coming out of this on C-SPAN. *Senatorial Gumshoes*. He's a committee chairman, she's FBI. They solve crimes."

"Mike." She hesitated. "Is there some other reason you called? Because you're not letting me off the phone."

"Two things, I guess." I took a breath. "There's this woman . . . from Kadmos Security. She's doing a consult for this Levin-Marcato thing. Plus a few other side jobs, apparently."

"Is this investigative work?"

"Nowadays my only investigative work consists of chasing down diners who don't tip," I said. "I was just wondering if you had anything on this Campbell guy. The CEO."

"Marty? He's a handful. If you believe his corporate bio, he founded Kadmos on money he made during a late-night poker game at MIT. Full house, aces over eights. I think it's what they call a dead man's hand."

"And if you don't believe the bio?"

"Then he stole it from a dead man's wallet," she said. "Nobody seems to know how they're planning to make their investment back on New Orleans. Security work is just a sideline. Their real money's in military technology. Drone surveillance planes, advanced weaponry—"

"Smart cards?"

"Yeah." There was a slight pause: I'd set off her alarms.

"Is he crooked?" I asked, jumping over the silence.

"No more than any other government contractor, I guess. He's got about half of Seaweather's committee in his pocket."

"As well as an appreciation for the liberal arts, it seems. Wasn't Kadmos that guy in Greek mythology who rebuilt the city of Thebes by sowing dragon's teeth in the ground? They sprouted up as a phalanx of warriors."

"Uh-huh. They mostly wound up killing each other, too." She paused. "What was the other thing you wanted to ask?"

There was a lot I wanted to ask, but I had to wait for the wind to die before speaking again. By the time it did, I found I'd lost my nerve.

"I miss you," I finally said. "You?"

"Every damn minute." She sighed. "Good-bye, Mike."

As we hung up, I saw Al's minivan waiting for me across the road. I ran straight to him through the rain, hoping the water would camouflage anything else on my face.

No turning back now.

TWENTY-THREE

"Mike, can I ask you an important question?" Al looked straight ahead as we parked in the shadows outside Cain's Grocery, while the night rain beat down like pinballs. "What is this object in my hand?"

"Al, that appears to be a McDonald's french fry."

"You know, I believe you're right." He held it under his nose. "Now don't think me an ingrate. I know how generous you were to buy me dinner. Considering that I might at this very moment be forced to eat an entire steaming plate of hot spicy crawfish, red beans and rice—not to mention an entire pitcher of ice-cold Abita—all prepared by my beautiful wife. Instead, I have these fries. As well as a delectable Filet-O-Fish, batter-fried and dipped in McDonald's own sweet-and-sour sauce, and two, count 'em, packets of fancy ketchup."

"Don't forget the Diet Coke," I said. "Good fries, aren't they?"

"Excellent." He popped one into his mouth. "If they don't serve 'em in heaven, I ain't goin'."

The Pandora's Box report gave no current address for Charles "Deadman" Carmichael. On a Monday night, Al told me, we were more likely to find him near his girlfriend's apartment on Dryades Street. It was enemy territory, but Deadman had faith in his destiny. I decided to go with Big Al's recommendation. I'd convinced Crawford to drive me uptown by pretending I was doing some hip-pocket surveillance for Kiplinger. So long as we kept driving around, Al seemed willing to go on pretending to believe me. But the stakeout at Cain's Grocery was making him nervous: In New Orleans, the corner shop was to drive-by shootings as what McDonald's was to drive-through dining.

"Cain's Grocery." I read the cracked sign above the market. " 'Home of the Butcher.' Now, I always thought that was funny. Wasn't Abel the one who offered meat?"

"Yeah, but Cain was the one with the bloody knife." Al slurped away the last of his Diet Coke. "You still didn't answer my question. Why are we sitting here in the rain—"

There were four diehards outside the grocery. One of them, a shaky young black man, leaned against the wall smoking a cigarette. He stepped forward as a white guy in a Honda drove past. They didn't make eye contact. The window rolled down, hands flipped past each other. The whole transaction took less than five seconds.

"Correction," Al said. "Why are we here in the rain, watching drug deals go down, when we could both be somewhere else, enjoying life?"

"We're waiting for Deadhead," I said.

"Deadman," he corrected. "You got it backwards. Cleanhead is dead. Deadman is clean. At least according to what his parole officer told me. So maybe we should let him alone to enjoy the company of his lady friend. Neither one of us is working for the law anymore."

"Doesn't it make you nostalgic to be here, fighting crime?"

He laughed. "No."

"Confess," I said. "You don't want to do something about the gangs? It's still your city, after all."

Al frowned, sensing I was trying to throw him off. "Maybe yes, maybe no." He looked around. "I'm starting to worry this town might be a lost cause. Della's even thinking about selling out, so's we can live near her sister in Baton Rouge."

"Della? You've got to be shitting me. Whatever happened to 'Never Closed'?"

"Things happened here," he said soberly.

"Must have been hell for you cops after the storm. I couldn't believe how many of your guys just walked off the job."

"Aw, Mike. Those boys just got pushed past the breaking point. You try dealing with that kind of madness. At least hell has a reason for existing."

I looked at him. Al had always been such a brave heart, such a man of force and optimism, that I never considered he might have serious troubles of his own.

"Anything you feel like talking about?" I asked.

"Let's just say that neon sign ought to be changed from 'Never Closed' to

'Too Close.' There's a lotta sick memories I got, since the storm. Some of
'em are . . . too close to live with."

He was silent a moment; then the shadow abruptly passed, and he was
the same old Al again.

"There's our man," he said.

Charles W. Carmichael was much as I'd seen him at Magpie's house, a
lean young prince of the alleyways. Even though it was raining, he wore no
shirt in the hot weather—just a pair of fatigue pants, a black bandana, and
some very expensive running shoes. He seemed to enjoy showing his bare
chest, as if to say, *Go ahead and take a shot if you feel lucky.* Something told me
he always got to shoot first. He nodded subtly in both directions, and two
young men at once got up from the pavement. I'd taken them for corner-
shop zombies, but now it was clear they were Deadman's personal bodyguard.

I half-consciously touched the SIG P226 under my arm. As I reached for
the passenger door, Al hit the locks.

"Mike," he said. "Don't be an asshole."

"I just want to talk to him."

"You see that graphite pistol stickin' out of that boy's jeans? That ain't
his John Thomas, my friend. That is the paraphernalia of purposiveness.
You would be dead before you got out of the car."

"I can handle myself."

"*I* can't handle you. I got a heart full of cholesterol and bursitis in my
shooting arm. Not to mention a wife who thinks I'm helpin' you stock up
on groceries. You said you wanted to see him . . . now you've seen. So
kindly release your hand from that door latch before I slap you dizzy."

Deadman stopped to light up. He seemed to be waiting for something to
happen.

"The paraphernalia of *what*?" I looked at Al.

"Purposiveness. It means his gat, son. His mind-fucker. His damn *piece*,
for chrissake. Scope out the thing. It could start a war."

"If you mean nine-millimeter, why don't you just say 'nine-millimeter'?
What's with all this street lingo?"

He laughed. "Aw, look at you, G-man. There isn't a word in the king's
English that you fellas can't screw up with some dumbass acronym. S-A-C.
A-S-A-C. Unsub. First time I worked with the FBI, I thought I'd swallowed
a gallon of alphabet—"

Then I saw Deadman's hand disappear behind his back.

"We've been made," I said. "Open the door!"

It happened before my mind could fully take it in. Deadman was staring straight at me, already crouched to a firing position. His two guards moved to block, and, as Charles Carmichael reached for his Glock, a five-year-old girl was standing in the open doorway of Cain's Grocery, holding a bunch of red vines. Screaming as Deadman seized her hard.

"Freeze!" Rain on my cheek told me I was on the street, the gun in my hand, even though I didn't remember getting out of the van. "*Freeze*, asshole! Let go of the girl and put the weapon on the ground."

There was a welter of yells. I was at once aware that not one but three handguns were now aimed at me. Deadman's voice rose above the rest.

"Aim that thing at me! Go on aim it the fuck at me!"

"Cop, you, fuck you up, cop—"

"Put it *down*, old man."

Al was standing beside me, unarmed but unafraid.

"Mike!" he called. "Back down. It's okay. I called my guy in Sixth District. There's a black-and-white coming."

"No!" I shouted.

"What?"

"Tell the police to go away, Al."

I stared straight into Deadman's night-black eyes. His hand tightened on the child's shoulder.

"Away from the kid, Carmichael. Right now. Or I will kill you where you stand."

My finger slowly squeezed the trigger. Deadman's Adam's apple pulsed. Then, as his bodyguards ran away into the night, he shoved the child brutally to the pavement and vanished into the dark rain.

"Leave him be," Al said. "Mike, the cops."

"We have to go after him," I said.

Even as I said this, I saw the child screaming on the sidewalk—tears running down her face, knees skinned; alone. Her red vines had fallen into the gutter.

"It's okay, kid. You're safe." As I reached down to help her up, someone was yelling at me.

"You *asshole*!" A young woman snatched the girl away before I could touch her. "You motherfucking leave my baby alone you goddamn cop you *asshole*!"

I suddenly realized what she and the girl were yelling about: I still had the gun in my hand.

"It's all right," I said. "I'm a federal . . . I mean, I *used* to be a—"

"He's an escaped lunatic." Al got between me and the mother. "God damn it, Mike, just put the gun down."

I took Al by the shoulder.

"Get behind the wheel," I said. "Come on, let's move."

"You cops leave my baby *alone*." The woman wrapped her arms around the child. "And *stay the hell away!*"

Al threw a tense look down the street, then a troubled look at the SIG SAUER. As we climbed back into the minivan, I could hear sirens approaching. The noise was lost in the screech of Al's tires as we hauled ass down Dryades.

"Great," I said. "For this they show up."

"We're fleeing the scene." Al shook his head numbly. "Jesus, Mary, and Joseph. Thirty years on the force, and now I'm helping a felon escape a drive-by shooting."

"And tourists think all the excitement's down in the Quarter." I took a flashlight from his glove box. "If you were Deadman, which way would you be running right now?" I looked at him. "Al, wake up."

He stared at the SIG SAUER. "Where did you get that *cannon*?"

"Even us middle-aged white guys have a little purposiveness," I said. "We're not fleeing the scene, okay? We're in pursuit. And we've got to decide which way to move—right now—or the real felon's going to slip past us."

"That does it." He slammed on the brakes. "Get out."

"Al—"

"Out of my minivan, Yeager. Right now. Or I am driving us both straight to Sixth District headquarters and you can explain that little noisemaker of yours to the captain."

"I have a private gun license," I said. "It's registered. I'm allowed to use it for self-defense."

He looked up with a smile of frank disbelief. "You know what? To heck with you. I think I'll just tell the cops you're a crack addict and you went down to Cain's Grocery with intent to purchase. Something tells me they won't have much trouble believing that."

"Okay. Okay." I opened the door. "You win."

"Leave the gun," he said. "Mother of God, I am an idiot."

"No, you're not. You came here for the same reason I did. You want to stop the bad guys." I tossed the gun onto the seat. "I'm still going after him, you know. If you drive away, you'll be responsible for whatever happens to me."

"Oh, no. Don't you even try that one on."

"Hey, an unarmed white guy alone in this neighborhood? On foot? I'll be lucky to last five minutes."

Al breathed out. "Yeager, which side of the law are you working here?"

"I'm not saying another word to you."

He thought about it. Then he set his jaw at me.

"Yes, you will," he said. "You'll tell me exactly what you're up to. That's my price for telling you where you're gonna find Deadman in the next five minutes."

I smiled. "No choice, huh?"

"No choice. The offer expires the second I take my foot off the brake. Then you just try finding another friendly black face within a mile of here, Mr. Renegade Special Agent." He waited. "My foot's moving."

I climbed back in. "Can I have my gun back?"

He grabbed the SIG before I could put my hand near it, then shoved it into the left pocket of his Windbreaker. Then he set the vehicle into gear, just as the red-and-blue flashers started to turn the corner down the street.

"Now buckle up." Al set his houndstooth cap. "Goddamn northerners bring nothing but trouble down here."

TWENTY-FOUR

Christ Resurrected Elementary School was one more shuttered building in a city whose children had largely vanished since the storm. It was spooky in the way that all school buildings are when the lights are out: You half-expected to see ghostly nuns stalking the grounds with their rulers. I silently prayed for my Protestant soul while Al searched for a gap in the fence. At least the rain was letting up.

"How sure are you that Deadman came this way?" I whispered.

"Sure as I know those french fries are doin' somersaults in my abdomen." He shook the fence, then pointed up to a piece of black cloth hung on the razor wire. "Tell me that ain't a hunk of Deadman's baggy dungarees up there."

"I hope to God that's not the way we're going in."

"Not on your life." He opened the back of the minivan and returned with a pair of bolt cutters.

"I don't believe he's here," I said.

"As the Bible says, 'Act as if ye have faith, and faith shall be given to thee.'" Al went to the padlocked gate. "Carmichael's a leader of Rize, and this neighborhood belongs to the Edge Sixty-Eight gang. He'd be a damn fool to show his face this time of night. But Catholic schools"—he set the bolt cutter to the lock—"they're neutral territory. He can take sanctuary here till morning. Now you got anything to say to this here padlock before I cut it in twain?"

"The Bible does not say, 'Act as if ye have faith.' Trust me, I know. I had to recite an entire chapter every night or I didn't get supper. The trouble with you Catholics . . ."

A clean, twanging noise cut the air, echoing around the schoolyard. Al caught the lock before it could hit the ground.

"Convert me later, preacher's boy. Right now we need to get quiet." The gate made an irate sound as Al pushed it open. "Just tell me this before we put our lives in jeopardy. You're sure Carmichael was mixed up in that English girl's kidnapping? 'Cause if he is, we're shit-stupid to be going after him without an army behind us."

"I have reasonable suspicion, but I can't name my sources." I cautiously followed him through the gate. "Deadman's connected to Cleanhead Duplessis. He's had counterinsurgency training, with an expert rating on the five-five-six assault rifle. From what I've seen of him, the guy's stone cold."

"What you've seen of him?" Al looked back at me. "When did you ever see Deadman in action before tonight? He sure as hell wasn't stone cold in front of that grocery."

"Come on. He used a kid as a body shield."

He thought about it. "You know, I could swear the way Deadman was looking at you, he'd seen you before. In fact, I'm positive he did." Al motioned me behind the school furnace. "You're not by chance still working for the FBI, are you?"

"Yeah, right." I laughed. "The Bureau screwed me with my pants on, Al. You saw it on television."

"Don't lie to a man who's holding a pair of bolt cutters. If the B ain't paying you, then it's gotta be the other B—as in, Barca. Either way, a little bird tells me you and Mr. Carmichael won't need an introduction."

"Maybe I should go in alone," I said.

"By all means. Keep in mind this is New Orleans, where emergency room ambulances move at five miles an hour. On the bright side, though, we do have drive-through funeral homes." He studied me. "You said you were helping Kiplinger with something. If I call him outta bed this late, what's he gonna tell me?"

"Good Christ." I took a long breath: Al was staring at me with his lie detector eyes. "He'll probably tell you that I penetrated FBI security and broke into his office earlier tonight and examined confidential files without clearance. I'm pretty sure he's figured that out by now."

"What?"

"I had to know if Carmichael's our guy. He is. So let's move before he finds another Catholic school to hide in."

Yet he wasn't moving. "Why'd you do it, Mike? Kiplinger's a good man."

"Why? Because I'm not sure how good he really is." I moved in close.

"They've got a psych file on me. I don't know what it's for, but it looks like they're . . . selecting me for something." I exhaled. "Now you know things you may have to testify to in open court. Can we please go inside?"

"No," he said. "For the last time, Yeager. Are you working for the FBI or the Cosa Nostra?"

"I'm pretty sure the answer to that is yes." I leaned around the corner for a better look at the main building. "You ever wonder why these Kadmos people want to put up all that money for New Orleans? What they're getting out of it besides a place in heaven? Would it at all surprise you to know that Simon Burke was on their payroll the day he died?"

"What are you talking about?"

"I have no clue what I'm talking about. And that scares holy crap out of me. There's a man inside this building who may have some answers. If we let the police take him, we'll never see him again. Kiplinger will seal this thing up like a steak at Schwegman's Grocery. Do you still have my gun?"

"Yeah, and it ain't going nowhere." He patted his side. "You ain't crazy, are you? 'Cause I don't like you crazy."

"I'm sure starting to feel that way. When I woke up this morning, there were three people in the world I could trust with my life. Peggy Weaver, Art Kiplinger, and you. At the rate things are going—"

"Mike—"

"—purely by process of elimination, you're the last man on earth I know isn't going to stab me in the back. So you better watch your ass, because I'm running out of friends."

He followed me onto the playground. "Damn it, you *are* on the pipe. Either that, or you're the most paranoid human being I've ever—"

Then his eyes lit on something above us.

"Mike, get down!"

I was already flinging myself out of the way when I heard the noise: the dry snap of a 9 mm firing. I saw a yellow spark as the second shot knocked Big Al's bolt cutters out of his hand. I crawled over to him. He was shaking from head to toe.

"Looks like we found . . . Deadman."

As his eyes closed, my hand came away from Al Crawford's chest slick with blood.

TWENTY-FIVE

There was a small hole in Al's jacket, but I couldn't find an entrance wound to save my life.

"Are you feeling it?" I asked.

He shook his head. "Shock's taking care of that. Reminds me of the first time I took a bullet. Back in my rookie year—" His eyes opened, suddenly fearful. "I could feel a sting in my side, Mike. Please God, tell me it didn't hit my liver . . ."

I ran my hand up his torso, finally touching warm blood under his arm.

"We might be okay." I breathed a ragged sigh. "You got it in the left deltoid cluster. Probably just missed the brachial artery. Can you move your arm?"

He shook his head.

"Don't try." I tore off my belt, strapping it tightly around his upper arm. "Okay, we're done playing Hardy Boys. Can you stand up well enough to make it back to the van?"

His right hand gripped my shoulder with astonishing force.

"Why am I not dead right now?" he asked. "Tell me."

I reached into the left pocket of his jacket and held up the answer.

"Looks like my little hand cannon took the bullet for you." I showed him the P226: a deep groove scored the gun's metal slide. "You can keep your damned graphite pistols. Stainless steel saves lives."

"That was a sign," he said in a solemn voice.

"That is what you call bastard luck. Now come on, hero. It's University Hospital for y—"

"No." He pulled himself up. "Do not disrespect a miracle, Mike. Especially not on God's holy ground."

"Okay, now I'm thinking that nine-millimeter round threw a fragment into your skull. Since when is there anything remotely holy about a Catholic school?"

"I'm fine." He took a steady breath. "I'm taking a bet on you, Mike. I don't think you've turned to evil, even if you are a hellbound heretic. Do you need to talk to that boy, Deadman?"

I nodded.

"Then get to it. And don't prove me wrong about you. I still got enough blood in me to . . . kick your sorry white ass."

I briefly checked the 226. "The slide's damaged. If I try to fire it, I'll probably blow my own hand off."

"You can catch him without shooting at him," he said. "Now will you stop lookin' at me with them tearful eyes? I'll be damned if my last supper is gonna be a Super-Size Number Twelve Value Meal. Delicious though it might be."

"Keep pressure on the wound." I held his gaze for half a second, then high-crawled across the schoolyard to the main building.

A heavy chain was looped through the school's rear door. For a moment I thought I might have to go back for Al's bolt cutters, then realized that Deadman had already forged a path: A window had been broken in, ten feet off the ground, chicken wire and all. How the hell had he made that jump? Suddenly the thought of chasing down an armed twenty-six-year-old combat veteran seemed insane. I'd run the obstacle course with guys like Carmichael during my Academy training, and even back then they routinely kicked my ass. I reholstered my useless weapon and jumped from the top of the metal stair rail, just barely catching the windowsill with my fingers. Forty-two years weighed on me like a cemetery vault as I scrabbled up the brick wall and hauled myself through the window.

The school smelled like disinfectant had been fighting a losing battle with mold; there was still a thick black flood line along the walls, just above the level of a child's head. Desks had been thrown across the doorways like revolutionary barricades. Deadman's footprints paced down the hall. Every few yards they darted toward a window, then away. He wasn't running scared: He'd been scoping for a firing position. The footprints ended at the stairwell. I took the steps in short sprints, gripping the SIG two-handed before me like it was still worth a damn.

Carmichael had abandoned his second-floor sniper's nest at the end of the hallway. Smart fellow. If he'd wanted to shoot me in the schoolyard, he could have done it. Instead he took Al down so that I'd either have to fall back or follow him alone. I was being drawn into close range for a clean kill.

I stopped cold at the top of the stairs. Someone was standing between two glass trophy cases, holding what appeared to be a rifle.

I approached cautiously. Two pale white eyes shone watchfully in the shadows. Then I realized that the figure before me was wearing the armor of a Roman legionnaire. What I'd taken for a rifle was nothing more than a carved wooden sword, cutting a cloak in half for an invisible beggar. I had come within a heartbeat of tackling a statue of Martin of Tours, patron saint of soldiers.

At least I know who's on Deadman's team, I thought. *Now where the hell is St. Michael?* Then I caught a faint reflection in the trophy case. I swung around and found myself taking aim at a fallen mop. The door to the janitor's closet creaked open. I dropped to the ground. Wood splintered in all directions as St. Martin took a 9 mm round to the head.

"Don't move." I held the SIG before me in a crouch position. I couldn't see who I was aiming at, but I could hear him breathing. "Down on the floor, Carmichael. You don't have any kids to protect you this time."

"Go ahead and shoot." From the sound of his voice, Deadman was maybe two meters away, standing over me. I saw—or thought I saw—a dim reflection against his graphite pistol, dark gray against black. "Kill me if you can."

"Put your weapon down or I will."

"Do it." He waited. "Come on, sonny boy. Rise and shine."

I flicked the slide lock off. *Maybe the damn thing will actually fire,* I thought. *Or maybe it'll just blow back and kill me dead.*

"My partner's still alive," I said.

"Yeah, I know. He crawled back to his little green minivan." The direction of his voice shifted; he was circling to my left. "I like your piece. That's an Elite Stainless, ain't it? Single-action only, if I'm not mistaken. Why don't you go ahead and chamber a round?" He waited. "Or is the slide maybe broken? Looks like it might be a bit."

Now I could see him. Deadman Carmichael, a warrior of the night. A bland thought crossed my mind: *So this is how I die.*

"You don't even know why I came for you," I said.

"I don't need to know." He was aiming between my eyes. Then I heard Deadman's voice echo in my head, what he'd shouted in front of Cain's

Grocery: *Aim that thing at me! Go on aim it the fuck at me!* And I knew that I had him cold.

"My partner," I said. "He's going back for the kid."

He didn't move. "Say what?"

"You heard me, bitch. The cute little girl at the grocery store." I was astonished by the coldness in my voice. "Is that what they teach scumsuckers like you in the army? How to hide behind children? Or just the ones you happen to care about?"

"Who gives a shit about her?" But the cool stealth in his voice had broken, replaced by a growing fury.

"Oh, I think you do. A girl that young doesn't go shopping for red vines at ten o'clock at night. Not by herself. Not unless her daddy's a made man."

There was a brief silence, and for a moment I was fairly certain he'd decided to waste me on principle—but the next sound I heard was a hammer easing back.

"Your fat friend better leave my baby girl alone," he said. "Or he's gonna lose his other arm. And he'll get you back with your dick shoved down your throat."

"I guess you can do that," I said. "I'm pretty sure you'll go to prison for it. Which means your baby girl grows up without a father. After that? Well, let's play the tape forward. In six years—ten, tops—Precious Little Angel will trade in her licorice and Barbie dolls for a crack pipe and a mac daddy. Just like her mother."

"Man, you shut the fuck *up*."

"Just like her mother," I repeated. "Five years on the street, and your baby will have the face and body of an old woman. She'll sleep inside a portable toilet on some construction site and give blow jobs to undocumented aliens for five bucks a pop. She'll also spit on the ground any time your name gets mentioned. Believe me, I kn—"

The butt end of the Glock whipped past me, cracking me on the left temple.

"You shut your cracker ass about my girl!" Deadman shouted at me. "You hear me? She ain't gonna wind up on no pipe. She ain't gonna—"

I knocked his legs out with a crouching kick. Locker doors shook as he landed against them. The guy was sixteen years younger than me, hardbodied, and trained to annihilate. He was also an enraged father, and I knew I no longer had to worry about the gun. He'd have to kill me with his bare hands.

I charged into him with a head-butt to the thorax; he seized me with both hands. Deadman was iron covered with leather. It took him maybe two seconds to hurl me to the ground. Then he started to kick. The first one landed in my ribs, the second in my kidneys. I went limp like a tackling dummy and let him land every single blow.

"You fuck!" Deadman screamed. "You leave my baby alone, don't you talk about nobody whoring her out, I'll fuck you so bad you don't have no call to talk about her that way!"

Then something flashed in the darkness as it connected with the back of Deadman's head. His eyes rolled back white and he pitched forward over me. As I pulled myself free, I saw Al Crawford standing over us both—one hand in an improvised sling, still using my belt as a tourniquet—the other one holding those big steel bolt cutters.

"About damn time," I said. "What, we weren't shouting loud enough for you to find us?"

"The wheels of God grind slow." Al smiled. "And if that ain't in the Bible, I don't care to know what is."

Over Al's strenuous objections, I drove the green minivan to University Hospital. He said he felt fine, but his left hand wasn't moving. Blood had spread across his shirt, straight through the bandage I'd jury-rigged from duct tape and napkins from McDonald's.

"You took a big risk, letting him beat on you like that." Al's voice was shaking; the adrenaline had worn off, and shock was setting in. "How'd you know she was his little girl?"

"He told me to aim away from her. Then he pushed her down to get her out of the line of fire. Guess that's what fathers are supposed to do for their kids." I glanced back over my shoulder. "You okay back there? Getting enough air?"

Deadman glowered at me. He lay on his side in the back seat, trussed up with plastic tie-down cord.

"Don't hurt my baby girl," he said.

"You damn knucklehead." Al looked back at him. "You call yourself a man—keeping that child where every badass with a rod can take a shot at her?"

"Fuck you, Fat Albert. Ain't they buried your old-school ass yet?" Deadman looked away. "I can't make that girl's mama do anything she don't want. Couldn't keep her off that glass dick, I sure as shit ain't gettin' my kid away from her. You think I'm cold, you should talk to that ragin' ho."

"What is she, your girlfriend or your wife?" I laughed when I saw the dull fury in his eyes. "Oh, this is too good. Ex-wife?"

"What can I say." He gave me an indifferent look. "Bitch got into some bad shit while I was off fightin' terror."

"You married her, pal." I eased back. "So is that how you bonded with Simon and Amrita? They talked about having a baby?"

Deadman cooled, sensing a trap. "Only talked to that Indian-looking chick one time. She never said nothin' about a baby."

"What did she talk to you about?"

"The storm," he said. "Just that. And the Superdome."

Al raised a surly eyebrow. "What about it?"

He snorted. "Cops shootin' people, and babies gettin' raped in the corners. Pilin' up bodies like beer cans. It was shameful. You should know, nigga. You was there."

"There's no niggers in this vehicle." Al was frosty. "Just two lawmen and a sorry fool who's gonna have a cryin' little girl at his funeral real soon. You best stay civil if you don't want that day to come any faster."

The sound in Al's voice was like metal on concrete: serious rage, bone deep. Even Deadman seemed wary.

"Al," I said. "Check it out."

He looked to see where I was pointing. An NOPD black-and-white was parked outside the emergency room. Right next to it was an armored personnel carrier from Kadmos Security.

"Guess we're just going to have to bite the bullet," I said. "Vouch for me at my trial, okay?"

"Let me out here," he said. "It's close enough to walk."

"Al—"

"If I go in there with a nine-millimeter wound . . ." He turned back to Deadman. "By the way, thank you very much for that." Al took a breath. "ER's gonna have to file a police report. I can tell 'em I got shot in close pursuit, and the perp got away—but you just gotta know who's gonna get the first phone call."

"I'll deal with Kiplinger," I said.

"Just don't try and deal with Della. She'll kill us both." He opened the door. "Bring it back with a full tank of gas. And Mike?"

"Yeah?"

"You know how they used to call the Lower Ninth Ward CTC—short for 'Cross the Canal'? Tell him what it stands for now, Carmichael."

"Cut Throat City," Deadman answered.

"Amen to that," Al said. "Every man for himself nowadays. You do the right thing, Michael Yeager. And for God's sake don't take your eye off this boy for a second."

I nodded. "I'll be by to check on you later."

"Full tank of gas," he repeated and stumbled painfully away. I watched him until he'd reached the white lights of the ER entrance. He stopped to chat with one of the cops. The patrolman walked him in personally.

"Why'd he leave you alone with me?" Deadman asked. "He knows I'm just gonna kill you soon as I get loose."

"No you won't," I said. "You won't even try."

He laughed. "Yeah? Why's that?"

I turned onto Poydras, taking care to see that we weren't followed.

"I'm much more useful to you alive," I said. "You know who I am, right?"

"Yeager-meister." He nodded. "You're that crazy-ass messenger boy Barca sent over the other night. Sure as hell ended that party."

"I was sent to bring Barca's daughter home," I said. "Maybe I can do the same for your little girl."

He took a slight pause. "Getting what in return?"

"Information," I said. "You were part of the crew that kidnapped Simon and Amrita. Don't bother denying it."

"Uh-huh. And if you work for Barca, why do you even need to ask?" He frowned. "In fact . . . why ain't I ever seen you workin' for him before?"

"I'm new to the game. But I learn fast. For instance, I know your buddy Cleanhead wasn't shot by the police."

He didn't answer. After a few minutes of silence I turned onto Tchoupi-toulas, heading upriver to the warehouses.

"What do you think your buddies in Rize are gonna do when they find out you helped murder one of your own gang, Deadman? Not to mention a former army buddy?"

"Kill me," he answered. "What do you think they'll do if they find out I made a deal with the Barcas?"

"Kill you," I said. "Logically, it makes as much sense to cooperate with me as not. Except that I know where your daughter lives."

"You best stop making threats," he said.

"This is what you call an offer. Probably the best one you're going to get." I parked. "Okay, end of the line."

He watched me. "This is where I die?"

"This is where we talk." I picked up the Glock. "You can die on your own timetable."

Deadman watched me carefully as I got out of the van and opened the sliding door. We were between two ancient brick warehouses, facing the dark Mississippi.

"Out." I cut the cord binding his ankles. "Come on."

Deadman narrowed his eyes. "Man, you sure don't talk like any wiseguy I ever met. Why don't you just cap me and dump me in the water? I ain't got nothin' to say to you."

"Sofia tells me different," I said. "Walk ahead of me."

He was silent as we approached the Mississippi. But it seemed like I'd dropped the right name.

"If I talk," he said, "what do I get?"

"Well, for one thing, you get to walk home, instead of floating facedown to Placquemines."

"Hell with that." He gave me a determined look. "I don't want my girl growin' up on the street—or windin' up with some child molester in a foster home. Understand? If I die tomorrow, or next week, or whenever—she gets a decent place to live. *That's* the deal."

"What makes you think I'll stick my neck out for your kid?"

"Would you have killed me to protect her?"

"Yes."

"There you go." He tilted his head. "We cool?"

I nodded.

"Word has it your man Barca's fixing to do a deal on the English lady," he said. "He shouldn't do it."

"Why not?"

"Reason one, it's a bad deal for him. I don't know what Barca's askin'— but it's gotta be at least twice what he promised Magpie for the job, and a hell of a lot more than what Magpie said he'd pay us. Trouble is, you gotta be alive to collect money. You see what I'm sayin'?"

I nodded. "What's reason two?"

"Amrita knows things," he said. "Almost like ESP. She knew those Kadmos people were coming to town, even before they did. She knew there was going to be trouble for us, like that police raid and shit. And she told me something bad was going to happen round about here in August."

"What's going to happen here in August?"

Deadman looked around before answering.

"Somebody is going to die," he said.

"Somebody usually is. Who exactly are we talking about?"

He shook his head. "All she said to me was, it would be bad for New Orleans. Worse than the storm, even."

"No offense, Carmichael, but I can get a better forecast from my daily horoscope. Didn't she give you anything specific?"

"She was about to, but she got scared. That Hispanic guy—Mexican, Honduran, whatever—"

"Ciro?"

"Mm-hmm. She wouldn't say a word around him. He was the one who did most of the actual mayhem. That was some hard shit to watch. First he put these wires on the guy's—"

"Yeah, I don't need the details of that, thanks. Was another one of Barca's guys there? White kid, young—"

"Looks like you?"

"A little like me," I said. "Not as handsome."

"Noah. He showed up to collect the girl." He grinned. "He's your boy, huh?"

"Did I say he was?"

"Didn't have to. I could see it in your eyes."

"Yeah, he's mine." I nodded. "So you and Amrita really hit it off, huh? What did you tell her about the Superdome?"

"That it was worse than bein' in the fuckin' war." His eyes grew hard. "Old folks died 'cause they couldn't get no air. We'd go stack their bodies up in the freezers. People had to take shits on the floor. It stank up the joint so much, you 'most had to vomit. They left us there to die, you know. Like animals at the zoo." He looked straight at me. "What the Dome does to you is this. It forces the human part out of you. And then it's just the animal left."

"Was your daughter with you?" I asked.

"Yeah." He nodded. "I told my baby girl to look at me. Any time she got scared, she should look at me. Finally I had to tell her to stop lookin'. 'Cause I didn't want her to see the animal that was comin' out in me." He looked away. "Anyway . . . that's what I told Amrita."

"Maybe that's why she decided to trust you," I said. "Do you wish you hadn't participated in her kidnapping?"

The question seemed to kick him in the stomach.

"I'd do anything to take it back," he said simply. "That woman needs to live."

"I'll keep that in mind. Turn around, Deadman."

He did so with what I had to call military precision. I pushed him down to his knees.

"We're now within the jurisdiction of the Sixth Police District," I said. "Go to the station house on Martin Luther King Boulevard. Use Sergeant Al Crawford's name. Make a deal to save your life. I can get your daughter into a foster home, but you're going to have to forget you ever saw me."

"You won't shoot me?"

I suddenly realized that the Glock was still in my hand.

"Why would I want to?" I asked.

"Amrita said . . ." He gulped air. "She . . . predicted you."

"She did what?"

Deadman shut his eyes.

"What do you mean, predicted me? She said my name?"

"She told me a guy named Yeager would come for her." His voice was starting to shake. "He'd pretend to be a bad guy, but he wasn't really. And I shouldn't be afraid of you if we ever met."

"Are you?"

"No," he said, "but I am afraid for you."

"Why?" I waited. "You'd better talk to me, Carmichael."

"I used to think I'd be one of the good guys." He stared at the river. "Eighty-second Airborne was my ticket out, y'know? Maybe I could be somebody my girl would be proud of?"

"Deadman—"

"My baby girl's name is Bessie." He was breathing hard. "We named her after my mama. She eats Froot Loops and she likes that . . . TV show. The one with the damn blue dog. Little Bessie wants to live on a farm and take care of horses and shit. Tell her I said her daddy's sorry for scaring her tonight."

I placed the muzzle of the gun against his temple.

"I didn't want you to know what else Amrita said to me. I was scared of what you'd do if I told you . . ."

"Tell me what?" I felt my blood pulsing. "Tell me what?"

Then he looked straight into my eyes.

"She told me you were going to kill your own son," he said.

A sick wave coursed through my head and landed in my gut. "That's bullshit," I said. "How? When?"

"That's all she said." He gasped. "You're gonna do it, Yeager. Sometime in the next few days, your Noah is gonna—"

I struck him hard against the ear with the butt of the gun.

"That's for Sergeant Crawford." I took a moment to breathe. "Go to the cops, Deadman. Confess to the kidnapping and give them every name you can think of. And for God's sake—have the guts to apologize to your daughter in person."

I hurled the gun as far as I could into the Mississippi river. Then I left him, facedown before the waters.

TWENTY-SIX

I started to get nervous when I saw the black Bureau car in the loading zone of University Hospital; more so when Art Kiplinger walked out, followed by a uniformed police captain. I waited until they'd driven well away before parking the minivan.

Getting into the ER was easier than I'd anticipated. For the moment, the trauma staff was distracted by a meth addict who'd tried to peel the skin from his arm to let the bugs out, and had very nearly succeeded. Unfortunately, Big Al wasn't in the ER. A private room off ICU, I noticed, was being guarded by two beefy young patrolmen. I was weighing the risks of taking them out when I heard a woman's voice behind me.

"Are you in pain?" she asked. "Lord knows you ought to be. You look half dead."

I turned and smiled. Vendella Crawford sat on a plastic bench, calmly eating a shrimp po-boy.

"Della," I said. "How are you holding up?"

"Don't you even try that charm on me." She gave me a wildfire look. "I'd slap you, but I'm too tired to stand up."

"I'll lean in close for you."

I offered my cheek. She merely frowned and wiped her lips with a napkin.

"Looks like somebody already beat me to it. Why're you dragging around like that?"

"I was kicking it old-school with Deadman Carmichael. Or rather, vice versa." I waited. "Is Al going to be . . . ?"

"Oh, that was a ton of delight. You ever try getting a doctor's attention for a middle-aged black man with a gunshot wound? They just looove takin' care of us folks after dark." She stood up, refusing my hand. "You just missed your old buddy Kiplinger. *He's* paying for Al to have a private room. What have you got to offer, Sonny Jim?"

"Trouble and misery," I said. "Can you get me five minutes with Al? Without bothering the guards, I mean."

"I expect I could." She gave an acid laugh. "You think I'm angry at you 'cause my Al got shot, don't you? Baby, I've been living with that fear for thirty years. That ain't it. He oughta been dead long ago, and that's a fact."

"He said it was a miracle that—"

"I don't wanna hear any more about any damn miracle." She tossed the remains of her sandwich into the trash. "You *left* him, Mike. You call your-self his friend and you left Al on the hospital driveway like a . . . bum." She turned away. "So my answer is no. You will not get five minutes alone with my husband."

I started to protest, then realized it was pointless.

"I'll give you two." She gave an airy tilt of her head. "*That's* fair enough. At two minutes and one second, I'll beat your head in with the heaviest thing I can hold in two hands."

I smiled. "Thanks, Della."

"Shut up," she said. "Damn cops will be the death of me."

There was one damn cop left on the door. As Della approached him, she was suddenly all smiles. He nodded politely and tipped his cap. Then he actually let her take his arm like a wedding usher and walked her down to the end of the hall.

Al Crawford sat up in bed, his arm heavily bandaged.

"They got you fixed up?" I asked.

He nodded. "Doc was real impressed with the field dressing you made. Pulled out every hair in my arm when they ripped that duct tape off."

"Are you all right?"

"I can't move my arm." A fearful tone stole into his voice. "They say there's damage to the nerve cluster."

"I'm sorry," I said. "I really am."

"Could be worse. Small price to pay, huh?"

"For what?"

He blinked, as if he hadn't realized he'd spoken out loud. "Nothing." Then he smiled and pointed with his right hand. "Three guesses who brought those flowers over there."

"Yeah, Artie always did have a thing for daisies." I pretended to admire the bouquet. "I'm not asking you to take the Fifth for me, Al. Whatever Kiplinger wanted . . ."

"They already knew you were with me at Cain's. God knows how, but they did. For what it's worth, the subject of your breaking into Kiplinger's office didn't come up."

"What did he have to say about me?"

"Oh, they want to 'help' you, Mike. Everybody's real worried you're gonna crash and burn." He rolled his eyes. "What I think they really wanted was to find out what Deadman told you. Good thing I don't know, so I don't have to lie."

"It'll come out soon enough," I said. "I told Deadman to turn himself in to Sixth District. You might want to phone ahead and tell them to give him special treatment."

"Think he'll do it?"

"He might. For his daughter's sake, anyhow." Then I found what I was looking for in the bouquet.

"Mike, if you—"

He stopped as soon as he saw what I was holding up: a tiny microphone, no bigger than a bluebottle fly, concealed in the flowers.

Al narrowed his eyes. "Sorry, my throat's a little dry. Can you reach me some water?"

I nodded and approached his bedside. I poured the water, carefully shielding my body from the ceiling, then scribbled a note on a magazine subscription card:

they're setting me up for murder

Who? he mouthed silently. I added two words:

my son

Al's eyes went wide. I dunked the note in his water glass, washing the ink away. Then I tore the wet card to pieces.

"You'd better get out of here," Al whispered. "Right now."

The door opened behind me.

TWENTY-SEVEN

It was Della, her eyes full of warning.

"I'll meet you outside," she said in a commanding voice before shutting the door.

"Damn windows won't even open." Al tried the window latch. "What are you gonna—"

As I reached for the red phone on the wall, the doorknob rattled. Then a pounding.

"Think he might still be in there." It was the cop's voice, the big one. A moment later, a key fumbled into the lock and the door swung wide. "Sir, you wouldn't by chance be a guy named Mike Y—"

"Crash team to the ICU, stat," I called into the phone. "Blue! Blue! Blue!"

Then I winked at the cop.

"You asshole." He moved to block me, but three pairs of feet were already tumbling down the hall. A moment later, he was swept out of the way by a team of running nurses.

"Don't let them defibrillate you," I told Al as I sidestepped into the hallway. By the time the cop had finished tripping over the crash cart, I'd run past two patients sleeping in the hallway and a hospital orderly reading about celebrity liposuction. The emergency exit was a quick sprint away.

"Attention all hospital personnel." A voice was calling over the intercom. "We have a security intrusion and we need everyone to sit tight till we give the all-clear—"

The voice was silenced by alarms as I pushed the fire door open.

Why the hell can't I ever leave a building without creating a state of emergency? I vaguely wondered as I ran down the handicapped ramp into the parking lot. Seconds later I saw a flash of green metal pass the gate: Crawford's minivan, Della behind the wheel. I pulled the passenger door open and leapt in just as the first cop tumbled out into the street.

"For God's sake!" Della said. "Buckle that safety belt. Didn't your mother ever teach you anything?"

"I remembered to fill the tank," I said as I clicked the belt home.

"Lord, I am done with the struggle." She frowned at me. "Soon as Al gets out of the hospital, I'm gettin' both you men out of my hair for good. Then I'm turnin' lesbian."

The Quarter was in full-insanity mode by the time we arrived. I couldn't help noticing how Della seemed to tense up as crowds of loud young men passed the minivan.

"So you really did come down here looking for trouble," she said. "How's it feel, now that you got it good and hard?"

"Better than running away," I said. "Guess I let you down."

"You only let me down when you didn't show up for work today," she said. "I just hope you don't think you're gonna ride off with that girl into the sunset, that's all."

"You don't like Sofia?"

"I've always loved her," she said. "I've always loved you. But that river keeps rolling, Mike. Only fools and hurricanes ever try to beat the waters back the way they came—and only the storm so much as makes a dent."

"I'll keep that in mind," I said. "You sure you want to go back to the restaurant, after the night you've had? You're already halfway into the graveyard shift."

"Even graveyard people get hungry." She set the parking brake. "I got two more hours till my relief comes, and then I still have to make the groceries for breakfast. Then I guess I better get back to University and see to it that Al doesn't run off with some young nurse."

I was about to get out, then stopped to look at her. It was only then that I noticed just how exhausted she was.

"Della . . ." I breathed. "I'm sorry I got you involved in all of this. And Al, too. I thought he could hold it together—"

"What makes you think he can't?" She raised an eyebrow. "Apart from having a fool head and a bum arm, I mean."

I weighed my words before speaking. "I didn't mean it like that," I said.

"He just seems . . . I don't know, defeated. He had a strange reaction when Deadman mentioned the Superdome. Maybe it was burnout, PTSD. I know—"

"Mike." The meaning was plain in her eyes: Don't ask.

"All I'm saying is, I know what he's going through. About a year ago, I hit my own wall. And you know us law enforcement guys are the worst when it comes to admitting we have a problem—"

"Not to him."

"Sorry?"

She exhaled. "You're almost right, Mike. Al had it bad during the storm, but . . ."

"It didn't happen to him," I said. "Oh, Christ."

Della looked at me, cool and unwavering.

"What happened to you?" I asked.

"I was raped," she said simply.

I sat for a moment, stunned, as the engine idled.

"Jesus, Della. I had no idea."

"We didn't want you to find out," she said.

"How did it . . . ?"

"Some kids down from the projects. That first night . . ." She took a long breath to steady herself. "My niece and her kids made it over the Claiborne Bridge to a house on the good side, up around where it wasn't flooding so much. There were maybe . . . I don't know, fifty people crowding in, everywhere we could find space to lie down. Most of them were friends and neighbors. Some of them . . ." Her voice failed her.

"Come on," I said. "Let me take you home."

"Back to the Lower Ninth?" She shook her head, amazed. "Mike, that's just where it happened. Why do you think I don't like to leave the restaurant?"

She looked away, touching her forehead.

"This was how it was," she said. "I was lyin' there on the living room floor, with my niece's two little girls sleepin' on either side. And those . . . raggedy-ass bastards just lay down on me with a knife, and . . . took turns. I didn't move or make a sound, because then I'd wake up the babies . . . and they'd see."

Her tears fell, snowmelt on a mountain face.

"One of the girls did wake up," she said, "and asked me, 'Who is that on you, Aunt Della?' And I had to say—'Go to sleep, child, go to sleep. It's just . . . ' " Her voice broke. " 'It's just your Uncle Al, lovin' up on me.' "

Vendella turned her face, keeping her dignity, while a boy in an LSU T-shirt whooped at us and pounded on the hood. I stared the little pissant down and he skulked away.

"The worst part," Della said, "was havin' to wait with those sons of bitches all day on the underpass, under that boilin' sun . . . till this bus came and took us all to the airport. FEMA folks actually tried to shove me on a plane with 'em. I was more scared for Al than I was for myself. Those boys were half his age. They'd have killed him."

"He's a cop," I said.

She thought about it for a long time. "No, Mike. What he is—what we both are—is two old people, staring at troubles we can't fix."

I gave her a napkin from the glove box. She wiped her eyes carefully before looking at me again.

"That English girl, Amrita, got kidnapped in our neighborhood," she said finally. "That's why Al wanted to help you. And if it matters . . . it's why I wanted to help you, too. A million terrible things happen here every day. Most of them never get justice. They just get washed away down the sewers, like rain. Don't you think it'd be nice to see one righteous thing happen in our city before we give up the fight?"

I nodded.

"Then stop apologizing for what you have to do," she went on. "This ain't Oprah Winfrey. It was rotten luck for me, and no mistake. Rotten luck for us all. But I just can't let anything rotten get into my restaurant. You see?"

"Talking could help," I said.

"Oh, that's what some 'grief counselor' kept telling me. Talk it out, baby, talk it out." She gave an ironic smile. "Maybe I don't need to think about it no more. Is that okay for me to decide, or do I have to ask permission?"

"Cook it out," I suggested.

She seemed to like that. "That's right, Mike. I'll cook it out." She opened the car door. "And what are you gonna do? Duke it out?"

"No." I smiled. "I'll just figure it out."

A moment later, there was a buzzing in my pocket from my Bureau cell phone. I scoped a quick look at the text message from Art Kiplinger:

you are making a mistake
call me while you still can

"Everything all right?" Della asked.

"We're good." I pocketed my cell phone. "Come on, I'll walk you to the restaurant."

TWENTY-EIGHT

He picked up on the third ring.

"You're not having sex, are you?" I asked.

Special Agent Yoshi Hiraka laughed. "I'm a married man with a new-born kid, Mike. Does that answer your question?"

"Just wanted to make sure I'm not making you regret taking my calls."

"Are you kidding? That smart-card chip was the most fun I've had since they canceled *The X-Files*. How's it working out for you?"

"Traded it for a voodoo doll at Marie Laveau's." I looked around. "Where's our ex-boss? She isn't answering her phone."

"You think I've got you guys on an electronic map somewhere? Little pink and blue dots for Peggy and Mike?"

"Okay, Jack Bauer. Where am I right now?"

"At a pay phone on the corner of Canal Street and Loyola." He growled, caught out. "Wearing a brown jacket."

"It's actually tan, but that was a good bluff. Back to my previous question."

"Peggy." He hesitated. "No idea. Last I heard, she was on some kind of political junket with Senator Starkweather."

I smiled inwardly. It was a purely Yoshi joke to mix up Seaweather's name with that of a notorious mass murderer.

"So she's unreachable," I said. "You are therefore under no ethical obligation to check with her before agreeing to any more knuckleheaded requests from me."

"Uh-huh?"

"Because you could get into a world of shit for doing that. Even though I'm the guy who actually recruited you for the squad and bought a much cooler gift for Rina's baby shower."

There was the sound of an office chair rolling across the floor. "Okay, I'm at my private workstation now. Shoot."

"How private?"

"Private." To Yoshi, that word meant something.

"This is the last thing I'm ever going to ask you for, and then you should probably delete any record of my calls. How tight would you say computer security has been in New Orleans since Katrina?"

"About as tight as a broken Slinky. Everybody's in such a hurry to rebuild their data pipes, they're bound to cut a few corners. I could probably use city hall's mainframe to host a Viagra Web site, and nobody would notice."

"So if I wanted to gain access to privileged communications within the FBI data or telecom networks—"

"Whoa," he said. "This is a test, right? You're not really asking for that."

"Absolutely not," I said. "Not even a little tiny bit."

He was silent for several seconds.

"Mike, you've come to me with some freaky requests over the years. And I've never once asked for—"

"I can't explain my reasons. And if you report this conversation, the Bureau will tell you I've gone rogue. You know what I've been accused of doing."

"I never cared about that," he said. "It's just this is the first time you've ever asked me to keep secrets from Peggy."

"Kind of new territory for me, too."

I could hear him tapping his finger on the desk.

"So what is it you're not asking me for?" he finally said.

"I'm not asking you to trap the cell phone records of a contractor in New Orleans by the name of Leah Varnado, V-A-R-N-A-D-O, senior consultant for Kadmos Security Solutions. Here's her number." I pressed the keys so he could hear the notes.

"Mm. Tuneful." Computer keys tapped on his end. "Anything else I shouldn't be doing?"

"The very last thing I'd want is for you to cross-check her against the Bureau numbers for Supervising Special Agent Arthur Kiplinger. Or any other numbers he might be using, either under his own name or dummy accounts."

"Don't forget about Internet long distance," he said. "Check your personal e-mail in fifteen minutes. I should have finished not sending you the requested items by then."

"Thanks." I exhaled. "God help us if you ever use your powers for evil, Agent Hiraka."

"Something tells me I just did," he said in a wistful tone. "Take care of yourself out there, Mike."

Art and I met in a tourist bar on Decatur. It was full of white people from Wisconsin—but for guys like Art and me, that was an advantage. We were more likely to blend in. As I sat down, he was staring at an untouched beer that looked like it had lost its head back in the days of Jelly Roll Morton.

"You're late," he said.

"And you're screwing Leah Varnado." I picked up the menu. "Boy, I could eat a skunk. Cajun-spiced buffalo wings, eh? I'm not a native, but is that really authentic New Orleans cuisine?"

He stared at me, betraying nothing. "Mike, are you done? Because I have very little to say."

"Good. Then I'll keep talking. As you've no doubt figured out, I was the guy who broke into your office and stole a look at the Pandora's Box report that Kadmos Security prepared for you. Which is first rate, by the way. I suppose you should get some of the credit for it. Because, after all—" I waved the server over to us. "You're screwing Leah Varnado."

Art looked away as the waitress approached, bouncy and fun. Forty strands of plastic beads covered her superstructure.

"Hey, sugar!" Her name tag said she was Sherry from Gautier, Mississippi. "Y'all want some Mardi Gras beads?"

"In August? Who wouldn't?" I handed her the menu. "Actually, I think I'll just have the Big Easy burger with spicy Creole mayonnaise. And keep serving up those Co-Colas."

"Pepsi okay?"

"When is it not?" I asked. "Art, you still good with that beer?"

Sherry's face went a little dead as she noticed Art's missing arm. He simply stared at the table until she walked away.

"Mike—"

"You're setting me up," I said. "The U.S. attorney's office is adding racketeering charges to their case. Guess they didn't get the memo that this is supposed to be a sham trial."

"It has to look real. If it doesn't look real—"

"They've also got the surveillance photo of me and Sofia at the Black

Pearl raid. You know—the one that was so secret that it could only be shown to me inside the field office?"

He seemed to be genuinely shocked. "There's only a handful of people who have access to that material, and all of them work for the Bureau. Who's going to be crooked enough to leak it to prosecutors?"

I suddenly realized that I had a pretty good idea, but I kept my mouth shut.

"Who told you this, anyway? Barca?" He gave me a tense frown. "And you believed him?"

"Not when he first told me," I said. "That was before I saw the psych profile you had on me in your file drawer. Why does—" I nearly blurted it out: *Why does Amrita Narayan think I'm going to murder my son?* But that, too, would take the conversation someplace I didn't want it to go.

"What were you about to say?" Art asked. "Why does what?"

"Why was the hero-homicide classification attached to my name?"

"You've got some balls." He leaned back. "Sorry, Mike. You don't break into a guy's house, steal his stereo, then call him up and ask for the owner's manual. The fact that you crossed the bright line does not entitle you to know—"

"Excuse me, but is this a lecture on personal morality?"

He bristled. "The last time I checked, adultery isn't against the law. Breaking and entering, on the other hand—"

"Stop right there. You started having joyous, midlife-crisis sex with young Lili Marlene right about the same time you hired her company to prepare that report. Which—depending on who you wind up pleading your case to—either constitutes quid pro quo sexual harassment or nice clean graft. Talk about opening up Pandora's Box."

"Can you prove that?"

"I don't have to prove it. I just have to announce it loud enough." I whistled to the bar. "Hey, everybody? Check who's getting some serious primo—!"

Art grabbed my arm. He wasn't angry. He looked terrified.

"Don't," he said.

I settled down.

"He warned me that you were off your rocker." Art shook his head, dizzy. "Vitale told me you'd failed every stress and anxiety test in the battery. I said I didn't care. You were my old partner and I knew I could trust you."

"You can trust me," I said. "The person you can't trust is that overpriced security consultant you're sleeping with."

"We're—"

"In love? Art, I don't care. I don't even mind that you were the 'friend' who asked her to set me up in D.C. Well, that's a lie. That actually sucked." I relented. "Whatever friendship you and I had is probably now over. Since I'm about to go to jail, I have nothing to lose. I hacked into Varnado's cell phone. That's how I knew about the twenty calls a day between you. In addition to the erotic text messages she's been sending. The girl really does have one hell of a—"

Art was staring at the table. As if he'd seen his future in the beer rings, and it wasn't worth facing.

"Vocabulary," I said. "No games, Art. Listen to me."

"I'm going to tell Rachel," he said. "This weekend."

"Tell her, don't tell her. You're missing the point. I know about Varnado's calls to you."

He looked up. "Jesus, I get it. How long do you have to keep twisting the knife?"

"Not just the X-rated ones, okay? All of them."

Finally it seemed to sink in.

"I can't justify the way I found out," I said, "but this has got to be dealt with."

He seemed extraordinarily calm. "What do you want?"

"What do I want? Some honesty between us would be nice. Agent to agent. Man to man." I gestured between us. "Exactly how were you planning to hide the fact that Kadmos Security supplied those armor-piercing rounds to Amrita Narayan's kidnappers?"

A strange astonishment began to spread across Art's face, from his one good eye to the edges of his mouth. Something almost like relief. But he didn't answer my question. Sherry from Gautier had returned with my burger and fries.

TWENTY-NINE

"We met last year at a Homeland Security conference," Art was saying as we walked down lower Decatur. "Leah was . . . electrifying. When I brought her in on Pandora, there was some internal resistance—at first— but damned if she didn't win them all over. Kadmos has been outstanding to work with. Like dealing with our own people. In some ways, better." He looked at me, dazed. "Over time, it just got easier to hand things over to them. They always came through. And Leah, my God. Whenever I needed anything, I turned around, and there she was. Then, one morning, I woke up—"

"And you turned over, and there she was." I looked around to make sure no one was listening. "Did you decide to bury the ballistics report on your own, or was that Lili's idea?"

He winced. I'd crossed a line, calling his beloved by her pet name.

"It was a mutual decision," he said. "For the last time, Mike, we did not suppress evidence on the APLPs. Our superiors—"

"Our superiors know jack shit about what you've been doing down here. Kadmos manufactured the five-five-six shell that killed Cleanhead Duplessis. They hired Simon Burke out to you as a special contractor. They're tangled up in your OC investigations like kudzu, and God knows what else. You sat there in the director's office and told me to find out who Barca was working with on the Narayan kidnapping. Well, I did. The same guy who somehow expects to make a fortune on the reconstruction. Leah's own boss, Martin Telfucking Campbell."

Art stopped. "You've got this cold?"

"Met him this afternoon at Barca's. Scotch drinker. Tell me you didn't know and I'll kick your ass."

"I didn't," Art said. "Mike, I swear it on my children. Are you absolutely sure that it was Campbell you saw—"

"Oh, God damn it, Artie!" It was all I could do to keep from punching him. "You let them in. There is a line between greed and the public trust, and you let them walk right over it. Have you actually convinced yourself that these Kadmos jerks are part of the team? Or are you just lying through your teeth?"

He started to answer me—then simply looked down at the dirty sidewalk.

"It's over," I said. "We have to tell the SAC and the director what's going on and take the consequences. And we're pulling Amrita out of danger. Tonight. That's nonnegotiable."

"The investigation—"

"The investigation's dead," I said. "Protecting the innocent is the only part of our job that ever meant anything. The rest is bullshit. I can't believe I'm the one who has to remind you of that."

"You forgot to mention the chip," he said.

"What?"

"The one you used to get into the building today. Kadmos manufactured that, too. Somebody must have looted it from Simon Burke's dead body. How did it get into your hands?" He looked at me. "Come to think . . . what made you so sure it would actually work? Someone else must have used it before you."

"Don't change the subject."

"You're the one who brought up our security gaps." He stared at me. "Not too many people could have gotten that surveillance photo out of the building. Really, only me and Noah Delacroix. Considering that he appears to have a faked birth certificate . . . I'm going to walk out on a limb and say it was your son."

A bray of laughter from some passing drunks punched the end of Art's sentence.

"You knew?" I asked in the following silence. "You're Noah's hook, aren't you? The one who's been covering for him on the inside? All this time, you knew he wasn't for real."

"I don't know what you mean by covering for him," he said. "Lately I've started to suspect his true identity. Your reaction to him today was the final confirmation. You knew he was yours the minute you saw him—and that's the real reason why you were scared to give him up."

I didn't answer. It wasn't worth denying.

"As for being for real?" Art held up his hand. "Define 'real.' He's sure got the talent, and he's probably better trained at nineteen than half the veteran agents in the field. Kind of a shame, actually. If he could have gotten in legally, I'd have had no trouble saying he was the real deal."

"Except that he happens to be working for his grandfather."

"Jumping to conclusions, aren't we?" There was Art's trademark sloping grin. "You see Noah feeding information to Barca and you assume that's where his loyalties are? How do you know he isn't acting on my orders?"

"Because you're not the one giving orders," I said. "Who put him inside the Bureau? Was it you, or Barca? Or was it Kadmos?"

"Maybe he put himself in. Like I said, the kid's smart. Maybe he just wanted to be like his old man." Art shrugged. "So I guess we'd better get back to deciding what we're going to tell the SAC, huh? Probably take a couple of weeks to get a new team up to speed. God only knows what's gonna happen to Amrita Narayan in the meantime."

"What happened to us?" I waited for him to meet my eyes. "Remember how we were gonna take on the world together, Artie? We were the good guys. What the hell happened?"

"Rotten luck, I guess." He looked away. "Tishah B'Av."

"Come again?"

"Today's the fast of Tishah B'Av," he said. "Sort of the Jewish equivalent of Friday the Thirteenth. Bad things happen on this day. It was on Tishah B'Av that the Romans destroyed the Temple . . . also the day Hitler ordered the Final Solution. And this year, I guess . . . it's the day the partnership of Yeager and Kiplinger finally ended."

"Yeah." I took a breath. "So how does it end, exactly?"

"You and I get off easy," he said. "We go to prison. That stolen ID card, on the other hand, is enough to convict Noah on murder one. While he's waiting out his appeals on death row, the lawsuits are going to bleed Kadmos dry, so no money for rebuilding New Orleans. Or maybe . . ."

"Maybe what?"

"Maybe we come out heroes," he said. "You show up for the handoff, a team from Hostage Rescue brings Amrita out safe and whole, Noah Delacroix drops out of sight. We make the case on Kadmos some other way. The good guys win after all."

"That's not gonna happen, and you know it." I watched him. "Why do they want Amrita, anyway?"

"I really don't know—and that's God's own truth." He held out his open palm. "Suppose that I really am as crooked as you think. Why would I ask you to find Barca's connection if I knew the answer was going to blow me out of the water? Where's the percentage in that?"

"Maybe you didn't expect me to live long enough to find out," I answered. "I don't need Hostage Rescue, thanks. I'll take care of Amrita on my own."

"You'll never get her out alive by yourself," he said. "Not her and Sofia both."

I hesitated. "Sofia's not mixed up in this, Art."

"She's not?" He smiled archly. "You don't think Barca's going to want revenge on the person who informed on him to the FBI?"

I pushed him back against a wall.

"Don't be an idiot." He didn't lose his cool. "People are watching, okay? They've got camera phones. I think you'd better let me go."

I had him by the throat; the urge to crush his windpipe was overwhelming. Finally I released him. A few tourists laughed and applauded.

"Sofia approached us." Art rubbed his throat. "She didn't want Amrita getting hurt . . . and she was worried for her son. So we struck a deal. Your bringing her home was part of the plan to get her close to her father. Worked out pretty well for everyone."

"Not for Officer Lenahan, it didn't." I turned away.

"The deal we made with Sofia is still good," he called after me. "You and I need to work together on this. If you're right, then Kadmos played me, and I'd like a chance to bring them to justice. I think we can do it, Mike. Just like the old days."

He paused, as if realizing that he still hadn't sold me.

"Sofia will be protected," he said. "Your son goes free, Amrita goes home to her family. Isn't that why you came here?"

"She said . . ." I took a breath. "Amrita said that I would murder my son."

He shook his head. "She's not a psychic, Mike. Just a psychologist."

My cell phone was buzzing.

"You gonna get that?" he asked when I didn't move.

I finally opened it. Two seconds of silence followed; then the signal died. The caller ID was blank.

"His Master's Voice," I said. "I'm being summoned."

"Mike." He watched me walk away. "At least take the offer to Amrita. She's got a right to decide this for herself."

As I looked back at him, I thought I saw a shadow of the brave young man I'd met long ago: good old Art, a clear-eyed voice of reason in the most unreasoning city God ever made. My very first partner, Agent Kiplinger, torn in half for my sins.

"Is it still Tishah B'Av?" I asked.

"Until sundown tomorrow."

"I guess we've got till then to turn our luck around," I said and turned my back on him.

THIRTY

"The fuck's wrong with you?" Barca stood still while Grady fitted him with a Kevlar vest. "You been cryin', or what?"

"I'm fine," I said. "Where's Sofia? She wasn't in her room."

He gave a dismissive wave: Forget about it. "We gotta move on this hand-over thing. Marty Campbell's people called an hour ago. Agreed to every penny I asked for, and then some. If that ain't the kiss of death, I don't know what is."

"I need to tell you some things," I said. "Alone."

Grady barely had time to open his mouth before his father silenced him.

"It's fine, Graziano. *Tutti e posto.* Go tell the doctor to make the girl ready."

"God willing, Mike can talk sense into you." For once, it didn't seem like I was the one Grady was pissed at. "Age doesn't always bring wisdom."

Barca gave his son a wizened look as the door closed.

"You better help me fasten this thing up." He struggled with the Velcro straps. "Weather's gotta be shrinking the material. Can't be that I'm gaining weight."

"The vest won't help you, anyway. Kadmos has armor-piercing rounds." I assisted him nonetheless. "It seems you were right to be suspicious. You give Amrita over, you're finished. That's the best information I have."

"Hell of a time to tell me." He finally succeeded in getting the straps around his gut. "You talk to your friend Kiplinger?"

I nodded. "He's in bed with Kadmos. Literally."

A wolfish smile crossed Barca's face. "What else?"

"He claims he didn't know about Kadmos's involvement, but I don't believe him." I watched Barca. "He's aware of Noah's real identity."

"Yeah, well, that was too good to last." Barca wiped sweat from his brow with his sleeve. "Nobody's seen Noah since . . . you know, what happened at dinnertime. Sofia's real worried."

I couldn't tell if he was looking for sympathy or playing on my guilt. Either way, I was being baited.

"It was stupid to put him inside the FBI," I said. "Kiplinger wasn't fooled. And if Kiplinger's gone crooked, then we're in twice as much trouble as we thought. You should cancel the meet. Either the deal's dead or you are."

"Bullshit," he said. "You know how much cash they're putting on the table? It could save our family, Mike. We need that money. You tell me how to make this work. 'Cause I don't see anybody else lining up to pay out for that English girl."

I shrugged. "Let me talk to her."

"We already tried talking. Hell, after you left, Ciro and Grady wasted an hour—"

"Yeah, I've seen your methods in action. This isn't a muscle job, Barca. Put me alone with her. I know how to get through. And when we've got the goods . . . then we'll have them over a barrel. Kadmos, Kiplinger, all of them. It'll be a pleasure."

He watched me for a long time with owlish eyes. Finally he ripped the Kevlar vest away.

"Least I don't have to fuck with this straitjacket any more," he said. "Grady!"

A moment later, his son appeared in the doorway.

"Take Mike out to the swamp," Barca told him. "He wants to meet a lady."

They still called it a swamp, even though most of the cypress and tupelo had been logged back in the 1950s. Really, it was nothing but an open marsh, and a sickly one at that. Grady navigated the airboat down the feeder ditches and canals, where dead nutria choked the oxygen-starved water. The only flourishing life was a cloud of mosquitoes, hungry as street beggars. My skin was going to look like raw hamburger from all the welts. The night sky was coffee-black: 2:00 A.M.

Nearly all of the slave cabins had long since subsided into the waters, consumed by a hundred and fifty years of flood and rot. One lonely cabin still remained on its wooden pilings, caught in the boat's weak yellow headlights.

Dr. Petrie waited for us in the open cabin door.

"She going to make it?" Grady lashed the boat to a scarred piling.

"She'll hold together, as long as she doesn't have to travel far." The doctor gave me a cautious nod as he climbed down into the boat. "You're the girl's escort, eh? Hope you weren't expecting to find her in satin and lilac water. This is no octaroon ball."

I pushed him off the ladder and hoisted myself level with the entrance to the cabin's single room. A pair of white eyes glowed faintly in the dark.

"Dr. Narayan," I said. "Amrita."

She didn't answer. I shut the door, hearing her shuffle in the darkness, against the far wall.

"You don't have to be afraid of me." I fumbled in my jacket for a penlight. "I think you know who I am. My name—"

I felt my heart seize as the light touched her face.

Dear God.

It wasn't the bruising around her swollen eyes and forearms that moved me so much as the withered gypsywort leaves she still clung to. Her eyes were red and cloudy, unable to close. Yet those eyes still looked at me with something like pleading. The Barcas had done far worse than beat or starve her: They'd left her with a feeble ration of hope.

"Come on." I moved toward her. "We're going."

"Please don't . . ." She shrank away, skittish. "No."

"Listen carefully." I leaned in close enough to whisper. "I can get you to safety, but you need to trust me. There are two men on the boat. If I can't disarm them, I'll have to kill them, and then we'll have very little time to get away. Can you—"

"Where are the others?" She waited fearfully. "The other men from the FBI. Sofia said there would be a . . . hostage rescue team. Where are they?"

I took a breath. "No one's coming. It's just us."

She shook her head. "She said her father might try to trick me. Unless she tells me it's all right, I won't go."

"I'm a friend of Sofia's," I said. "Mike Yeager. Do you remember my name?"

"You're Noah's father," she said. "He helped them kill my husband. At least . . . I believed that's who Simon was. He turned out to be a very different person than he seemed when I married him—"

"Amrita, please. We're out of time."

She stared at me with her wide, intense eyes. "How do I know I can trust you?"

"You told Deadman I was a good person pretending to be a bad one. Isn't that enough?"

"Deadman. That isn't really a name for a person, is it?" She smiled faintly. "Everyone thinks a psychologist is someone who looks into a man's eyes and finds the monster inside. When so often it's the other way around. Would you care to know what I see when I look into your eyes, Mr. Yeager?"

"Why don't you tell me on the boat ride back."

However, she held firm. "I know all about you," she said. "You think you let your mother die. You believe that makes you a murderer. Doomed to be alone in the world. Don't you?"

I didn't answer.

"You're wrong," she said. "The earth is full of boys who failed to protect their mothers from cruel men. Many of them—"

"Amrita."

"*Listen.*" Her hand took mine, hot with fever. "Many of these boys grow up thinking they have to be just as cruel as their fathers. A few of them, too few, devote their lives to kindness. Then there's you. You think that if you deny yourself all happiness—choosing nothing but pain—then it will stop you from ever hurting anyone, ever again. But you're wrong. Do you know how I know all this about you?"

"You read my FBI psych profile?"

"No," she said. "I wrote it."

For moments the only sound was a distant buzzing, like the night song of cicadas.

"It was Simon who convinced me to take the job," she said. "The FBI gave me all the documents and interviews, and I . . . became quite familiar with you, I think. They all believed you could be corrupted, but I knew you better. I knew that, at the moment of truth, you would destroy yourself rather than—"

"Why am I going to kill my son?" The noise outside was louder, fighting against my heart's rhythm. "Why?"

"Because it will be the only way to stop him," she said.

"Stop him from what? From—" Then I listened. It wasn't cicadas, after all. "There's another boat coming. Let's go."

"No. I won't. Not like this." She pulled away, determined in spite of the terror in her eyes. "If I go with you now, they'll kill me. Or Simon's employers will take me, and then I'm dead anyway. And I have to live. I must talk to Senator Seaweather."

Until that moment I thought she might be delirious. Yet as she spoke the senator's name, there was something in her voice that rang hard and true as iron bells.

"Please," she said. "Many people's lives depend on it."

"If I promise to call in a Hostage Rescue team from the FBI," I said, "will you do exactly what I tell you to? No matter what I ask, no matter how strange it seems?"

"Yes," she said with perfect trust.

"Then—"

The engines suddenly stopped.

As the rough wooden door fell open, it was my son, Noah Delacroix, who stood smiling at the top of the ladder.

"That's good enough," he said. "We'll take it from here."

THIRTY-ONE

Emelio Barca was waiting at the house, his eyes brimming with compassion as Amrita was brought to him. He stroked her frayed hair and inspected her bruises, enraged to learn that his men had so badly mistreated her; he thanked me for bringing her suffering to his attention. Then he humbly asked my permission to speak to the girl alone. Feeling Grady's hot breath on my neck, I nodded. Just as I feared, Amrita seemed to take it as a sign that she ought to cooperate. The two of them, Barca and Amrita, disappeared into his private study. The last sound I heard was the door closing. Then silence.

Barca returned twenty minutes later, alone this time, smiling as if the weight of twenty years had miraculously lifted from his shoulders.

"You get what you wanted out of her?" Grady asked.

"And then some." He grinned like a young lover. "You were right as rain, Mikey. Gaining her trust was the right way to go. This deal is gonna work out a lot better than we thought."

He waved, and the men at once began to follow him out of the room.

"Barca." I stepped forward to catch his arm. "What did she say to you?"

He only smiled.

We rode in three vehicles. Grady and his men were in the lead. Barca was in the second car with Amrita, with Noah behind the wheel. That left me and Ciro to bring up the rear. We drove along a narrow access road north of Slidell, somewhere between the West Pearl river and the National Guard training center at Camp Villere. My Bureau phone was still in my pocket. Now and again we'd come within range of a cell tower, and then my throat would go dry. All I had to do was make one call, say two or three words, and FBI Hostage Rescue would know precisely how to find me. Trouble was, we weren't stopping long enough for me to make that call, and I kept losing the signal.

Ciro wouldn't stop talking.

"You and I got a lot in common," he was saying from behind the wheel. "Same U.S. government trained you as me. Trained me very well. I come from a good family in El Progreso—sugar plantation. Learned my English at the Honduran military academy. And you thought I was just some *pinche* farmboy, heh?"

He laughed when I didn't. Ciro was in an unusually expansive mood. He'd been talking about his home a lot—almost as if he expected to return there pretty soon.

"Best years of my life," he said. "CIA made me a man."

We were in an abandoned industrial belt, littered with old refineries and factories from the glory days. The sky was charcoal-pink, scattering haze from the airport lights a few miles to our south. *That's how Kadmos is planning to get Amrita away, I realized. Slidell's runway is five thousand feet. A Gulfstream V could just barely make the takeoff. Has a range of six thousand miles. With a jet, they'd have no problem getting her out of the country, staying ahead of ICE.*

"I remember my first job with Battalion Three-Sixteen," Ciro said in a voice of sweet nostalgia. "The target was a young girl, beautiful. Small tits, you know? I don't like 'em that big anyway. She and her man were dressed like tourists—but we had good intelligence they were leftists, headed for El Salvador . . ."

Honduras is only eleven hundred miles away, I calculated. Friendly, right-wing government. They could be there by morning.

". . . raped her right in front of her man, but that didn't do any good. I think he might have been *mayate*—you would say, faggot. So we put the electricity to her . . . not a word. Dunk her head in the water, kick her around a little . . ."

It will take twenty minutes for Hostage Rescue to get here by helicopter. The airfield is only ten minutes away. If I'm going to make this call, I have to do it now.

"So . . . we start to cut her. Didn't even scream." Ciro groaned, as if recalling an unpleasant chore. "Then we find out—she and her boyfriend, they're both fucking deaf! Can't even talk. Didn't even know we were asking them questions. And all that time, we thought they were these tough kids." He smiled, waiting for my laughter, as if he'd just told the punch line of a dirty joke. "You don't get it? Shit, man. Least my CIA handler had a sense of humor."

The red light of a cell tower glowed in the distance ahead.

"That's some story," I said. "Did you try anything like that with Amrita the night you killed her husband?"

He grinned. *That's for me to know and you to find out.*

"Because she told me you couldn't," I added idly.

"*Qué?*" He frowned. "What do you mean, couldn't?"

"She said you tried to ball her, but you couldn't get the motor running. Thought it might be because you had those shriveled little gonads. Or . . . what was it she compared it to . . . what's Spanish for 'soggy french fry'?"

"You're full of shit, Mike." His hands tightened on the wheel, white with anger.

"Listen, Ciro, I don't pretend to know how your brain's wired into your dick. Maybe Amrita's breasts just weren't small and boyish, the way you like them—or maybe you can only rape a woman when she's terrified of you. Or could it be . . ." I nodded. "Tell me that word again? *Mayate?*"

"Shut your hole, okay? I'll fuck you up so bad—"

"You'll fuck me?"

Ciro slammed on the brakes. The other two cars immediately slowed to a halt. We were less than a quarter mile from the cell tower.

"We're gonna finish this job," he said, his voice boiling. "Then I'll show you who's *mayate*. Maybe I'll even show the boss's daughter. For that you get a front-row seat."

Noah had left the car and was coming toward me—reaching for his pancake holster with smooth polish, like the federal agent he never had been and never could be.

"Look, my son's watching us," I said. "Can't you act just a little butch while he's around? He still hasn't learned about what men in prison do to each oth—"

Ciro flew at me like a jaguar. Just as he sprang, I hit the door handle and we both tumbled out. Under the circumstances, it probably would have been courteous to let him get in just one shot to save his manhood—but I'd already gone a round each with Noah and Deadman Carmichael, and I wasn't sure how much more my ribs could take. I punched Ciro's larynx with the ridge of my knuckles and sent him tumbling into the ditch. After that, getting into his pockets was easy.

"What the fuck!" Noah bore down on me. "Holy Christ, what the hell are you doing?"

He nearly drew his weapon. Then the car door slammed, and Grady was standing in the dust of our headlamps. Noah instantly withdrew his open hand from his jacket.

"What happened?" Grady asked, in no mood for shit.

"He was talking smack about Sofia." I pointed to Ciro, who had struggled to his knees, choking. "Started joking about how he was going to rape her. What would you have done?"

Grady cooled. "Ciro?"

Ciro didn't respond, and Grady evidently chose not to press the point. A dark fire kindled in Noah's eyes.

"I suppose we'd better split you two up," Grady said. "Get him into my car, Noah. We don't have time to screw around."

Noah pointed at me. "You're gonna leave him to drive there alone?"

"Will you shut *up* with that bullshit?" Grady slapped the back of Noah's head. "Jesus and Mary, if I didn't already know you were Mike's brat, this clinches it. Stay with Pop, okay? That's your job."

I saw Barca's silhouette in the passenger seat of the car ahead, his eyes narrowed in the sideview mirror. Ciro didn't resist as my son pulled him roughly to his feet, then forced him into the backseat of Grady's car. As he slammed the door, Noah turned and spit at the dust before me.

"You're such a fucking disappointment, Dad. You know that? Worse even than I expected."

Moments later, the caravan was back in motion. Finally alone, I put the car into gear and opened the cell phone on the seat beside me.

"Yeah?" Art's voice.

"You'd better not screw me over on this," I said. "You won't believe what I just had to do to make this call."

"Yeager? What are you—"

"I'll explain later," I said. "Is the team ready to move?"

"Yes," he said. "How far away are you from the rendezvous?"

"Maybe fifteen minutes. They wouldn't tell me where it's happening, but I'm going to say it's somewhere along County Road Nineteen. It's got easy access to Slidell Airport. You'd better close down the runway, just to be safe. And check for any private jets preparing for takeoff."

"The team will be there," he said. "Your code word is 'Dido.' That's Delta-Indio-Delta-Oscar. Mike, are you armed?"

"No." Which wasn't strictly true. I had the .38 I grabbed from Ciro while he was trying to rip my face off. But I didn't know who else might be listening in, and it bothered me that Art wasn't asking about Amrita's condition. It should have been his first question.

"Keep the phone turned on so we can follow your signal," Art said. "Godspeed."

As I hung up, a wayward thought suddenly crossed my mind. Noah had called me a disappointment. Worse even than he'd expected.

But he'd also called me Dad.

THIRTY-TWO

We stopped at the railroad tracks. There was open ground on both sides for about a hundred yards. Past that was a stand of cypress trees, and enough low brush for me and Amrita to dive into if things got rough. Half a mile down the tracks was a single black SUV, its lights off.

"Why do you keep looking up at the sky?" Barca asked me. "You expect Superman to fly down? Santa Claus?"

"Skylab." I looked around. "Where's Amrita?"

"She's coming. You know what to do, right?" He pointed down the track. "You walk her halfway there, no further. They'll meet you with the cash. Make sure you count it a little, so they know you got your eyes open. Don't waste too much time on it—but don't run from 'em, either. You carrying?"

I shook my head.

"It's probably best that way. Don't worry, we got your back. If you get in trouble, give the signal. Remember, you're worth a lot more to me than the money." He put a fatherly hand on my shoulder. "Things are looking up for our family, Michael. You steered me in the right direction. I won't forget that."

Half a dozen different responses struggled to my lips, most of them liable to get my teeth broken. "Thanks, *padrino*. That means a lot to me."

"You went a little hard on Ciro back there," he said. "I don't blame you. I know you been under stress, and . . . he's not respectful of our women. Still, you gotta learn restraint if you want to be in charge. If it hadn't been for Ciro, we wouldn't even have that girl to bargain with."

I finally realized what was bothering me about Barca. He didn't look worried. For days he'd fretted about Kadmos trying to kill him—and now that I'd finally confirmed his worst fears, he seemed as happy as a kid play-ing hooky at the zoo.

"What did Amrita tell you?" I asked, trying not to sound desperate. "Just to be practical. If something happens to you, God forbid, and you're the only one who knows—"

"What do you FBI types always say? Need to know?" He laughed and pushed me toward the track. "Nothing's gonna happen to me now, Ein-stein. Thanks to you, I'm bulletproof. Now get the hell out of here. Don't keep a girl waiting."

I turned to see Amrita standing a few feet away—barefoot, clad only in a white nightgown, hands bound before her. *Like Joan of Arc for the burning,* I thought. *Or a bride.*

"Come on, Doc," I said to her, trying my best to sound comforting. "It's almost over."

Someone was approaching us from the other end of the tracks, a dark-ened figure whose face I couldn't see. I don't know why I expected him to carry a valise. He simply walked with his arms at his sides, keeping both hands in view.

"Are you all right?" I held my hand to Amrita's back—partly to steady her, but also to check her breathing. I was surprised to find it slow and steady, if a little shallow.

"There's ants on the railroad tracks," she said in a distant voice. "They're biting my feet."

Drugged her, I thought. *Smart move, Barca. And very bad for me if this doesn't go just right.*

"I'm going to tell you a couple of things, Amrita, and I need you to listen carefully." My own heart was easily beating twice as fast as hers. "We're pulling you out. If Hostage Rescue isn't here by the time the bad guys take you, I don't want you to resist or run away. I want you to do exactly as they tell you to, so you don't get hurt."

"You won't leave me?" She seemed to be fighting to gather her concen-tration.

"I'll stay as close to you as I'm able. I will do everything I can to protect you. But the second you hear gunfire—you drop to the ground, you hug the earth like it was your mother. Understand?"

"Yes." She stepped uncertainly over the wooden ties. "Why did you want me to . . . tell my secrets to Sofia's father?"

I took her arm just in time to keep her from stumbling.

"I didn't, Amrita. I didn't mean for you to do that." I looked ahead: We were twenty yards from my counterpart. "What did you tell him?"

"I don't remember," she said. "He gave me water. Tasted salty. It might have been . . . gamma-hydroxybutyrate . . . I mean . . ."

"Can you remember what you wanted to tell the senator?" I asked. "Something about . . . someone about to die?"

For a moment, she was so quiet that I couldn't even hear her breathing. At last she shook her head.

"The senator," she said. "I'm sorry, Mike. I can't think."

Now I could see the face of the dark-jacketed man coming toward us: His cropped hair was sandy brown, his stride loose and assured. I was mildly surprised to see that he was wearing aviator glasses. As we closed the distance, I did my best to seem like Amrita was only a hindrance to me, a piece of luggage that I was eager to throw off.

Amrita stopped cold.

"Where are they?" she asked in a voice of childlike terror. "Where is the rescue team? You said—"

"Please be quiet. Remember what I told you. If there's trouble, let me—"

"This is wrong," she said. "I want to go back."

The other guy was less than a dozen yards away—and starting to get curious.

I yanked her forward. "Please listen. I will die if that's what it takes to save you, but you have got to trust me for a few more yards. Once we're through this—"

"I know what I have to say to you." Amrita's voice was suddenly clear as winter ice. "It's like that song I learned when I came to New Orleans. 'God gave Noah the rainbow sign . . . no more flood but the fire next time.' "

"Yeah? Where's the fire going to be?"

"Jackson Square." She looked at me. "You have to tell her, Mike. Tell her it's going to happen at—"

"Agent Yeager?" The man nodded grimly as he came within arm's length. His eyes were dark behind smoked lenses. I pulled Amrita close to me, giving me just enough room to draw if I needed to.

"Who wants to know?" I asked.

"I'm Special Agent Owens from HRT," he said in a steel whisper. "The men in the SUV back there are from Hostage Rescue as well. How's our girl here?"

"They've got her on narcotics," I said. "Possibly GHB. She needs medical."

"She'll get it." He cast a rapid glance over my shoulder. "We were able to subdue the group from Kadmos before you arrived, but we still need to distract Barca long enough to position our second team. I'm going to reach slowly into my jacket and try to hand you a bank card."

"That isn't what Barca negotiated," I said.

"Exactly. You'll get pissed off, we'll argue for a while, then I'll get on my cell phone and somebody else will come forward with the cash. You leave the victim with us. Then you walk back. It's very important that you not allow any of Barca's people to approach us."

"Understood," I said. "So I'm not being pulled out."

Owens shook his head. "We need to keep you inside for a while longer. Kiplinger's call. Now if you're ready . . . let's start the show."

He began to reach into his jacket. Suddenly, Amrita seized my arm.

"I don't want to go with him," she said. "Please, Mike."

Owens smiled. "It's okay, honey. Mike did his job, now let us take o—"

"Why didn't you ask him for the code word?" Suddenly she sounded not at all drugged. "Simon told me . . . there's always a coded signal between agents."

Owens froze like a computer getting faulty instructions. Then he eased up. I noticed he was wearing an in-ear mike.

"She's got a point." I glanced back over my shoulder. Barca's men were pacing nervously. "Technically, you should have requested my code word, even before establishing your own identity. Who knows, I might have been under duress."

"Fair enough," he said. "Do you have it?"

"Yeah, but . . ." I rolled my shoulders, as if from a stiff back. "Since you already know it's me, why don't you go first?"

"Dido." He looked nervously past me. "Okay, Barca's men are starting to come this way. You'd better stop them before they get any closer."

"Actually, I'd better not." I reached into my jeans, drawing my .38 before he could move. " 'Dido' is my code word, jerkwad—not yours. Kiplinger should have told you that, if he'd sent you. Did he?"

"You'll never know, will you?" Owens merely cocked his head. "Should have played the game, Yeager."

At once there was a rush of noise, the engines from several vehicles as they broke through the low brush. We were frozen in the crisscross of white searchlight beams. Owens's aviator glasses suddenly reflected black: some kind of transition lenses. He was reaching for a weapon.

"Mike!" Amrita screamed. "He's—!"

I fired, clipping Owens in the right shoulder. Then, too late, I saw what he'd dropped at my feet. A hexagonal steel tube, pierced with round holes. *Flashbang*.

"Amrita, cover your eyes!"

I turned to her just as the stun grenade went off.

Amrita Narayan froze in a brilliance of white light; the noise ripped through my ears like razors. For long seconds, her image was burned into my retinas: Her eyes were little moons, her mouth gaping at something I couldn't see. Something terrible. I felt her slip away from me.

Then the image finally faded into red darkness as my eyes recovered from the assault. I tried to move, stumbling over something soft and heavy. I looked down and saw her.

A single bullet hole pierced Amrita Narayan's forehead. Her eyes stared wide into the night sky, seeing nothing.

I opened my mouth to yell and heard only a dull ringing. I looked back down the track: A black vehicle had cut off our retreat. Bullets were noiselessly striking the tree branches. Two of Barca's bodyguards lay dead on the ground. Grady was firing back. Then I felt a hand on my shoulder.

Noah. He was shouting at me, his lips forming the words: *Come on*. I was already running with him alongside the tracks. The beam of a cherry-red laser sight picked him out. I pushed him down and a chunk of dead cypress exploded to dust. "High-crawl it," I called to him—feeling my voice vibrate in my chest, hearing nothing. He instantly complied.

Barca was in front of his car, dazed in a swirl of light and smoke. I could see the whites of his eyes as he groped for a hiding place. Two black-uniformed guards were nearly upon him, rifles drawn. *If something happens to you*, I'd said to Barca, *and you're the only one who knows—*

The uniforms weren't FBI. I silently thanked God for His left-handed gift: If I was going to have to kill anyone to save Barca's worthless neck, at least it wouldn't be my own guys.

It happened in a brace of seconds. The guards wore ballistic armor, probably with titanium plates. Armor would catch the bullet, but it wouldn't cancel the force of impact. At least I hoped to Christ it would catch the bullet. Throwing myself between the first man and his target, I pressed the muzzle of my .38 right against his chest and squeezed the trigger.

He was instantly flung backward, stunned by the sudden impact, but the fabric of his vest hadn't broken—and now I had his rifle. I turned to the second guard and fired. The APLP round went straight through his shin guard. He landed on his shattered leg, his mouth in a wide O. Then he fell.

And Emelio Barca smiled.

". . . into the car . . ." Grady was calling to us when a bullet struck him sideways. I could actually hear him faintly, a distant voice in a swarm of locusts. I hurled Barca into the front passenger's seat, then jumped behind the wheel and drove. Noah leapt into the backseat and slammed the door. I threw on the brakes, making a wild J-turn in the soft dirt, then gunned it through the brush over open ground.

The pursuing vehicles had fallen well back by the time I was aware of any sound but my own breathing. It took me a moment to realize that I could hear again: Barca, speaking to me in a dazed whisper.

"Shoulda listened to you, Mikey," he was saying. "Shoulda listened to you right from the start."

THIRTY-THREE

Grady was bleeding from a graze on the neck. We laid him across the backseat, stopping only briefly to change cars at an auto yard near Abita Springs. Barca ordered Noah to take over the wheel and we headed east, deep into the Louisiana pine barrens. At first I wasn't sure if we even had a destination. Finally I recognized the darkened roadhouse at the crossroads: the Bottom Dollar Social Club.

A GREAT PLACE TO GET YOUR BODY DOWN! read the faded sign on the side of the building. A lot of shady characters had been knifed or shot in that club over the years—so many that we used to joke that the sign should have read A GREAT PLACE TO DUMP A BODY! Like everything else in Barca's universe, the roadhouse was long abandoned, a last grim relic from the days of Bunk Johnson and bootleg rum.

Noah and I carried Grady between us like a drunken sailor. I could feel his warm blood crawling down my shirtsleeve. The kitchen door opened . . . and it was Sofia waiting for us in the dim light. She didn't meet my eyes as we took her brother inside.

"Put him on the pool table," Barca said. The dizzy élan in his eyes had vanished, replaced by a cold, predatory certainty. For the first time since coming home, I felt like I was seeing the real Emelio Barca, no games or pretenses. It reminded me of something that Uncle Paulie had said to me during our brief acquaintance: Death was Barca's only true consigliere.

"You gonna pull through?" Barca slapped Grady's face to wake him up. "Come on, kid. You gonna die, or what?"

Grady opened his eyes, showing no fear. "I'm okay."

"You're bleedin' straight through the felt on the pool table," his father said. "I can't afford to send you to the hospital, and who the fuck knows where Doc Petrie is now. So either you gotta die, or we gotta sew you up here. Understand?"

His son nodded. "You have to get the . . . traitor, Pop. Whoever screwed us over . . ."

"Don't you worry. I got a few ideas about that." He stroked his son's hair, then gestured to Sofia. "Over here, sweetheart. You remember how to do this, right?"

"I'll have to use the sewing kit." She nodded gravely. "Is Noah all right?"

"Yeah, I put him on the door to keep lookout. He did good, though. Both of your men did good. Mikey, you take care of Sofia. I gotta make a couple phone calls."

He went into the back, alone. I looked around the empty room, realizing for the first time that Ciro wasn't with us.

"If you're going to stay, you need to help." Sofia spoke to me, but her eyes were on her brother. "See if there's any hard liquor under the bar. Vodka would be best."

I searched the shelves. "You knew we were coming?"

"Papa sent me here earlier, in case there was trouble. Looks like he was right again, huh?" She opened the sewing kit, checking her needles. "Make sure it's an unopened bottle. It has to be strong enough to clean out the wound."

I brought her a dusty bottle of Popov. She opened it, smelling its contents before holding it over her brother's neck.

"You'd better hold him down," she told me. "This is about to get ugly."

"I can handle it." I took hold of his shoulders.

"Speak for yourself," Grady muttered. "Asshole."

Then he screamed.

Thirty minutes later, Grady lay unconscious on the table, his neck sewn and bandaged. The first gray light of morning filtered through cracks in the boarded windows.

"So you saved my father." Sofia filled my cup from a thermos. "Why did you do it?"

"Before they shot her . . ." I took a swallow of weak coffee. "Before she died, Amrita told your father something in private. Right now he's the only person on earth who has that information. If I'd let him die . . ."

"That was quick thinking, all right. Tell me—why didn't you use that same quick thinking to save Amrita?" Sofia stared at me, stone cold. "You promised me you'd protect her, Mike."

I looked over at Grady. His chest rose and fell, slow and even, his eyes closed.

"I promised her, too," I said. "I tried, but it was an ambush. She wouldn't come with me unless a rescue team—"

"You should have known better than to trust the FBI." Her eyes narrowed. "Who told you he'd send a team? Was it Kiplinger?"

I nodded.

"If you're any kind of a man at all," she said, "he'd better die for this."

Then the office door opened. As Barca entered, he slipped his cell phone into his pocket. If his circumstances had been any better, I would have sworn that he looked happy. He rapped on the outer door; Noah opened it. Barca joined him outside, and they spoke in tense whispers for several minutes. Then the two of them came back inside.

"In here, Mike." His eyes darkened a little. "We got some things to talk over."

We followed him into the back office, a windowless room filled with aging invoices and beer crates. The only light was an electric lantern on the desk. I was a little surprised to see Uncle Connie sitting in a wicker chair, watching both of us with his amazed goggle eyes.

"Close the door," Barca ordered Noah. He complied—then stood directly behind me, where I couldn't see him.

"We're in trouble and no mistake." Barca spoke directly to me. "Right at the same time those Kadmos bastards started shooting at me, they also sent a team to raid my house. Killed a lotta my guys, busted the place up real bad. Good thing we didn't stay home last night, huh?"

"Good thing," I answered.

"You were right about Kadmos," he said. "They're in bed with the FBI. Reason I know that is, somebody made a phone call from your car, maybe twenty minutes before the handover. Take a look at what Noah found."

He held up a cell phone.

"Call went to Kiplinger," Barca said. "You know anything about this, Mike?"

I shook my head.

"You sure about that? Absolutely one hundred percent?" He waited. "Because a reasonable person might think otherwise."

I laughed. Barca gave a rapid upward glance to Noah.

"You think this is funny?" Barca raised an eyebrow. " 'Cause I sure ain't laughing."

"Whose phone is it?" I asked. "It sure isn't mine."

Which it definitely was not. I didn't know for a fact that anyone would suspect me of calling in HRT—but I figured if they did, it would be better if it was from somebody else's phone. Barca motioned to Noah. I held up my hands while he frisked me. Then he handed my own cell phone to his grandfather.

"Check my SIM card if you don't believe me," I said. "I think you'll find that other phone belongs to Ciro."

"Ciro?" Noah said it a few inches from behind my ear. "You're telling me he's—"

Barca raised his hand for silence. "Go on, Mike."

"If you have any contacts at Slidell Airport, see if Kadmos had a private jet with a registered flight plan to Honduras. Because I was sitting next to Ciro on the ride, and I got the distinct feeling he was looking forward to seeing the folks at home. At least that's how he sounded when he made his call."

"What exactly did you hear him say?"

"Hell, I don't speak Spanish. Ask Ciro." I shrugged. "By the way, where is he?"

Barca solemnly examined my phone before tossing it back to me.

"Wouldn't make much sense to dick me over and then save my life," he mused. "Not to mention getting that pretty little lady shot, and almost yourself in the bargain. You're not that fucking dumb."

"Glad to know you think so well of me," I said.

He pointed to a chair. A moment later, Noah sat down where I could see him, watching me with his mother's searching eyes.

"So there's good news and bad," Barca said. "Good news is you're maybe not a rat after all. So I can tell you there's more good news. I just got off the phone with Marty Campbell."

I exhaled. "No shit."

"Yeah, the sonofabitch flat-out denied he tried to whack me. But he was plenty pissed to hear my voice, let me tell you. Probably his guys are all gonna be fired on Monday morning."

"If they're not dead already," I said with a glance to Noah.

"Damn right." Barca laughed. "So here's the more good news. It seems we got a deal with Campbell, after all."

"What?" I couldn't help myself. "Are you out of your mind? After what—"

Noah shifted uncomfortably. "I hate to agree with him, Grandpa, but what the fuck."

"Calm yourselves, both of you. This is a good thing." He held up his hand. "Campbell thought his troubles were over when the girl died. Now he knows I got all her secrets out of her, thanks to Mike. That makes me very valuable to him."

"Or very dangerous," I said.

"Or very dead," Noah added. "I wouldn't have made that call, Grandpa. They can triangulate the signal and send a crew here in no time flat."

"I took precautions, no worries. Grady has a friend at the telephone company who handles all our phones, and mine is switched around six ways to Sunday. The point is this. Before tonight, we were just some dumb mutts who did a kidnap job. Now—we got a real partnership. Fifty-fifty on this Levin-Marcato money. Campbell doesn't like it, but he'll pay. Proper tribute, like in the old days. Share and share alike. And when it all comes down, the Barcas will be running the show."

Noah threw me a tense look. "I still don't like it."

"That's because you're only half Italian," Barca answered. "That pig-headed heinie blood is fucking with your head."

"But, Grandfather . . . our enemies . . ."

At once there was a strange sound, like wood creaking: Barca's uncle Constantino was laughing.

"We men of the Barcas have always had to deal with our enemies," the old man said. "My grandpapa, rest in peace, was solid Italian. He drove a horse cart for White Rose Ice Cream. He bought us a house in Gentilly through shares in the Italian Homestead. And he kept his money only at Banca Italiana. Always he would say to us children . . . do you remember, Emelio?"

" 'New Orleans was founded by our *paisano*,' " Barca said.

"Exactly. It was Enrico de Tonti, the man with the iron hand, who first explored Louisiana. Don't let those Frenchies lie to you." Connie's face darkened. "But when he was a little boy, it was . . . not so good to be Italian. On March fourteenth, 1891 . . . my grandfather was forced to watch as eleven Italian men were murdered by a mob—lynched! Like animals, like *mulignani*. Cut like meat and left to rot before the smiling eyes of Mayor Joseph Shakespeare . . . and only because they were falsely believed to have murdered a police chief. *Morte*."

He stopped for a moment, his voice choked with emotion.

"A murderer from the crowd asked Nonno his name," Connie continued. "He answered—'I am Barker.' If he had told his true Italian name, they would have killed him, too—and he only a boy of nine. He had to live, though, so that he could one day take revenge. This he did; this he finally did. Today the name of Barca is feared. One must be patient in order to survive."

Then, having said his piece, Constantino Barca settled himself back into his chair and closed his heavy eyelids. Soon after that, he began to snore.

"So we're gonna do this deal with our enemies," Barca said after a respectful silence. "Like Uncle Connie said—we're gonna be patient, and then we'll have our revenge. There's work for you in this, Noah. I'll explain it all later."

"Excuse me," I said, "but Noah isn't your responsibility—"

"I'm old enough to speak for myself," Noah said.

"You're old enough to kill. That doesn't make you a man. What exactly are the terms of this deal, Barca?"

He raised an eyebrow. "So I'm 'Barca' again. What happened to *'padrino'*?"

I braced myself before speaking. "You are alive right now because of me. I warned you against the handoff, and you went ahead and did it anyway. So I think I'm entitled to be heard."

"You've been heard," Barca said coolly. "But right now, you got a trial coming up, and people looking for you. So you're just gonna have to cool your jets. Go home, take a bath, call that lawyer lady—"

"And wait for the goddamn phone to ring," I said. "No thanks. If I'm in, then I'm staying in."

He thought it over for a long time.

"Your choice," he said finally. "You're in."

"You said there was bad news," Noah said. "What's the bad news?"

"The bad news is we still got a fucking traitor to deal with," Barca answered. "Somebody's sure as hell informing on us to the FBI. And if it ain't Mike . . ."

He searched my eyes, then Noah's, for a long time.

"Well, it seems like maybe you boys need to take some family time together. Maybe run a couple errands in the city for me." He lifted his bulk from the chair. "Now if you don't mind . . . I'm going to see how my only surviving son is getting along with the stitches in his neck."

Then he left us, taking the light with him.

THIRTY-FOUR

The sun was well up by the time Noah and I left, and the August heat was already making jackets unbearable, so we stowed our guns into our jeans like button men. Noah drove, keeping a constant eye on the rearview mirror. Once again I was impressed to see how careful he was. Living on the run seemed to come naturally to him.

We had little to say to each other on the road. He paid cash for a cheap hotel room in Covington, where we showered and changed. Supposedly we were there to grab some sleep, but I don't think I shut my eyes once in two hours. I was pretty sure Noah didn't, either. At eleven o'clock, he sat up and announced that it was time to get moving again.

"Where are we going?" I asked as he used a slim jim on the door of a parked Toyota Camry.

"Back to the city, like Grandpa said." The lock slid open, and Noah went straight to work on the ignition. "Have you still got that microprocessor you stole from me?"

"I can get to it easily enough."

"Good. We'll need it." He twisted a couple of wires and the engine sparked into life.

The rest was silence until we reached the southern end of the Causeway.

"I've been hoping you'd solve a minor mystery for me," I said. "How'd you manage to bluff your way into the Academy? I guess you could have faked your application documents, bribed people to give you good interviews, lied through the polygraph, and convinced real agents like Bill Bly that your acne scars were really cordite burns—but that theory does seem to violate Occam's razor."

"You're misinterpreting Occam," he replied. "It's not the simplest explanation that's most likely true. It's the one that requires the fewest as-sumptions. And there's just one assumption too many in your question." He overtook a family van in a no-pass zone. "*How* I did it isn't that exciting, once you know. It'd probably be more revealing if I told you why."

"All right. Why?"

"I said *if*." He laughed. "I'll tell you this much. It's not what you're thinking. It wasn't so I could be like you, or prove myself to you, or any of that Dr. Phil bullshit."

"What about proving yourself to your grandfather?"

"Not even that. Don't get me wrong. He's a tough old bastard, and I've learned a lot from him. Still, there's things going on here that are way be-yond my grandfather's understanding." Noah looked at me. "And if you think I'm teasing you because I secretly want you to figure me out, think again. Far as I'm concerned, we're just two guys killing time in a car."

"Fair enough," I said. "What if I figure you out anyway?"

He didn't answer for nearly a quarter of a mile.

"You won't." Then we pulled off the bridge into Metairie. "Okay. Let's get to work."

I retrieved the smart card from a locker in the Greyhound bus station on Loyola, under the looming shadow of the Superdome. Half an hour later, Noah gave two thousand dollars cash to a guy working in an electronics warehouse in the Central Business District. The employee handed him a laptop computer and assorted hardware. Then we got fast food at the Mc-Donald's on Canal. While we ate, Noah took advantage of the restaurant's wireless network to reprogram the card.

"We're not going to be able to use it to get into the FBI field office," I said. "Security won't fall for the same trick again."

"We don't have to go inside." He studied the monitor. "This thing will go inside for us. Right into the network."

"Nice little gadget," I said. "Was it worth murdering Simon Burke for?"

"Pretty much, yeah." He smiled. "Okay, we're good."

He stowed the card, and we drove on. Finally I realized where we were headed: the Crescent City Bridge.

"What's in Algiers?" I asked as we crossed the river.

He shrugged and said nothing.

"Look, Noah, I can handle the silent treatment. I can even handle you hating my guts. But if we're on this job together . . ."

"You can go home if you want to," he said.

I nodded. "You still think I'm a rat, don't you?"

"I know you made that call to the FBI," he said. "It may have been Ciro's phone, but the number was Kiplinger's private line. Far as I know, Kiplinger doesn't speak Spanish either, and I know something else that Grandpa doesn't: You called that girl of yours yesterday. Agent Weaver. Very interesting chat you two lovebirds had. One might almost think you were trying to get her attention."

I laughed. "Boy, was your mother right about you. Why are you so determined to believe I'm still loyal to the Bureau?"

"People don't change," he said.

"Yet here I am," I said. "Strange that you didn't give me up."

After that he fell into a brooding silence.

Finally we reached the West Bank. Noah left the car beneath the overpass, dumping the computer into a nearby Goodwill bin. We walked past schoolyards and vacant lots toward the river levee. Noah seemed to know exactly where he was going.

"I don't blame you for not trusting me," I said. "Growing up without a father all those years must have been hell."

"I did okay," he said over his shoulder. "How'd it work out for you, having a father all those years?"

"Shitty."

"Yeah? Wasn't your dad some kind of Nazi? That's what Mom said. She said he used to kick you around."

"He was a weak man," I said. "Weak and cruel. Even before my mother died, we never got to leave home except for school and church. No talking to anyone outside the family. And forget about dating or friends coming over. It was pretty much all apple picking, the Bible, and . . . paranoia."

Noah stopped, as if checking his bearings. I pretended not to notice as he stole a quick glance at the display on his cell phone: a map with a GPS readout.

"Everything all right?" I asked.

"Hunky-dory," he said. "Sorry. Tell me more about your fucked-up childhood."

"It wasn't always bad for me," I said as we resumed walking. "Sometimes I'd take a beating. Sort of his way of telling me how much he hated my guts for letting his wife gas herself in the garage."

I hated the flippant tone in my voice worse than talking about it. Peggy was right: I did get smart-ass whenever it started to hurt.

"Was it your fault she died?" Noah seemed mildly curious.

"She'd tried it a couple of times before. I was supposed to watch her. One night . . . I kind of fell asleep on the job."

He looked at me. "So in a way, it was your fault."

"In a way, yeah." I shrugged it off. "The weird part is . . . the more he blamed me, the more determined I was to shine in his eyes. I had to be perfect at everything. First one up for chores, last one to stop praying and go to bed. Straight A's across the board. I guess that's why the scrapbook—"

I stopped, suddenly realizing we were maybe six blocks from Sofia's old apartment at Algiers Point. Mardi Gras World was dead ahead.

Noah looked back at me. "Scrapbook?"

"When you make Eagle Scout, you get all these letters and commendations from various VIPs. Your local congressman, Lions Club, local sports heroes—all congratulating you on your big achievement. I even got a letter from George H. W. Bush."

"The one who got us into Iraq?"

"His father," I said. "I put all the letters and stuff into a scrapbook. Even embossed the Boy Scout logo on the cover. Then I did a very stupid thing. I left it on my father's desk. You know—not wanting to rub his nose into it or anything, just . . . wanting him to see. He didn't say a word about it all day. Then that night, really late, he woke us all up. Made us line up in the living room, like the von Trapp children. And he said to us, 'Michael has committed the gravest of all possible sins against God. He has committed the sin of pride.'"

As I said it, I could hear my father's flinty Pennsylvania Dutch twang. The way the candlelight carved shadows in his cheeks and eyelids. The curious smile on his face. The smell of raw bourbon on Calvin W. Yeager's breath.

"'And the only cure for pride,' my father said, 'is shame.'" I took a breath. "'So let us all aid in Michael's correction.'"

"What happened? He knocked you around?"

"I could have handled that." I shook my head. "He made me drop my shorts and take a piss on the scrapbook. Each of us had to take a turn. Even the girls had to squat down. When we were all finally done . . . the old man went last. Just whipped out that German sausage and took the longest, rankest, foulest piss of his life. All the time smiling with relief—like it was the best he'd had in years."

Noah stopped walking. We were near the loading dock of the unguarded Mardi Gras warehouse. A row of giant fiberglass heads, gaily painted, grinned down on us.

"You didn't beat the shit out of him for that?"

"He'd have taken it out on the others," I said. "Anyway, the next morning, I got up before anyone else, and I spent hours trying to clean it all up. Never could get rid of that stain."

Noah considered it. "What happened to the scrapbook?"

"Buried it," I said. "Three years after that, my father died of heart disease. I was at college. Right before the end . . . he wrote me a letter."

"Let me guess. You pissed on it."

"Just threw it away without opening it," I said. "I'll never know if he wanted to apologize or . . . what he wanted to say. I didn't want to give him the chance, I guess."

"Gosh, I wonder where this is going."

"It's just a story, Noah. How I learned my lesson. You got one of your own?"

He laughed. "You don't want to hear about that."

We moved on into the scrap yard. A row of broken floats, crusted in mud, listed against the concrete flood wall.

"I remember all these floats from when I was a kid," Noah said. "I must have been six or seven. They were all stories out of Greek mythology. Happiest time I ever had in childhood was getting my mom to explain these floats to me." He pointed to one of them. "Recognize that one?"

"Dido and Aeneas," I said. "Dido was the founder of Carthage. Aeneas made love to her, then abandoned her because the gods commanded him to build the city of Rome."

"Then she killed herself," Noah said. "God or no god, a guy who will do that does not deserve to live. You disagree?"

I shook my head.

"You really want to know how I learned my lesson?" he asked. "Is it gonna make any difference between you and me—any difference at all—if I tell you?"

"I hope so. I can't promise anything. I'll listen if you want to tell me." I turned away from Queen Dido, streaked with filth. Noah led on, more cautious than ever.

"When I was nine years old," he said in a low voice, "I got to watch a man bleed to death."

I didn't answer—just waited for him to look at me. Which he never did.

"He was one of my mom's boyfriends." Noah bent down to inspect the ground. "He thought that gave him a license to fuck with me. A lot of guys thought that—and she never stood up to any of them, you know? Not one time." He stood up straight. "So this one night, I was woken up by some noise and yelling, and I came down from my room. My mom's in the kitchen with a big fat lip, and her shirt's torn down straight to her waist. The fucker made my mom sit there crying with her tits hanging out. Big biker—strong guy, you know? Name was Ricky. Ricky from Atmore, Alabama. Nice fat beer gut. Confederate flag tattoos. And he was making my mom cry. So I took a steak knife . . . and I put it right into that sack of shit, right between his hairy nipples."

I didn't respond.

"Yeah." Noah laughed. "Couldn't get the knife all the way in, 'cause it stuck on a bone or something. Plus I wasn't that strong, I was only nine. So he's all running around, trying to kill me . . ." He shook his head. "Mom wanted to call the hospital. But the noise woke up Grandpa and Uncle Grady. They were mad at me, at first—but as soon as they heard the whole story, they took my side. We were hiding out on a farm in those days. So we dragged Ricky the biker out back and—"

"Watched him bleed to death," I said. "In other words, your grandfather and uncle helped you kill a man when you were nine years old."

"In other words—" He checked his watch. "You have no fucking clue what I had to deal with because of what you did to my mom. And I'll tell you something else. Your father may have been an asshole—but he had ten times the balls you had. I wouldn't have let that old cocksucker push me around."

"You'd have refused to piss on the scrapbook?"

"I'd have cut off his dick and made him eat it," Noah said without expression. "If anybody tried to make me piss on something I cared about, father or no father, I'd have killed him without a second thought."

Then Noah drew his 9mm Beretta.

My first impulse was to reach for my .38. Then it hit me: *Is this when I'm supposed to do it? Kill him? Like this?*

"You asked me why we're here," he said. "This is why. We're here to deal with the traitor in my family."

I'd allowed him to lure me out of public view. We stood behind an enormous float depicting the fall of Troy, well hidden from the street. The distant roar of the Canal Street ferry drifted toward us. High noon.

"Noah." I held my hands up. "I should have been there for you. Believe me when I tell you . . . that I'm sorry."

"Believe me when I tell *you* . . . that I proudly don't give a shit."

Then he aimed the pistol up at the huge Trojan horse.

"Get the fuck down from there," my son said in a commanding voice. "Come on, shitbird. Fool me twice, shame on me."

Moments later, a trap door opened. Ciro Garra crawled down from the float. His empty hands trembled.

"How did you find me?"

"I'm magic," he answered. "You know the drill, *teniente.* Hands on your head, palms up. And don't trip on your way down, or I'm liable to kill you just for being clumsy. *Comprende?*"

"I got friends coming. They work here. They'll see—"

"Nobody's here. Siesta time. Kneel down, okay? I don't want to damage the float. It's got sentimental value to me."

"You're wrong about me, Noah. Wrong. He's the traitor." Ciro nodded to me. "Fucker took my gun and my phone. I tried to warn Grady—"

"Yeah? What else did you tell Grady?"

He hesitated, as if realizing his mistake.

"Nothing, I promise. *Nada.* My word on this is golden."

"Premium bullshit is still bullshit, Ciro. Did you spill anything to my uncle or didn't you?"

"Noah," I started to say.

Ciro looked at me fearfully.

"You're a government agent," he said. "Please. You can't let him do this, or you're accessory. Don't let him—"

Noah pressed the muzzle against Ciro's head. Ciro obediently dropped to his knees.

"Talk to *me,* asshole. Yeager isn't gonna lift a finger for you. You'll fry his ass if you live long enough to cop an immunity deal." Noah lowered his voice, cool as Christmas. "For the last time . . . what did you tell my uncle?"

"I didn't. I didn't tell him anything."

"Noah," I said. "Don't do it."

Then he saw me, aiming the .38 at him. Noah smiled.

"Gosh," he said. "Is it still a Mexican standoff when the guy's from Honduras? You gonna shoot me, Dad? Is that your big plan to get back into God's good graces?"

The ferry horn blared again, louder this time. My gun lowered just a fraction, away from my son.

"I knew you wouldn't," Noah said. "Tell him why, Ciro. Tell him why he can't afford to kill me now."

"Please don't," Ciro said.

"Fucking tell him."

"Your mother . . ." Ciro gasped. "Your mother made a deal with the FBI. Sofia's the informant. She's the fucking rat."

The ferry horn reached a crescendo.

Noah put two shots through Ciro Garra's skull.

For several seconds I didn't move—just watched the dead man's white brain matter cling to the Trojan horse's flanks. Finally, I lowered the .38 until it pointed at the ground.

"Weak," Noah said to me—and walked away.

THIRTY-FIVE

"What the hell are you doing?" I followed Noah at a fast walk down Powder Street, toward the ferry landing.

"Give me a break." He sneered at me. "You ought to be the happiest guy in the world right now. I just solved all your problems."

"Because you killed Ciro instead of me."

"Because of my mom, you bastard." He exhaled a breath. "You heard the man. My mother's the fucking rat. Jesus H. Christ. If Ciro could figure that out, how long is it gonna take Grady and my grandfather?"

"When did you figure it out?"

"Kiplinger let a few things slip. It sure wasn't hard to guess, after all the whispering you and her have been doing over the past few days. Like two schoolgirls."

"We have to pull her out." I had to struggle to keep up with him. "You can't control this. If you want to protect your mother, we have to get her into custody—"

"Yeah, that worked out great for Amrita Narayan, didn't it?" He laughed. "I saw you take on those Kadmos guys at the handoff. If you'd killed that fucker instead of just winging him, he wouldn't have had time to throw that flashbang. Not to mention those other two guards you fought away from my grandfather. They'll be maimed for life, but at least you didn't *kill* them. Very noble, Agent Yeager. Very merciful."

"Noah, you just murdered an unarmed man."

"You let me do it," he said. "Same way you let your mother die. History repeats, huh?"

"You don't know what you're saying." I could feel my temperature rise.

He finally stopped to face me.

"Neither do you," he said. "You don't even know the moral of your own story. The defining moment of your life wasn't when your mom killed herself. It was the day you tried to make up for it with a scrapbook full of letters, telling your dad what a great kid you were. No wonder he pissed on it. Hell, I'd have taken a *shit* on it." He shook his head in disgust. "And you tell me that story hoping I'll throw you a little pity? Is that why you keep fucking up? So people will feel sorry for you?"

I put a hammerlock on my rage, hoping to God it would hold.

"I told you that story to warn you, Noah. About what your emotions can do to you, if you're not careful."

"What emotions? The guilt again? The shame?"

"The anger," I said. "You didn't stab Ricky-from-Atmore because he mistreated your mother. You did it because you couldn't protect your mother. If you don't find a way to cage that anger . . . one day it'll destroy everything you're trying to save. Believe me, I have been there."

For a moment, he seemed to waver. I got the feeling I was close to getting through. The next words out of my mouth would decide.

"Let me help you protect her," I said. "Damn it, Noah, we've got that much in common. I love her, too."

"Love." He rolled his eyes. "Let me tell you something about love, old man. I could live without it. As bad as it was growing up with jerks like Ricky around . . . there are times when I think I'd have been a lot better off if my mom had the guts to take care of herself the way your mother did."

I punched him straight in the jaw.

There was no moment when I decided to do it. One second I was a grown man, trying to talk sense into a boy of nineteen. A second later he was reeling from the blow, his eyes full of hatred.

"God," I said. "I'm—"

He cracked me on the chin. Not a planned strike. A swift, savage uppercut that ought to have torn flesh from bone—but I'd stepped back just as he began to swing, and it stole some of his momentum. Which is not to say that it felt like a kiss.

"You like that, you faggot?" He flexed his hand painfully, his knuckles already turning red. "How about you shut the fuck up now?"

"Thank you." I rubbed my mouth.

"For what?"

"I don't have to feel guilty about this anymore."

By the time I said it, I was already on him. I grabbed him by both shoulders and head-butted him, feeling an explosion of white pain through my skull. He was still reacting to that as I threw him hard against my knee, driving it upward. A final downward slice against his kidneys, and he was over and out.

Just a kid, I thought. My head was throbbing, and the sick feeling in my stomach was back.

I rolled him over; Noah was gasping for breath, but he wasn't spitting blood. I had time to rifle quickly through his pockets. I tossed the Beretta down a storm drain, leaving him the cash in his roll, close to a grand. Then I stuffed the cell phone and card into my own pocket.

"Wake up," I said, shaking him. "How bad does it hurt to breathe—"

He drove the edge of his knuckles into my right eye. Black flowers exploded in a scarlet cloud. I fell back.

"About that bad." Noah tried to stand—then dropped, holding his rib cage. "*Jesus.*"

My hand came away from my eye slick with blood. *That's going to be one hell of a bruise,* I thought. *Good one.*

The ferry's air horn went off, a block away. Noah painfully pulled himself to his feet.

"Noah—"

"Stay the hell away from me and my mother," he said. "If you try to come back again, I'll kill you."

I sat on the pavement and watched him stumble away for the ferry. He got there just as the gate began to close. Moments later, the boat started to move away from the shore. By then I could hear police sirens.

THIRTY-SIX

I ran, paying very little attention to where I was going. All I knew was that I had to get away from that police car before it turned the corner. I shouldn't have been too surprised to find myself at the corner of Socrates and Vallette. Right in front of the narrow shotgun house where Sofia lived during our all too brief romance. In a way, I'd been trying to find that crumbling old dump ever since I left it twenty years back.

The house was still painted god-awful lavender, and the dormer window was still patched with plywood. Probably still had the same family of inbred cats living under the floorboards. A lot of dirt had subsided from the pilings, and somebody had finally gotten around to repairing the porch swing, but it hadn't changed that much. As I circled around back, I imagined myself reaching for the spare key under the geranium pot, carrying a six-pack of Goebel's beer and a bag of Della's hell-flavored pork rinds. Sofia would be listening to Lou Reed or Miles Davis, or maybe Patsy Cline if she was having a particularly rotten day. Singing along with "Back in Baby's Arms" in that wandering soprano. I'd sneak up and put a cold beer against the back of her neck, and she'd yelp. Then we'd both laugh . . .

The kitchen door was hanging halfway open. I put my head in, then stepped inside as the Doppler whine of the sirens continued to rise. No refrigerator. There was a pizza box on the stove, but its coupons had expired six months ago. The lights weren't working. I carefully shut the door behind me.

The police car slowed down as it passed the house, but that wasn't what was setting me on edge. It was that strangely detached feeling you only get when you return to a place that used to matter to you. For years you will visit it in your dreams, imagining how you'll feel when you finally see it again. What troubled me most was that I felt so little.

I watched my son kill a man. The words stared at me like B-movie titles, but I couldn't summon the emotions that ought to have gone with them. I supposed that I was still in shock: A mere twenty-fours before, after all, I didn't even know I had a son. That was also when Amrita Narayan was still alive.

The black-and-white NOPD prowler kept moving down the street, then finally disappeared from view. Then I heard a woman's voice.

"You're scaring me," she said. "Don't, okay? I can't . . ."

My heart seized. The girl sounded young. Something shifted and thudded against the thin plaster wall. She was in the next room: Sofia's old bedroom.

"Please," she said. "You have to promise me. You have to promise you won't . . ."

Even before I stood in the half-open door, I could hear the soft wet sounds of open mouths, the give and slide of cloth against flesh on an old mattress on the wooden floor.

"So nice." The guy's ass was shifting up and down between the girl's legs, bare inches away from where he wanted to be. "Don't worry, *mi cariña*. I just want to hold it there for a second. Just a second. You feel so good inside—"

"No, baby, please. I don't want to . . . omigod!" A Hispanic girl of seventeen suddenly hoisted herself up in the bed, scrambling to get her bra back in place. Her runt of a boyfriend turned over, already grabbing for his jeans.

"For God's sake," I said. "Do yourselves a favor and use a condom."

Then somebody started pounding on the front door.

"Oh, Jesus," the girl said. "It's my brother—"

"Relax." I put my head into the hallway. "It's just a cop."

Or rather two cops. One was trying to see through the dusty foyer window while the other one worked on the lock. I went right past the two half-naked kids and lifted the window.

"What's happening?" the boy said. "Oh, fuck, what is this?"

"You'll know in about twenty years," I said and jumped out into the side yard.

The police weren't stupid. They'd seen me disappear behind the house and were probably just waiting for me to relax a little before they flushed me out into the open. The real question was how they'd known to start looking for me in the first place. I could hear the crackle of their radios in the backyard: One of them was circling around back. I jumped the chain-link fence into the next yard and heard running feet. Sure enough, one of the cops was right on my ass.

"Slow down." The policeman was about my age, in no mood for a chase. Which meant he'd gladly use that gun on his belt if it meant saving his cholesterol-ridden heart. All that stood between us was that rusted fence. "Come on, buddy. Don't be a jerk about it. Right now we just want to talk. If you make us chase you down—"

I didn't run. I walked steadily backward along the fence, keeping one eye on the cop and my ass to the house behind me. He stalked me, a friendly dogcatcher trying to coax a rottweiler into his net.

"What's the rush, eh? Better slow down. You'll live longer." Then he gave himself away: He broke eye contact and looked over my shoulder, just a moment too soon. I slammed my elbow back and cracked his partner right in the nose, then I turned and gave the poor bastard a headlock throw. He bounced against the fence, and I started running for the street.

The police car's engine was idling. *Drive or shoot?* I wondered—then decided in favor of the latter. I drew my .38 and put two rounds into the prowler's front tires, then a final bullet into the radiator for good measure. Then I flung the gun away as hard as I could. Being caught running would get my ass kicked—but getting caught with a gun would absolutely get me killed.

I bolted headlong for the fork in the road between Verret and Vallette. If I could get to the cemetery, I might be able to hide out among the crypts for a few minutes. The police would probably stop the ferry from taking me back across the river—but there were small boats at the wharf, and some of them might not be locked up too well. *So, where do you go from there?* I didn't want to think about that. I was trying very hard not to consider anything in my immediate future when a black Land Rover swung around De Armas Street, right across my path.

Jesus wept. It had smoked bulletproof windows and the kind of tires that could drive across iron spikes without slowing down. The beast stopped right in front of me, warming its eight-cylinder engine, waiting to see which way I was going to jump.

I could feel a stitch in my side. I was getting winded. The cops were behind me, closing in.

What do I have left? I wondered. Noah's cell phone? I could call Della and tell her to come save my ass—or maybe just call the Catholic archdiocese and ask if last rites were available for unbelievers. I searched the empty streets in both directions. *Where are all those goddamn tourists with camcorders when you really need them?*

The Land Rover's driver's side door opened . . . and it was a woman's slender foot that first touched the pavement.

"It's okay. We got him." The policeman said it from about twenty feet behind me. The next sound I heard was the whish of a gas cartridge. The probes pierced my right bicep. I took fifty thousand volts and every muscle in my body seized up. Then again. Then I felt my head hit the street.

Taser? A blinding question. *Since when do New Orleans cops use Tasers . . . ?*

Then it was over. As I lay there waiting for the cuffs to go on—or the bullet to enter my brain—I stared glassy-eyed at the legs of the woman approaching me. I couldn't turn my head to look any higher, but I was pretty sure I recognized those calves. No wonder she ordered them to give me a double shock. I was surprised she didn't press the button herself.

"Pick him up," she said in a neutral voice. "Please be careful."

I started to black out as soon as they lifted me up. Even as I struggled to stay conscious, I dimly realized how it was they'd found me.

The card. That damned smart card, still in my stupid pocket. Damned technology was the bane of my miserable existence.

THIRTY-SEVEN

The room I woke up in was too clean for a prison infirmary and too quiet for a public hospital. All the other beds were empty. The overhead lights were out, but I could still catch a little daylight through the drawn shades. As I drifted in and out, a guy in green scrubs would occasionally check the fluid in my IV drip and shine a light into my pupils. Finally the straps were taken off, the needle withdrawn, and I was able to inch myself up to a sitting position. As I did so, I could hear low-heeled footsteps in the dark, and a sound of fizzing water. Then the scent of Weber's Superior Root Beer reached my nose. Noah was dead wrong about me and root beer. On any other day, it might have reminded me too much of my father. At that particular moment, it was my rope ladder to God.

"Thanks." I drained off half the can at a single pull. "Nice and cold."

"The flight attendant put it on ice for me," the woman at my bedside said. "If there was any law and order left in this country, root beer would be a controlled substance. I don't know how you manage to swallow that stuff."

"You close your eyes and pretend it's mouthwash." I finished the bottle. "I'd say it's good to see you . . . but right now you look like a big gray blob."

Then she came closer.

"And you look like a meatball, my friend." Peggy Jean Weaver was using her supervisor's voice, the mom-is-angry voice. Even so, I could hear the concern she was trying very hard to disguise. "You ready for the light?"

"Let her rip."

I squinted as she turned the bedside lamp on. Peggy was in her working clothes, a trim black suit and ivory blouse. You didn't need to see her badge to know she was an inspector now: Her power was all in those hazel eyes.

"You must have been pretty wrung out even before you got the Taser shock," she said. "Not my idea, by the way. How are you feeling?"

"They took my underwear," I said. "I can feel my bare butt on the sheets. That's not nearly as exciting as it sounds."

"Don't worry. Nobody peeked." She touched my forehead with the back of her hand. "In case you're curious, we were already tracking you when we intercepted a ten-seventy-two homicide call to the police. At least . . . we were tracking whoever was holding that card. When I heard them talking about someone firing a round into a car radiator, I knew exactly who we were after."

"We have a long-standing tradition of trashing automobiles in this city." I finished the root beer. "Did you check out that swell new piñata they've got at Mardi Gras World?"

"Ciro Garra, yeah. They just now got him back to the morgue." She sat back. "Who killed him, Mike?"

"My son." I set the empty can at my bedside.

"Ah." She took the can over to the wastebasket. "I guess we have a few things to talk about, huh?"

"I guess we do."

The aluminum can made a hard clang as it bounced around. I waited until she sat down again before speaking.

"His name—"

"It's okay," she said. "I'm familiar with the Noah Delacroix situation. And . . . his mother's, too."

I caught a quick glimpse of pain before she dismissed it.

"Kiplinger briefed you?"

"The director did." She looked away. "You're in a lot of trouble, Mike. I didn't know how bad it was until I got down here this morning. Somebody has video surveillance of you at last night's gun battle in Slidell. They've sent excerpts to the prosecutors on your case. We've put a lid on that—for now. Yet there's also a rumor it's been leaked to the tabloids."

"Do they have footage of Kadmos employees murdering Amrita Narayan?"

"No. But they have you shooting two armed guards and escaping with Emelio Barca." Her face darkened. "They also have video of you at Barca's lakefront estate over the past couple of days. With members of his family."

"With Sofia," I said. "Have you seen it?"

She nodded.

"Peggy, I'm not going to try to defend myself by pretending that everything I did was in support of my cover—"

"Don't." Suddenly there was real pleading in her voice. "I'm serious. Please don't finish that sentence."

We sat there for close to a minute, caught in one of those silences where every breath starts to feel like a step into a minefield. Finally, Peggy gave me what had to be the worst possible response under the circumstances: She smiled. That was my sign that the shields were up, that her feelings had been hidden away somewhere safe where I couldn't get to them.

"We'd better get back to work," she said.

"Peg—"

"I put some clothes for you on the next bed." She stood up again. "You can get a shower down the hall. Yoshi's here, and . . . we need to do a debrief. The sooner the better, for your sake."

"I'm ready whenever you are." I started to climb out of bed, my legs still rubbery beneath me. "Who's the subject of the investigation I'm debriefing on, Peg? Is it me, or Barca, or . . . is it Noah Delacroix?" I waited. "It's my son, isn't it?"

"Yes and no," she said. "Your son is wanted on a lot of charges. Homicide's by no means the worst of them. But we're not looking for anyone named Noah Delacroix."

I swallowed. "I don't understand. Why aren't you . . . ?"

"Because Noah Delacroix died last year," she said.

Then she left me to clean myself up.

THIRTY-EIGHT

The debrief turned out to be me, Peggy, and Yoshi. She informed me that I was being recorded, although I didn't see any devices: probably something Yoshi kept in his key ring. Peggy showed me a memo from the chief inspector, informing me that Special Agent Weaver had been authorized to make certain inquiries. I was instructed to cooperate but not to discuss any details of my initial meeting with the FBI director. Evidently the old man was keeping himself in the clear. Peggy duly avoided this topic. She also seemed to be skirting any direct questions about Sofia Barca.

Finally she showed me a photograph of the real Noah Delacroix.

The young man in the Colorado State yearbook was, by anyone's standards, a prime candidate for special agent training. He had done everything my son bragged about, and more. Valedictorian. Track and field. Debate team. He'd spent his summers doing internships in the U.S. attorney's office and volunteer work for a children's mission. He was well liked and well rounded. Those weren't the qualities that cut his life short at twenty-three. What got him killed—much more than his very slight resemblance to my Noah—was having the incredibly bad luck to share my son's first name. I could only guess that Noah thought it would be simpler if he didn't have to answer to anything but his own name: Occam's razor again.

"Noah Delacroix—the real Noah—applied to FBI Academy during his senior year of college." Peggy walked me through the relevant files, one by one. "Nobody's sure why he decided to do it, but he sailed right through the process. Then, at some point during his cross-country drive to Quantico, the original Noah Delacroix disappeared. The one who showed up for special agent training was your son."

I examined the two photographs, side by side. My son had copied

Delacroix's hairstyle, his clothes, even his confident smile. It was as if he'd somehow managed to absorb some—if not all—of the dead boy's spirit.

"Here's the truly Orwellian part," Yoshi said. "The database manager at Quantico told me he'd scanned in Delacroix's photo during the enrollment process—and then a virus got into the network, so he had to go in and clean up the files. After that, he could have sworn the picture of Noah had changed. This all happened inside maybe fifteen minutes. My guy was tired, he was cranky from dealing with the virus, and he figured he'd seen so many earnest young faces, he just got confused. He'd practically forgotten about it until I called."

"So what pointed you in Noah's direction? Was it—" Then I stopped. "Yoshi, you dick. You ratted me out on the card? Jesus, whatever happened to loyalty?"

Yoshi cringed. Peggy gave me a hanging judge's stare.

"Stop talking like a gangster," she said. "We already knew about the card. It was Delacroix's mother, of all people, who tipped us off. She'd gotten suspicious when her son stopped calling. His e-mails didn't sound like him, she said. Finally she hired somebody to trace the correspondence. It turns out they weren't coming from the FBI but from a law enforcement training facility in Roanoke, Virginia. Right down Highway Eighty-one from Quantico. Kadmos Security Solutions. She went looking for him." She handed me another photograph. "This is the person she found."

It was a blurry cell phone picture of Noah in black fatigues, crossing an outdoor firing range. He was half-turned to the camera, eyes narrow with suspicion. The weapon in his hands was a 5.56 assault rifle.

"How did he handle it when she confronted him?"

"Mrs. Delacroix said she felt pretty threatened. At first she thought this fake Noah might hurt her, but he finally just let her go. He told her it was national security, and he wasn't allowed to explain where her son was, but she should keep her mouth shut for his sake. Evidently he thought he'd scared her sufficiently to let her go." Peggy took the picture back. "Lucky for us, she decided not to keep her mouth shut. Otherwise, we might never have made the Kadmos connection."

And he didn't kill her, I realized. "Maybe we should recruit Mrs. Delacroix for special agent training. She took this photo?"

Peggy nodded. "She's also the one who found the mistake in his documentation. Her son's full name was Noah Faraday Delacroix. Your son's ID card reads Noah Francis. We're not really sure how he could have made a dumb mistake like that."

I was starting to think that I did. "Not to mention how we could have made a dumb mistake by missing it for so long?"

She nodded, taking the point.

"It was Kadmos that infiltrated him," she said. "They recruited him when he was seventeen and trained him in secret for two whole years before Noah Delacroix was murdered to give him a false identity."

"Then why did he need to steal the smart card from Burke?"

"He wasn't stealing the card. He was stealing it back. Burke got killed because he decided to go free-agent. He wanted to get himself and his wife out of trouble, so he boosted the card and tried to offer it to the highest bidder. Needless to say, Noah was determined to recover his favorite toy."

"Which means you got off lucky," Yoshi offered.

"No shit." I breathed out. "So were we one of the high bidders for the card?"

"That's above my pay grade," Peggy said. "My job has principally been to shine a light on the FBI-Kadmos connection. God knows how many other agents they've tried to slip past our barriers. Well . . . God and somebody else."

"Kiplinger," I said.

"That's right. And last night, Kiplinger sent you out to die." She retrieved the photographs from me. "On paper, he did everything he was supposed to. He dispatched the Hostage Rescue team to look for you somewhere along County Road Nineteen, just north of Slidell—exactly as you suggested—but first there was a fifteen-minute delay while they shut down the airport. We also believe Kadmos was listening in on the call, which gave them just enough time to finish the job."

"So why am I not dead?"

"We don't know," she said. "They must still need you."

I thought about it. "Have you spoken to Kiplinger?"

She shook her head. "Missing in action. The New Orleans SAC says that there's been rumors about Kiplinger and this Leah Varnado, but you're the first one who's actually managed to find proof. How'd you do it?"

She genuinely didn't seem to know, and I stopped just short of answering. From the corner of my eye, I saw Yoshi blush: no damn poker face.

"I bluffed." I gave an absent shrug. "I told Kiplinger I had the goods on him and Leah, and he spilled the beans. I made a blind guess and it turned out lucky."

"Good guess," she said.

"I'd seen them together already. You know how people act around each other when they've been . . ." *Hiding an office romance* died on my lips. "Hiding something."

She gave me a dull stare. "Is that how you plan to answer the question in a courtroom, Mike? Because that would be something to see."

"Why? What am I being tried for now?"

"Not my decision, thank God." She looked over at Yoshi. "Okay, I think we're done here. Let's get ready to roll."

Yoshi stood up and stretched. "Hey, do I have time to visit that sno-cone stand out front?"

"Only if you're quick," she said. "Five minutes and then we're driving off without you."

"No worries," he answered on his way to the door. "What flavors do you guys want?"

"We're good." She waited until the door closed before looking at me again.

"Peg, if you don't believe what I just told you—"

"It's something else," she said. "I don't want Yoshi having to corroborate what we're about to discuss."

"Which is?"

"Be honest, now. How does it feel, hearing the truth about your son?"

"Like crap," I said. "I keep telling myself that it wasn't my fault, but . . . I dunno. DNA. I can't help but feel guilty for the way he turned out."

"Enough that you want to try to save him from himself?"

I didn't answer.

"During your debrief," she said, "you told me that you didn't know Noah was taking you along to an execution this morning. What did you do when he pulled a gun?"

"Drew my weapon and ordered him to stand down."

"And when he refused?"

I exhaled.

"I couldn't shoot him, Peg. It was a deadly force situation, and I . . . couldn't make myself do it. That's all."

"A witness in Algiers saw the two of you fighting," she said. "Told the police that you threw the first punch."

"Yeah. Noah said something kind of shitty . . . about his mother. I can tell you what he said, or you can take my word that it's immaterial to the case."

"Don't worry about it." She leaned forward, less the interrogator now and more the dear friend. "But are you absolutely sure that's the only reason why you knocked him out?"

"What else would there be?"

"I can see the kid's hard-core. Still, it's like I said to you in Washington. You don't always plan things very well, but you improvise better than anyone I've ever seen. When Noah was lying on the ground, half-conscious . . . what was the very first thing you did?"

"Well, I disarmed him. Believe me, he was mad enough to . . ." However, I could see it wasn't washing with her. "Shit."

"Yeah." She flipped back through her notes. "Police questioned everyone on the ferry after it landed at the Canal Street Wharf. Among them was a young white male with a fresh bruise on his jaw. He wasn't carrying any identification. Wasn't carrying anything, in fact—except for a roll of cash and some loose change."

"What happened to him?"

"Miscommunication. By the time we got Noah's description, they'd already let him go." She closed her book. "The police probably would have been more likely to detain Noah if they'd found him carrying the nine-millimeter Beretta that killed Ciro Garra. Unfortunately, somebody threw it down a storm drain."

Another painful silence followed.

"You tell a board of inquiry that you couldn't bring yourself to shoot your son," she said in a low whisper. "They won't like it, but they'll probably let it go. You tell them that you concealed evidence of homicide after the fact . . ."

"I exceeded my limits," I said.

She nodded.

"I'm not your supervisor anymore, Yeager. I'm not the one who keeps the rain off your back so you can do your job. This time, I'm the person who has to inform the chief inspector if anyone broke the law. And I'll tell you something, this is much worse than Madrigal. Based solely on your actions, there's no one on earth who can prove that you didn't know your son was going to Algiers to carry out a mob execution."

"There's no one on earth who would care," I said. "Unless Ciro was somehow of value to the FBI. Are you telling me he really was working for our side?"

"No—but we think he might have been working for Kadmos. And Kadmos is the elephant we're trying to bag."

I took a moment to absorb that. "What makes you think so?"

She stood up.

"Come along and I'll show you," she said. "You know I'll stick up for you as much as I can. You did some good work these past few days—and the higher-ups are going to know about it, if I have anything to say. But you also crossed the line."

"And it doesn't equal out," I said. "Tell me this. Would anyone have gotten this far with the investigation if I hadn't crossed the line?"

Yoshi entered before she could answer, carrying three cherry sno-balls.

"What?" He looked between us. "What did I do?"

THIRTY-NINE

They called it the Taj Mahal of forensic science: In the immediate aftermath of Katrina, with initial death estimates at six thousand or more, the federal government had rushed construction of the St. Gabriel morgue at a cost of seventeen million dollars. It was state-of-the-art, the envy of coroners everywhere. It was also something of a white elephant. Turned out those initial estimates were somewhat exaggerated. After precisely ten weeks in operation, the morgue was already in the process of being boxed up in preparation for the next big catastrophe. A few of its facilities were still in working order, though, and that's where they took Ciro Garra.

"The swamps took a lot more bodies than people want to believe." The morgue attendant, a small and precise woman in her late thirties, spoke of terrible things in respectful tones as she ushered us into the cool room. "Perhaps as many as a thousand people got washed away as far as Bayou Sauvage. We may never get a complete casualty list for the storm."

Peggy nodded, quietly sympathetic. I drew Yoshi aside, letting the two women walk ahead of us.

"Peggy asked me how I knew about Kiplinger's affair." I spoke as casually as if we were discussing air-conditioning. "I just wanted you to know that—unlike you—I didn't throw my friend under the bus."

"I already threw me under the bus." He shrank away. "Sorry. I guess when it came down to it . . . I just couldn't lie to Peggy Weaver."

I started to tell him he was a dope—then smiled. "Don't sweat it, Yosh. I know how it feels."

"Yoshi." Peggy looked back from the swinging door. "Have you got that microprocessor thing?"

"Right here." Yoshi took the smart card from his pocket and slid it into a handheld computer. "Tremble, mortals, and behold your future."

No shit, I thought as I followed Yoshi into a room filled with the dead.

There is something weirdly compelling about a dead man's tattoos. *I loved this person,* they seem to say; *I served in this branch of the military; I thought this looked great one night in Cabo when I was bombed out of my mind.* It's as if you've been left one final message, a cryptic flourish as tantalizing as a suicide note.

Ciro Garra's tattoo was pale blue against his graying skin: a skull and a simple 316, identifying him as a member of the Honduran death squads. That was all that remained. Everything else—the memories of a deaf girl's silent screams, the tormented execution of Simon Burke—had been splattered like oatmeal against a plastic Mardi Gras float. At my son's hands.

The world was not a poorer place without Ciro. But I did wonder if he'd ever wanted to be anything more than a mindless executioner for his government. I did wonder about that.

"Here's how Noah tracked him down." Yoshi was showing us his handheld computer's screen. It displayed a map of the St. Gabriel morgue, a small red dot glowing at the center. "Right now, the microprocessor is accessing a network of transponders with RFID tags—"

"English," Peggy said.

"Radio frequency identification," Yoshi said. "Little microchip implants that contain information about the bearer. Medical data, personal history—sort of like you'd get for your pet. Or those annoying antitheft tags they put into your DVDs at Wal-Mart. Except that these are implanted in human skin."

"Where's the implant?" I examined the naked cadaver.

"Right here." The morgue attendant handed me a small plastic bag. It contained a clear tube, half the size of a grain of rice, filled with copper and silicon. "We took it from beneath the victim's right arm. If you look closer . . ."

She set the implant under a microscope. Peggy looked first, then motioned to me. A logo was etched into its side.

"KSS Technologies." I looked at Yoshi. "So this is part of the Kadmos employee package? A tracking implant?"

"This is what makes it so amazing," Yoshi said. "There's never been any such thing as a real live GPS tracker that lets the government find you at all times. The implants just can't broadcast a signal far enough. Fortunately, Kadmos seems to have solved the problem."

"Fortunately?" Peggy raised an eyebrow.

"Well . . . fortunately for those of us who geek out on this stuff. Maybe not so fortunate for humanity. Don't you want to know how they did it? I promise you, it's mind-blowing."

"Go ahead."

"Cell phones." Yoshi smiled. "All the implant has to do is get a signal out as far as the nearest cell phone—which, nowadays, is rarely more than a few feet away—and then it hops onto the signal like a flea jumping onto a rat's back. Then the rat climbs onto a ship, the ship sails over the ocean—"

"And everybody dies of the plague," I said. "So the smart card is able to track down . . . who? Just Kadmos employees?"

"Let's find out," he said. "I can surely find anyone in this building who's got a similar implant."

"Do it." She pulled me aside as Yoshi went to work. "Did Simon Burke have anything like this?"

"In his teeth—we think—and the smart card, of course."

"Hey, I got one." Yoshi's smile faded. "No, wait. It's gone. Boss, can you take a step back to where you were? I think it's piggybacking onto you."

"I'm not crazy about something in a dead guy's arm talking to my phone." Peggy stepped back uncertainly. "How's this?"

"Bing." Yoshi held his thumb up. "Bachelor Number Two will now take your questions."

"Where?" Peggy cast a cautious glance around.

Yoshi pointed to the steel drawer behind her.

"That's John Doe Thirty-three," the attendant said. "He's a floater. Nothing special about him. We pull a lot of guys like him out of the river when there's trouble—"

"Show me." I was already dreading the answer.

She pulled the drawer open. Even before I saw his face, I already knew him from the neck down. Not a mark on him anywhere—except for those ligature marks on his wrists.

"You won't believe this." Yoshi stared only at his display. "I can give you a name for this guy."

"So can I," I said with a nod to the corpse. "Charles Wesley Carmichael."

Deadman.

"Very little fluid in the lungs," the attendant was telling us as she completed her examination. "No bullet wounds. A few contusions, including a bruise on the right temporal area."

From where I pistol-whipped him with that 9 mm, I realized. Carmichael lay on his back, face slightly bloated. Was it fear I saw in his closed eyes? Resignation? As I stared down, I began to see something like determination—the grim certainty of a bullfighter who's finally met his match in the ring.

But that was probably wishful thinking. He was dead, that's all.

"So he likely didn't drown," the attendant continued in her sparse monotone. "Probably died before he hit the water."

"Could he have been killed by the blow to his head?"

Peggy homed in on the sound in my voice. "Why, Mike?"

"I questioned him the other night," I said. "Down by the river. I—"

"Excuse me," Peggy said to the attendant. "Could you and Yoshi maybe see about finding this gentleman's implant?"

The woman nodded uncertainly. Peggy yanked me into the hallway.

"Don't," she said. "I mean it. This is not a good time for you to self-destruct."

"Peg, I hit him. I didn't think I hit him hard, but—"

"You ask a medical examiner a question like 'Do you think the blow to the head might have killed him?' and you're only going to get one answer. 'Possibly.' Then you'll see what a prosecutor does with that word in front of a jury."

I looked down at my feet.

"I know what you're doing," she continued. "You're trying to make yourself a bigger target than Noah. Stop it. Your son isn't going to help us crack this case. You just might."

"It's good to know you're so interested in my welfare," I said, feeling the blood rush. "Is that why you told Amrita Narayan about my psychiatric treatment last year?"

"What?" She blinked. "Mike, I would never do that."

"I read some of her profile on me. It quotes you saying that you told me to see a shrink after Madrigal. You never spoke to her?"

Peggy shook her head. "I never even knew anything about her until after she died."

"So did you maybe tell Uri Vitale? Our ASAC in Philly? Yoshi?" I waited. "Your mom? That grumpy old news vendor on Arch Street? Anyone?"

She passed a hand over her forehead.

"Mike, I'm so sorry." She sighed painfully. "I did tell somebody about wanting you to see a psychiatrist."

"Who?"

"You," she said in a measured voice. "Jerk."

I watched Peggy walk away, feeling about ten inches tall.

"Hero homicide," I said to her back.

"What about it?"

"I don't know what in the profile is true and what's hearsay, but the bottom-line number is one-twenty-eight-point-oh-two. Supposedly that's me. Hero homicide. I kill so that I can get a medal for solving the case."

"Yeager, what are you talking about?"

"Let's say you were the one on the witness stand right now, and somebody asked the question, 'Do you believe that Mike Yeager is capable of cold-blooded murder?'"

"I'd refuse the question as calling for speculation."

I shook my head. "Ciro and Deadman had something in common besides a subcutaneous implant. They both knew something that could get Sofia Barca killed. As did Damien Corveau, for that matter. So let me finish asking the question. Do you believe that I'm capable of cold-blooded murder . . . if it means I get a chance to save someone I failed to protect a long time ago? In other words, solving a problem that I helped create?"

"Yes." She nodded grimly. "I do."

"As it happens, so do I." I released a long breath. "So maybe that profile wasn't total bullshit, after all."

The door opened. Yoshi motioned us both in.

"You found the implant?" Peggy asked, back in command.

"And then some," he said.

He turned the handheld so we could both see it. A sea of red dots floated over a map of New Orleans, slow as hornets.

"Turns out there's a lot of these little guys buzzing around," he said. "Maybe it's those Kadmos security teams?"

"Maybe some of them." I examined the map. "Not all."

"What's that big cluster right here?" Peggy pointed to where I was looking: a mass of red points, congregating just west of City Park.

"That's Holt Cemetery," I answered. "Potter's field."

FORTY

We lost because we underestimated the enemy, Noah told that room full of policemen. No doubt he was only playing a part, maintaining his cover as a bright young FBI agent, but what he was saying was true nonetheless. *If we're not prepared to match them—dollar for dollar, weapon for weapon, tactic for tactic—then we may as well admit we lost this war a long time ago.* And Leah Varnado had led the applause.

"How many of those implants are out there?" I asked Yoshi on the ride back to New Orleans. It was late afternoon, near about five o'clock: the green hour. I wondered if Barca was still honoring the ritual without his son to fill the cup.

"Couple hundred," he answered. "I'd say maybe half of them are still moving around, and the rest . . . aren't."

"What's your theory on this?" Peggy asked me from the driver's seat.

For some reason, I couldn't get that image of Barca's bug zapper out of my head.

"Pandora's Box," I said. "Kiplinger told me they rounded up most of the gangsters on the list but had to let them all go after sixty days. It's possible that Kadmos has found a way to bypass all that pesky due process. Obviously the criminals couldn't die while in policy custody . . ."

"So they got tagged and hunted down like animals?"

"The device is pretty tiny," Yoshi said. "It wouldn't be hard to disguise the implantation procedure as something else—a mandatory HIV test, for example. The subject might not even know they were carrying it around."

"With or without involving the police?"

"Without," I said. "Kadmos handles medical services for all law enforcement agencies in greater New Orleans. That's what Leah Varnado told me."

"Sounds like it's time to track down Leah Varnado," Peggy answered. "Have you got her description?"

"You met her in D.C.," I said. "She served you champagne."

"Holy shit." Peggy thought for a moment, then laughed. "The things some people will do for a government contract, huh?"

"You have no idea," I said.

In a city replete with bizarre place names—Desire, Tchoupitoulas, Terpsi-chore, and the ever popular Peniston Street—the unlikeliest of all has to be Bunny Friend Playground in the heart of St. Claude. It actually had been a playground before the storm, grass and everything. Now it was covered in gravel for the convenience of white FEMA trailers. They were lined up like cemetery crypts, row upon row, temporary housing for people whose homes had been lost in the flood. Several hundred ordinary citizens milled around the central courtyard, as well as a few local TV crews. The police were providing crowd control, supplemented by men in dull gray Kadmos uniforms.

REVIVE. REBUILD. RENEW. A team of orange-vested workers cheerfully hung the banner across Desire Street. The crowd was in a celebratory mood. Ten flavors of music played from a hundred boom boxes. Strings of chili-pepper lights glowed in the dusk. Smoke from the grills was keeping the mosquitoes down, filling the air with the aroma of burgers and hot sausage. It reminded me that I hadn't eaten much since my fast-food meal with Noah that morning.

Yoshi and I stood beside the Land Rover, waiting for Peggy to reemerge from a chartered bus parked down the street.

"So what were you guys doing all day today?" I asked Yoshi. "Before you got around to chasing me down, that is."

"A little tourist stuff, here and there."

"Yeah? You went to see the Quarter?"

"Went to see the Wizard." He gave an enigmatic smile. "Got to tag along with the senator's entourage for the big tour of the Kadmos facility in Michoud. You wouldn't believe the shit they've got down there. I felt like that kid in *Charlie and the Chocolate Factory* who steals Fizzy Lifting Drinks. What was his name?"

"Charlie," I said. "Did you get a T-shirt from the gift shop?"

"No, but I hacked into their network and downloaded a map of the building." He patted his handheld computer—then pointed to the bus door as it opened. "Okay, here she comes."

But it wasn't Peggy. I withdrew to the relative shelter of the Land Rover as Leah Varnado stepped down from the bus . . . followed by Martin Telford Campbell. They didn't look like they'd be hanging around for barbecue. He got into a waiting Town Car and drove away. Leah stayed behind, casting a determined eye around her. Then, as Peggy joined her on the street, she broke into the biggest toothpaste smile I'd seen since *Up with People*. Damned if Peggy didn't let Lili give her an air-kiss good-bye.

"How was that?" I asked Peggy as she returned to us.

"I need a shower," she said. "That's the woman who set you up in D.C.? You actually let her into your hotel room?"

"Who knew that Appalachian girls were so evil?" I asked. "Oh, right, you're from Tennessee. How'd you ladies get along?"

"She pretended not to recognize me. I pretended not to imagine her roasting on a spit." She shrugged. "The meeting served its purpose. She and her boss are now convinced that we've got our heads up our asses on the Narayan investigation."

"So where exactly are our heads?"

"Yours will be on the end of a pike if you don't get on that bus," she said. "Go on, Yeager. Do right and fear not."

"Are you crazy? Have you seen all those security guards? Those bastards will shoot me on sight."

"If I made it out alive, so can you. Relax. What could possibly go wrong in a place called Bunny Friend?"

"The nearest cross street is Desire." I walked away from the Land Rover. Leah was gone, but the Kadmos logo was everywhere I looked. I could feel eyes on my back as I stepped up into the bus.

"The mayor wants to speak first." A sandy-haired young man in shirt-sleeves and necktie was chatting with his counterpart, a middle-aged black woman. "We have to consider protocol."

"Protocol, hell," she answered. "This event wouldn't even be happening if it was up to— May I help you?"

Both of them turned to me.

"Who are you here to see?" the young man asked.

"My name is Yeager," I said. "I'm—"

"Where's security?" She looked around. "Weren't we supposed to have people on perimeter, protecting us from—"

"Mike." A deep voice behind me.

Christ, no, I thought as I turned to face him. *Peggy Jean, if I live through this, I will dedicate my life to your misery.*

The aides instantly straightened up as Senator James Seaweather of Pennsylvania strode toward me down the aisle. And I thought he looked big on television: In that confined space, the man was like some kind of optical illusion.

"Mike." He clasped my hand in both of his. "How have you been, Mike? So good to see you again."

"Jim." I gave him two brisk shakes. "Jim, we've actually never met."

He laughed, a subwoofer roar that shook the windows. "You'll forgive me," he said. "So many people claim to know me, I figure it's best to err on the side of caution." He released me, gesturing to his aides. "It's all right. Mike and I are going to talk alone for a few minutes."

The young man stood up. "Senator, the mayor—"

"Yes, yes. Let the mayor enjoy a brief moment in the sun, that's fine. Hopefully the crowd will have used up all its rotten tomatoes before I get to the podium."

He led me into his private compartment at the back of the bus. Two plates of pork barbecue were waiting for us.

"I understand you're a root beer man." He produced two cans of Barq's from the mini fridge. "Mind if I join you?"

"Suit yourself," I said. "I actually don't drink root beer anymore."

"Yeah? Since when?"

"Since you opened that refrigerator and offered me one." I pointed to the food. "On the other hand, I wouldn't mind having a dig at that pig."

"My sentiments exactly." He smiled. "Let's not bother with silverware, if you don't mind. Some things just beg to be eaten with a man's own hands."

"No argument there."

For five minutes we concentrated on our food. I sensed that I was being bribed like a dog getting a chew-toy. If I had any dignity left, I would have rejected his hospitality on principle. But a guy has to stay alive.

"Peggy tells me you're a good person," he said as we cleaned our plates. "She cares about you, Mike. You ought to know that. God knows we've all fallen in love with her over the past few months. My kids, especially."

"So you wanna arm-wrestle for her?" I waited. "Why are we even talking, Senator? I didn't vote for you."

He nodded, glancing soberly at the locked door behind us.

"I just got off the phone with the FBI director." He reined in his baritone voice. "He's given me permission to read you in on the situation with Kadmos and the Roanoke Group. Do you mind if we proceed?"

"Do you routinely sweep this room for bugs?"

"Twice a day," he said, "and the bus is shielded against remote listening devices. If you think Kadmos is nosy, you should see what my opponents in the last election were up to."

"So what am I being read in on? Your latest attack ads?"

"Levin-Marcato," he said. "We lost in committee this morning. We don't have the votes to defeat it on the floor, and the president's already promised to sign. So—barring a miracle—it will soon become the law of the land."

"Which is why you're down here in the city of miracles."

He nodded. "The bill is enormously popular down here. Which makes me enormously *un*popular. A few of my colleagues are still on the fence, though, and the media's watching. Which is why I'm about to stand up in front of that crowd of people and tell them why they should refuse to accept six billion dollars. Think I've got a chance?"

"I think you may as well cancel Christmas." I picked at a spare rib. "I mean, why should they refuse? I know there's some constitutional issues . . ."

"You don't know the half of it," he said. "Yes, they're federalizing New Orleans, and that's against states' rights. Quite frankly, I've never been much of a fan of states' rights myself. And yes, Martin Campbell is matching federal funds to the tune of three billion dollars, and he's probably expecting some nice fat government contracts in return. I'd say he's entitled. On paper, the bill is . . . not perfect, but no worse than some others we've passed lately."

"So what's the real beef?"

"The real beef is the part that isn't on paper," he said.

"Which is?"

"There's a secret provision in the bill," he said. "Proposed by Martin Campbell, and agreed to by Senator Levin of Connecticut and Senator Marcato of Texas. Call it a gentlemen's understanding. It's been blocked from public debate on grounds of national security. I'm a committee chairman, and I'm not even allowed to allude to its existence during my own hearings. Basically, it confers immunity from prosecution on any Kadmos employee or its subcontractors and licensees, for any actions taken in the line of duty—even if such acts were committed before the law took effect. Do you see the implications of this?"

"Kind of a get-out-of-jail-free card."

"More like a never-go-to-jail-at-all card. Currently, if a New Orleans cop shoots an unarmed man without cause, he can be indicted for excessive force, wrongful death—even first-degree murder. His family can sue the city for damages. But under Levin-Marcato, if a Kadmos employee kills someone in cold blood . . ."

"No one can touch him." I thought of Amrita Narayan, lying dead on the tracks. "Why is this a matter of national security?"

"It's been standard policy for contractors in Iraq ever since the War on Terror began. We're just bringing it home, that's all." The senator shook his head. "It gets scarier. Depending on how you interpret the law, it actually becomes a felony for any government employee to disclose the identity of any Kadmos employee so accused . . . or even to acknowledge that the crime occurred at all. You, me, the cop down the street—we're all under a gag order. And Kadmos will essentially be the law of the land in greater New Orleans."

I pushed my plate away, my appetite suddenly gone.

"I got into this job to serve the public trust." He leaned toward me. "Something tells me you did, too. But that's not the way things are going in this country. Bit by bit, that trust is being outsourced for private gain. Our health care's in the hands of HMOs that refuse bone marrow transplants for children because it would affect the stock price. Mercenary armies are fighting our wars for us, for profit. We're paying foreign countries to torture our enemies—everything's open for business. Now here comes Levin-Marcato. It's not the United States I pledged to serve. If it keeps up like this, we may as well change the name of the country."

"To what?"

"El Dorado," he said. "Do you want to know what's even more alarming? I seriously doubt that New Orleans will be rebuilt at all. Why should they spend the money? You don't need a city to manage oil platforms or shipping canals, and that's where the real profit is. Oh, I'm sure Campbell will put up a few showcase homes. They'll look great on television. He's even dropped hints that he could do a better job with the levees and floodgates than the Corps of Engineers. But you don't really need people here, except to work in the bars and casinos. Everyone else can be more efficiently relocated to Houston or parts unknown. And when there's nothing left to bleed dry—no wetlands or neighborhoods, just a theme park surrounded by the world's biggest salt marsh—they'll abandon what's left to the next hurricane and move their medicine show right down the line."

"You really think that's going to work?"

"Oh, I think it'll work real well. It'll probably become a model for the entire nation. And guess who ponies up the money for that?" He moved his index finger back and forth between us. "It's like asking a condemned man to provide his own rope."

I sat back.

"So what's your take on this, Mike?"

"Honestly, Senator? My take is that you're the head of the sixth richest family in Pennsylvania. Nothing against that, but I don't think you've got a clue about what's going on with people down here."

He gave me a stern look. "When I was a kid in Pittsburgh, we weren't the sixth richest family on the *block*—but that's neither here nor there. This man, Martin Campbell, is a criminal. He has friends in high places, his operations are vital to homeland security—and he needs to go to jail. If you care about the people of New Orleans, you'll help me put him there. This city deserves more than a second chance. It deserves justice."

I tore open a moist towelette and wiped my fingers.

"Last night," I said, "a woman named Amrita Narayan was under my protection. She said she had to live so that she could tell you something in person."

"Tell me something?"

"She said that somebody was going to die. Maybe you, maybe me. I wish I could say more. The fact is, last night I failed to protect her. She's dead. Where's her justice?"

"I can't answer that for you," he said gravely. "A lot of people are dying now, and none of them are getting justice. Pandora's Box is a coffin. If you and Agent Weaver are right, these men are being murdered so that Kadmos can claim victory in the war on crime. The victims are scum of the earth, so nobody cares. On the other hand . . . maybe some of them aren't scum. Maybe a few innocent people are being executed without trials or lawyers. Maybe we're next. Where's the justice for anyone, if not for them?"

I thought about that for a moment. *What the hell,* I decided, then cracked the root beer open.

"I knew one of them." I took a drink. "Charles Carmichael. He was all right. He was a soldier—fought for his country. Lived through the Superdome. His daughter's name is Bessie. Her mother's got a drug problem. Bessie likes red licorice, and she watches the cartoon show with the blue dog."

"*Blue's Clues*. My youngest girl likes it, too." He smiled a little. "My daughter's name is Celeste, by the way. I know you helped save her life last April. And . . . I never thanked you for that, did I?"

"We don't take bows in the FBI," I said. "I appreciate the food, Senator. Good luck with the miracle."

"Mike." He waited for me to meet his eyes. "If you could do one thing to help Bessie . . . what would it be?"

"I guess I'd make sure she didn't have to grow up in the life she got stuck with," I said. "The one you're describing doesn't sound too good, either. I guess I'd like to see her do a little better, if she can."

"Then you'll help me."

"You don't have to convince me to help you." I put my hand on the door. "As somebody recently reminded me, it's my job to support the Constitution."

Then we nodded to each other—a mark of respect—and that was dinner.

FORTY-ONE

I left the bus just in time to catch the end of the mayor's speech. There was plenty of applause—but, typically for New Orleans, the real show was in the crowd. The MAX School marching band—melded from the remnants of three local high schools—played a raucous drumline, spiced with occasional trumpet riffs on "Jazz Police." So many schools had been forced to close down, and so many children had been dispersed since the storm. Still and all, the MAX band kept burning on, and everyone around me seemed to treat it as reason enough to celebrate. Sofia, I thought, would have loved to hear it.

Sofia. Where was she? I wondered with a sudden panic. And what the hell was I doing at a cookout, when she might be in danger of her life?

Stay the hell away from me and my mother. Noah's last words to me, cold as a rusted knife. *If you try to come back again, I'll kill you.*

I jumped half out of my skin when Yoshi tapped me on the back. Somehow he'd managed to acquire a string of Mardi Gras beads.

"Nice," I shouted over the music.

"Yeah. Didn't even have to take my shirt off to get them. How'd it go with Senator Sewerweather?"

"He was using me to try out some new campaign material, I think. Where's Peggy? I need to get out of here."

He pointed to the podium. Peggy was in the process of receiving a bottled water from Seaweather. As he handed it to her, she said something into his ear. He nodded, leaning closer to listen. Then he put a hand on her shoulder, covering her completely.

"What's the matter?" Yoshi asked.

"Just tell her I had to go," I said.

"Don't you need a ride back to wherever—?"

Then the mayor stepped back, and a roar swept through the crowd as Senator James Seaweather took the stage.

God knows it wasn't all cheering. There was plenty of booing mixed in, and a lot more people just getting poleax drunk. Even so, I couldn't help but notice how the senator's presence seemed to focus the crowd. It was as if the electricity had finally come back on after a long darkness.

"Thank you!" The senator clasped his hands together, a gesture that was somewhere between praying hands and a boxing champ's moment of triumph. "Thank you so much, New Orleans. God bless you!"

He pretended to call for silence, but his smile kept egging them on. Why did Peggy make me sit down with that grinning popinjay? Was it some new form of punishment, or . . .

Something's wrong.

I was smelling something in the air. A burning odor. Not barbecue smoke, or cigarettes, or even pot—though God knows there had to be enough of all three to get one mother of a contact high. It was chemical, irritatingly familiar.

"Thank you." The senator raised his hands as the applause finally faded. "I want to thank the mayor, and all of you, for your wonderful hospitality this evening. There's so much to rejoice in . . . and so many important things to discuss . . ."

I looked around. Cops were pacing among the spectators, bored but alert. Some of them chatted with the Kadmos guys like old buddies. A trumpet player in the band was cleaning out her spit valve. A father was helping his son climb to the top of a stepladder. Whatever I'd smelled (fireworks? creosote? motor oil?) had faded, leaving a nagging ghost-odor in my mind.

Peggy was a few yards away from me, talking into her cell phone. I briefly caught her eye, and she motioned me toward her, her eyes filled with concern. I waded through the crowd.

"Before we begin that discussion," the senator said, "I want to tell a story from the Bible that I learned long ago, as a boy in the Hill District of Pittsburgh. It's a story of father Abraham and his God."

"Hey, bubba, slow down." A copper-skinned man in a black cowboy hat stopped me from knocking his drink out of his hand.

"Sorry."

He chuckled. "Cheer up, son. Maybe it won't happen."

I looked around. Peggy was gone.

"The Lord told Abraham that he would destroy the city of Sodom with fire." Seaweather's voice resonated in the summer air. "A lot of people back then must have thought that Sodom had it coming . . . just like a few ignorant folks seem to think New Orleans had it coming last year."

A chorus of boos. He waited for them to subside.

"Fortunately, Abraham was not so coldhearted as that. He could have shrugged his shoulders and said, 'Thy will be done, Lord.' But he didn't. Abraham pleaded for the lives of the innocent, those who were still living God's word. 'That be far from thee to do after this manner,' he said to his Lord, 'to slay the righteous with the wicked . . . ' "

Peggy Jean, where are you? Then I saw her again, yards away. I rushed straight to her. As our eyes met, we both shared a single terror. I knew what it was that I'd smelled on the air a moment before.

The senator had reached a crescendo. "And Abraham said to God, 'Shall not the judge of all the earth do right?' "

"C-4 compound!" I yelled. "Peg—"

"We have to get everyone out of here," she said.

A moment later, a ball of flame tore the crowd apart.

The explosion happened in an instant. First the ground trembled. Then it broke beneath my feet, and Peggy and I were falling. The light was intense, scorching. Something screamed past my ear, trailing smoke.

The next thing I was aware of was a burning in my eyes. Dust. Cordite. That acrid, oily stench of plastic explosive, foul and poisonous. I could taste it in my mouth.

I had fallen shielding Peggy. Her heart was racing.

"Are you okay?" I coughed. "Can you move?"

She nodded to me.

As I pulled myself up, I began to see what the bomb had done. The senator was still on the stage, staring wildly. His podium fell sideways as his bodyguards pulled him away. People were running for their lives in all directions. Many others lay where they fell, struggling to move. Some weren't moving at all. A white plastic sousaphone lay broken on its side, splattered with blood. Fragments of metal and ball bearings lay everywhere. And, oh my God, blood.

I tripped over something in my way. A human arm, severed at the shoulder. Gold on the third finger: a wedding ring.

"Mike." Peggy stumbled toward me, recovering herself. "Come on, we have to call in the EMTs. People are—"

Then she fell silent. We could hear it on the wind from all directions. Screaming.

FORTY-TWO

" 'God gave Noah the rainbow sign,' " I muttered, leaning on the edge of an overturned park bench. It had been almost two hours since the bomb, and I still couldn't get that damned song out of my mind.

"What's that?" Peggy asked me.

"Something Amrita sang to me just before she died. 'God gave Noah the rainbow sign . . . ' "

" 'No more flood but the fire next time.' It's just the blues, Mike." She put a hand on my shoulder. "Come on. They're waiting for us."

I looked at the miniature wasteland the bomb had made. EMTs had taken the most seriously wounded to Bywater Hospital—and the dead to the county morgue—but there were still so many left behind, waiting for attention. A woman held a bandage to her bleeding head, crying her eyes out while an EMT knelt in front of her. Smoke rose from the stepladder I'd seen a father set up for his child. A FEMA trailer was torn open, thrown onto its side like a broken toy.

Most of the other dignitaries were long gone, but the senator had refused to evacuate as long as there were still wounded people on-site. So we held our situation conference inside the sacristy of a church down the street. A portrait of Jesus smiled down on our undertakings, opening his sacred heart to all.

"What's the latest word?" the senator asked as we both sat down.

"Six dead," Peggy told him. "At least thirty wounded, probably more. Expect that number to rise."

"We're not doing any good sitting here," one of his aides said. "I think we need to make a statement."

"The mayor's already beaten us to it," another replied. "And the governor. Probably for the best. We're guests here—and not entirely welcome. One reporter actually asked the mayor if our coming here was what triggered the violence. So now that's in the atmosphere."

"Sir, you need to decide," the first one said. "Do we stand out in front of this, or not?"

The senator thought a moment before responding. "I'd like to visit the hospital as soon as possible."

His aides shifted nervously.

Peggy leaned in. "Sir, that just isn't feasible. We really shouldn't be here anymore. We're taking up police and security resources that are badly needed elsewhere. Even the mayor has withdrawn to City Hall."

"If we go to the hospital," one aide suggested, "it could send a message that we're involved in the welfare of New Orleans."

"Or make it look like we're grandstanding," the other replied.

"What's it going to look like if we turn tail and run?" The senator fumed. "Enough about the spin, guys. I don't want to 'send a message.' I'd actually like to do something."

"Boss, we're getting killed in the media right now. Every moment we sit here at the bomb site digs our grave—"

"People. Died. Here." Seaweather cooled a little. "Agent Weaver, what do we know about the bomb?"

"Low-yield explosive," Peggy said. "Ball bearings and fragmentation metal were packed in to create shrapnel. One of the trailers absorbed some of the impact, so the damage was less than it might have been. Also, the C-4 explosive has a chemical marker that can tell us where it was manufactured. NOPD Fifth District is sending a forensic team over to recover samples."

"Any idea who planted the bomb?"

Peggy gave me a rapid look before answering.

"No, sir. However, your security detail believes that it was planted some hours in advance of your arrival."

"But we only announced the rally this morning," one of the aides said. "I personally watched them sweep the site. With bomb-sniffing dogs. How could this happen?"

"Senator?" Peggy gave him a meaningful look.

"Folks, can we have the room for a moment?" he asked.

After a moment's hesitation, the aides left. Then it was just him, Peggy, and me.

"One of the bodies we recovered belonged to a policeman inside the trailer," Peggy said. "We don't think he was killed by the explosion. Our theory is that he was murdered with a blunt object and then left near the bomb to cover the unsub's tracks."

"I see." He mulled it over. "It's Kadmos, isn't it?"

"It's too soon to tell," she said. "You should know that we found a second bomb. It was meant to go off after the first one, but the police dogs sniffed it out just in time."

"Where was it?"

"Under the bus," she said. "The bombers must have known that your security detail's first move would be to take you there for safety. It's very likely that second blast would have killed you."

"Um." He shot a nervous look between us. "I'm assuming this is no longer a problem."

"The New Orleans bomb squad deactivated it," she said, "but no, I don't think you should be using the bus. I don't think you should be in New Orleans. In my opinion, the trip's over."

"Peggy, we've been through this. If I leave now, it's going to look like I got chased out of town. Not only does it defeat my whole purpose in coming here, but it defeats . . . everything." He looked at me. "Mike, what do you think?"

"I think you're wrong," I told him. "It wasn't Kadmos. It was Barca."

They both watched me intently.

"Campbell can't afford to take a shot at you," I continued. "You're his most public opponent, and right now you've got a big fat spotlight trained on him. If there's a marker in the C-4, then it's there because we're meant to find out where it came from, and chase off in the wrong direction. Trust me. Martin Campbell has ways of killing you that wouldn't leave such an obvious trace."

"No doubt." The senator considered it. "But why Barca?"

"He seems to have forged a new partnership with Campbell—the terms of which were loosely described to me as 'share and share alike.' Even if I didn't know that, I'd still say it was him. What happened today was exactly Barca's style—big, loud, and nasty. And you are right about one thing. If you leave now, it will make you look like a coward. I'm starting to think that was the whole point of the attack."

"Agent Yeager," Peggy said.

"It's all right," he said. "How so?"

"People think you're the Grinch who stole Levin-Marcato. Now you're also a bomb magnet. Even the ones in this town who support you will be afraid to come within a mile of you. So my belief is that the whole plan was designed to chase you out of town, force you into hiding. Shut you up." I paused. "Killing you might just be the backup plan."

"And this is what you think Barca would do."

"It's exactly what he did to me and Art Kiplinger twenty years ago. He couldn't stop the indictments against him—but he sure as hell kept either one of us from taking the stand. Believe it. The day Emelio Barca planted that bomb in our Chinese takeout was the day we started to lose the fight. Because he succeeded in making us afraid of our own shadows."

He seemed to appreciate that. "What do you think I should do instead?"

"Don't hide," I said. "Don't be a Katrina tourist on a bus, they get enough of those already. Get to know these people. And for God's sake, stop allowing vague euphemisms like 'national security' to decide what you can and cannot say in the public interest. You're a leader, Senator. Lead."

Senator Seaweather fell silent, seeming to disappear into his thoughts. Then his phone rang. He listened to the caller for a moment, then hit the mute button.

"It's Marty Campbell," he said. "Calling to express his great relief that I wasn't killed today."

"I'll see myself out." I stood up. "If you want to rattle his cage, ask Campbell how he likes his scotch."

"His scotch?"

"Yeah. Ask him what he's got against putting a little water into a glass of single malt." I opened the door. "Excuse me."

I went out into the night. Emergency lights had been set up around the playground to assist the forensics team in their search for evidence. Yoshi wasn't around; I vaguely remembered Peggy sending him back to the field office. Too bad, I thought. I would have liked a chance to say good-bye.

"Mike." Peggy followed me down the block. "Why did you do that?"

"Jimmy's a big boy. He can handle a little straight talk."

"You didn't give him straight talk, you called him out. You told him he'd be a sissy if he didn't stand up and spread his arms in front of his enemies. That's not our job."

"No. Our job is to catch bad guys. Which is why you came down here, isn't it? To lead the team into battle? You're the war chief, Agent Weaver. That's your job, not mine."

She looked at me uncertainly. "Why are you saying that?"

"Because 'chieftess' sounds funny. Tell the truth, Peg. Why does an internal investigation on Kadmos require you to personally body-block an attempt on the senator's life? You're not Secret Service. Were you ordered to protect him—or is that just what you do for love?"

She rolled her eyes. "Mike, come on."

"Hey, it's okay. It's obvious that Seaweather likes you, and he should. You're amazing. You're twice the agent I ever was." I paused. "Feel free to disagree with me on that."

"Actually, I was kind of enjoying it." She gave me a tense smile. "You're good at what you do. You don't have to be jealous of me."

"I'm not. I'm jealous of him. He's an action figure. Seaweather's gonna save America's soul, and I hate him for it. The fact that you like him just ices the cake."

"Now you're being childish."

"I'm not blind to the way things work. You rescued his daughter, he gets you promoted, and now—hell, I saw him grab you on his way up to the stage. It's like he was . . . claiming you."

Her eyes darkened. "You've got some nerve, you know? You keep forgetting I've seen pictures of you kissing that Barca woman. That I've—" Her voice fell. The anger traveled across her face, burning white. Then, just as suddenly, it faded. And she actually laughed.

"Did I accidentally say something funny?"

"No," she said. "Does this make it easier?"

"Make what easier?"

"If you think I've found somebody else," she said, "is it easier to go back to her?"

My mouth opened. Nothing came out.

"Oh, boy." Peggy sighed. "And you're actually suggesting that I rescued his daughter so I could get close to him? 'Hey, Jim, the kid's fine, let's jump in the sack'? You don't think that badly of me." She gave me a daring smile. "You made me cry in that D.C. bar, you bastard. I'm not doing it again."

"I didn't want you to cry."

"No. You wanted me to tell you to go to hell." She shook her head. "Won't work, Yeager."

"It's okay," I said. "I'm already going there anyway."

Then the smile failed her.

"I was going to marry you," she said. "I would have stood before God and claimed you for my own. Now you're gone . . . and I don't have a damn thing to put in your place. So if this woman Sofia is the real reason you left me . . . she'd better be worth it. Or so help me, I will beat you up."

"I don't know," I said. "But Leah—God rot her—was right about you and me. The marriage just wasn't going to last. And it would have been my fault. There's always been this door that Sofia's had into my heart. Even when I thought she was dead, it never closed. I thought that door didn't matter, except to me. Then I found out she was still alive—and I did what I thought I had to do. Or what I gave myself permission to do. Apparently there's a difference."

We looked at each other for a long time: old friends, old lovers, old comrades.

"What *are* you going to do?" she finally asked.

"I have to get Sofia out of there," I said. "Before you start raining down thunderbolts."

"Yeah? When am I going to do that?"

"When they try again to kill the senator. It's gonna happen, sure as my people invented blitzkrieg."

"Bad things happen when Germans and Italians get together," she said. "My father always warned me about that."

"Sorry I never got to meet him," I said. "What do you think he'd have to say to me right now?"

"He'd tell you to go to hell," she answered plainly. "There's something else I've been wanting to say to you, ever since Washington. I couldn't until now."

I nodded. "You mean, when you told me not to take the assignment here, but you couldn't tell me why? Because Kiplinger was already on your watch list, and you were bound by your oath of confidentiality?"

"That would be it."

"Don't sweat it, okay? Seriously. At least somebody in the family knows how to follow rules. That's why you're the war chief."

She didn't answer. The light of command was in her eyes.

"I'm not your kind of hunter, Peg. I can't just 'do my job.' And I can't keep making you wait for me to change. Please don't hate me for it."

"I don't hate you, Mike. You know I still—" She sighed. "That door you were talking about. Is it still open?"

"It's not closed," I said.

"Okay." She nodded, determined. "We can't go back to where we were,

Mike. Not ever. I don't hate you for it. But the minute you left me to find her . . . that's when it ended for us."

There seemed to be nothing more to discuss. One of the senator's aides was standing in the church doorway.

"He's off the phone," the aide said to Peggy. "He wants to see you."

"We'll be right there," she answered.

The aide shook her head. "Just you."

The door closed.

"Mike—"

"See you when the lightning strikes," I told her.

Then I kissed her good-bye and walked away.

FORTY-THREE

"What do you want?" An elderly Korean man wandered toward me across his auto yard. "Closed. Night time. Go home."

"I need to buy a car." I nodded toward the selection of prime junkers. "How much?"

"Nothing. I don't sell cars at night." He reached out to quiet the Rhodesian ridgeback that had been barking its head off ever since I opened the gate. "You got cash?"

I held up the money from my wallet. I had the grand Barca gave me for delivering Sofia, plus Grady's five hundred in get-acquainted money. Besides that, I still needed to buy a gun, and it would probably cost more than the car.

"Twelve hundred," I said. "That's fair."

He made a dismissive gesture and turned away.

"Okay, fifteen. But I want something good for my money."

He grinned. "We don't get good here. We get shit. Better go someplace else."

CLEAN NORTHERN CARS, read the sign over his shop: which they probably had been, when that sign was painted back in the 1950s. I pointed at a two-toned red Ford pickup that looked like it might have soaked up a little less flood water than the others. "How about this one?"

"Two thousand."

Then the dog started barking again.

"Oh, brother." I turned in the direction of the noise and saw Yoshi Hiraka coming toward me. He carried a gym bag over his shoulder. His right wrist was in a brace. "Hey, what happened to your beads?"

"They clashed with my bandage," Yoshi said. "How's the negotiation going?"

"Great for him. We started at nothing and now we're at two grand."

"Hey. Hey. You talk to me, okay?" The auto dealer excitedly grabbed Yoshi by the sleeve. *"Hangukmal hal jul ani?"*

"Hab SoSlI' Quch!" Yoshi gave him a quizzical smile.

A furious exchange of verbiage followed. The auto dealer repeatedly pressed his point. Yoshi nodded frequently, smiled a couple of times, and made occasional comments in a guttural voice. At last they shook hands like old friends.

"How much have you got?" Yoshi asked me.

"Fifteen hundred," I said.

"Fifteen hundred, sure." The dealer held out his hand.

I gave him the money. He counted it twice, then fished a set of keys out of his pocket.

"Title's in the glove box, okay? So get the hell out of my yard." He grinned at Yoshi, making a thumbs-up sign and cackling like a madman as he left.

"What the hell were you guys talking about?"

"Beats me. I don't speak Korean." He shrugged. "Don't even speak much Japanese, come to think of it."

"Well then, what—"

"And Shoreh thinks *Star Trek* conventions are a waste of money." Yoshi smiled. "He asked me questions in Korean, I answered in Klingon. *'Hab SoSlI' Quch'* means 'your mother has a smooth forehead.' Very big insult." He handed me the gym bag. "Anyhow, enjoy the ride to wherever you're going."

"Who's this from? Peggy?"

"Nope," he said in a tone that implied otherwise. *"Heghlu'meH QaQ jaj-vam*, Mike. And I hope for your sake that isn't true."

"Which means?"

"Today is a good day to die," he replied.

As I examined the gym bag's contents, I quickly understood why Yoshi wanted to give Peggy a little plausible deniability. With my status still listed as TERMINATED, even the least harmful item in the bag was officially off-limits to me. There was a thermoplastic vest: it wouldn't stop an armor-piercing round, but it would take care of most everything else in my way. I also found a brand-new SIG SAUER 226—better than the one I'd lost fighting Deadman—with a spare ammunition clip. As well as Yoshi's handheld computer, still containing the smart-card chip.

Then I found what she'd left at the bottom of the bag.

FEDERAL BUREAU OF INVESTIGATION. The raised letters shone gold on a shield crested by the American eagle. U.S. framed a blindfolded woman, holding her sword and scales above the words DEPARTMENT OF JUSTICE. My hand trembled as I took hold of it. How on earth had Peggy gotten it back? Still, there it was.

My FBI badge.

The computer showed several red lights glowing on the grounds of the Bonangela Marina. One of them corresponded to a name I recognized: Owens, M. T., the fake Hostage Rescue agent who threw that stun grenade. I watched his red dot circling back and forth on the map, as though walking sentry duty.

The other icons were apparently members of Owens's team. I remembered Barca telling me that they'd raided his home at the same time we were ambushed in Slidell. So what were they still doing on the property?

There was one more light that kept flickering in and out. The computer registered it as UNKNOWN. From what I could tell, it belonged to someone inside the house.

The Ford pickup rattled up the Causeway like an old man trying to reach the toilet, never once getting past 45 mph. All that kept it from sliding into the lake was a load of strategically placed cinder blocks in the bed. Beyond doubt, it was the worst getaway vehicle I'd ever driven. On the other hand, it had one virtue: Nobody would be looking for it.

It was near ten o'clock when I finally arrived in Mandeville. I stowed the truck in an abandoned gas station that adjoined Barca's property, put the vest on beneath my shirt, then set off into the cypress woods. I ignored the mud in my shoes and concentrated on trying to remember if alligators' eyes glowed when you shone a flashlight on them.

The lights were out at the Bonange place, and I soon found signs of a recent stealth attack. Several shell casings from a HK-911 sniper rifle lay half-buried in the sand: definitely not a law enforcement weapon of choice. I didn't see tire tracks, so the invasion must have come from the water. A few windows had neat little bullet holes in them. Not too many .38 shells on the ground, though. Whatever happened to Barca's men must have been over before they had time to defend themselves.

I scoped a quick look at the handheld, then froze in the tall brush. If the computer was right, one of the attackers was standing less than ten feet behind me.

I pivoted back to see him, black against the night sky: a tall sentry, leaning on a wooden piling, aiming his rifle at the deck. His back was to the water, so there was no way to sneak up on him from behind. If I took off running, I'd likely be dead before I got twenty yards.

I picked up a stone and slung it past him. It landed on the sand, making barely a sound. He didn't react. *To hell with it.* I flicked the slide lock of my 226 and punched a single round right between his eyes. He spun sideways, then went down into the water as the report echoed loudly around the lakefront. Then silence.

That was just too easy, I thought. No return fire, no comrades scrambling to check out the noise. No anything. I pulled myself out of hiding and high-crawled to the end of the boardwalk. My guy was bobbing in the water, faceup. He had an entrance wound in his forehead, but no blood came out. And no wonder. That big chest wound must have done the job hours ago. *Congratulations, Yeager. You just murdered a dead man in cold blood.*

Then I found Owens.

The handheld display showed him moving in circles—and that he was definitely doing. He hung from the branch of a river oak, his neck broken by a length of plastic cord. Swaying gently in the night breeze.

What went on here? There was one red dot on the display that was still moving: the unknown soldier inside the house. Heading slowly but steadily in my direction.

I circled around to the kitchen entrance, then flung the door open and aimed straight ahead. Nobody there. Yet the handheld display was telling me that someone was right in the room with me. Upstairs? There was no room above the winter kitchen, and I'd already scoped out the roof. So where . . . ?

The basement. Christ, I wasn't looking forward to going down there. Probably half-flooded, clogged with tree roots and God knew what else. Then again, it wouldn't be the world's greatest sniper's nest, either. Whoever was confined in the basement wasn't there by choice. It might even be Sofia.

The only problem was finding a way in. The basement had been constructed for hiding slaves, so naturally the door had to be well hidden. Then I recalled what Yoshi had said about the implant chips feeding on cell phone signals. If I was getting a read, then whoever was down there must still have a way of talking to me. Assuming that I had their number.

The more I thought about it, the more certain I was that I did have his number.

I dialed. Listened. Then I heard it ringing, muffled beneath my feet. I had to call twice before I got an answer.

"Mike?" A bloodless voice, faint.

"Art, I'm here. I'm in the house. Are you okay?"

"I can't . . . sorry, I can . . ." A muffled noise. "The phone keeps slipping away. Can you hear me?"

"Yeah. You've got to tell me where the basement door is."

"I think it was through . . . the pantry, a bedroom. Something like that." Silence. "I'm kind of messed up."

I was already heading for Sofia's room off the kitchen. "I'll get you out of here. But you've gotta answer me truthfully or I'll blow a hole in you. Are you armed?"

"No," he said with what sounded like a dry laugh. "Got a few knives with me, but . . . don't worry."

The signal died. Then I understood what he was talking about. All of the kitchen knives were missing.

"Holy Mother of God," I whispered.

The basement was dark, and that was a mercy. Art Kiplinger lay in a pool of liquid, formed of groundwater and his own thick blood. A meat cleaver stood from a stump of cypress wood, a hacksaw not far from it. He'd fought hard for his life, but they'd still ripped him apart.

Then he looked at me.

"Didn't want to let me . . . bleed to death." Art gasped. "Almost got there by myself. Another hour . . . I'd have made it."

My heart stopped when I saw the blood trail behind him, leading toward the meat cleaver. He was halfway there.

"Art, what happened?"

"It was after the shit went down in Slidell. I was investigating the damage here . . . lost contact with my team, and then . . ." He coughed, his naked torso convulsing. "Then I ran into an old friend."

"Noah?"

Art closed his eyes. He didn't seem to want to answer the question.

"I'm taking you to a hospital," I said.

"*No.*" He paused, catching his breath. "No."

"You don't have a choice, Art. You're a criminal. You have to stand trial and rat on your buddies at Kadmos."

He exhaled, looking up at me so that the whites of his eyes showed. He had to be in agony, but that wasn't what I was seeing in his face. Art was afraid.

"I said there was a way . . . we could both come out heroes. Remember, Mike?"

"Yeah. That was before you sent Amrita Narayan into the belly of the beast. With me for an appetizer."

He shook his head violently. "Wasn't meant to . . . happen that way. If you'd handed her over without violence . . ."

"Sorry I didn't get the script." I knelt down to his level. "Let's just say that bad things still happen on Tishah B'Av, and leave it at that. Come on. We'll have years to chat it about it when we're sharing a cell block at Super-max."

"Not going to prison." He steadied himself. "I've still got my phone, Mike. Why do you think I haven't tried to call for help?"

"I understand that. But you've got a wife and kids to think of."

"Damned right I do," he said. "When you die in the line of duty . . . FBI gives you a really nice funeral. You know, with a flag on the coffin, and . . . they fold it up for the widow? Eulogy from the special agent in charge, phone calls from the director and attorney general . . . stuff that your kids can be proud of. What do you think . . . happens to bad agents?"

"This," I said plainly. "What am I supposed to do with you? Leave you alone so you can keep trying to cut your throat?"

"Had something a little more . . . direct in mind." He looked at the gun in my hand. "Nice weapon you've got there."

I shook my head. "Can't do it, Artie."

He wouldn't stop staring at my gun. I put the safety on the SIG and re-holstered it. A tear welled in the corner of Art's glass eye, cutting a path through the blood as it trickled down his cheek.

"Do you remember the old days?" He smiled faintly. "The old man kick-ing our butts on the Barca case? Putting us in competition with each other, so we'd knock ourselves out trying to be the one who made the collar?" He shook his head. "I was so jealous of you. Even after I found out how you did it—how you used Sofia—it never stopped burning in my gut. And when I took the bomb and you didn't . . . just added injury to insult."

"That's why you sold out to Kadmos? Jealousy?"

He shook his head. "I really believed in what they wanted to do for New Orleans. They offered me money—a lot of money—but I didn't want it. I just wanted to be part of something bigger. Saving the city where I raised my kids. And Leah . . ." Art coughed. "She was the only woman I ever met who never treated me like a cripple."

"So if they had you—why'd they need Noah?"

"He's their . . . secret weapon. A sleeper. They've spent two years getting him ready for his mission . . . and now . . . they've got him right where they want him."

"What do you mean?"

"Sofia," answered. "Barca knows she betrayed him. Kadmos has her now. So Noah doesn't have any choice. He's got to fall in line." Art started to shake. "They're tying up their loose ends, Mike. For chrissake, watch your ass."

"Art," I said. "Who did this to you?"

He didn't reply. Just stared up at me—and, as he began to see the answer he wanted, his fear seemed to vanish.

"The gun can be traced." My voice choked. "I'll have to do it some other way."

"Just make it clean." He closed his eyes. "Got . . . phantom pains after I lost my arm. Always wondered . . . what kind of pains do you get when you lose . . . everything?"

I stared at the meat cleaver for a long time. Finally, I took hold of the grip and pulled it out of the wood. It felt nauseatingly heavy in my hand, slick with moisture.

"You'll get that flag," I said, "but first we need to talk."

FORTY-FOUR

Half an hour later, I stumbled out of the basement. The water wasn't working in the kitchen taps, so I ran into the yard. Down across the front lawn, down to the water's edge. I tore off my holster, tossed my gear aside, and threw myself headlong into the brackish waters of Lake Pontchartrain.

"Artie," I whispered to no one who could hear me. "How the Christ did we wind up like this?"

I didn't come out until I was certain that all the blood had washed away.

The moon was a hazy August red as I drove the highway south to Michoud. There, between the NASA facility and an old sugar plantation, was an anonymous white building that had gone up while no one was paying attention.

There was no gigantic sign announcing that I'd arrived, just a narrow road that plunged deep into the cypress woods. Every so often, I'd pass a radio transponder, like you'd find at a tollbooth. Each one read the signal coming from the device in my hand and sped me through. My only tense moment was when one of those gray armored vehicles drove by. It took up the entire road and nearly forced me into the swamp, but it didn't slow down. Either I checked out as a friend, or I was too insignificant to bother with.

I left the truck at the bottom of the parking garage and approached the building on foot. There she was: four stories above ground, and God alone knew how many below; twenty-four acres of granite, steel, polarized glass, and prestressed concrete. The southeast regional headquarters of Kadmos Security Solutions, Inc. Big enough to make its own gravity.

I didn't see any guards, but that didn't mean they weren't around. I sent a text message from Art's cell phone:

surprised to see me?

She showed up five minutes later. Not exactly hurrying, but I supposed she needed a little time to make sure that really was Kiplinger's cell phone outside the building—the high-tech equivalent of pebbles tossed at a bedroom window. For the first time since I'd met her, Leah Varnado looked afraid.

"Security's on its way." She froze at the sight of the gun in my hand.

"No they're not. You don't want to risk involving anyone else in your little tryst—at least not until you find out who managed to get hold of your boyfriend's cell phone."

"Where's Art?"

"Right where you left him," I said. "Don't worry, he's dead now. I finished the job you started. Christ, and I thought you guys liked each other. Couldn't you have just shot him twice in the head, like a normal breakup?"

Then the fear was gone. She gave a faint little smile.

"Not and make it look like a mob killing, no." Leah's voice was impenetrably calm. "I didn't necessarily agree with my orders, but it was decided to stage the crime scene so as to resemble Barca's more . . . theatrical style." Then her eyes dropped a fraction. "I didn't think he'd live that long. I tried to make it easy for him."

"If that isn't love, I don't know what is. I can see why he wanted to leave his wife for you."

"You killed him." Her eyes brewed little thunderstorms.

"I let him go the way he wanted to," I said. "Now take me to Sofia. I know she's here. Barca gave her to your boss as a security deposit. Second underground floor, northeast corner of the building. Art told me everything before he died."

She walked ahead of me to the door.

"Put your hands down," I told her. "You're giving a VIP tour. See if you can be as playful and charming as the day you planted that kiddie porn in my room."

As she approached the glass door, the light turned green and the lock slid open.

"I was right about you," she said. "You're bad luck for anyone who gets close to you."

"Guess that makes us two of a kind." I pocketed the gun as I followed her in.

The enormous lobby was dark and empty, except for a single light falling down on a huge architectural model of Greater New Orleans. I recognized the river and the lake, but hardly anything else. Rising up between the waters was a swirl of villages and low-density gated communities, as colorless as a field of mushrooms. There were a few public parks and a lot of golf courses and boat marinas. One thing I didn't see was anything remotely resembling a city: just a few rows of mansions, and a dense little warren of streets that I finally identified as the French Quarter. Huge concrete levees encircled the city like the Berlin Wall.

"What the heck is this?" My voice echoed in the cavernous room.

"It's where we're heading," she said. "The future."

Leah took me through the inner security door into a long white hallway. We passed a few people working late, all of them as friendly as Disneyland employees.

"You should ask me questions," Leah said with a precise smile. "You're getting a tour. Tourists ask questions."

"Here's one for you." I stayed within arm's length of Leah—close enough to grab her if I had to, far enough away to avoid any sudden kicks. "What's your interest in my son?"

"He has potential," she said with the slightest smile. "Martin asked me to scout for talent—his name came up. Don't you think we chose well?"

"For what? A mole? A hired killer? I thought you guys were supposed to be big-time patriots."

"We might have used you, only you're so trammeled by conscience." She smiled simply. "Your son is much closer to our way of thinking. Don't equivocate in a crisis. See what's right and do it. That's how we're going to save New Orleans."

"Save it for what?"

"Proof of concept," she said. "The old model of government—collectivist, bureaucratized, your tax dollars not at work—it's all failed. We believe we can do better. And what better place to start than the city America failed to protect?" She threw me a sly look. "Be honest. Who did more for the people of the Gulf Coast after Katrina? The federal government or the private sector? FEMA—or Wal-Mart?"

"Wal-Mart hasn't actually killed anyone," I said. "Unless you count its lack of an employee health-care plan. Anyhow, I doubt your motives are all that altruistic."

"True. Actually, they're quite opportunistic."

An armed guard crossed our path. He grinned at her and she winked back.

"We'd been forecasting the potential effects of a Category Four hurricane on New Orleans for years," she said. "In 2004, we helped the National Weather Service launch a mock-emergency drill called Hurricane Pam. It confirmed all our findings—right down to the levee breaches and the resulting breakdown in emergency response. Everyone knew the storm was coming, sooner or later. We were simply the only ones who made any preparations for it."

I wasn't imagining things. She was actually pleased with herself.

"All the legislative language for Levin-Marcato was drafted well in advance—just waiting for the right trigger event." She tilted her head. "We were less than six months from completing this facility when the storm hit. Smart planning, eh?"

"You built your headquarters on the fastest-sinking piece of real estate on the Gulf Coast," I said. "How smart is that?"

"Smarter than your Mafia friends." She opened the door to the stairwell. "Art was obsessed with the gangs, you know. He actually thought they were a serious threat to our operations here. But do you see how easily we took them out of the equation? And do you know why they matter so little in the long run?"

"Stupid nicknames like Fat Poppa?"

"They don't know the first thing about genuine partnership." She turned to me at the foot of the stairs. "You don't gain influence over a politician because you've bribed him, or blackmailed him. You gain influence over him—over an entire government—by making yourself indispensable."

She reached for the door. I stopped her long enough to take a look through the inset window. All clear.

"Right here in this building, Kadmos is designing the next phase of the War on Terror—and beyond." She led me through. "Our contractors are the pride of the armed services. If we were to disappear tomorrow, America's wars might have to be fought by ordinary citizens, using outdated weapons. Can you imagine how that would turn out?"

"Good point. We might have to quit fighting so many of them." I put a hand on her shoulder. "Whoa. Stop right there."

Two words were stenciled on a pair of swinging doors: JACKSON SQUARE.

"It's our indoor target range. It's not on our way."

"It is according to the map. There's a door on the other side, close to the holding cells." I held up Yoshi's handheld. "Come on, VIP tour."

"The airlock's got a firearms detector," she said. "It can smell the chemicals used in ammunition. You'd have to leave your weapon behind."

I laughed. "Lady, I don't think so."

She wordlessly removed her security tag, hanging on its cloth lanyard, and handed it to me.

"Tie me up," she said.

I did as she instructed, knotting her hands behind her, then dumped my ammo into a trash can. We walked through the doors, and there was a loud rush of air. After that a green light came on as the other end of the airlock opened.

"Holy shit," I said.

We were back in New Orleans.

Or a studio backlot version of it, anyway. The room contained a full-scale replica of Jackson Square, as big as a city block. All of the principal landmarks had been re-created, from the Cabildo to the Mississippi River levee. A fiberglass Andrew Jackson reared back on his horse. Papier-mâché live oaks and crepe myrtles were decked with plastic leaves. Their version of St. Louis Cathedral, I noted, was only a facade held up by scaffolding, cut off at the bell towers. Even so, the center steeple was built out fully in three dimensions—as if it played some special part in the masquerade.

It wouldn't fool anyone who'd seen the real thing. But it was the best tactical training facility I'd encountered outside of the Bureau's own Hogan's Alley.

"We can simulate anything here." Leah's voice echoed in the empty space. "Any time of day or year, any weather conditions—including storm winds. Want to see a demonstration?"

"No thanks." I took hold of her wrists. "And you'd better not have anybody lurking behind the palmettos."

"It's like I said. Live ammunition isn't permitted in the simulator. Hence the detection systems. For training purposes we use modified—"

"Paintball markers." General Jackson, I noticed, had taken a bright pink splotch in the right temple. Several more splattered the pavement in front of him, closely spaced. "Why did you build this room?"

She simply smiled and tilted her head—just as she had in my hotel room, weeks ago.

"All right, I've seen it," I said. "Let's go."

Leah didn't lose her nerve as we approached the far exit. She kept her eyes straight ahead and didn't strain against the lead. Still, you can always tell when somebody's trying not to look in a certain direction. Just as she reached the door, I saw what she wasn't looking at: a tiny convex lens set into a café's faux-iron balcony.

She opened the inner door of the airlock. Another loud rush of air, sniffing us for cordite. Then I saw Leah take a deep breath and hold it.

As she did, a shadow darted past the door. I grabbed Leah's security badge—then pushed her through, just as the gas began to seep in.

"*Down on the ground! Now!*" Two laser sights sliced through a greenish cloud: armed guards, faces masked. I dove at one of them, catching the muzzle of his handgun as it fired; hollow-point lead streaked past me. He was already off balance and I helped him in that direction, hurling him between me and the bullets. He took two in the chest from his partner's rifle. *Good armor,* I thought. The gas was giving me cover, but it was also starting to get into my nose with a stink like dead cat. Leah Varnado lay on the ground, retching.

I took the guard's handgun and fired directly at the ammunition sensor on the door. Red alarms went off. I ran, holding my free hand to my face. Whatever that gas was, it was working. I could feel my guts twist into the worst fucking stomach cramp of my life.

The room at the end of the hall was unguarded and unlabeled. I used Leah's ID badge to open the door.

"Sofia," I said. "Sofia, we've got to—"

The first thing I saw was the hypodermic needle. Plus a few thin drops of blood on the white tile floor, leading to her.

Sofia lay on the bed like a broken doll, the tourniquet slack on her arm. Still cradling the glass ampoule. She wore a thin hospital gown—eyes half-lidded, staring past me.

"Oh, God." Then sickness overwhelmed me. I could feel the acid rise in my stomach. Someone was running toward me down the hall. I turned just in time to see him aim his rifle: not at me, but her. After that, it all became simple.

The guard was armored head to toe, a small mask covering his mouth and nose, but there was a thin sliver of exposed skin between neck and helmet. I fired at it point-blank. The bullet plowed through his right carotid artery, spilling bright blood. I picked up his rifle and scattered bullets down the hall. There was no movement after that, only the red strobe of the alarm lights.

"Sofia." She was out of it, and no wonder. The ampoule's label indicated that she'd shot up with Dilaudid, drugstore heroin. Her breathing was too shallow, her skin too cold. Her pupils had contracted to needle points. I grabbed the dead guard's filter mask and put it over her face. Then I lifted her over my shoulder and stood in the doorway.

"I'm coming out," I said. "I will kill any son of a bitch who fires at me or attempts to get in my way."

No answer. I took my last clean breath and carried Sofia down the hall. The gas was beginning to dissipate. The first guard lay faceup on the ground, quivering with shock. Leah was gone.

The door to the stairwell was falling shut. I caught it just in time. As I set Sofia down, I heard the last echo of a woman's footsteps, two flights up. Then another door clicked shut.

Art's cell phone was ringing in my pocket.

"Kiplinger residence." I carried Sofia up the stairs.

"You can't get out of the building." Leah was steady, back in control. "We're in lockdown now. Put your weapons down on the ground and re-main—"

I dropped the phone down the stairwell. With any luck, she'd think I'd gone down, not up. I carried Sofia cautiously up the stairs. Finally we were at ground level. She started to groan as I set her down.

"Mike?"

"Yeah, baby." I took out Yoshi's handheld computer and started pressing keys. "It's Mike. Your personal bad luck charm."

"I didn't wanna . . . shoot up. They left it with me . . ." Her eyes opened dimly. "I'm so . . . shamed . . ."

"Shh. It's all right. I don't want you to be ashamed. But you gotta stay awake for me, okay? Keep breathing and stay awake." I ejected the card. "Okay. If this doesn't work, at least you won't be feeling much pain."

A door crashed open four flights down, followed by a noise of running feet: bingo. I held the card to the security panel next to me. A second later, the light turned green.

"What did you do?"

I threw the door open and fired twice with the handgun. Two plain-clothes security went down. Then I took Sofia back into my arms and ran for the parking garage. The glass doors opened automatically.

"I created a new identity." I carried her up the garage ramp, where the Ford pickup was still waiting. "The security system now thinks I'm Martin Telford Campbell. Officially, those guys just got killed by their own boss. Only in America, huh?"

Sofia ripped the mask away. "I feel sick."

"I'll take you somewhere you can throw up safely." I set her down on the concrete as gently as I could; I was getting winded. Then the guards poured into the garage.

"Step away from the vehicle!" one of them commanded. They were thirty yards away. Just far enough.

"That tears it. No Christmas bonus." I grabbed a cinder block from the bed and jammed it against the accelerator. Then I cranked the engine, gave the wheel a hard turn, and sent it careening down the ramp. Too late, they saw what was happening and began to scatter. I shouldered the rifle and fired two into the gas tank. One of the guards slipped on a stream of gasoline and his sidearm went off. Then I flung myself against Sofia as the fireball burst.

The flames were hot on my back. Sofia coughed.

"Those men," she said. "Those men are—"

"Don't look back." I pulled her to her feet, the exit right ahead.

"You killed them," she said.

Then we were out of the building, out into the night.

FORTY-FIVE

The journey through the swamp was fairly close to hell. Even if I had been alone, it would have been hard to keep moving, with mosquitoes at the corners of my eyes and thick green water straight to my chest and unseen things moving past my legs. Sofia was barely conscious—her skin too cold, her breathing too unsteady. I wondered how much of that Dilaudid was swimming around in her blood. Every few yards I stopped to make sure that she hadn't inhaled any water. Once in a while, she'd beg me to put her down. I pretended not to hear.

Eventually we reached soft ground, then dry ground, and after a few false starts we found the road I was looking for: right on the borders of the old sugar plantation.

My cell phone was waterlogged, no signal. Yoshi's handheld computer was in the same fix. It was maybe ten miles to the nearest pay phone.

"We have to keep moving." I slumped down at the foot of a dead cypress. "I'm gonna need you to walk from here on, okay? We'll rest a while, and then . . ." I waited. "Sofia?"

No answer. She lay on her side, not moving.

"Sofia!"

I grabbed her tight under her rib cage. She coughed up water, her lungs weak and heavy. Then I held her up so she could lean forward. After several minutes, her breathing finally began to clear.

"Mike." Her voice was paper-thin, barely any wind behind it. "You gotta go, baby. I can't go with you. I can't . . . do it anymore."

"Hey, what are you complaining about? I've been doing all the heavy lifting up to this point." I exhaled. "Not that I'm implying anything about you being—"

Her hand took mine.

"My brother . . . left the works with me." She breathed. "Grady thought it would be funny. Wanted to prove a point. I held out for a while—"

"I'm not judging you about the needle, Sofia. It was fucking cruel, what he did. Please don't blame yourself."

"Baby, I've got a problem." She pushed herself up on her elbows. "I'm dirty, Mike. I'm an addict. I kick, and then I get healthy, and I start to think I can get on top of it, and then I pick up again. Grady knows who I am. Do you?"

"Yes." I smiled. "You're the girl who got away."

She started to cry. I put my arm around her, warming her.

"I'll help you," I said. "I know you hurt, sweetie. It's okay. Sometimes I hurt, too. Maybe we can—"

"Help each other?" She put her head against me. " 'Two wounded birds can't share their broken wings.' "

"What?"

"Oh—it's a line from an old song. Some guy used to play it at Della's sometimes. I'd sing it for you, but I don't want to break your eardrums." She concentrated. "The rest goes . . . 'I can tell you're hurting, I know the needle stings . . . but I can't fly for you, baby, on my own broken wings.' "

"Hey, that's cheerful."

"There's a lot of songs about people trying to help each other," she said. "Not too many about people who can't help each other. That's you and me, Mike. I wish you could. When you're around . . . I feel safe. But you're broken, too, like me. We've got to find a way to put ourselves back together . . . or we're just no good to anybody."

We clung to each other for several minutes, sharing our warmth. All that lay between us was the thin cloth of her hospital gown and the ballistic vest Peggy had given me.

"We better keep moving," I said after a long quiet.

"Not yet, okay? Not yet." She nestled herself against me. "I just wanna . . . feel you with me a while longer."

"Okay, hon. We'll do that."

"I was so scared that you were gonna . . . use me. When you said you loved me the other night . . ."

"I meant it, Sofia. Every word. It's why I came back."

She smiled. "Do you want to make love to me, Mike?"

"Yes."

"I wish we could." She stroked my face. "I tried to hate you. Then sometimes I'd . . . dream about being with you—and, you know, it was nice. In spite of that I'd wake up feeling like such a traitor to myself. Because I wanted you then . . . and I still do." She breathed deeply. "I wish we hadn't done things to make it so difficult. I wish we could make love like we used to."

"Me, too."

Then she released me. Her eyes were clearer now.

"You should try to find a phone," she said. "You have to get back to New Orleans. Do you know what's about to happen? What they want Noah to do for them?"

I nodded.

"Then you have to stop him," she said. "Be his father, Mike. Be strong."

"I'm not leaving you again. Either we both start walking, or we wait here until you're able to move." I gestured to the space around us. "Or maybe we just build a shack here in the woods and never leave. We'll live on possum."

"That did it." She smiled weakly. "Okay, I'll walk."

I lifted her up and we both moved, stumbling a little, down the road.

"In some ways, I guess it was a little easier for me than you." She steadied herself on my arm. "At least I had Noah to remind me of you."

"That made it easier?" I steeled myself. "Noah and I had a pretty bad fight in Algiers today."

"I know." She looked at me, subdued. "He said you thought he was angry because he'd failed to protect me. From Ricky."

"Was I wrong?"

"Not entirely. I mean . . ." She caught herself from falling. "He'd hate me for telling you this. But there was a time when he idolized you, Mike. You were this fantasy hero, and I was just a . . . disappointment. When he really wanted to piss me off, he'd talk about joining the FBI."

"I guess he did, in a way."

"Do you remember the time . . ." She steadied herself. "That afternoon we made Noah?"

"Yeah." I put her arm over my shoulder, my hand around her waist. "Who knew how that would turn out, huh?"

"Young, horny, and naive," she said. "Fatal combination."

We were mostly silent as we carried each other along that empty plantation road, but it wasn't hard to guess that both of us were thinking about the very same thing. Yes, I remembered that afternoon. Barely a month went by that I didn't think about it at least once. Sometimes, in my most defenseless moments, the memory would come at me with terrifying force. Yet I guarded that memory fiercely, even from myself. It was sacred space, uninhabited, the last fading fragment of a life I'd rejected long ago.

It was near the end of March, the first shy promise of spring. One of those wet New Orleans days when you feel just a bit drowsy and lost, and the gray light makes everything seem just a little more real. Sofia and I had reached a good place with each other. The shadows of Mardi Gras were behind us, and my introduction to her family was still in the unknowable future. On that particular Saturday afternoon, it seemed that both of us had briefly become what we wanted to be: happy and open-hearted, two young people with no past to regret and everything to hope for.

There was still a little sunlight when we started walking down Magazine. We were on a weekend hunt for used records; she'd made a few sharp trades at her favorite music store. I can't even remember what she bought. I do remember that she'd just cut her hair above her shoulders, and it suited her. Sofia was wearing a loose white skirt with a tank top that I loved on her, and an old oxford shirt that she'd stolen from me that morning. Then it started to rain down like a drunken sailor. We tried to use our shopping bags for rain hats, but it was no good. By the time we reached Lawrence Square, both of us were soaked through. Then she looked up and kissed me.

Take me to your room, she said. We never go there.

Her warm brown eyes held a teasing light, and she twined her hand in mine in a way that I found impossible to resist. I protested that my apartment was a mess, which was saying nothing. It was always a mess. Still, I had to admit that no other solution made much sense. We were a lot closer to my place in Carrollton than hers in Algiers. And we both seemed to know where the afternoon was going.

So we went to my studio apartment, the one with the stove next to the bed and empty bookshelves that reached to the ceiling. I made coffee with chicory, and she put piano jazz on the stereo. Then she started looking at the photographs on my shelf. She wanted to know who the pretty, sad-eyed woman was.

I'd never told her anything about my mother, and she wanted to know everything. So I told her. Things I'd never said to anyone outside my family until that day. I said most of it with my back to her, paying a lot of attention to the cream and sugar. I ended by suggesting that maybe some good had come of it, after all. If my mother hadn't died, maybe I never would have become . . .

Wouldn't have become what? she asked.

The person I am today, I said after a fearful silence. I trembled to realize how close I had come to telling her, right then and there. Then Sofia put a hand on my cheek and turned me around. She told me I had my mother's eyes: wounded eyes. Until that moment, she'd never realized just how sad a person I truly was. She hated to think of me carrying that sorrow through life, all alone.

You can be happy, Sofia said to me. Your mother would want you to be happy. You deserve to be.

We never got around to drinking the coffee. Instead we kissed in front of the open window, listening to Chet Baker. Then she led me to the shower. Nice, hot water ran down her back as I traced my fingers along the cleft of her spine, the curve of her bottom. Her smile was sweet and simple as I washed her thighs. Then she got that teasing look again. Sofia slid her hand between my legs and started to lather me. Making soft cooing sounds in my ear, rubbing the end of my shaft against her. Saying with each kiss, Do you like that, baby, do you? Urging me into her.

I'd like to believe I said something tender and romantic, but I'm pretty sure my reply was along the lines of, Are you insane? She'd always joked that the women in her family could get pregnant from a kiss on the cheek, and right then we were doing a lot more than that. Until that afternoon we'd been careful, layering ourselves in protection, skirting around the dangerous days. Now I was just shy of slipping into her. I'd never felt her bare, not once; and it was glorious.

Do you want me to keep doing that? I asked breathlessly. Uh-uh, she said, this is what I want you to do.

Then she put her tiny foot on the edge of the tub, and her arms around my neck. She slid down on me, biting her lip with pleasure. Tight around me, warm and caressing. Laughing.

We stayed in the shower until the water ran cold. Then we dried each other off, a little playfully, and I carried her to the bed. Be slow, she said, please be slow. So I took my time, kissing each soft breast, warming her flat belly, lifting her leg over my back so that I could my work my tongue into her. Then I took her. She lay caught beneath me, pale in the rainlight, looking at me with complete acceptance, complete trust. We rode each other until suddenly her eyes closed tight and she cried out, every muscle tensing. She smiled, openmouthed, and her heart beat wild.

Do you want to . . . ? she asked, and I said it was okay, I'd pull out before it was too late. But somehow that wasn't what I was doing. Then she pressed her hands against my back and asked me again. Looking into my eyes with absolute compassion, taking all my hurt into herself.

Go on, baby, she whispered. It's okay, you can stay in me. Come on. Just come on in. And I told her that I wanted to stay in her. Wanted to stay with her forever.

Sofia.

Then I fell, exhausted, and she cradled me to her.

The time after love was always shaky and a little vulnerable. Sometimes she'd cry for reasons she couldn't explain. That afternoon, she simply twirled my hair and whispered to me until we both fell asleep. Two hours later, the telephone woke us up.

It was Art Kiplinger. He'd finally tracked down a friendly judge who would grant us the surveillance warrants we needed on Barca, but we'd have to hustle. Also, if I didn't get my goyish ass downtown, he'd gladly take all the action for himself.

I waited until Sofia went to the bathroom, then told him I'd be there in an hour. I was working on something for the case. Bullshit, he said. You've got a girl in there, don't you? I told him it was none of his fucking business. I hated that I sounded so damned spiteful about it.

Sofia turned frail and quiet when I told her I had to leave. She sat naked on my bed while I knotted my tie, asking if she could stay in my apartment until I got home from my meeting at the bank. I told her that would make me very happy. I'd be back in an hour, and we'd go have dinner at Vincent's. But it was near eleven when I finally stumbled back in, numb from overwork and sick from the smell of the judge's cigars. By then, she was gone. She'd kissed the bottom of the note she left for me.

There would be more love after that, and a few more Saturday afternoons searching for old and lost records at the music stores on Magazine—but not enough, not nearly enough. You only get two or three days like that in a lifetime, and it can take years to figure out that you've used them up. By then, you've been to the free clinic so the doctor can confirm what your girlfriend's body has been telling her for weeks. You've remembered the oath you took to defend the U.S. Constitution. You've spoiled the magic by suggesting that both of you are too young to be parents. You've made arrangements for the problem to go away, you've drawn cash to pay the clinic so the charge won't show up on your credit card. All the while you're pretending that you didn't want it to happen, that it was a mistake; when you know damn well it was exactly what you wanted. You knew it even before you released your seed into the depths of that girl's body. You knew you wanted to find some way, any way, of staying with her just a little while longer.

Maybe it happened to you some other way. This is how it happened to me. The lesson it taught me has never gone away. You can make love to someone a thousand times, but only three of them really matter in the end: the first time, the last time, and the time when you held absolutely nothing back. It wasn't until I found myself alone with Sofia again—walking down that muddy road past the sugar plantation, fleeing for our lives—that I finally accepted that we'd already had all three.

"Did you call again?" Sofia asked as I handed her a cup of convenience-store coffee. "Did they answer this time?"

"Yeah, we're good. They'll be here any second. Stay out of the light, okay? I don't want anyone being able to identify you from the road."

We'd said nothing to each other on the walk back. We made ourselves believe it was for safety. More likely we didn't talk because it would have meant asking questions we didn't want answered. Such as which boyfriend first made her a junkie. Or who this Agent Weaver was that I kept mentioning as I talked on the store's pay phone. Questions that were bound to awaken painful thoughts. It was better to feel nothing and say nothing and stay numb.

As a pair of distant headlights approached, I finally got my nerve up to ask her one question.

"Noah told me something," I said. "When he was nine . . . he said that he stabbed a boyfriend of yours. A biker named Ricky. And that your father and brother stood around until Ricky bled to death."

"Yeah, that's true." She shivered. "Except that Noah wasn't nine when it happened. He was six. And he was crying the whole time. He didn't want to look, but my dad made him watch."

She took me by the hand.

"He didn't fail to protect me, Mike. I failed to protect him."

Then the green minivan pulled up to the front of the store. Sofia Barca smiled like a timid child as Al and Vendella Crawford opened the door to her.

FORTY-SIX

We took turns showering in my cramped quarters over the oyster house. By the time I finished dressing, clear warm light was beginning to spill through the window slats. Morning.

"Why aren't you in the hospital?" I asked Al as he met me on the stairs. "Did the Bureau stop payment on your private hospital room?"

"Got bored without you." He gave me a meaning look. "How's Kiplinger?"

"He didn't make it."

We walked down the stairs to the back room, where breakfast was waiting for us.

"Kiplinger was in bed with Kadmos for a year at least, maybe longer." I swallowed coffee, strong as road tar. "This joint operation of theirs—Pandora's Box—is a smoke screen for an urban cleansing operation. They've been tagging and killing top gang leaders as part of an overall campaign to impose law and order on the city. That's just phase one. Levin-Marcato is a federally funded plan for turning New Orleans into the world's largest suburban nightmare. They're gonna save the Quarter and those big houses on St. Charles, but pretty much everything else is up for the wrecking ball."

I went to refill my cup. Al stared into space.

"Simon Burke was assigned by Kadmos to gather intelligence for the Pandora report," I said. "Apparently he convinced Amrita to assist them in creating a psychological profile on me, the purpose of which I still don't completely understand. At some point, he got cold feet and tried to do a deal with our side. Which made them both very dangerous to Kadmos."

"So they hired Barca to kidnap Burke and his wife?"

"Actually, they hired Barca to kill them both. During the torture and interrogation, Barca's people learned that Amrita might be more valuable alive—so they decided to ransom her back to Kadmos. Pure opportunism."

"And now she's dead," Al said.

I nodded. "But now I know what she wanted to tell Senator Seaweather. I also know what's supposed to happen in August."

Al opened his mouth to speak. Then Della came down the stairs.

"How is she?" I asked.

"It's gonna be a long road home for her," Della said quietly. "My youngest brother wound up like Sofia. Couldn't stay off the needle, but we finally brought him back. We'll get her back, too, Mike. Just don't expect any overnight miracles."

"Is she awake?"

"You can go up for a minute. Only for a minute, okay?"

"I can't stay long anyway." I gave her a kiss on the cheek. "Thanks, Della."

"Mike." Al called to me up the stairs. "What's gonna happen in August?"

"It's going to happen sometime today," I said. "Unless I'm very badly mistaken, Senator James Seaweather is about to die."

Then I went upstairs to check on Sofia.

She lay on my bed, wearing an old shirt of mine, covered by a quilt I salvaged from my Philadelphia apartment. Sunlight fell on her from a gable window.

"This is where you sleep?" she asked.

"Not lately," I said. "I have to go now. Della and Al are going to look after you. I've arranged for some money to come to you if . . . well, just in case."

"How are you going to do that?"

I showed her Yoshi's handheld.

"As of twenty minutes ago, you've got a new name and Social Security number. Also a fairly nice money market account at Bank of New Orleans. I've written it all down for you. As for how I did it . . ." I took the chip from the computer. "Let's just call it a miracle."

I knelt down and rifled through my suitcase until I found a spare ammunition clip for the SIG. Sofia watched me lock and load.

"We won't see each other again, will we?" She spoke with blunt sincerity. "I've been feeling it ever since we came here. One of us isn't coming back."

"You won't get rid of me that easily." I holstered my weapon. "Did you think you'd see me again after I put you on that bus?"

"Yes," she said, "but I don't anymore."

I knelt down to her bedside.

"You're going to live through this." I stroked her hair. "Just like Uncle Paulie said. You're going to get out of here, and you're going to get healthy, and stay healthy. And someday you'll be happy. And you won't be alone."

"My father won't leave me alone," she said. "He keeps bringing me back, and he keeps throwing me away. As long as he's alive, he won't leave me alone."

"I haven't kept too many promises in my life, angel—but I'm going to keep this one. The men of your family will never have the power to harm you again."

We kissed each other softly on the lips. Then once more.

"You've got to stay alive, too. I'm serious. I'll curse your grave if you don't." She laughed. "You listen to me on this, okay? My mother was a conjure woman. I can do it."

"I believe you," I said. "Maybe I haven't learned how to care less about you over the years—but I hope to God I've learned to listen."

"A little," she said.

"More than I used to." I stood up.

"Mike." She waited for me to turn back. "What are you going to do about Noah?"

I took a long breath. "That depends on Noah."

"You can't let him hurt anyone. That's your promise to me, okay? Promise that."

"I do," I said. "I will."

"Tell him I love him. And ..." She smiled. "I'll always love you, Michael."

I smiled back at her.

"See you around," I said. "Once in a very blue moon."

FORTY-SEVEN

Al walked with me as far as Chartres Street, where the crowds were beginning to gather. You could hear a raucous calliope ahead, and occasional bursts of distant applause. I saw the lights of a police cordon near Toulouse.

"This is where you turn back," I said. "I've gotten superstitious ever since Carmichael shot you in the arm, okay? I can handle myself from here."

"Okay, hero." He smiled. "You feeling guilty about what happened to Carmichael?"

"I feel guilty about everybody. In his case, however, I think I might know a way to do something about it. That kid of his—"

"Mike." Al gave me a warning look. "Don't even."

"All I'm saying is, Baton Rouge is a nicer place to grow up than the front of Cain's Grocery. Or the Lower Ninth Ward. I'm not telling you to take a child away from her mother, but maybe it wouldn't hurt to pay a visit with Child Protective Services."

"God love you for a troublemaker." He exhaled. "I already raised four kids, damn it. You think I wanna push a little red wagon while I'm sitting in a wheelchair?"

"Talk to CPS. That's all I'm asking." I waited. "Maybe Vendella could go with you to meet the kid."

"Mike Yeager, will you please quit tryin' to heal my pain?" His laughter died on his lips. "You better get moving."

"I'm already gone." I gave him a hug. "Thanks for getting my back lately, Alvin. Or is your name really Alcatraz?"

"It's Alligator. And I'm gonna bite your head clean off if you mention that child in front of Della."

I smiled as he walked away. Then I headed straight for the police.

The first person I recognized was Yoshi. He stood on the other side of the barricades, talking on his cell phone.

"Yoshi!" No answer. "Yoshi!"

He couldn't seem to hear me over the noise. The cops were passing people through a metal detector, but it was taking too long. I walked straight up to the wooden barrier.

"Whoa. Whoa." A policeman's hand on my chest. "Back of the line, skipper."

I reached for my badge. "FBI. Special Agent Yeager. I gotta get through to my people, okay? It's important."

"Nobody told me anything about FBI. What did you say your name—"

"Yeager." I waved over his head. "Yoshi! For chrissakes, will you look over here?"

Finally he turned back. As he did, his eyes filled with warning.

"Hang on." The cop reached for his radio. "Just cool your jets while I check this out, okay? We got a lotta weirdos trying to crash the line, and . . . hey!"

I'd finally had enough. I put one foot on the cross-tie and launched myself over the barricade. The cop was right on my heels.

"Yoshi," I said as I reached him, "will you tell this bozo who I am? I've got to find Peggy right now. Whatever's going on here today, we've got to cancel."

"You need to get out of here," Yoshi said. "Some shit's going down and you don't want to be here for it."

"Why? What's—"

The next thing I felt was the policeman's hand on my back.

"Yeager, huh?" Another cop got in my face. "Got a lot of people looking for you, dickbrain."

"Leave him alone," Yoshi said. "He's not—hey!"

They shoved him out of the way. I tried to run, a half second too late. Two policemen pinned my arms behind me. The crowd began to applaud.

"Go find Peggy," I yelled to Yoshi. "Tell her to stop—"

Then I was facedown on the hood of a police car. The cuffs snapped on.

"What the hell is this?" I asked.

"Conspiracy to commit murder," the cop said. "And if you're so fucking stupid that you need to ask, maybe you really are FBI after all."

FORTY-EIGHT

I knew I was in trouble when the Bastard came into the NOPD interview room. Even with the bad patch job on his broken nose, Uri Vitale was grinning like he'd just discovered blow jobs.

"Vitale," I said. "You know why I'm here, for Christ's sake. Tell these jerks that I'm working undercover."

"I have no idea what your assignment was supposed to be." Uri Vitale sat on the other side of the table. "The director kept me out of the loop on that. What I do know is that any immunity from prosecution your assignment might have given you ended the moment you murdered Supervising Special Agent Kiplinger."

"Kiplinger's dead?" I asked. "Jesus, that's awful. What happened?"

"Mike. Mike." He shook his head. "Anybody ever tell you that you can't keep bluffing after you've shown your hole card?"

He nodded back to the two-way glass. I was still cuffed, and lucky for him. Something told me that he'd give an interesting shriek as he crashed through that mirror.

"I want Agent Weaver in the room," I said. "Bring her in here and I'll tell you anything you want to know."

"I'll just bet you will." He laughed. "Your girlfriend's got her hands full. She can't help you any more than Kiplinger can. You're mine, Yeager. First-degree homicide of a federal agent. Conspiracy to homicide of an elected official. Accessory after the fact to felony homi—"

"Go screw," I said. "You think I came here to kill Seaweather?"

He gave me a prissy frown as he took the digital recorder from his pocket—then placed it on the table and hit PLAY.

"Where's Art?" It was Leah Varnado's voice.

"He's dead now," my own voice answered from the recorder.

"You killed him."

"I let him go the way he wanted to." Then silence.

"Give me a fucking break," I said. "You accepted an edited audio recording from Kadmos as evidence? Put it through voice analysis, Vitale. It won't stand up, I promise you."

"It's not just the audio file." Vitale cued to another track. "You were very careful about wiping down the meat cleaver and the kitchen taps at Barca's house. Fortunately, we also found the body of that guard you shot—and ballistics on your SIG SAUER places you at the marina at the time of Kiplinger's death."

Then he pressed the button again.

"It's going to happen sometime today." My voice again. "Senator James Seaweather is about to die."

He turned the recorder off and slipped it back into his pocket. "We've already got more than we need for indictment. The senator told us that you recommended he appear at this morning's rally, despite the bombing. Apparently you've developed some sort of . . . fixation on Seaweather ever since Weaver started traveling with him. And, of course, there's the rifle."

"What rifle?"

"The five-point-five-six assault rifle we discovered this morning, during a routine sweep." He folded his arms. "With your fingerprints on it. Oh, you might also be interested to know that the chemical marker in the C-4 explosive matches traces we found in your clothing. Gotta love FBI Crime Lab."

"Of course you found it in my clothes, you moron. I was close enough to smell the C-4 when—"

Then it hit me: Vitale hadn't mentioned the guards I shot during my breakout. Of course not. That would have meant mentioning Sofia.

"How much is Kadmos paying you?" I asked him.

"What?"

"Skip it," I said. "Let's say you're right about everything. I'll cinch it for you. I'll tell you where they found the rifle. That's something only the assassin would know, right?"

"No doubt." Vitale narrowed his eyes.

"St. Louis Cathedral," I said. "In the central steeple. That's where the sniper's nest is. With a clear line of sight on the senator's speaking platform, right in front of the statue. Am I right, or was that one hell of a guess?"

His eyes brightened. "You'll sign a statement?"

"Give me a pen," I said, "and I'll tell you something else, because I'm that darned eager to be helpful. I'll tell you what the motive is."

"Yeah?" Vitale laughed. "Yeager, if you're bullshitting me—"

"Subjects in this type of homicide are likely to be wannabe cops—or former law enforcement, like me. The motive is to stage the murder in advance, so as to allow the perpetrator to prevent the crime from taking place—or to be the one to solve it. I plant a bomb, then I tell the senator he has to stay in public. Then I show up and try to warn everyone that he's about to be assassinated. So that when I really do kill him, I get to stand up and say I told 'em so." I nodded to him. "Hero homicide."

"That's the statement you're willing to sign?"

"It's either that or my backup theory," I said. "Which is that Kadmos set up all this evidence to frame me, so that nobody will be looking for the real assassin."

Vitale smiled. Whatever god he worshipped had been kind to him that day.

"Give me a minute." Then he left the room.

I stared at my own warped reflection in the two-way mirror. Vitale was leaving the room to call somebody, a salivating boast that he'd finally nailed Yeager's coffin shut. But who was he calling? Then it hit me: *why is he the only one talking to me?* It definitely wasn't FBI standard procedure—and Lord knew the NOPD would want a piece of me. Finally inspiration took hold.

"New Orleans police are a bunch of fucking pussies," I said to the mirror. "Katrina didn't kill enough of them. Those shit-for-brains did more looting by themselves than half the people in this city. Cops suck dick. FBI rules, okay?"

Vitale returned with a printed sheet of paper: a confession that must have been drafted for me some time ago.

"Who were you talking to?" he asked.

"David Berkowitz's dog," I said. "I'll sign on two conditions. Is the senator still going ahead with the rally?"

"Your appearance has caused a delay, obviously—but yes, I believe he's decided to address the crowd. They seem confident that the threat has abated, now that you're in custody."

"You have to stop him from taking the stage."

"I'll pass the word along." He slid the paper to me.

"I said two conditions. The other parties in that second audio recording have nothing to do with this. I want them left alone."

He sighed. "Yeager, you used to be a halfway decent investigator. You really think it's wise to allow Emelio Barca's daughter to walk around—after her father hired you to kill a U.S. senator?"

Bastard. "I'm not talking about her, Vitale. I'm talking about Al Crawford. That old spook set me up. I don't want him arrested. I want to kill that punk-ass cop myself."

"Sorry, Yeager. No deal."

Finally I was sure of my guess.

"I can't sign until you take the cuffs off," I said.

He hesitated a moment before walking around behind me.

"Try not to be an idiot." He slipped the key into my cuffs. "We've already got you on tape confessing to the cr—"

I drove my fist straight into his jaw. As he collapsed, staring thunderstruck at me, I took his sidearm and badge.

"In case you're wondering, this is the Eighth District," I said. "Crawford's district. I promise you, if there were any cops listening to me make that threat—I'd be dead right now."

I cuffed both hands through the table, then choked him with his own necktie.

"Now answer the question I asked earlier. How much is Kadmos paying you to set me up for Seaweather's assassination?"

He stared fearfully, struggling to breathe.

"Not . . . him."

"What?" I waited. "Bullshit."

"Seaweather's safe." Vitale gasped. "Nobody cares if he dies. He'll get the message when . . ."

He started to faint. I slapped him back to life.

"What message is he going to get?"

"When they . . . take out the real target," he said. "The one who's been investigating Kadmos . . . all along . . ."

I let him fall, already moving for the door.

FORTY-NINE

I was all right until I got to the tourist information desk in the police station lobby. Then damned if I didn't run smack into the same cop who put those cuffs on me.

"Hey!" He took off after me. "What the fuck—"

The metal detector went off as I ran out the front door.

Eighth District headquarters, at the corner of Royal and Conti, was just inside the police cordon. A festival mood reigned in the streets, somewhat more freakish than the family crowd at Bunny Friend. I pitched a gold-painted street performer into the path of the cops running after me. I got makeup all over my palms, but it gained me a few seconds to grab a stupid-looking baseball cap and oversized sunglasses from a gift shop rack. Then I blended in with the crowd and tried very hard to look drunk.

By the time I reached St. Peter's, I was reasonably certain that I'd thrown off my pursuit. There were still plenty of police around, though a few of them were on horseback—and they were starting to get urgent signals on their radios.

"*In just a minute,*" a woman's amplified voice was calling from the direction of the square, "*we're going to hear from a man who has gone through a great deal of trouble to be here today. And while some of you may not agree with him—*"

I ran down Pirate's Alley, nearly knocking over a whole troupe of guys in black vampire capes. RESURRECT NEW ORLEANS, read the blood-dripping letters on their picket signs.

"*—I think he needs a chance to tell us his side of the story.*"

Then I saw her at the near end of the park, conferring with one of the senator's bodyguards: Special Agent Weaver.

"Peggy!" I ran to her, throwing my disguise away. "Peggy, you've got to listen. I know what's about to happen."

"Mike." She dropped what she was doing and came to me. "They called me from the station. I don't know what you think you're up to, but you—"

"You have to get out of here. Right now."

Peggy stared at me doubtfully.

"Not the senator," I said. "You. You're the target. You're the one who's about to die."

"Mike, what the hell are you talking about?"

"Kadmos wants you dead. Ever since you took them on in Tennessee, you've been getting closer to exposing them. Don't you see? If they shot you in an alley, there'd be an investigation. The FBI wouldn't let it drop until they found the shooter. Hell, *I* wouldn't sleep till I personally killed the bastards, but if you're just one more random casualty in a failed assassination attempt on the senator—"

She looked away as the police caught up with me. I held up my hands.

"Do not go near that platform or you're dead. The shooter's up in the cathedral. I'm almost positive it's Noah. Promise me you'll have someone check it out—and I'll go quietly."

She stared at me for several seconds. Then she looked at the bodyguard next to her.

"Who do we have in the bell tower?"

He took a moment to check his list.

"Last-minute replacement," he said. "Sharpshooter from HRT. Guy named . . . Owens."

"Owens isn't an agent," I said. "He worked for Kadmos. And he's dead."

She looked back to me.

"Let him go," she said to the police, then turned to the man beside her. "Make contact with this Agent Owens. If he doesn't respond immediately, send a team into the cathedral. Yeager, you're with me."

I followed her through the iron gates of the square, to a tent set up behind the speaker's platform.

"You broke out of a police station to talk to me?" She kept to a brisk stride. "You ever hear of a little thing called the telephone?"

"I didn't know who'd be listening in." I struggled to keep up. "I get paranoid when you're not around."

She threw me a withering look. "You sure as hell get something when I'm not around."

"Peggy, what is this?" Senator Seaweather emerged from the tent. "I just got word you want to cancel. What are—" Then he saw me. "Oh, no. What the hell is he doing here?"

"Sir, Agent Yeager claims there's immediate danger. Supposedly you're not at risk, but until we check it out—"

"And you want to put me five feet away from the man they accuse of trying to kill me?" He bore down on me. "God above, Yeager. Are you a hired killer or not?"

"Hold on." Peggy answered her ringing cell phone. "Okay, this is the confirmation. Sir, if you could get back inside the tent—"

She turned to speak to someone. Seaweather didn't seem to want to get too close to me.

"Now let's all give a warm New Orleans welcome," the woman on the loud-speakers said, *"to a very dear friend of mine—Senator James Seaweather of the great state of Pennsylvania."* Her voice ended in applause.

"My God," the senator said. "She's still on the platform."

"Who is?" I asked.

"The mayor." He started to run into the open. "She doesn't know—"

Peggy snapped the phone shut. "Jim!"

She moved into the clearing to block him. I threw myself at her. As I pulled Peggy Weaver to the ground, blood burst from the senator's chest. A moment later, gunshots echoed all around Jackson Square.

Hell followed after.

There were two more shots, but they went wild. I saw the senator, crawling to safety through his own blood. Two black-suited men rushed in to carry him away. By then, we were at the center of a human cyclone. A scream rose through the crowd, like cheering for a home run. People moved in waves, knocking over wooden barriers in their panic.

Peggy Weaver walked in the direction of the gunfire.

"What's the situation?" She spoke into her cell phone, listened. "Roger that. The senator is critically wounded and is en route to the navy's trauma center on the USNS *Comfort*. Our priority now is to protect the crowd. Get these people away from here."

She turned to me.

"There's two men in the tower," she said. "One of them's guarding the second-level stairwell. He's armed and claims to have a bomb. Shooter is also armed and dangerous."

"Description?"

"Any visual contact, Lieutenant?" She waited, then looked back at me. "No description on the assassin. The guy with the bomb is a white male, dark hair and mustache, bandage on the right side of his neck."

"Grady," I said. "The shooter's Noah."

"Lieutenant, hold for my orders. Repeat. Do not make any aggressive moves without my explicit instructions."

She closed the phone.

"Peg—"

"We gotta take him out, Mike. Both of them. If there is a bomb—"

"I'll bring them down," I said. "Are you in touch with Eighth District?"

She nodded. My heart was racing—but my head was clear.

"Send a team to Della's Original Oyster House at Bourbon and Iberville. Sofia Barca will be there. Tell her that I'm keeping my promise to her—but she has to come here right now."

"Come *here*? Mike, we're trying to clear the square. If your guy really does have a bomb—"

"She'll understand that," I said. "Do it now. And keep the hell down, okay? He's not done with you yet. Give me ten minutes before you send in the troops."

"It may not be up to me," she said. "The SWAT teams are trained for these kinds of situations. If there's a clear shot, they're going to take it." She took a breath. "You have to be right about this."

"Understood," I said. "At ten minutes and one second, you unleash the wrath of God."

"Mike . . ."

She grabbed me by the arm.

"Don't screw this up, Yeager. I don't want to have to replace you."

"I love you, too." Then I walked out into the open.

Armored SWAT police were in crouch position against the cathedral doors. A few more ran for cover around the side buildings. Several of them stared at me, waiting for my approach. I stared up at the church tower.

There was a gap in the blinds of the steeple window. I could just see the end of the rifle muzzle. Pointing down directly at me. I made a careful show of taking out my weapon—the 9 mm I took from Vitale—and slowly laid it flat on the ground. Then I held my hands up.

A flat pop. A chunk of concrete broke at my feet, knocking the gun away.

I waited several seconds. Then I walked, hands up, to the south door of the cathedral.

"He's here," the SWAT lieutenant said quietly into his radio. "All units, we have a man going in. Hold your fire."

The door was cracked open. As I reached for it, he leaned in to me.

"I've got two men down in there," he whispered. "One was still alive at last count. Watch out for him, okay?"

I nodded.

"Anything you need from me?" he asked.

"Do you pray?" I pushed the door open and walked in.

The narthex of the cathedral was cool and quiet, smelling of rosewood. Its diamond-patterned floor sloped upward to the altar of God. A dead New Orleans policeman lay semifetal against the baptismal font, staring into the middle distance. Someone had disarmed him in a hurry.

"Yeager!"

Grady's voice, echoing. I turned to the open stairway door. He had to be at least one flight up.

"Up here, Yeager. I know it's you. Come closer so I don't have to shout in God's house."

I cautiously went up the steep concrete steps. It was too dark for me to see more than a few feet ahead, but I could hear someone wheezing in the hallway above.

"How do you feel about shooting in God's house?" I called up.

"Even Stonewall Jackson fought on Sundays." He coughed. "Do me a favor. There's a cop lying near the entrance to the choir loft. His breathing's driving me crazy."

"What am I supposed to do about that?"

"Shut him up," Grady said. "Seriously, Mike. You can't miss him. Big colored guy with a sucking chest wound."

"I'll see what I can do." I started back up the stairs, feeling something sticky beneath my feet. "By the way, Grady. You are aware that nobody under the age of ninety says 'colored' anymore."

"I have a special reverence for the old ways."

There was a short, narrow passage at the top of the stairs, at the end of which was another hallway. A pair of heavy black boots protruded from the right-hand side. I turned the corner—and looked down into the terrified eyes of a young black man, clad in ballistic armor. He held both hands to his chest, trying to plug the hole in his right lung.

"Have you found him yet?" Grady asked.

"Yeah. Mind if I take him outside? He won't bother you."

"Hm. How much time did they give you to talk us down?"

"Not long."

"You won't make it back in time," he said. "Hurry or you'll miss the grand finale."

The cop took his eyes off me, and I saw what he was looking at. The pepper spray canister on his belt. I quietly took it from him. Then I silently mouthed, *Hang in there.* Cupping the spray can in one hand, I turned back to the door behind me. KEEP LOCKED AT ALL TIMES, it read. The steeple entrance. Someone had recently pried the lock open. I gently pushed the door wide and started up the second flight of steps.

I checked my watch. I had three minutes left. Maybe three and a half, if Peggy was feeling generous. Which I hoped to God she wasn't.

"So Grady," I said. "Why don't we take a second to consider our op—"

A small-arms round struck sparks off the stone wall, the noise ringing in my ears.

"Did I say come up? Huh? Did I say come up here?"

I held my course up the steps. Then I saw that Grady did, in fact, have a bomb.

He leaned against the stairs, his arm looped through the iron rail, hanging on for dear life. Sweating like a kid at the eighth-grade prom. And no wonder. A suicide vest was tied around his waist with Velcro, hung with large silver canisters. High yield: It could blow the facade of the cathedral clean off. A detonator wire ran to a pen-sized switch in his hand, which he pressed down with his quivering thumb. In his other hand was a .45 semiautomatic.

"Why the Christ did I let Papa talk me into this? Some partnership." Grady laughed. "Should have been you pulling kamikaze detail. You're the fucking new guy."

"Grady—"

"It's a dead man's switch," he said. "You shoot me, my thumb comes off the button, and it's bye-bye St. Louis. So tell me, smart-ass. How do I get out of this one?"

"They can freeze it down," I said. "You walk out with me, the bomb squad's waiting. They'll take care of you."

"What have you got in your hand?" He aimed the pistol at me. "Aw, Mike, what is this shit? *Pepper* spray? Do you know how stupid it would be to fuck with me right now? Do you—"

"Grady, don't move!"

Then his brains sprayed in all directions as a bullet tore through his head. I dove to catch his hand—pressing my thumb on Grady's dead one just in time.

"Noah?" I waited. "Noah!"

"It's got a forty-five-second fuse," Noah said calmly from the darkness above me. "If you let him go, you've got just enough time to get your ass out of here. Maybe even save the cop—if you're feeling particularly heroic."

Gingerly, my fingers slick with blood, I slipped my thumb beneath Grady's. Now I was holding the detonator. I pulled the strips of Velcro away, lifted the vest over Grady's lifeless body.

"Looks like a lot of shit's going down out there," Noah said. "Maybe you don't have forty-five seconds after all."

With my other hand, I reached for the can of Mace. I closed my eyes and pressed the button. Two long bursts misted the air. So at least that was working. I pocketed the .45 and started up the stairs again.

"Think my grandfather will be pissed at me?" Noah asked. "I mean, family loyalty's so important to him. Although it sounded like Grady was having second thoughts about his mission. I don't guess he was likely to give Grandpa any grandchildren anyway. You ever get that feeling about Grady?"

"I try not to judge people that way," I said. "Anyhow, what family loyalty? You're never going to make it out of here alive. Meanwhile, your grandfather's safely far away, planning his new 'partnership' with Kadmos. What's that old Sicilian bastard done for you lately?"

"Well, I do get to spend a little quality time with my dad." Then Noah came out of the shadows.

He wore the battle dress of an FBI Hostage Rescue sharpshooter—full body armor, Kevlar helmet, goggles, balaclava—and he'd never looked so young to me: like a child soldier. The weapon in his hand was a 5.56, aimed straight at my heart. He whistled as soon as he saw the suicide vest.

"Oh, that's good." Then he laughed. "What is this, tough love? Do we go out hugging the bomb?"

"We've got about a minute and a half to live," I said. "I don't want to waste it talking about anything that doesn't matter. Just consider this. Agent Weaver's still alive. Kadmos is going down. Your grandfather's an old man without any more sons to throw between him and the Grim Reaper. You don't have anything left that's worth dying for, Noah. You might as well live."

"Yeah? And what do you have worth dying for?"

"You," I said. "God, look at you. I only wish you'd lived the life you stole from the Delacroix boy. I'd be proud to have a son like that. If I'd stayed with your mother—maybe you'd have gotten that chance, maybe not. But if I could die to give you that second chance . . . hell, I'd do it in a heartbeat."

"One minute," he said. "You just wasted thirty seconds."

"Noah, I know there's a part of you that doesn't want to be what you are. You're doing all of this hoping it will keep your mother safe from the bad guys. Kadmos, your grandfather . . . me. Just like you tried to protect her from Ricky. That's why you couldn't kill Delacroix's mother—as stupid as it was to let her live. There's still a part of you that can't stand to see a mother's suffering. And that's something you get from me. You can't do a damn thing about it."

He almost seemed to hear me. Then his face hardened.

"My mother won't be suffering after I finish this," he said. "So go ahead and kill us both. The blast will take out that FBI girlfriend of yours—and Kadmos will keep its end of the bargain."

"They won't do it, Noah. They can't."

"Yes they *will*. They'll let my mother go, and . . . that'll be the end. I don't need you in this with me, okay? Either get the fuck out or kill us both."

"She's not with Kadmos." I waited. "Not kidding, Noah. Look out the window. By now, your mother should be right in the middle of Jackson Square. Right in the blast radius."

For a moment he was wary, sensing a trap. Finally he looked out into the square.

"You fucking bastard." His voice rose to a scream. "Mom, get the hell out of there! Jesus fucking Christ, get out!"

Dead silence. Noah leveled the rifle on me.

"You shoot me and my thumb comes off that switch," I said.

"You won't kill her. You said it yourself. You came all this way for my mom. Fucked up your own life to save hers."

"So did you, Noah. So did you." I stared him down. "Do you want to know what it means to be a man? You might as well find out before you die."

I took my thumb off the switch.

"It means deciding," I said. "Decide."

Noah froze.

"Get her out of here." He was turning pale. "Please."

"Your mother said to tell you she loves you," I said. "You get her out of here. Now."

He finally looked me in the eye. He had my wounded face, the tense set of the jaw, that pinched and thoughtful expression—but his eyes were his mother's, soulful and deep.

Then he put his rifle down on the ground, and moved past me, down the stairs.

"Peggy!" I called out the window. "Peggy Jean!"

"*Mike?*" Her voice, amplified.

"We've got a man coming out," I said. "Don't shoot, okay? He's unarmed."

I pressed the switch. Then I waited. Ten seconds . . . five . . .

Come on, come on . . .

A moment later I heard rifle bolts being pulled back, followed by Peggy's voice on the wind.

"*Get down on the ground,*" Peggy commanded. "*Keep your hands over your head, fingers locked. You will not be harmed.*"

Forty-five seconds. I breathed the longest sigh of my life. Sometimes the propellants in chemical mace will make a dead man's switch stick a little . . . sometimes they don't. Maybe Al was right about miracles after all.

A minute later I came from the cathedral, carrying the wounded officer. EMTs rushed forward to take him from me. A news helicopter buzzed overhead. Noah stood handcuffed, watching me.

I saw her only for a second—a pale shadow of her face, a pair of dark eyes. Watching us both together. Then—as she always did so well—Sofia disappeared from view.

FIFTY

"Was it a trick?" Noah sat on his handcuffs, surrounded by flashing lights. "You tricked me to get me out of the tower, didn't you? You and Mom both. A fucking trick."

"Just keeping a promise," I said. "You were right about me, Noah. I do want to keep my promises. And the highest one an agent makes—the only one that matters—to protect the innocent. Even at the cost of his own life."

"Yeah?" He frowned. "What do you think the shrapnel from that bomb would have done?"

"Well, my arm isn't bad. I guess I could have tried throwing it into the river. Or maybe just tossed it back into St. Anthony's Garden."

"The one with the statue of Jesus?" He laughed weakly. "You know, that statue lost two fingers in the hurricane. People say Jesus broke them off knocking the storm away to the east. Saved the French Quarter."

The cops were ready for him now. He stood up without being told to.

"Don't you think . . ." He looked away, then back at me. "Don't you think it would have been worth Jesus losing his whole arm to save everybody else?"

"Probably, yeah."

They started to lead him away. He held for just a moment.

"I guess you're going to prison, too," he said. "Maybe they'll send us to the same one, huh? Guess we can look out for each other."

"We can try, son." I smiled. "We can sure as hell try."

With everything we now had on Kadmos, the warrants for Martin Telford Campbell and Leah Varnado were a fairly simple matter. Finding their partner in crime took a little longer.

Three weeks after the Jackson Square shooting, I had the privilege of attending the arrest and interrogation of a heavyset old man named Charles Edward Barker as he attempted to charter a private boat from a marina in Port Isabel, Texas. In his suitcase were five hundred thousand dollars and Martin Telford Campbell's private cell phone number. I requested, and was granted, permission to speak with the arrestee for a few minutes alone.

We met in a shabby lounge at Huntsville Prison, normally used for final meetings between death row inmates and their families. Barca sat impatiently on a green armchair. He looked unexpectedly good in his khaki prison scrubs, like some kind of generalissimo in exile. All he needed was a sword to fall on.

"So what the fuck, Mikey. How's it hangin'?" He smoked a cigarette, back in the habit. He wouldn't meet my eyes.

"Around my neck, Barca." I sat across from him in a wooden chair. "You're going to be moved in a couple of days. Most of your crimes turn out to be federal, so it's Beaumont for you until your trial. Texas is proud to offer its hospitality."

"Fuck Texas. Fuck all fifty of 'em. I got a good lawyer."

"No argument there. By the way, how do you plan to pay her now that you're flat broke?"

He blew smoke in my face, then stubbed his cigarette out.

"I still can't figure out how the hell you did this to me," he said. "Fool me once, fine. This time, I had you pegged from the start. I had Noah watchin' you from the inside, I had Sofia for insurance—and those dopes at Kadmos said they were gonna set you up but good. I figure, if I had anybody's nuts in a bag, I had yours. So how'd you fuck me this time?"

"This time it wasn't me. It was Noah. He's the one who told us how you were planning to get out of the country."

"Noah. Noah. Shit." He leaned on his elbows. "I said he had your brains and my balls, didn't I? Bad luck for me."

"He also inherited his mother's eyes," I said. "At the end of the day . . . I think he saw you for who you really are."

"Stupid kid." He nearly smiled. "Would have been beautiful if he'd had the guts to pull it off, huh? That black sonofabitch politician runs for cover, Levin-Marcato goes clean through—and I've got enough on Campbell that he doesn't dare blow a whistle on me. We coulda run the whole country that way, Mikey. Voting with bullets. Coulda worked."

"You forgot one important thing," I said. "You tried to take down Peggy Weaver. I did try to warn you about that."

I stood up to leave.

"Hey, what's this shit? Here's your hat, what's your hurry?" He held out his hands. "C'mon, Mikey. Siddown. Don't you gotta wait for your own trial somewhere? Might as well be here, eh? They got steak tonight."

"I have to get on the road," I said. "They're expecting me for a debrief in Washington. And then . . . who the hell knows?"

"Yeah, okay. Listen, if you see her . . ." His voice faltered.

"What?"

He drew a deep and painful breath. "If you see Sofia. If you see her . . . tell her the old man's sorry, okay? Tell her I got no reason to be forgiven, but . . . I'd take all those years back, if I could. Tell her that her papa loves her, and he's sorry."

"I seriously doubt I'm going to see Sofia again," I said. "She's had three weeks' head start, and I don't plan on looking for her. But I promise you this. I'll burn in hell before I pass along a message like that. She's had enough knives stuck in her without your twisting that one."

He stared at me, stunned and forlorn. I made it all the way to the door, then thought, *Screw him.*

"There's an old story my mother told me," I said. "It's about a man who knows he's about to die. Each year, when Death comes, he convinces somebody in his family to go in his place. First his parents, then his brothers and sisters, and finally his wife and children. Suddenly there's nobody left, not even the family dog. So when Death comes for him the next time, the guy's petrified. But Death says, 'Don't worry, my friend, I won't take you. You've been so good to me over the years. You gave me everyone you ever loved— and now it's just you and me.' If that isn't worse than dying, Barca . . . I don't know what is."

For a long time, he didn't respond. Then he suddenly looked at me, as if waking from a bad dream.

"My brother Paulie used to tell me the same story," he said emptily. "Of course . . . it was much funnier in the original Italian."

I gave him a nod. Then I knocked twice on the door, and the prison guard let me go.

One of the guys from the resident agency gave me a ride to the airport, and I rented a car from Enterprise. The lady at the desk said that one-way cost more, but I told her I didn't mind. I preferred it to flying. I needed the time alone.

It was six hours from Huntsville to New Orleans, and I got there just before sunset. For the first time in God knew how many years, the old neon sign at the oyster house, NEVER CLOSED, was dark. In its place was a new banner, black letters on white vinyl: UNDER NEW MANAGEMENT. I got oyster loaf and a microbrewed beer. It wasn't that bad and it wasn't that great. I guessed if I wanted Della's cooking, I'd have to get my butt up to the restaurant she was opening in Baton Rouge. The new manager, a corporate lackey from Texarkana, let me upstairs so I could collect some belongings I'd left behind. Among them was a small, flat plastic chip I'd wrapped in aluminum foil and stuffed between floorboards. I don't know if Yoshi actually believed me when I told him I'd lost the magical microprocessor in the swamp—but at least he'd done me the courtesy of not looking too hard for it. A good thing, too. The way things were going, I might just need a little magic in the months to come.

Sofia had left me the shirt she wore the last time I saw her. Still smelled like her, too. I held it to me for a few seconds, then packed it away. As I did so, a folded piece of paper fell from the pocket. I put it away for later.

A man at the Mandeville animal shelter told me that, yes, a young female beagle with JOSIE on her tags had been brought there a few weeks back, but some people had already claimed it: a black couple in their early sixties. He believed they were moving to Baton Rouge. Apparently they wanted the dog as a welcome-home present for a foster child they were taking in.

I asked him if there was a woman with them. White lady, dark-haired, about my age. Sad eyes. The clerk said he hadn't seen her.

I kept on driving along I-10. First to Slidell, with its silent city of empty homes. Then I caught Interstate 59 into Mississippi, where the casino billboards made MacArthurian promises to return to Biloxi. Morning found me in a cheap hotel in Meridian. That night I slept on the downstairs sofa of Peggy's mom's house in Avalon, Tennessee. Peggy was there for a meeting of the Avalon College board of regents, on which she was now apparently a very big wheel. A couple of times, her mom asked when we were getting married. Peggy found polite ways to change the subject. From there we shared the ride to D.C., talking about everything except what we had done on our summer vacation.

Then we came to Washington, that shining city, and for three days I answered questions and spoke my piece. On the final afternoon of my deposition, I was told that Senator James Seaweather wanted to say hello, if I had time for him. I stopped by his office on the Hill. I knew he was in the room when I heard the whirr of an electric wheelchair.

"Are the doctors hopeful?" I asked when we were alone.

"They're cautiously optimistic." His voice had a new rasp to it. His breathing was steady as ever. "Apparently, I have to be the hopeful one. If you're asking, 'Will I ever stand up from this chair?' Who knows, Mike. It would be nice. But I will run in '08—and just between you and me, I intend to win."

"Good to know there'll still be one honest man in the Senate."

"Hell with the Senate," he said. "The wheelchair facilities in this building are abysmal. They're marginally better on Pennsylvania Avenue, of course. Choice little piece of real estate I've got my eye on. Way I hear, I wouldn't be the first handicapped guy to live there."

The phone rang. The senator wheeled himself over to his desk and picked up the receiver. His face instantly brightened.

"Yes? Well, that's just wonderful. No, no, I'll be there this weekend. Just because New Orleans tried to kill me doesn't mean I have to hold a grudge. You put me down for every block meeting and fund-raiser you can schedule. I'll bring extra batteries for the Batmobile." He laughed. "Love you, too, babe."

He hung up.

"Batmobile?" I asked.

He patted the sides of his wheelchair. "I took some of your advice. Not enough of it, I'm sorry to say. But I am going to do my level best to get to know the people of New Orleans. Whatever happens next—I'm done hiding behind vague euphemisms like 'national security.' "

"Senator." I briefly looked at my feet. "I owe you an apology. My son—"

"I can't do much to help your son." His voice grew quiet. "I'd be lying if I said I didn't have a . . . lot of anger against that boy. But you can't be responsible for what he did. Heck, I've got a nephew in prison, and you can bet my opponents made political hay out of that. You gonna let it weigh on your conscience?"

I nodded.

"But you will speak for him at his trial?" he asked.

"Yeah." I took a breath. "I am responsible for my own actions, sir. I don't . . . feel right about the deal we made. I don't think I deserve to be rewarded for—"

"For shooting some guys because they were gonna kill the mother of your child? For helping an old friend die so his kids didn't have to be ashamed of him?" He raised an eyebrow. "I used to be a district judge before I got into this racket. When you render a verdict, you either decide that motives matter—or they don't. I happen to believe they do. More to the point, Yeager, you got results. Campbell is going down, thanks to you. Good will come of what you did. That I definitely believe."

"I failed to save Amrita," I said. "I should be punished for that, if nothing else."

He looked away, then back to me. "You are being punished, Mike. Just not by your country, that's all."

The intercom buzzed. "Senator, your children are here."

"Be right there." He looked at me. "You don't mind?"

"Not at all." I stood up. "If I could ask—who was that woman you were talking to on the phone a minute ago?"

"Oh." He smiled fondly. "That's Her Honor the mayor of New Orleans. Guess we got a little friendly through this whole business. But now, that's between us guys. I start reading about her and me in the tabloids . . ."

"A man has a right not to get teased about his girlfriend."

"You must have a family like mine." He pointed to the door. "Celeste is here, by the way. My youngest. You want to say hello to her?"

"No, that's—"

"I think she wants to meet you. I think she'd like to say hello to the man who helped save her life."

Finally I nodded. "I'd like that, too."

"Then it's settled." He motioned me to him. "I'd prefer to save my batteries for this weekend. You don't mind . . . ?"

I smiled. "It's my privilege, sir."

Then I took the handles of the senator's wheelchair and escorted him to his children.

FIFTY-ONE

Peggy waited for me on the Capitol steps.

"Where to now?" she asked.

"I'm going home," I said. "You could have told me that 'Jim' already had a girlfriend, you know. You could have mentioned that at least once. That way, I wouldn't have been stewing over the way you called him 'Jim' for the past three weeks."

"Just because it's none of your business doesn't mean I had anything to hide." She stood up. "How did it go with him?"

"He has nice, polite children," I said. "And don't even pretend you didn't stage-manage that. How did it go with the director?"

"Better than expected," she said. "The prosecution's deal with your son has been approved. Kiplinger's getting his posthumous decoration for valor. Yoshi—no thanks to you—was already covered by a blanket surveillance warrant from the chief inspector's office. More than that, you're not going to jail."

"No medal for me, huh?"

"You're out, Mike. And don't act so forlorn. Something tells me you're not entirely unhappy about that." She took a moment to straighten my tie. "So which home are we talking here? Home as in your gloomy little apartment in Philly? Or maybe home in New Orleans?"

"Home as in home. As in where I came from. Lancaster, P-A." I walked a few steps below Peggy, then looked up at her. "It's been a long time since I said hello to my family."

"Can I come with?" she asked. "Purely out of morbid curiosity. I've never met any Amish people."

"Lutheran."

"Whatever. Unless you're ashamed to be seen with me."

I laughed. "I think you've got it backwards, Peggy Jean. Sure you want to be seen traveling with a broken wing?"

"Everybody has to, sooner or later."

She stood beside me on the long walk down.

My brother and his wife and kids were waiting for us at the farmhouse. Soon after, my baby sister Jessie and her girlfriend Camille stopped by with pound cake and *kartoffelsalat*. They gave me crap about never visiting, and told Peggy embarrassing stories about me, and we all ate hamburger casserole. Everyone was jumped-up excited to meet the famous FBI agent—Peggy Weaver. Nobody mentioned my recent troubles in New Orleans. Then my brother took me out to the garage, where my mother killed herself behind the wheel of her car thirty-three years before. He'd converted it into a rumpus room. We shot pool.

"Your friend Peggy's nice." He chalked his cue. "Something cooking there?"

"Just friends," I said. "And all I can say is, thank God for her friend-ship."

"She keeps calling me Samuel. Like I'm some kind of Old Testament prophet. Why don't you let her use the family nickname?"

"Because I don't want to give her the opportunity to start making jokes about two brothers named Spike and Mike." I broke, then pointed to the corner pocket. "There. I just set you up a honey of a shot, but only because I feel sorry for you."

"What a guy." Spike laughed with his entire face, a younger and happier version of his bulldog brother. "You don't mind us putting a pool table in here, do you? You don't think it's disrespectful to Mom?"

"You have to let things heal, I guess."

"That you do." He nodded soberly. "You did okay by us, Mike. You looked out for me and Jessie when we were little. God knows we'd have caught a lot more hell from the old man if you hadn't taken most of the hits."

"I notice you didn't mention our other two sisters."

"Debbie and Fran still think Pop hung the moon. They deny any of it ever happened. What are you gonna do." He took his shot, avoiding the easy one I'd left for him. "You should come to the cemetery. We just put up new stones for Mom and Pop. Jess picked out the inscriptions—from

Shakespeare, I think. Real good ones. You maybe feel like taking a look-see?"

"Sounds good," I said. "After I finish kicking your ass."

"Dream on," Spike said and sank a three-corner shot.

Peggy shared the ride with me and Spike to the graveyard. Before we left, I asked if I could have a couple of minutes alone. I nodded first to the old man's spare gray stone.

CALVIN WOLFRAM YEAGER

1933–1985

Seek Not Thy Mortal Father in the Dust

Then I put my hand softly on my mother's smaller marker, of rose-colored granite:

ARIEL FRANCES DEMOUY YEAGER

1944–1973

For That Thou Wast a Spirit Too Refined

I checked around briefly. Peggy was chatting warmly with my brother, giving me privacy. Then I cleared my throat.

"They kicked me out of the FBI, Pop." I paused, trying not to sound bitter. "I dunno, maybe I could have fought the decision. It just didn't seem right after . . . what I did. So you got me cold, I guess. Pride goeth before a fall, and all that bullshit. Anyway . . . I'll find something else to do, don't worry. Maybe not right away. But I'll figure it out."

The stone glowered at me. I hadn't said enough.

"I feel stupid doing this," I said. "I don't even think you're listening, or you'd have told me to shut up by now. For what it's worth . . . I wish I'd read that last letter you wrote to me. Maybe you weren't trying to apologize, maybe it was just more guilt. If you were apologizing . . . I'm sorry I didn't give you a shot at it."

Then I turned to my mother.

"I hope to God you are listening." I reached into my pocket. "I've got a son, Ma. He's got troubles. I don't know how he'll wind up, but . . . his mother's a nice girl. She left you a note. I'm pretty sure she wanted me to read it to you. So . . . here goes."

I unfolded the slip of paper in my hand, covered with Sofia's wandering script.

"'To Mike's Mother,'" I read. "'Your son is a good man. He doesn't know this. He thinks he let you down. He blames himself for what happened to you. Sometimes he . . . sometimes he is sad because he doesn't think a mother can forgive a son for such things. He doesn't know how mothers really are. I hope you find rest . . . and I hope your son finds happiness, wherever he looks for it. He deserves some. My name is Sofia and I thank you for bringing Mike into the world. There was some pain but there was also joy. I'd do it all again.'"

I folded the paper and put it back into my pocket.

"She signed it with a kiss, Ma." I touched my fingers to my lips, then to the gravestone. "She does stuff like that."

Then I walked away from them.

We were quiet on the ride back. The grown-ups had a few glasses of wine; then everybody went to bed. The next morning, Peggy and I got up early so we could have breakfast alone. She drove me to the Greyhound station and waited while I bought my ticket. I gave her the keys to the rental car, and then I kissed her on the cheek, and held her for a very long time. Peggy didn't ask where I was going. All she wanted to know was when she might see me again. I told her it could be a while, but I'd call before I went to bed.

Then I saw Peggy on her way, watching her taillights vanish down the Gettysburg road. And caught my own ride to wherever I was going next on God's green earth.